A LESSER LIGHT

ALSO BY PETER GEYE
PUBLISHED BY THE UNIVERSITY OF MINNESOTA PRESS

The Ski Jumpers

A LESSER LIGHT

A Novel

PETER GEYE

University of Minnesota Press

MINNEAPOLIS

LONDON

Published by the University of Minnesota Press
111 Third Avenue South, Suite 290
Minneapolis, MN 55401-2520
http://www.upress.umn.edu

ISBN 978-1-5179-1637-4 (hc)
ISBN 978-1-5179-2065-4 (pb)

A Cataloging-in-Publication record for this book is available from the Library of Congress.

Printed in Canada on acid-free paper

The University of Minnesota is an equal-opportunity educator and employer.

31 30 29 28 27 26 25   10 9 8 7 6 5 4 3 2 1

For Emily
—moon, and moonlight on the water

CONTENTS

The Gininwabiko Light 1

Mare Crisium 53

"Quasi una fantasia" 85

Seiches 113

Stellar Aberration 143

A Long Shadow Behind 179

Seventh Sunday 217

The Serpent's Tail 227

The Storm 247

Anima 271

Fog 291

Inheritance 309

Dead Stars 337

Magnetic 353

Mariage Blanc 377

Where Does the Light Go? 401

The Thousandth Watch 413

At Loggerheads 425

Ripeness 453

Queen of the Highway 469

Offing 481

The Fawn 497

Undertow 507

Spindrift 523

THE GININWABIKO LIGHT

APRIL 20, 1910

I'll tell you about the moon and the comet and the lighthouse and the light; the storms and the softest hours.

I'll tell you about the clockworks and the watchworks; the shipwrecks and survivals.

I'll tell you about the wolves and the fawn; the drownings and the orphan.

I'll tell you about the sacraments and the sins; and the most beautiful song.

I'll tell you about the station master and his wife and the child she fell in love with and the mother she despised and the man who rescued them both.

I'll tell you about Kitchigami and all her moods.

And if you're still of a listening mind, I'll tell you about the dying.

But first I need to report a most peculiar arrival.

S HE'D LEFT TWO HARBORS in snow before dawn. Some hours had passed with only the magnetic pull of the lake beneath her, and now the *Nocturne* was surrounded by fog as dense as paraffin. Despite the chill, she unlatched the porthole, pushed the window open, reached outside and clenched her fist, trying to hold the fog in her grasp. That's when she heard the basso profundo of the ship's whistle, and a faint echo answering from the distant shore.

She brought her hand back inside. It was slicked by the fog and she wiped it dry on the sleeve of her blouse. The ship's whistle blew again; there again, the answer.

The purser came through steerage. "Next stop's the Gininwabiko light," he called, opening his leather pocket ledger. "Mrs. Sauer?"

She startled at her name but managed to acknowledge him with a quizzical look.

"Keeper Sauer asked me to escort you personally. We'll drop anchor in five minutes. The lighthouse launch will meet us shipside. I'll fetch your trunk now. May I have your baggage ticket?"

She withdrew it from her handbag. "There are two trunks."

"Find yourself to the forward gangway. Portside." He threw his thumb over his right shoulder. "Thataway." He pocketed his ledger and looked over the top of his pince-nez at the open window. He reached over and latched it shut. As he did, the ship sent another moan into the day. After this third call, she didn't hear the distant echo, but rather felt, even from amidships, the vibrating deck as the anchor chain ran out.

"I reckon Cap found his spot. Better make haste." He turned and hustled through the cabin as she stood and walked the other way.

3

She found herself alone at the railing, the black water rolling beneath her as slow and gentle as the orbiting night sky. The ship's whistle blew every third or fourth swell, calling her husband through the fog. For a moment, she fancied stepping into the killing water. She even leaned over the railing and glanced once in each direction. No one would see her. She could end her trial before it began. She gripped the railing more firmly and sent the water a beseeching query.

The answer came from the secreted shore—a lament calling back, a chorus of howls belatedly harmonizing with the whistle. They were so close she could reach out and hold their music.

"That's not your mother's lap dog," the purser said, standing there as suddenly as the howling had found her.

She acknowledged him by peering harder into the fog.

"Wolves," he said.

As soon as he said it, she heard a different sound: a symphony of splashing oars and dissonant whistling materialized into an ill-shapen boat, lit by a single lantern and rowed by Theodulf. The din on his lips was meant to be Beethoven.

"A big pack's up in those hills," the purser said. "Dozens, is what I heard. Reckon there's been no need to kill them yet. Or no one around to do it."

Now Willa did turn to him. "Whyever—"

"Lo!" he shouted, cupping his hands around his mouth. "Master Sauer! Lo!"

His whistling stopped and the oarlocks complained.

"*Nocturne*," another voice shouted back. Her husband's. Theodulf's.

"Lo!" a different voice added to the choir. The captain, if she understood his regalia. "Aye, Master Sauer! Come abeam. We'll trice up."

He had a line in his hand, ready to toss to the launch. The lantern light grew brighter until it was no light at all, and Theodulf was there, in full uniform, standing astride the thwart, the long oars still in his hands, his eyes steady on the gangway, though not on her. Not at all.

Defiantly, Willa turned to look at the purser. But he was gone, replaced by one of her trunks and the distinct sensation that he had had no more substance than the fog.

"Toss the line," Theodulf said.

The boats triced up.

"Excuse me, Mrs. Sauer," the captain said, unlatching the gangplank and lowering it to the launch's gunwale. Then he said, "Ma'am?" and offered the crook of his arm.

A mere six feet separated the *Nocturne* and her husband's boat. Six feet that may as well have been the whole length of the lake for as much as she wanted to cross it. But cross it she did, reaching down for Theodulf's offered hand, pausing to note the brass buttons on the cuff of his peacoat, the starched white collar and necktie, the gleaming visor of his peaked cap. When he took her hand, it was not with gentleness or kindness or love—as any other man might have greeted his new wife—but rather as though her arm were a hawser, and he a stevedore bitter at his labor.

After hoisting her aboard, he fetched the first trunk, and waited aboard the *Nocturne* for the second, speaking to the captain. When finally he loaded the second trunk, he said, "A fair load for one lady."

Not hello. Not sweetheart.

He uncoupled the gangplank and watched as it was hauled back aboard the ship, where the captain stood holding the railing with one hand. The other was raised in a half-hearted and unofficial salute. Theodulf, misunderstanding the gesture, straightened himself and said, "We'll watch for you going home tomorrow, sir. Here's to clearing heavens and fair breezes."

Willa didn't say that the fog would relent soon but give way to snow. She didn't say the calmness they all bobbed in now was exordium to stiff northern winds sure to bring unkind seas. She didn't warn him, or say a proper hello herself, or stifle her unhappiness. She only sat on that seat and stared at her worn brogues, knowing how the wind would blow, hoping for an hour's reprieve sometime in the middle hours of the night so she might catch a glimpse of the perihelion of Halley's Comet.

Theodulf said nothing, not even when the *Nocturne* sent up its farewell whistle and the wolves answered one last time. No, he didn't say anything until Willa, seeing the shore materialize through the fog some five minutes later, observed another man on the dock, his dark form silhouetted against the whiteness of the boathouse, and asked, "Who's that?" and he replied, "That's Father Richter."

"Why's he here?" she asked.

Theodulf looked over his shoulder, whether to lay eyes on his beloved priest or to take measure of where the dock was, she could not know. "He's here to bless the light."

"To bless the light?"

He finally looked at her then, his unkind gaze coming up from under the shadow of his hat. "How would this light shepherd even a single vessel if it were not itself blessed by God?"

"Why didn't you signal the station foghorn for the *Nocturne*?" she asked.

"She's not commissioned until sundown."

"Not even in this weather? Not even for your new wife, to guide her safely?"

"Contrariwise to regulations," he said, then pulled harder on the oars. As if to shorten his time on the boat with her. His legs were spread wide, his boots planted firmly on the burden boards, one on either side of a trunk. He kept his chin tucked on his shoulder. His mustache was hoary gray and long, and it hung limp around his lips. His hands squat and rough and gripping the new oars.

"Father Richter's blessing of the light, that's regulation?" she pressed.

"My service is first to God," he said.

As if God were rewarding his piety, the fog started rising. All of it this time. As the last tendrils evanesced, the lighthouse came into relief atop a sheer granite cliff. Theodulf steered toward the boathouse, which she could see sat some eighth of a mile up the shore from the base of the palisade. Father Richter was close enough now that she recognized the stole hanging from his narrow shoulders, a brilliant green at odds with the dull gray hills above.

"Just a few more minutes," Theodulf said. He sculled easier now that the fog had lifted, and the launch sliced through the water. "One more thing," he added. "You'll tell Father Richter confession before you settle in."

"Pardon me?"

"He's here to bless the light, as I say. But we'll take the opportunity to visit the sacrament of penance. Who can say when next the good Father will call on us?"

She turned and watched the wake of the boat lag behind, watched the steam from the *Nocturne* rise with the retreating fog. It was her turn for reticence. Not because she was chastened or acquiescent, but because she knew her husband was immovable on this, the subject of his piety and the decorum he pretended. She also knew he was a fraud—in the matter of his faith, to be sure, but also in a slew of other ways—and to expose him all at once would rob her of what little promise the years ahead possessed. There'd be time to parley with Theodulf. She'd wield her secrets like strychnine.

So instead of extending their quarrel, she turned her attention to the lightening sky. It was quick to move on this wild shore. Her father had taught her a long time ago to sense barometric pressure, and between the weight of her blood and the arcus clouds hauling down, she reckoned the weather would remain all day. That this realization broached as much unhappiness as her general circumstances was almost a relief, filling her, as it did, with a sense that the blood coursing through her would indeed funnel through her own heart.

Just before they came into earshot of Father Richter standing on the end of the dock, Theodulf offered a sudden remark. "We should want absolution, Willa. We should want God's grace and goodness. Asking forgiveness and doing penance is a way *to* that absolution."

She had other notions about absolution, but only smiled at Theodulf as he rowed for the shore.

His first condition of their engagement had been her conversion to Catholicism. She supposed his evangelizing, with its elementary logic and somber flourishes, was a fact of life now. The only time he'd held her hand was on that morning in her mother's parlor, while he spoke ardently about the mysteries of God and the joy of belief. Then and now, Willa might have quailed—she no more believed in God or thought herself Catholic than she believed she would one day love the man rowing this boat—but instead of despair she channeled a kind of resolve she'd not known she possessed. Oh, she would be devout, not to her husband or God, but rather to her sacred sciences. To reason. To her own true self.

Theodulf stood with one hand still on the starboard oar and the other clutching a coil of hempen line. The robed figure of Father Richter stood on the dock, ready to help them land.

A moment later, the priest greeted them. "I daresay, I wondered if you'd find your way back in the fog."

"We followed the wolf song," Theodulf said.

"They sing heresies!"

Theodulf tossed the line and Father Richter tied the boat to a cleat. "Mrs. Sauer, you look hale. Welcome home," he said, and then offered his hand, which Willa took as she stepped onto the dock.

"Father Richter. You're a long way from Sacred Heart," she said.

Father Richter helped get Willa's trunks dockside before putting a hand on her shoulder and saying, "I need go where the sinners are. And this"—now he spread his arms wide, east and west, as though to encompass the shoreline and the wilds above it—"is rich territory for reprobates and degenerates."

At this, Theodulf joined them on the dock. Despite the cold, a gloss of sweat glazed his brow. He held up one finger as though he were about to make a point, removed his hat, and wiped away the sweat instead. "Welcome to Gininwabiko, Willa. I hope you'll be happy here." Without waiting for her response, he said to Father Richter, "She's ready to repent. Shall we go up to the house?"

Father Richter only nodded, took one end of the first trunk, and followed Theodulf up the path to the lighthouse.

It was a steep five-minute walk to the top of the palisade and the compound atop it. There were three identical brick houses backed by three wooden sheds and fronted by a walkway that led to a concrete bunker she assumed was the oil house. The foghorns were mounted on the roof of another brick building, which sat on one side of a staircase. On the other, the lighthouse loomed, eight-sided and magisterial and ready for service.

"This is our residence," Theodulf said, pausing before the stoop of the house farthest from the light. "I thought it would offer the most privacy. The first and second assistants will be here on Sunday. Their families will live there and there." He pointed at the other dwellings one–two.

"It's more than I was expecting," Willa said, glancing up at the house, a two-story foursquare with dormered windows overlooking the grounds and the lake from the second floor.

"I told you it was lovely," he said. "Did you doubt me?"

"Doubt you? Whyever would I?"

"Good," he said, oblivious to her mocking, then nodded at the front door and the stoop before it. "Father, will you help me with this? Willa, wait just one moment."

And again she was dumbfounded. Would she really not be permitted inside her home without first saying confession? In as much time as it took her to understand this truth, Theodulf and the priest were stepping back out. Now her husband had a captain's chair, which he set on the porch. Father Richter trailed with a folded blanket in one hand, and his bible in the other. He arranged the blanket next to the chair.

"Child," he said, offering the blanket.

Theodulf was already hurrying back down to the dock for the other trunk. She watched him, his shoulders set and sloped, his stride lumbering, until he crested the hill and disappeared downslope. Willa turned to the lighthouse. Wisps of fog still licked the windows of the lantern room, as if it were exhaling, its breath plenty, for the fog no sooner ended than the clouds did commence. She scanned the rest of the sky to discern the time, but there was none.

"Please, Mrs. Sauer. Kneel. Say your confession."

Father Richter gathered his cassock and sat down, gesturing at her spot, which was turned away from him. They would be shoulder to shoulder, he facing the house.

She glanced again at the empty trail.

Father Richter saw what she did. "Your husband is a good and pious man. His virtues and the virtues of this light station will help save countless lives. It is a storm-ravaged and wild place you live now." He clutched his bible, brought it to his lips. "God's grace will be your most faithful companion."

For a moment, she fantasized about Theodulf disappearing. Of him never cresting the hill again, with or without her trunk. She could live here alone. Happily. She might even consign herself to a life of prayerful devotion. Again she glanced at the lighthouse and the sky forever above and beyond it. A glimpse of heaven, without her husband there to sully it. She could have daydreamed for an hour, but Father Richter's rotten breath rode a sigh from the cauldron of his throat, choking her back to her place on that stoop.

"Child," Father Richter said again.

As the priest had gathered his cassock, so Willa now gathered her skirts. She knelt on the blanket, there at the door of her new home. Father Richter peeked at her, and then made the sign of the cross and whispered, "In nomine Patris et Filii et Spiritus Sancti."

She wanted to howl. To make music with the beasts, to sing harmony to their heresies.

His eyes were still closed, but Father Richter leaned toward her and said, "Begin with your venial sins, Mrs. Sauer."

I am full of anger, she thought. *Is anger a sin? Envy, yes. Pride and greed, yes, sins, and I am full of these. But more than anything, I am full of wrath.*

"We are all impure. Each and every one of us," he said, as though reading her mind.

Now there came from the near distance wolves barking. Short and warning. It sounded like they might be on the other side of the house. Six or eight yelps.

Father Richter looked quickly heavenward, then just as quickly down at Willa. He kept his gaze on her, as though by force of will he might divine her secrets. When she didn't budge, he said, "If you do not repent, you will be—"

"Bless me father, for I have sinned," she began, recalling the rules she was expected to abide by. "This is my first confession since January." She saw an inscrutable smile rise in his beard. His eyes were closed again, and she could sense as much as see a kind of ecstasy in his fluttering lids at having won her voice. This sickened her— that she should be so unfaithful to herself, that she should let this man and his simplemindedness prevail upon her—and in order to quell the nausea, she had a fiendish idea.

"I have had impure thoughts," she lied. "I have been covetous and I have been desirous and that's not the whole of it." She saw his own eyes glance sideways at her. If he was dubious, she couldn't tell, so she pressed on. "I have lain with another girl. I would do so again." She feigned a caught breath.

At this *he* gasped, but because he was genuinely surprised. Perhaps even stricken.

Before he could regain his bearing, she added, "I have injured. I have taken the Lord's name in vain." She felt gleeful and hurried through a litany of false sins. Idolatry, envy, blaspheming, sloth. What else was forbidden?

Across the grounds, Theodulf reappeared with her chest. He set it on the path and continued to the lighthouse, avoiding her gaze as he passed. During their courtship, such as it was, he had spent their Saturday afternoons not promising primroses and complimenting her beauty, but proselytizing and praying and laboring over the ten commandments, as though *her* conversion meant *his* salvation. That she so easily convinced her husband of her righteousness, well, it was a small thrill. Especially now, as she paid this entry toll into her new life.

"Is that all, child?" Father Richter asked.

What she didn't confess was that her true sin, born only in those moments with Father Richter, staring at her husband beneath the lighthouse, in full regalia, was that she felt *murderous*.

Instead of confessing anything more, Willa merely nodded in answer to the priest's query. And as he prayed over her soul—granting her pardon, assuring her absolution, and assigning her penance—she made a silent vow: her covenant would be with the wilds—the wolves and water and celestial bodies. She would remain as agnostic as nature. And as cunning.

L OOK AT HIM OVER THERE, the master at his station. His right hand is clenched in the pocket of his standard-issue peacoat, his left raised to block the cascading sky. But it's not the heavens he's studying. Not the deliquescing fog or the cut of strange clouds or even Willa giving her confession. It's not even the lighthouse itself, cocked and stalwart and ready to be lit. What he *sees*, what he's in fact ruminating on, is the machine inside. The symphonic apparatus that will compel the light not to *shine*—that is the provenance of the incandescent oil-vapor lamp nestled in the honeycomb of the lens—but to *rotate*.

He understands his duty to this mechanism. He can catalogue its parts from the heavy weight hanging beneath the watch room's concrete floor to the manifold glass of the lens with its forty refracting and reflecting prisms perched in the lantern room like a king's righteous crown. There's the chariot upon which the lens is mounted, and the mercury vessel and the 250 pounds of quicksilver on which the lens and chariot float. Beneath this, the clockworks proper, the source of his narrowing attention now: the drive drum and gears and springs and pulleys, the annulus and pawl, all the brass and steel and braided cable, the tallow used to slick it up, the hand crank he'll wind every other hour from dusk to dawn. He can take it apart and put it back together again without understanding *how* it works. Only that it *does*. In this way, it's like faith. It's a miracle—a word he does not use lightly—that some mind comprehends so much. That some man conjured it all. A Frenchman, in this case, employed by the firm Barbier, Bénard & Turenne, at 82 rue Curial in Paris, France.

"Paris," he says aloud, then brings his hand down from its salute to rub the word from his lips. He would forget that faraway and long-ago place if he could. Would unbind himself from the shame of his memory. But he can't. Of course he can't. And so with his right hand, he thumbs the watch that came home from Paris with him. It's a Longines La Renommée he found in a jeweler's shop just off the Avenue des Champs-Élysées during the Exposition Universelle in 1900. The savonnette cover is a work of art unto itself: an embossed trumpeting angel rising above clouds and the earth in solid gold. There's also an hourglass with wings in the design, a feature he's rubbed dull in the decade since he returned from France.

He's marked many an hour with the ticking of this watch, hours that have tethered him to the earth second by second, hours that have brought him further and further from his month abroad and the ignominy that trailed him home. That trails him still, if his present malaise is any indication. He takes the watch from his pocket, flips it open without noting the time, and holds it to his ear. The *tick-tock*, it speaks for God. He listens for ten seconds, then closes the watch and holds it in his pocket again. It's the surest reminder that he's here on earth. Surer even than the cathedral of granite beneath his feet. Time has delivered him again to simpler things. His duty, for example. The role his meticulous disposition will play in the operation of this lighthouse. The fundamental and profound importance of this particular station. He thinks again of the machine inside. Of the clockworks. For now, they will remain as mysterious to him as his own true nature.

He would be embarrassed to admit this, but since he has never yet failed in his duty to the Lighthouse Service, not in the nearly ten years of his employ (first at Devil's Island, then Ontonagon and Two Harbors before his stint as first assistant at Rock of Ages), he hides his ignorance in the same way and place he hides so much else. And who's the wiser?

Lord God, he answers, and swipes at his lips again, as if suddenly a bee had landed there, as if he had spoken the words and not merely thought them. He must stop these careening thoughts. He *will.* And to help himself he clicks his boot heels and does an about-face and in a split second turns to the row of three houses behind him, hoping to rout from his mind the infectious thinking.

But there's Willa, kneeling before the priest. She exudes confidence. If only he could summon the courage to trade places with her, to genuflect before Father Richter and make his own confession. Then perhaps these dizzying memories would vanish forever. But he's never uttered a word about what he harbors deepest. Not to anyone, but least of all the priest. Father Richter raises his hand above Willa's bowed head and makes the sign of the cross. Theodulf can as much as hear the prayer of absolution being uttered, can feel the wash of forgiveness as though he has repented himself.

He takes a deep and steadying breath. He should pity her, he knows. But he also knows he never will. He has developed a fine ability to repress his noble instincts, to stand tall when he thinks people are admiring him and to let his position in the world speak for his righteousness. So, he straightens. He will let his wife—his *wife!*—regard his authority and rank. He will indeed be the master of his station.

And he will not agitate the question of why she's here, or why they are now husband and wife. He knows, and presumes she does too, that if he wishes to one day head the Lighthouse Service, then he will need a family. Appearances are tantamount to abilities, after all. In this or any endeavor. His mother taught him that. So he did what any prudent man would and got himself a wife. Even a pretty one. Who cares that she's overeducated and recalcitrant? Their audience here will be most trifling. Only the two assistant keepers—Misters Axelsson and Wilson and their wives—and the two fishing families living in their shanties on the cove a quarter mile west of the station. All this is a domain he's suited to govern, of that he's quite sure.

He smiles across the snow-crusted grounds. Willa does not smile back but turns away from him, opens the door to their home, and walks in alone. *Let her look,* he thinks. *Let her see how lovely her life will be.*

On the ridgeline a hundred paces above the houses, the trees commence again. Several acres had been cleared in preparation for building the station. There are no roads from here to anywhere. Only footpaths and game trails through the wilderness in all directions. Two Harbors is twenty miles by boat to the west. There's a settlement at Otter Bay three miles to the west, and a few others between here and Gunflint, the only other proper town between Two Harbors and the Canadian border, fifty-odd miles down the shore. But to the north—the direction he's cast his gaze now—there's nothing but wilderness all the way to Hudson's Bay. He removes his cap and strokes back his hair and returns the cap to his head. This wilderness, he fears it. Especially the wolves that seem intent on singing back at any sound. Just yesterday, while he was alone at the station and testing the foghorns, they answered that bellowing with their own urgent and louring howls. And then again today, when the *Nocturne* called, they did the same. He could hear them even from the station boat out on the water. He'd need to warn Willa about them. He supposed he'd need to protect her. Add this to his duties.

CAN YOU IMAGINE standing in the entrance of your new home, atop the varnished wood floors, with the ghosts of April trailing you, and seeing—first, and above everything and without doubt—*violence*? With Father Richter's stinking breath coming over her shoulder sure as the breeze, Willa saw it as vividly as the fog that had attended her all morning. It emanated from the vacant rooms, the violence did. As though the wolves howling on the hillside had come inside to fill them.

It wasn't the first time she'd witnessed something like this essence. This *aura*. It had been the same at her parents' house in Duluth, on that cold morning seven months ago. Though she hadn't seen her father strung up from his laboratory ceiling, she'd felt the brutality of his act as if the same cord had gripped her own neck. That morning, as now, a rage attended her. In both instances, she blamed her mother.

The house in Duluth had also been empty. By the time Willa got home—for two days she'd traveled by train from Boston—her mother had cleared the laboratory not only of his lifeless body but of all his meteorology equipment, his papers and books, his desk and chair.

"What did you do to him?" Willa asked her mother the morning of her arrival.

"Do to him?"

Willa turned to face her. "This is your fault."

Ann Brandt, Willa's mother, was the sort of woman who had enjoyed her husband's station in life without ever taking much pleasure in the man himself. Ann's father was an Iron Range miner who seldom spoke, her mother a zealous Lutheran and termagant whose only amusement in life was derived from the misery of others. Especially her pretty daughter. Ann had done well to marry into the Brandt family, and not only because it meant escaping the misfortune of her own kin, but also because she'd found a man who could tolerate her bitter moods and absent charms. Willa, much to her mother's irritation, could not.

"My fault? I suppose at Radcliffe they teach you to assign blame?"

"You wouldn't know anything about what they teach me at Radcliffe."

"Not logic, certainly." Her mother moved to the window overlooking the harbor and funicular tracks. "Your father was a man besotted by the shame of his failures. He was lily-livered and selfish, and the fact that he thought it better to strangle himself than to make things right, well, that any of this could be viewed as my fault shows how partial you are." She pulled the curtain closed and added, "Partial and imprudent. But enough of that, we have important things to discuss."

"Where's his equipment?"

"Gone to the new bureau meteorologist."

"What about his papers and books? What about his desk? What about his telescope? That wasn't the property of the weather bureau."

Her mother looked at Willa with some perfect combination of loathing and condescension. "Nor any course in common sense either, I see." She walked to the spiral staircase that led to the observatory balcony. When she reached it, she put one hand on the railing, and signaled Willa with the other. Together they walked up the stairs and went out onto the balcony. Below them, the city and harbor lay still in the autumn morning. Her mother pointed at the roof of the Thibert Hotel. "We'll be staying there until I can find a suitable, permanent room." She looked at the clock tower above city hall. "We'll be taking a tallyho ride this evening, with the Olaussen family. They're Norwegians, sadly, but they've a son. Georg is his name. An accountant. A bachelor." Her mother turned with an unapologetic gaze. "Willa, you need to find a husband." She bunched the collar of her cloak into a fist to stave off the harbor wind. "Practically speaking, I do too."

"I'll meet no one named Georg Olaussen, or anyone else you'd pair me with."

"I'll grant you the shortcomings of the institution—even of men in the main—but we're bankrupt, Willa. *Failed*, altogether. And unless you have a secret fortune, well, we'll soon be unhoused, too."

"But we can afford to take rooms at the Thibert Hotel?"

Her mother glanced again at the rooftop of said hotel and then closed her eyes against what she saw there. "Your father found your naïveté charming. I find it troublesome, and even alarming."

"Which is no answer at all to my question."

"Troublesome because for all your intelligence, you fail to see what is plainest. You always have. You know algebra and trigonometry, but you couldn't tell me how much a loaf of bread costs. You can imagine the dark side of the moon, but not the prospect of being penniless." She shook her head. "And alarming because you cannot fathom the consequences of your ignorance. You're just like him."

"And yet *he* never managed to bankrupt us. *He* managed to keep us in bread and in pennies while you've managed to clear us of both. If what you say is true." Now Willa shook her head. "And you equivocate. You avoid answering any question put to you."

Ann Brandt sighed and unclasped her purse and removed a handkerchief and touched her nose and cheeks with it and looked at the cloth as though she expected to find specks of blood. "I've made arrangements, dear. Temporary, but all the same." She returned the handkerchief and straightened. "I've called in our last favor." Now she glanced around the balcony for what would be the last time. "If that's what it is and if you must know. But it would be best if you not press me on the matter. Instead, put some of your famous conviction to the use of finding a well-heeled beau. He needn't be handsome or charming, and you certainly needn't *love* him. Just make do. Find someone who'll provide a nice home. And other small comforts." As she alighted the spiral staircase she paused midway and turned again to her daughter. "You're pretty, Willa.

And not without other qualities." She took another step, stopped a second time. "Who knows? You might even find something more than the moon and stars."

That morning had been only seven months ago, and here she was now, her husband suddenly standing beside her in the entryway. "The rest of the furniture should arrive next week," Theodulf said, gesturing straight ahead, then leading the way into the kitchen when she did not budge. It was Father Richter who finally took her by the elbow and ushered her in. Theodulf was adding wood to the stove.

"The rest of our monthly larder should arrive with the furniture, but for now there's still some pork down in the barrel, and there're plenty of comestibles in the pantry." He set the damper on the stove, brushed his hands and unbuttoned his coat, and said to Father Richter, "Lend a hand with these trunks?" Then to Willa, "Please, have a look around."

Willa followed the men out of the kitchen and watched as they carried the first of her trunks upstairs. She wandered the main floor. The kitchen and entryway and two other rooms furnished only with a desk and captain's chair, a banjo clock and Christ on the cross hung above it, and, in the parlor, hidden beneath thrown bed linens, an upright piano.

"For you," Theodulf said from across the house.

"I'm speechless," Willa said, taken aback by the unexpected kindness. There passed between them a clumsy silence. The boyish smile he was capable of in candid moments came over him, and she smiled in turn. "Thank you."

He hefted the second trunk and said, "I'll show you upstairs."

There were three bedrooms, two of them empty except for lace curtains hanging on the windows. In the third, a folding cot made with a woolen blanket and thin pillow gave the appearance of a barracks. "I'll be on duty nighttimes," Theodulf said as he came out of one of the other bedrooms. "So, until delivery of our furniture, you can sleep here. I'll slumber during the day. Once everything arrives, that will be your bedchamber." He pointed at the room next to this one. Willa stepped into her bedroom and walked to the window and pulled the curtain aside.

The lighthouse stood dispassionate against the backdrop of the lake. To her right, the weather fairly galloped east so that the shoreline came clearer and clearer with each moment. There were still patches of snow on the beach and in the hills. The forest held black and shadowless up into those hills, and beyond, but as she stood there, she thought she could see it shifting. As if it were its own weather. Or as if it had its own confused heart. It was from this direction she'd arrived. Only an hour ago, but already it seemed ten years past.

Theodulf removed his pocket watch, checked the time, and said, "I'll take advantage of the fair weather to row our friend back down to Otter Bay. It's eleven now, I should return by two. I'd like you to have supper ready. And make a plate for me to bring on watch tonight, yes?" He turned to the priest. "I'll ready the boat. You gather your things and meet me down at the dock in ten minutes." Theodulf stopped in the doorway, turned back, and added, "Willa, come down to see Father Richter off, yes? I'll also show you where we keep the perishables." Now he made a passing survey of the mostly empty room. "It's a far sight homier than the Thibert Hotel, there's no doubt of that." Then he left, his boots clomping down the stairs.

When Theodulf reached the main floor, the priest spoke in a hushed voice. "Just remember, though you can't see God, He'll be watching after you. And anyway, Mr. Sauer is not mistaken." He spread his arms as though to welcome the Holy Spirit. "It's a lovely home. Make it a happy one for your husband." And then he, too, turned to go. His own footfalls on the narrow stairs were as a ballerina's.

Willa looked at her trunks pushed against the inside wall. All of her personal belongings reduced to what they held. It was a thought that might have brought some grief, but then she looked around the room as Theodulf had, and took a small comfort in knowing that she at least wouldn't need to sleep with her husband.

Theodulf had raised the mast and rigged the sail, which hung slack on the boom. She heard him rooting around in the boathouse as she reached the dock with Father Richter, who carried his leather valise and a folded blanket no doubt intended for his lap. The sky was still brightening, but the faint breeze off the water was cold, and an hour in the boat would be chilling.

Emerging from the boathouse with the tiller, Theodulf walked to the skiff and lowered it into the water. "Father, go ahead and hop aboard," he said, then to Willa added, "I'll show you our store of provisions." Without waiting for her to answer, he walked halfway out the dock where a four-foot square of cast iron hunkered like a hatch coaming. Theodulf dropped to his knees, unbolted the lid, and lifted it open.

Her curiosity roused, Willa stepped closer and looked down into the dock. There was a barrel in there, someways submerged in the lake water, and Theodulf was unclasping the head and pulling it up from the cavity in the dock. "This hogshead is watertight, and the cold water acts like an ice box." He reached in and removed a package wrapped in butcher's paper and marked with an *H*. "This is a ham steak. You'll no doubt become acquainted with our larder, which is delivered quarterly." He returned his attention to the barrel again, reclasping the head and then sliding the cast iron cover into place and bolting it. "The lake kicks up and this lid's not in place, our meat will end up down the shore. If the lake's calm and this lid's not in place, our meat will end up in the mouths of wolves." He nodded at the ham steak. "There are canned goods in the pantry, and potatoes and roots and such in the cellar." Now he looked over at the skiff and nodded. "Very good, then. We'll be off."

As the station boat rounded the headland, looking like nothing so much as a Charles River dinghy, another boat came scudding into view, this one under the engine of a single rower, a man in a knit sweater and an oilskin hat pulled down over his ears and cinched under his chin. He rowed a simple herring skiff, the long oars like two thin wings beating against the gentle water. His strokes were effortless and potent, and as he came abeam the station dock, he glanced her way without missing a stroke. She could see he was clean-shaven and that his galluses held up oilskin pants that matched his hat. He was not fifty feet from her when he flashed a kind smile and then steered for the cove another quarter mile up the shore.

Thinking the cold air would help preserve the pork, she left it wrapped in butcher paper on the stoop and went back into the house to drift through its vacancy. The pantry was well stocked. The windows in all the rooms were covered with the same lace curtains as the bedrooms. She went back up there, into the room with her trunks, and opened the larger of the two. Her wardrobe, once grand, was paltry now. Just two summer skirts and a pair of trousers, three plain white blouses, one with short sleeves, and a chambray work shirt, a housecoat, two sleeping gowns, stockings and undergarments and petticoats, the cloak she only just realized was still covering her shoulders, one pair of house slippers, another pair of brogues. A pitiable trousseau, but what matter? She didn't much care that her gowns and fine hats had been sold one at a time. Given her druthers, she'd dress like a college professor. Of course, her new lot necessitated a certain ladylikeness, which explained the blouses and petticoats.

She arranged her clothes in the closet and then stowed the empty trunk beneath the hanging garments. Before returning to the second trunk, she stopped at the window again and looked up the shoreline to the cove. How had she missed those fish houses at first glance? From here, she had a clear line of sight. There was a thin ribbon of smoke coming now from the one on the left. Likely that man had landed his boat and gone inside to stoke his woodstove. Did that mean he lived alone? Why was there no smoke from the second shanty? She turned to the other trunk, removed her cloak, and sat on the floor beside the rest of her belongings.

There were her shampoos and soaps and powder for her teeth; a box of stationery and inkwell and pen and a stack of journals, some blank and some filled with her jottings and equations; a portrait of her mother and father in a small gilt frame; a pair of decent gloves and a bonnet to wear against the sun. There were seed packets to plant when the weather turned, turnips and tomatoes and cucumbers, basil and thyme and peppers; her father's collapsing brass telescope; and the last gift he'd given her, a rosewood music box that played six airs. All of this she removed from the trunk and laid on the floor beside her. She then rose to her knees and reached into the silk lining of the trunk, along the back at the bottom edge, and used all of her fingers to pry up the false bottom her father had installed before she'd departed for Radcliffe.

Packed neatly in the real bottom were two clandestine books (Theodulf, she felt, would not abide a learned woman, a fact he made clear during their engagement). The first was a copy of James Nasmyth and James Carpenter's *The Moon*, which she'd cleverly unbound from its original case and glued into the covers of a Douay-Rheims bible. The second was Louis Agassiz's *Lake Superior*, similarly transformed to fit between the covers of Augustine's *The City of God*. In a felt-lined box, whose lid she unclasped and lifted, was a Smith & Wesson Model 10 and a box of .38/200 bullets. This a parting gift from her mother only yesterday. There were three diaries, two of them yet to see a word, and the other, which she set aside, less a diary than her own observations and hypotheses about her most recent fascinations: Halley's Comet (and comets generally) and the moon and stars. And last, the score of Beethoven's Piano Sonata No. 14, its pages turned a hundred times—a thousand times?— the only vestige of her happiness to make this journey with her.

She sat cross-legged on the floor, opened the score on her lap, and ran a finger along the first ledger line of the sonata. But before she could conjure the notes, before she could summon them through the memory of her fingers, she closed her eyes and then the score, and placed it back in the bottom of the trunk. She returned the gun and the books and then the false bottom. She returned everything else and slid the trunk across the floor to the window. Before closing it, she took the telescope and extended it and trained it on the fish house up the shore. That man was loading herring into wooden boxes, a pipe pinched between his lips, his movement easy and efficient. Now she shifted her sight to a young girl sitting on an upturned fish box, her feet dangling, her hands in mittens but her legs bare beneath a shabby dress. Willa watched her for a moment, then saw her rise and shield her eyes and apparently say something to the man on the other dock, who, when Willa retrained the spyglass on him, had stopped loading his catch and was talking to the girl. Then he laughed, or anyway smiled, and bent back to his labor. The girl was smiling back.

Willa felt a reprieve from what she already understood was loneliness. She took one more look at each of them before packing the spyglass away again. She straightened her skirts and tucked the wisps of her hair behind her ears and descended the narrow staircase to the main floor, where she went to the kitchen to consider how to make supper.

Taking an apron from a hook beside the sink, she hung it over her shoulders and tied it behind her back. From the woodbox, she lifted two pieces of split birch and stoked the stove fire again and then lit the lamp and followed that flame into the cellar. Behind the cistern, which was full of black water as still as bedrock, she found the boxes of potatoes and onions, apples and carrots and radishes, the cans of lard and bottles of vinegar and molasses and the jars of pickles. She put two Irish spuds in her apron pockets and a jar of lard under her arm, then lifted an apple with her free hand. She took a bite of the apple, which was mealy and bland.

Back in the kitchen, she set the potatoes on the table and finished the apple. Where to begin? Had she ever actually cooked a proper supper? Certainly she had no instincts beyond warming the cast iron skillet. So, she lifted it from a hook and scooped a spoonful of lard into it. Could she cook the pork and potatoes together?

In any case, she'd need the ham steak, which she went to fetch from the stoop.

But it was gone. She turned and looked down the path to the lake, retracing her steps of only a half hour before, remembering the butcher paper and string. She glanced out over the grounds, and then sat on the porch railing and felt the chill of the air, which had been the reason she'd left the ham outside in the first place. She closed her eyes and lifted her face to the still air. Instead of weeping, she stood up and glanced around once more for the ham. Over the stoop rail, on the ground beneath her, she saw the paper and string. Hurrying down the stairs and around the balusters, she discovered that the package had been torn open. She bent down and picked it up, and only then saw the muddy paw print. It was as big as her own hand.

She did not, as she looked across the grounds and into the dark woods up on the hill, feel the terror that might have accompanied this thievery. She did not admonish the guilty wolf. Instead, she admired its stealth and daring. She took pleasure in it, and let it raise in her some resolve of her own. She smiled across the yard and lifted a hand to the locket hanging at the neckline of her dress. Perhaps her father was with her after all.

Back inside, she went to the pantry and took a can each of mutton and corn from the shelf. She found the can opener and uncapped them and then emptied them into the hot skillet. The sizzle that arose had an almost pleasant odor. There was a knife on the drying rack in the sink, and she used it to slice the potatoes, which she added to the stew in the skillet. Back in the pantry, she found a jar of mustard and a canister of pilot bread. She brought them back and put them on the table, and then she took the apron off and hung it back on the peg. She went upstairs to retrieve the masquerading copy of *The Moon* and brought it with her to the kitchen table. Before she rested, she fetched tea from the pantry and made herself a cup. Finally, she sat down and opened her book.

HER UNCLE MATS was as gentle as goose down and as sweet as the sarsaparilla he brewed by the firkin. Silje loved the evenings they spent in his fish house. She loved the sound of his deep voice humming those fishing songs from the old country. She loved more than anything the smell of his pipe smoke and the glint of his kind eyes behind it.

He pointed the mouthpiece at her and said, "Mind you wrap the barrel and the stock before you put it in the vises."

"Wrap it with what, Uncle?"

He fetched two remnants of the last moosehide he'd tanned and offered them. Stepping back to his own labor, he said, "And don't set the vise too tight. Just strong enough to hold it."

She wrapped the stock first, set it in the vise, and cranked the handle until it held firm. She did the same to the barrel of the Winchester, then fetched the brass brush and slid it down the bore. She knew her uncle watched through the haze of his smoke, so she worked deliberately. Carefully. After two passes, she attached a cotton patch to the brush and slid that through and back. It came out black, so she repeated that step three times more, until the patch, held up to the window, came out more or less clean.

"How much oil, Uncle?"

"Just a drop or two."

Uncle Mats had strung two shuttles and was now collecting the floats and putting them in a fish box. He'd set the first nets of the season tomorrow. Before or after they hunted the Gininwabiko Creek, depending on the lake's mood. He'd promised his niece the hunt, but their stores were grim, too. A moose or a deer in the cache would stay a season of hungry nights.

"When will they return?" Silje said.

"We had fog most of the day. Likely they waited it out in Two Harbors and we'll see them tomorrow morning."

"The fog lifted before noon."

"Maybe your mother needed more than her tooth pulled."

She loosened the vises and removed the gun and folded the moosehide. "They're not coming back," she said.

"Nonsense, Silje." He set the last of the floats in the box and tapped the ash from his pipe, which he stuffed into his shirt pocket. "There's a hundred reasons they might've stayed in Two Harbors and only one explanation if they left. Fog sunk a lot of freighters, but hardly ever a skiff." He lifted the box of floats and pushed the door open with his boot. A cold gust of air whooshed in.

Silje added a log to the woodstove, grabbed the Winchester, and followed her uncle outside. "If they don't come back, you'll take care of me?"

"You'll be taking care of me, then."

She turned to look across the water. Into the hardness of the evening. It settled like the *Lisbon*, sunk five years ago now, right under her feet at the Big Rock. She was only eight years old then, heading back from Otter Bay afoot, the snow like hammerblows off the lake, the wind harder than she'd ever felt. Her mother, desperate for laudanum after a sprained wrist, had insisted on the trek to Winkler's store despite her father's warning that it was foolhardy to go out in the coming weather. Silje had turned to look back only once, her father's fists knuckling into his hips and a rash of rage flaring on his neck.

"Remember when the ship sank down the shore, Uncle?"

Uncle Mats set the box in his boat and turned back to her. He took his waxed canvas hat off and ran a hand through his matted hair. "Don't carry that rifle around. It's not a toy."

Silje took a step back as though he might grab it from her.

Mats put his hat back on and said, "There's a loaf of rye in the breadbox. Why don't you bring that and the cheese into the fish house? We'll sup in there."

"It's warmer in the fish house," she said.

"Go on," he said. "I'll bring the nets down boatside and meet you at the counter. Warm the coffee, aye? Put the gun on the rack."

He started for the net reel and was halfway to it before he heard the shot echoing across the water. He flinched and turned and there she was, looking back over her shoulder, the Winchester still aimed at the lake. He did not smile. And she felt no relief, only the jolt in her shoulder.

Mats hurried across the stones. He grabbed the rifle by the fore-stock and slung the barrel over his shoulder. "The lake out there, she gives you everything. And here you are, shooting her full of lead?"

"The lake, she takes, too, Uncle."

"I'll hear no more of that, Silje Sigrid. You'll go get the bread and cheese, and we'll have a bite before we sleep. Go on, I said."

She glared at the rifle then Uncle and then the house before stomping across the beach and into the line of trees and the cabin dark among them. She found the rye bread and the last of the cheese and headed back for the fish house. She set dinner on the counter and looked out the window, imagining the lighthouse keeper's wife's skirts billowing in the breeze off the water.

"What's got your eye, child?" Uncle Mats asked as he came back inside.

"Did you see that lady come?"

"The keeper's wife?"

"Why would she marry that ugly frog?"

"You've a sharp tongue."

She turned to him and said, "He's rotten, too."

Mats shook his head, chancing a smile. "You know an awful lot."

She came over to the counter and took her knife out of its sheath and cut the bread into three slices. She cut the cheese, too. "I can't help I have the sight."

"You *think* you do." He brushed her wild hair from her eyes. "It's sometimes better not to."

"I've no choice, Uncle."

"No choice. *Harrumph.*" He put the cheese on a slice of bread and took a big bite as he walked to the window himself.

"I bet she's pretty. You should marry her."

"You can't marry another man's wife."

"The devil or Fenrir will take him."

"Fenrir, that's your furry friend out in the woods?"

"Fenrir is no friend to me. He'll eat us all if we let him."

"Those wolves don't want anything to do with you, Silje."

"If we see him up on Gininwabiko Creek tomorrow morning, we should shoot him."

"We won't see him. Or any of his gang, either. They're like ghosts."

Silje picked a piece of bread and cheese from the counter. "I forgot to put the coffee on to warm." She slipped over to the stove and put the kettle on.

"If the weather's right, I'll set nets before we hunt."

She nodded and finished eating and cleaned her knife. From her shelf above the counter she grabbed the woodcarving she'd lately been working on. She climbed onto the counter and rested by the window with her back against the wall, her knees drawn up.

After a while Mats said, "You know, Fenrir is a strong name. We tell stories about a wolf called that."

"How do you think he got his name, Uncle?"

"And how do you know about that old beast?"

"You've books in the cabin. And winter's long. Long-long-long."

"There's still plenty of snow up in the hills."

"Easier to track the moose," she said. "And more snow falling now."

Every thirty seconds she glanced out the window, as if the woman might actually be there.

The carving she held in her right hand while with her left she whittled the snout. Her lap was covered in curls of birchwood that smelled better than the cheese dinner had. She'd cut away to the ears and eyes and a long, sleek neck. Next would be the lips and sharp teeth and last the wolf's sleek coat. She'd need the fine gouge for that.

"What's her name, do you think?" she asked.

He quit humming. "The keeper's wife?" He was smoking his pipe again and using some of the hempen line to attach a gaff hook to the long handle. When Silje didn't answer, he glanced up at her. She was looking down. Expectant.

"She's a man's name. Will, or something like that. Keeper Sauer told me when he visited that day." He swiped his own hair off his forehead. "He said he'd trade haircuts for fish."

Uncle Mats set his work down and came over to look at the carving. Together they glanced out the window.

"Tonight he'll light the beacon," he said.

"The water, the light, our sight . . ." Silje sang in a whisper. After too long a pause, he answered, "Ay, it is a damn-ed sight." She leaned back in laughter.

"We'll sleep out here tonight? So I can finish my work? You can keep at yours?"

She nodded and climbed into the cockloft and fluffed the pillow she kept there. She set back to work carving, caricature fangs twice as big as they ought to be.

ALREADY THE HOUSE FELT LIKE HOME, and not because his wife was in it. As he stood in the doorway, his arms and shoulders and back twitched, remembering the six-mile row. Sometimes his body got like that. Alert. Aroused by his labors.

In the entryway, he removed his coat and hung it over the radiator. As he walked into the kitchen, he looked at his watch.

"What time is it?" Willa said, closing her book and rising from her seat in one motion. She straightened her skirts and went to the stovetop, where she stirred the stew.

Theodulf opened and closed his watch again, as though much time had passed in that instant. "It's two o'clock," he said, taking the seat opposite Willa's, pocketing his watch, and arranging the linen napkin in his shirt collar. He sat with great posture and poise, had the mien of a man raised by a strict father.

Willa had earlier set the table, and she took his plate and went to the stovetop and scooped a ladle of stew onto it. A geyser of steam rose from the mush. She placed it before him, then took two pieces of pilot bread from the canister and laid them on the edge of his plate.

Theodulf squinted at his food. "What's this?"

Willa took her seat. "It's mutton. There're stores of it in the pantry."

"What about the ham steak?"

"It was pilfered."

His gaze lifted from the table to her face. "Pilfered, you say?"

"Some critter or other."

"Stole a pound of ham?" He looked once around the room, as if the offending rascal might be about.

"I left it on the stoop when I came up from the lake. Because it's cold out, and I thought it would stay fresh. I was going to bring it in after I unpacked. When it was time to make supper, the ham was gone."

"You say you thought it would stay fresher? Out on the stoop?"

"Yes. Naturally."

Theodulf moved the stew around with the tines of his fork. "That was the last of our pork until the tender next comes."

"When will that be?"

"A week from today."

"In the meantime, there's plenty else to eat."

"But the ham steak was to be our first meal here together. I saved the best meat." He stirred the mutton again.

If she appreciated his gesture, he didn't notice. Though in fairness to himself, he'd not spent much time alone in the company of women. And if they were inscrutable in public, in private they were horrifying. Or anyway Willa had so far proven to be. When he chanced another glance at her, she was staring right back, her hands folded on the table where her own plate of mutton might have been.

Her hands thus composed reminded him he'd not yet said grace, so without aplomb he made the sign of the cross, folded his own hands, and bowed his head. "Bless us, O Lord, and these thy gifts, which we are about to receive, from thy bounty, through Christ, our Lord. And eternal rest grant unto them, O Lord, and let perpetual light shine upon them. May the souls of the faithful departed, through the mercy of God, rest in peace. Amen." He opened his eyes and blinked at her.

She took her own plate to the stovetop and scooped up some mush.

Theodulf appeared perplexed. "I thought I smelled ham when I came in just now."

"Well, I burned the butcher's paper. Maybe that put up a scent." Back at the table she lay her napkin on her lap and took a small bite.

He watched as her eyes closed and her lips stopped moving and she swallowed. After a moment, she opened her eyes and looked at him and if he'd had to declare, he would have said she smiled. Tempting the moment, he smiled back.

"It's terrible," she said.

Theodulf raised his napkin to cover his mouth. "The texture alone could have slayed me," he said, dropping his napkin as quickly as he raised it, pushing his plate away, and allowing an awkward laugh.

"It tastes like tin. The potatoes are cooked to mush." She took a piece of pilot bread from the canister and broke it in half and ate it. Her smile waned as she chewed. She sighed. And as quickly as she'd appeared happy—or at least at ease—she suddenly looked a scared child again.

Theodulf, eager to maintain the lightness of the moment, picked up the jar of mustard and said, "What was this for, then?"

She only shrugged.

"Your mother told me you weren't much in the kitchen. And that's just fine. I have simple tastes. And anyway, the Lighthouse Service provides only the basest provisions. In fact"—and here he rose and retrieved from the front room a list of those very rations— "this is for you, to plan our meals and manage our larder. There's a mercantile in Otter Bay, and we'll have what we can hunt and grow in our garden, and of course fish from the lake, but this is the bulk of it. And all provided as though a God-given right."

Willa set the list of provisions on top of her sham bible. "My mother was not much in the kitchen herself. Or anywhere else, in the house or about town, if we're telling the truth." There was a sharpness in her voice that suggested more than the animus Ann Brandt had counseled him about. He knew Ann to be an unpleasant woman, a heathen, but also shrewd and resourceful. She'd weathered her husband's suicide when it would surely have been easier to follow him right into the grave. Willa sitting here at his table, while Ann was settled in an apartment at the Thibert Hotel, a largesse at Theodulf's expense, was proof of all that.

"You know, your mother is welcome to visit whenever you like," he said.

She answered with a piercing stare, and despite his cocksureness, he wondered if he'd overplayed his hand.

"Of course, if you'd rather she not—"

Willa stood abruptly and scurried into the pantry, where she took a hunk of cheese from a shelf and brought it back to the table. She used the same knife she'd cut the potatoes with to slice the cheese and moved the cutting board to the middle of the table before lifting the two plates of mush and setting them on the drainboard beside the sink. "My mother will, of course, never be invited here." She sat back down and selected the smallest piece of cheese and took a small bite.

He felt like he was watching the weather change, so unexpected and moody was this woman. But he was practiced at just this sort of observation. In fact, his whole occupation was predicated on it, and so he set about studying her as though she were a storm cloud coming off the lake. "Very well," he said, as though granting her permission.

She paused eating, clearly aggrieved, and then set her cheese down on the edge of the board and said, "You told me there were no neighbors for miles around."

He raised a questioning eyebrow and then caught her meaning. "Of course. You saw our fisherman coming up the shore this morning. I saw him myself."

"There're two places over there." She gestured in the direction of their fish houses.

"The one you saw is Mats Braaten. He's a bachelor. There's another family over there called the Lindviks. Arvid and his wife and their daughter. I believe they've taken advantage of the first fair weather and ice-out to make a run for supplies. Her name's Bente. A meaner woman you've never met. But they're all God-fearing folks. Lutherans, it's true. But I suppose when a man calls on God out on the big water, a little something is better than nothing."

"Should I expect them to come around?"

"I told Arvid I'd gladly trade haircuts for fish, so I believe you might."

"Haircuts?"

He made a scissoring motion with his first two fingers. "Did I not tell you I spent some time barbering?"

"You did not."

"It's a noble profession. A democratic one."

She nodded and reached for another bite. If he was honest with himself, he felt her looking right through him. As though he were glassine, and all his lies and secrets were written in black ink across his flesh.

"I'll look forward to meeting them," Willa said. And now she stood and retrieved another plate from the pantry. She sliced more cheese and fanned it on the plate. She added some pilot bread and a dollop of mustard and covered it with a tea cloth. "This will have to suffice for dinner tonight."

"It'll be fine."

"What time is it now?"

Theodulf checked his watch, thinking an hour must have passed since he sat down for supper. The Longines told him otherwise. "It's only two fifteen."

"It seems much later."

"I was just thinking the same." He put his watch back in his pocket.

She tilted her head and looked out the kitchen window, up at the sky, and with that simple glance was gone. He knew it even if she didn't.

"What's outside?" he said. "You went away all at once."

She kept her eyes on the clouds, now wisps against the cold blue above them. The weather was in retreat.

"Willa?"

"The sky's clearing," she said without looking at him. "It wasn't going to."

"Fairer skies to see the light!" Theodulf exclaimed.

As if she hadn't heard him, Willa said, "Today's the comet's perihelion."

"Halley's Comet?"

Now she did look at him. "You know of it?"

"Certainly I do. Every educated man does."

"Have you observed it?"

He straightened his cravat and affected an air of superiority. "I close my eyes when I stare heavenward. The better to see God."

She sighed and turned back to the sky.

"Perihelion?" he asked.

"When the comet's orbit is closest to the sun."

"Where it might gather more poisonous gas to shuttle back to earth."

"You don't honestly believe that?" Willa said.

"One of the most learned men I know—one who studied at the Sorbonne and at Harvard, who's now an apothecary down in Gunflint, and with whom I conduct a regular correspondence, a certain Hosea Grimm, a Papist himself, as devout as the prophet for whom he's named—he told me all about it. He's gone so far as to develop his own treatment for what he's sure will be a sickness born of that serpent comet's trailing vapors."

"A sickness? From trailing vapors?"

But Theodulf was undeterred. "Pope Pius has appealed for prayers against the destruction of the earth. He's asked that bells be rung against it. Should the comet strike earth, well, he prays that it finds the Turks, not us faithful."

Finally, she turned again to him. This bedlamite. This quibbling gasbag. This dullard.

"What is it?" he asked.

"The Turks? A pill to protect us from *vapors*?"

He pinched a toothpick from the breast pocket of his shirt and with a dramatic pause levered it between molars.

"I'm tired from the long trip." She put the list of provisions on the tabletop and picked up her book. "I think I'll go upstairs and rest."

"You'll not," he said, replacing the toothpick.

"Excuse me?"

"There's a mess here," he said.

She looked at the skillet on the stove, the dirty plates on the drainboard. The knives and forks and cutting board still with the block of cheese and apple core.

"Our duty is to the Lighthouse Service, Willa. In fulfilling that duty, I put a shine on the water. And you put a shine on the tinware and crockery. You'll be faithful to the Service, and not to fanciful comets or anything else in the sky save God." He held out his coffee cup and nodded at the stove.

As if drawn by the heat of it, Willa's gaze settled on the percolator and lingered for a moment. When she turned again to look at him, she said, "You'll command me as though I were one of the assistant keepers? Is that it?"

"If I must," he said, a kind of exasperation in his voice. "But now I'm merely instructing."

"And you can't fill your own cup?"

He slammed his free hand down on the table. "There will be no petulance." He smoothed his hand over the board, as though flattening a linen not there. "We each have our responsibilities. It's as simple as that."

She walked to the stove, donned the oven mitt, lifted the percolator, returned to the table, and filled his cup to the lip. Then she returned the coffee and set about the rest of her chores, starting a pot of water to boil first. She scraped the plates and dumped the stew into the mess bucket. The cheese and mustard she returned to the pantry. Impatiently, she added another piece of wood to the firebox and stood above the stove, waiting for the water to warm. All this while Theodulf sipped his coffee, contented in her obedience.

"I hope you found comfort in your time with Father Richter? He believes you'll be happy here."

She turned to face him, a look of sheer vacancy drawn over her fair eyes.

"We should expect to see him from time to time. It's astonishing, really, the lengths he travels to meet the needs of his congregation. Why, tomorrow he'll be going back to Two Harbors, later this week to Gunflint. He'll even pay a visit to the Chippewa village up there. It's almost as if the whole shore is his parish. Even us, here at this lonely station." He worried a piece of apple from his back tooth. "That's duty." He spat the apple rind onto his plate. "That's devotion."

She had to choose her words carefully. "He seems a humble man."

Theodulf smiled. "Humble, indeed. And pious. A true servant of God. We should all aspire to be so good." Now he nodded at the chair and her faux bible. "Speaking of such, I'm happy to see that. I find the isolation of this station to be the perfect place for reading scripture. The perfect place for *prayer.* We mortals stand out against the beasts and endless wilderness."

"Doesn't God hear our prayers wherever we say them?"

He smiled. "Yes, naturally. But I imagine that here, they find special resonance. Like the light will shine upon the lake at night, so will our prayers lift from this spot." He paused and rested a finger beneath his eye as though to wipe away a tear. "It brings me such joy to believe that. Tell me, what book were you reading from?"

She had rehearsed her answers to such questions and quickly answered, "Genesis."

"Our primeval history," he said. "God's creation." He spread his arms again, as though preaching. "Do you find solace in the simplicity?"

This sort of question she'd not rehearsed an answer to. Her response came spontaneously. "Simplicity? There's hardly such a thing."

"*Our* faith? *Our* reverence for God? *Our* belief in the word of God? Nothing could be simpler. Nothing."

Willa didn't reply, only turned back to the stove and lifted the lid on the hot water reservoir, thinking of the comet and where it came from and where it would return. Was there anything simple in that?

"That's to warm water," he said. "You can fill it when you start your preparations. Then, when it's time to scrub the messes, you'll have hot water ready, instead of needing to wait for a kettle," he said.

"I know what it is," she said. She stepped to the sink, put the plug in, turned on the water tap, and soaked a cloth. While the sink filled, she wiped the table. Theodulf, meanwhile, stood. He straightened his trousers and checked his watch again.

"Sunrise is shortly after six tomorrow," he said.

She turned to him.

"There's oats for breakfast."

"Breakfast shortly after six," she said, then turned her attention to the sink full of dishes.

"I've a few things to attend to before I go on watch," he said.

Willa merely nodded.

A half hour later, Theodulf returned to the house and climbed the stairs. He walked past the bathroom and stopped at his bedroom's closed door. For a moment, he waited just outside, his nose nearly touching the jamb. He didn't know how to do this. How to be kind or generous. He wanted to leave. Everything would be simpler if he did. But then he pulled out his watch and tallied the tasks still undone and marked them against the hour. He needed to act, and knew he'd be relieved once he had. The door swung slightly open as he knocked. Willa lay on the cot, facing away. The shape of his young wife's body was supposed to arouse him. He understood she was pretty and shapely, but at best the object of his gaze brought curiosity. Certainly it was a gaze without desire. Even the thought of the ham steak had stirred him more.

He stood in the doorway, waiting. He felt the ticking of his watch in contest with his own nerves. A full minute must have passed before she sensed him—or woke—and looked over her shoulder.

"Excuse me," he said.

She answered by sitting up on her elbow.

Without further explanation, he crossed the room to retrieve his black leather holdall, then held it up as explanation and stood by the window, unmoving and unspeaking.

"What is it?" she asked.

He reached into the pocket that held his watch. This time, instead of the Longines, he removed three Silvertop Chocolates and brought them to her. "I nearly forgot. I bought these for you in Otter Bay." He handed her the prize.

She sat up further and looked at the candy. "You're full of surprises today."

He felt the blush run up his neck and into his cheeks. "Anything so frivolous as chocolate we must arrange for ourselves," he said, as though reciting a statute. For good measure, he added, "Those are the rules of the Lighthouse Service."

She unwrapped one of the chocolates and popped it into her mouth. Her eyes closed slowly, and he understood she was savoring the sweetness. When she opened them a moment later, she said, "Rules aside, it was kind of you to bring these for me. I'll do my best to make them last."

Now he smiled, too. It was the first moment of unfettered gentleness that had passed between them since her arrival, and he was amazed to discover that he'd orchestrated it himself. He raised his holdall again, nodded, and turned to leave. At the doorway, he said, "Well then, until morning."

B EFORE HE MIGHT ATTEND TO HIS DUTIES, Theodulf with-drew from his holdall a single slip of Lighthouse Service letter-head, uncapped his pen and ink bottle, and wrote furiously:

April the 20th, Year of Our Lord 1910

My Dear & Fair Sir,

Salutations from your humble friend and servant at the Gininwabiko station, in the hour before its commission. With God's grace, and in His everlasting image, we'll soon be a bea-con for all the boats what ply these troubled waters. I wish that you could witness her blazing light this very night. But since I alone will be here to strike the first match and marvel at her effulgence, I invite you to her twentieth illuming, at the jubilee of May the 9th. I would be happy (indeed, proud) to consider you a guest of honor.

But I write on another matter of great urgency. As you no doubt know, tonight marks the occasion of the perihelion of Halley's Comet, when that cursed ball of brimstone will be closest to the sun. As my own investigation into the matter has yielded most troubling findings (viz., that the poisonous tail of the comet, when it explodes into earth, will doom us all, and that even those of us inoculated from damnation will suffer the heat of hell), I wonder if you might confirm some few of my theorem. Or, should your own learning on the matter not be sufficient to the queries herein, perhaps you might steer me wisdom's way.

To wit; (1) Is it true that the comet's tail is rank with enven-omed ammonia; (2) Is it true that cataclysm is inevitable, by way

42

of that poison splashing across the earth, or by mere impact; (3) Is it true that you yourself have conjured some antidote to those very gases and poisons, and that something as simple as a pill might protect us; (4) Is it true that His Holiness Pope Pius X has issued a Bullarium against said comet, and further asked for prayers and bells both to be sung against it, as I read in the *Ax & Beacon* not more than six months ago, in an article written by none other than yourself; (5) From what authority did you pen said article; (6) And, forthwith and if I may, are you a Papist yourself; is that the source of your conviction?

I appeal to your wisdom on these and any other matters germane to that cursed comet, and send my gratitude for your time and consideration.

Yours in faith & affection,
Theodulf Sauer
Master Keeper, Gininwabiko Station
The United States Lighthouse Service

Postscript: Are you suffering the scourge of wolves in your county?

He folded the letter in perfect thirds, slid it into an envelope, and paused to bite saliva from his tongue before slowly wetting the glue and pressing the envelope shut. He laid it on the center of the small desk and nodded as though the note stared back in agreement. After addressing the letter, he put the cap back on his pen and turned to his other and more exigent duties.

Closing his eyes and pressing the pads of his thumbs together at the tip of his throat and wrapping the rest of his fingers around his neck until the nails of his middle fingers met at his nape, he squeezed until he felt the bloodless prickle all over his scalp. He held himself thus for six seconds, then released his hands and watched the static emerge behind his closed eyes.

S HE PULLED THE LINEN from the piano and let it pool on the floor beside the bench. Three recessed alcoves on the upper panel were backed by crimson velvet set in rosewood, which seemed, in that twilit hour, to give a bloodlike essence to light the room. Above the fallboard, which was closed and missing one of the two brass knobs, only the G and CK of the George Steck emblem remained. The ornate legs were chipped and the middle pedal missing. The water stains emanating in concentric circles atop the piano gave the impression of a full, bright moon spreading against the black night.

She toed the bench out from beneath the piano and sat and let her fingers hang poised above her legs, the fallboard still closed, as though from the sanguine air alone she might draw a few notes. The irony of this gift could have been the subject of its own symphony. And yet, she couldn't help seeing it as a kindness. Same as the chocolates still sitting upstairs on the pillow of their cot. A kindness, certainly. But one that came with a price. One she had already begun to pay. A debt impossible to settle.

She shook her head firmly against the indignity and turned instead to the sound that would have arisen from the adagio she imagined. The plaintiveness mined from the left hand, the ostinato of the right, played pianissimo even when her fingers were on the keys and not just the air around them. She felt the music in the bottom of her gut, despite it not being there at all. Her father used to tell her that she was never as beautiful as when she played, by which he meant she was never so at ease. But this piano, in this house, bestowed by Theodulf? She wondered if she'd ever be able to play it at all.

44

She made her hands into fists and the sound she imagined was replaced instead by the echo of its absence. It made her uneasy, so she stood and picked the linen off the floor and folded it as though she might be able to capture the silence in those threads and banish it. But by the time she laid the folded linen atop the water stain, the echo was only louder and more lamentable, and she hurried upstairs to flee it.

At the window again, she pushed the curtain aside and searched the gloaming for some quiet. The clouds banked on the quarter sky rising from the edge of the horizon, up over the water, meant she'd miss the comet again. Another insult on this damnable day. She let the curtain fall from her hand. What was it her mother had said as she walked with her daughter out of Sacred Heart on Willa's wedding day? "Marriage is contrivance best endured with a smile"? When Willa scoffed at her, her mother added, "Pen me a letter the first time you want to scream but pretend happiness instead."

She went to her chest, whether for the Beethoven score or gun or something else she wasn't sure. But as soon as the false bottom was lifted, she took from its hold the collapsing brass telescope and went back to the window. If her mother's advice was usually reserved for some sleight, her father's was always practical. Even beautiful. And when he'd given her the telescope some years ago, he told her its use was simple: to bring the faraway near. He further advised that she'd find uses for it almost wherever she looked, if she was only looking hard enough.

In Boston she'd used it to study the ships in the harbor, the sculls on the river, and the birds nesting high in the trees on the Commons. But mostly she'd train it on the moon, so much the object of her curiosity. She'd wandered around the grounds of the Harvard College Observatory with the telescope collapsed in her satchel, waiting for the moon to rise or the skies to clear. On the best nights for observation, she'd spend hours with her head craned to the sky, looking down only long enough to add layers to the maps she drew. On more than a few of those same nights, Professor Pickering—famous professor Edward Charles Pickering—paused during his evening constitutional to engage her in conversation. He even brought her, on one occasion, a facsimile of Athanasius Kircher's map of the moon, and recommended Nasmyth's tomb. But ever since her father's death, the telescope had hardly come out of her trunk. Now she trained it on the horizon to the northeast, up the shore. It came to her emboldened, the water dull under the heavy sky. The shoreline limned with the stingy hour's light. The moon and the comet no more in evidence than a semblance of contentedness in her thoughts.

Down the shore a lighter sky, another freighter steaming toward her—already the third she'd seen today—bordered by the inland woods ebony with evergreens and shadows. There was no pull toward home. Toward Duluth. But rather an indignation as sprawling and many pointed as her gazes up and down the shoreline. And there'd be no heavenly reprieve. No phantasm passing in the night sky. Or at least not one she'd be able to witness. The snow now moving ghostlike into her view through the telescope would see to that.

As she brought the lens back up the shore, the glass passed over the fishermen's dwellings. Smoke still rose from the tin chimney, and the skiff was up on the ways on the rocky beach. Two stacks of fish boxes rested from the dock deck to the eaves trough. They were newly made, the sawhorses and bucksaws still sitting outside suggested. Everything was tidy. The roof of the fish house had new tarpaper and a stack of shingles ready to be hammered on.

Willa focused the lens on the fish house's lakeside window. It was too dark to see inside, but as she focused evermore on that glass, she saw the reflection of the lighthouse. Then the houses, her own included. She lowered the telescope and strained her gaze across the suddenly great distance. With the long view again, she saw another house set back in the woods. Or at least the shape of a house, silhouetted against those pitchy pines.

Without so much as a second's hesitation, she ran down the stairs and out the front door and turned right for the path to the dock. Not until she got there did she feel the chill in the air, biting and fresh, the snow spitting against her downy cheeks. Like winter again. The planks were slick, and she had to slow her gallop after slipping on the first step. At the end of the dock, she extended the telescope again and turned it on the settlement. From water level she could see fewer particulars but confirmed a cabin in the woods, perhaps thirty yards back from the shoreline. It was made of stone and had windows on either side of the door. There was firewood stacked in mountainous piles all around.

There were two fish houses, and two boat ramps, but only one boat. Between the fish houses an empty net roller settled into the dusk. She knew this scene from all up and down the lakeshore. The familiarity helped her catch her breath, and looking again at the fish house, she concentrated on the same window she'd earlier studied. Whether it was a sixth sense or something else, she imagined the girl's profile in the dark glass. She watched for a long time, hoping to catch a movement or some other evidence of her being there. But nothing materialized. Not until that same pane of glass was suddenly lit from inside, and the girl's head fell back in laughter, framed in amber lantern light.

OVER THE NEXT FOUR HOURS, Theodulf made final preparations for the night ahead. He shoveled coal into the basement furnace, then filled the scuttle and brought a load to the lighthouse cleaning room, where he started the stove beside his desk. Noting the chill on the late afternoon, he fetched another scuttle and dumped it in the bin for later use. He delivered his plate to his desk in the cleaning room, moved his holdall and the letter he'd written aside, and readied the lamp and logbook for the evening ahead.

From the oil house, he retrieved the requisite kerosene for the vapor lamp in the Fresnel lens. He transferred stores of gasoline for the fog signals and stood in the doorway for ten seconds trying to read the weather, which was lowering again. At the hoist and derrick, he made sure the winch was locked and the cables taut even though it hadn't been used since Sunday, when the barrels of gasoline and crates of coal had been delivered. At the dock, he put the boat up and double-checked the lid on the cache, now empty of meat. The weather vane staked to the outermost piling showed a sputtering northerly breeze.

Back in the cleaning room, he rinsed and soaped his hands over the chamber pot before setting his holdall on the desktop and opening the pouch on the clasp side of the bag. He removed first the linen cloth and wiped his hands and the desktop. Next he spread the black silk napery and smoothed it over the blotter. Sitting down now, Theodulf withdrew the rolled leather pouch and arranged it above his blotter. It held a Swiss-made wrench with six pins, four screwdrivers and spare blades, a flat nose pliers, a seventy-five-millimeter ruler, a holding block, a leather buff, two different fine-point tweezers, a pair of pin vises, cutting broachers, and the fine-bladed pocketknife he used to remove the case backs. Last he took from the bag the loupe and magnifying glasses and finally the reason for all this, the Hamilton railroad watch he'd been using as his most recent subject.

He lit the desk lamp and brought the flame up. Satisfied that everything was arranged just as he liked it, he shifted his knees out from under the table and set his plate on his legs to eat. After he finished he put the kettle on the stove and readied the coffee and sugar. When the kettle whistled ten minutes later, he made a full pot and poured a cup, stirring a spoonful into it. He drank the coffee at the window, and when he finished he put the cup back on the desk and moved the pot to a trivet also on the desk. Over the course of his first long watch, that coffee and the tools spread across the black silk would be his only companions.

Back in the lighthouse, he swept the floor and dusted the window ledges. Up in the lantern room, he took the buff-skin to the lens one final time. As if those layers of glass could be any cleaner. He adjusted the vents on the lantern room walls and attached the hand crank to the clockworks. When all of this was done, he stepped out onto the catwalk and cast his gaze over the sheer lake nigh two hundred feet below him. He didn't pray. Or castigate himself. Or even think a mean thought. He did not reach for his watch. Or grow dizzy from the height. He only looked at the enormous vacancy before him, waiting for the night.

And he felt it as much as saw it. The gloaming, rising from the eastern horizon, coming up as though it were a sunrise. He scanned the lake. The water was leaden to the north, a dozen vicissitudes of pearl and gray that met the sky in a calm line of darkness. The islands thirty miles across the lake—the Apostles: Sand and Bear and Rocky and Devils, his old stomping grounds—which had been ensconced by fog all day, were now visible only as variations in the coming darkness, no more distinct than the snow now flecking the evening. And to the south, a lone freighter bearing northeast steamed, its coal smoke a perfect accompaniment to the twilight.

That ship—he could have named it with the light of an hour earlier—was the whole reason he stood on the deck. Things could be so simple as this. A lake and a ship and a light to guide it. Not everything need be rotten with ambiguity or duplicity, with self-doubt or loathing.

It was this that brought him back to the moment at hand. He took a deep breath and thought to pray, but checked his watch instead. The perfect movement of the second hand in the sub-dial, the intricate, miniature scrollwork of the minute and hour hands, unmoving to the naked eye, but keeping time with the second hand all the same, these things soothed him. They brought him back into the moment, and he knew that in four minutes it would be time to light the lamp. He closed his watch and walked back inside.

The fuel assembly rested on the lens pedestal, the brass reflecting the jade-green glass above so it appeared the faintest layer of patina coated the mechanism, though it certainly did not. Theodulf levered the pump once–twice–three times, removed the box of matches from his pocket, and struck one against the pad on the box. Holding the flame above the Bunsen burner, he finally twisted the knob to loose the kerosene. The flame took beautifully, and he brought it up, slowly, slowly, so that by the time the match, still pinched between his thumb and forefinger, burned his finger, the glass all around him refracted the light and filled the womb of the lens with splendorous incandescence.

He stepped down the ladder and attached the hand crank to the clockworks and wound it. Above him, the pedestal danced and the whole perfect machine began to rotate. He checked his watch—eight o'clock sharp—and stepped to the window and witnessed the first rays from the light spread across the lake.

It was beautiful—like the blooming of a greater moon, one that danced and danced.

He counted sixty revolutions of the light—six per minute—at the end of which he found his hips shifting in time with the light. A slow, ecstatic, solitary dance matching the light's own waltz. When he stopped moving, a wash of dizziness came over him, and he had to hold the railing as he descended the spiral staircase.

He passed through the hallway and the cleaning room and went outside to see the light from that vantage. Standing now atop the cliff, he watched again as the light shone far across the lake. He looked north and east and watched as it came off the hillside and splattered across the water, sweeping in an easy arc past the darkness in the offing and the snow falling through it before finally shining on the cove just up the shore and back on the hills before the steel plates to the shoreward side of the lantern room snuffed it out. Ten seconds later, it passed again on its fated course. It would forever mark that angle with its brightness, the only variation from now on the shape of the water or woods on which it would fall.

Satisfied and with his hands stuffed deep in his peacoat pockets, Theodulf watched a final rotation of the light. When it came ashore in the west, he noticed Willa, standing on the end of the dock, beholding, he presumed, the same trajectory that he observed.

MARE CRISIUM

APRIL 21, 1910

Who among us hasn't beheld the moon of a spring night and wished to tread her sands? To swim in her hoary, weightless, and waterless seas? To look back upon the earth and see from there all the things we cannot know from here?

H E WAS NOT A MAN given to musing upon the water. The lake was his livelihood and his life. He knew this simply and without emotion. He knew it was there each morning. He knew it was cold. In December, in July. He knew of its kindness. And its meanness. He knew it could swallow you as though you were rainfall. He knew it better from the middle thwart of his skiff—a hand on each oar—than he did from shore. He knew it like he did the wind and sunlight. He trusted it less than either. Which is why, on this morning of utter calmness, the likes of which came rarely, he could still sense, through the soles of his boots resting toe-to-heel on the keelson, the water's capriciousness. Like it was biding its time.

It was always biding its time.

He was rounding the waters of his island, steering for the grounds off the mouth of the Bunchberry River, the nets in his boat already four days behind schedule. Arvid should've set them the morning the ice was gone. Instead, his brother-in-law himself was gone. And Bente. Left Silje with bread and cheese and coffee. Two days alone at their homestead. Alone. All because of Bente's toothache.

Not only had Arvid failed to get the nets in the water, but he'd neglected most of the chores they'd discussed in November. No shingles on the roof of the cabin. No cords of wood laid in. No new fish boxes. Mats had spent the winter hewing trees with a band of sorry brothers on the Burnt Wood River. Five months sleeping in a rotten bunkhouse with the likes of Adolf Zinzler, that psychopathic blacksmith who pulled his pud each night before the lanterns were doused. Mats had labored that season with those rotten men so that he could carry a time check valued at $108.54 (he'd had $18.39 deducted from the camp account for tobacco, mittens, and

a new pair of Red Wing boots) into the town of Gunflint, where
he spent another twenty dollars on supplies and two nights at the
Traveler's Hotel before boarding the *Nocturne* on its first pass back
up the shore.

And now here he was, the lighthouse above the cliff and nearly
out of view, already the muscles in his shoulders and back protested. Different muscles from those he had honed all winter, but
they were in the same body. His body. And on the heels of a nearly
sleepless night—the passing of the lighthouse beam had been like an
interminable lightning storm from sundown to sunup—still early in
the morning, cursing his brother-in-law for the third time already
that day. All he'd had for breakfast before he left the fish house that
morning was a cup of tepid coffee and one of the butterscotch can-
dies he'd brought back for Silje.

At least the lake was giving this morning. He skulled around
the island and the lighthouse was gone. In half an hour he'd be setting the nets.

Most of the men leaving the Burnt Wood River Camp had hopped
off the sleigh at the Toboggan Road, headed for a place up that
track called the Shivering Timber. Some of them would squander
half or more of their winter's earnings on Canadian whiskey and
molls. The world's lonely souls, those brutes.

Mats rode all the way into Gunflint. He bought a new shirt and
a bar of soap at the Apothecary, a loaf of bread and a pound of bologna, and a jar of mustard and one of pickles and sat on the edge
of the soft bed in the hotel and ate half of his stores. Then he took
a long bath and slept for eighteen hours. The next afternoon he
went back to the Apothecary and with the slight woman behind
the counter arranged his passage on the *Nocturne* (thirty cents to
the Gininwabiko station) and requisitioned his sister's list of provisions sent with her last letter: flour, sugar, salt, yeast; a new bread
pan and measuring spoons; a bolt of green gingham and a package

of shank buttons and one of wooden toggles; aspirin and laudanum; a new hand drill, a six-pound maul head, and five boxes of
nails; spectacles for Arvid; books and carving tools for Silje; a pot
of Vaseline for Bente's cracked feet. He packed it all in a wooden
crate and spent the rest of that warm evening sitting on a bench
on the Lighthouse Road watching the fishermen. It would likely
be his easiest hour of the year.

The next morning, he was back on the quay before the sun
rose. Even in that hour of dawn the bustle was enough the wharf
vibrated. The *Nocturne* had docked overnight, and here a handful
of stevedores loaded banded bundles of sawn pine onto her deck.
He wondered for a moment if it was wood he had felled, but more
likely it came from one of the gyppo camps now more prevalent
around here. Erlandson's operation up on the Burnt Wood would
shutter permanently now, and if he was going to find more work
in the woods next year, it would have to be with one of the smaller
outfits. Probably for less pay. The mere thought of it soured him,
so he turned his eye out to harbor beyond the ship. He recognized
Arne Johnson and his young apprentice haggling with the fishmon-
ger. Arne's skiff and the monger's boat were triced up on one side,
the monger on the *Nocturne* on the other. How Arne already had
boxes packed and ready for market Mats did not know, but if any
fisherman on the shore was likely to make first nets, it was Arne.

Mats heard the clomping hooves of two horses and turned to
watch them lead a cart up the Lighthouse Road. They stopped right
before Mats and he counted ten barrels of what he did not know,
but he watched still as the stevedores turned their attention from
the lumber to the barrels. The horses stomped their shod hooves,
their withers twitching against the morning chill. When the barrels
were loaded and the sacks of mail delivered by Rebekah Grimm,
the same woman who'd wrapped up his bread and bologna two days
ago, the same who'd sold him his passage yesterday, the ruckus of
the quay was replaced by the din of the distant mill. Likely the new
bucking saw he'd heard so much about.

When the purser of the *Nocturne* called the queue of passengers aboard at half past seven, Mats took his seat and watched through the porthole as Arne and his apprentice brought their skiff up onto the ways across the harbor. If he felt any pleasure in watching them, it was only in the notion that his own labor would soon be on the water, a place he much preferred to the thorny woods.

Now the current from the Bunchberry was the only disturbance on that sweet water. He shipped the oars and stood and cracked his back and peered down into the clear, clear water. The shapes of the reef were but shadows six fathoms deep, but still he knew them.

The lake was up from last fall. The fenders on his dock were half in the water now. Another thing he'd have to tend to back at the homestead. He pondered this as he took a sounding. With the same wet line, he readied the first marker buoy and the gunnysack of rocks that would serve as anchor. He'd run the nets east–northeast along the edge of the reef. Three thousand feet of them, up to the mouth of the river. It might yield a hundred pounds of herring that he'd use as baitfish for his hook lines. If the weather remained fair, he'd have fish to bring to market in five or six days.

He tied a miller's knot onto the anchor and coiled the line on the stern sheets, after which he tied the end of the line onto the buoy and lifted it into the water. It sent ripples wide and quick, and before they dispersed, he hefted the eighty-pound sack of rocks, making sure the line was clear before he dropped the anchor. The line unspooled. A mist rose around it. For fifteen seconds he watched the line slither into the lake. The mist rising from water caught the pink light of the morning, and he turned to study the eastern horizon. The lower edge of the sky was flaming red.

Now he fed the lake the first of his nets. The float line hugged the surface while the weighted lead line brought the length of it down into the water. For the better part of half an hour he doled the net out. He'd row a few strokes of the oars, then lay the net out.

Row then lay. By the time he lowered the second marker buoy, the warmth of the sun rode through his shirt on an easterly breeze. He dropped the second sack of rocks into the lake and cracked his back again and turned his sweating face to the gentle wind.

When he sat on the center thwart, he dipped his tin mug into the lake and gulped the frigid water. He dipped it again and set it beside him and shook his hands. He'd have a smoke before rowing home. So he drew on his pipe and sipped the second cup of water in turn. The sun ever friendlier. The kindness of a morning like this, it didn't come routinely. When it did, it was oftenest upset sooner rather than later, and this morning was no different.

After he finished his pipe, after he tipped the ash into the lake and pocketed his pipe, he swung his legs over and faced the stern. Before he even had the oars back in the water, he saw it. A shape among the snow-shrouded rocks and very much like them. But grayer. A shape he recognized even if not at first. He felt the contours of his own boat and the form it held in the water as if it were merely an extension of his own body. It was the same thing ashore. A boat. He unbuttoned his trouser pocket and reached for his watch. He couldn't have said why he did this, but he noted the time. Half past eight.

Half past eight and he knew Silje was right.

Half past eight and he was turning his skiff to shore. He kept his chin tucked on his shoulder, watching the shape, which was becoming more and more another boat.

Five minutes it took for him to reach the edge of the lake. He didn't know what he was preparing to see, but it wasn't the empty vessel he found, its bow knocking ever gently on the rocky shoreline despite the lake's perfect calmness. It could've been any of a hundred fishing boats from this lonesome shore, but it wasn't. It was the one he cared about most. The only one he'd know by the missing quarter knee on the portside. And by Arvid's cracked oar. And by Bente's shabby blanket caught on the rowlock and spread across the water as though it were a seining net.

He removed his hat and rubbed his hair back. He looked up and down the shore, as though the two of them might be picnicking on the rocks.

Of course they were not.

ALL NIGHT she tossed and turned as though her bunk were a skiff on rowdy seas. The light spilled from the cliff above and through her window as if on a pendulum. Only in the pair of hours since sunrise did she find deep sleep, waking at eight thirty like a bucket of lake water had been tossed on her, knowing all over again.

Silje climbed down from the cockloft and untangled her skirt from between her knees. She pulled the pot from under the counter and peed and set the pot by the door. The certainty spun in her belly. The only thing left to wonder was whether her uncle had gone out to set the nets. Curious, she stoked the fire in the stove and grabbed the pot as she went outside. His boat was gone, too. The cove was glass-like, the sky pink and guileful, the woods and shore blanketed by downy snow. She walked back and behind the cabin.

"The wea-ther, my mo-ther . . ." she sang, tossing the contents of the slop bucket into the woods. Before she could finish her rhyme, she felt the eyes on her. The woods were scant, but her observer as shifty as the wind itself. Silje looked from tree to tree. She tried to peer through the boulders half-buried in deadfall.

She started whispering, as though the sweetness of her voice might call it out. "Now there're two moons. Did you see? All night long, blinking like that. Did you think it was awful? I hardly slept myself." She set the pot beside the stone foundation of the cabin and took a few cautious steps toward the feeling from the woods. "It'll be with us until winter comes again."

Their cache was built on four stilts, and she climbed halfway up the ladder. Something caught her attention just ahead, and she stared through the rungs, intent on finding him. "How will you

61

know when to howl? Or where?" Was that a twitching ear? "Uncle Mats has gone out to set the nets. He'll be back soon. We're going to go hunting when he returns." She set her chin between her hands on the ladder. The woods and rocks and the lichen clinging to the rocks, even the lake on the other side of the isthmus, all of it was white. "Where's the rest of your family?" she asked. "How come it's only you that comes down here? What did I ever have to offer?" She thought of stepping off the ladder. Of going deeper into the woods. Up the hill. But then she heard a snapping sound and turned her gaze toward shore. The water through the trees caught a band of sunlight and flashed brilliantly. In the doze of shadow that came just as suddenly, she saw him. His tail twitched, his face turned back over its right shoulder, and she caught the glint of one eye. She could have run to him in five seconds.

Neither moved. Not until the wolf sat, still peering back. Its tongue ran down the flank of its hindquarter once, twice, and then it let a cavernous yawn. Silje yawned back, then smiled. "Mamma and Pappa died. Drowned, I think," she said, to which the wolf turned and faced her completely. "They went to get Mamma's tooth pulled and should have been back yesterday." She sighed. The same spun feeling in her belly came again as the wolf bounded into the woods. She watched it go parallel to the shore. Watched it until it leapt and was gone.

In its place, she saw her uncle some ways offshore, his own skiff towing another.

"Ma-mma og Pa-ppa . . ." Silje whispered, her voice not in song but rather something like the prayers Mamma used to put into the night. Silje regarded the air vacated by the wolf's shadow—had the lake's reflection caught it?—then looked once more out at Uncle Mats rowing his skiff. "In-to the lake they drop-ed . . ."

A FTER SHE PUT THE BOWL of oats on the table, after she cored and cut the apple and placed it beside the oats, after she watched him eat his breakfast and wipe his mouth, after he adjourned for his morning's nap, and after she scrubbed the dishes and placed them on the rack to dry, she went outside and crossed the grounds and stood at the clifftop. She wedged the toes of her brogues right up to the lip of the tallest step of granite and might have leapt to the smooth water and scree a hundred feet below if not for the dueling sky spread out before her. To the east, a tender pink lip all across the horizon, lit by the sun then clenched behind a bank of soaring and milky clouds. And to the west, the moon, as low to the horizon as the invisible sun, and as pale as her sleep from the night just spent.

Less than twenty-four hours into her durance, and already the prospect of a fall like this—a *leap*, rather—seemed practical. She looked again down the craggy face. With the water this high, she might live. The image she regularly conjured of her father slung from the rope in his laboratory crossed her mind, and she stepped back. She regarded again the setting moon and lifted from the surface of the water what might have been a mirage: two skiffs and one sculler, his oars like wings, a line taut between the stern of his boat and the bow of the other. She tried to blink the image away, but he was still there when she looked again. She'd already seen as much of that man as she had her husband.

Theodulf. She risked a glance at their house. At the window she knew him to be sleeping behind. He'd not even expressed thanks for breakfast.

Again, she shook her head. Where had this clarion sky been last night? If it had risen, instead of the heavy clouds, the comet in its perihelion would have arced across this sector of the heavens right at eye level. Now it was a new day's blue, lightening in the west as it cascaded toward the horizon, where the moon drew her eyes and their wetness as though they were the subject of their own peculiar tides. She loved the moon best in this repose. In its faintness she most clearly saw its astonishing features. There, in its northwestern hemisphere, half of *Mare Crisium,* the Sea of Crises, dissolved into the light. It was about the size of Lake Superior. The shimmering surface of the water below flashed, and for an instant it might've held the reflection of the moon. All seventy-three trillion tons of her. The sort of number she delighted in. One most people couldn't comprehend, but helped her solve countless riddles, few of them mathematical. Here now, for example: the moon's burden in the heavens, despite the heft of those seventy-three trillion tons, was minuscule. Even microscopic.

Perhaps that was why she believed it could hang there, like little more than a shred of onionskin paper the size of her thumbnail it resembled now.

With a hand at arm's length, her gaze was once again arrested, this time by the young girl crouched on the path like a wolf poised to ambush its prey. A rifle strap crossed her chest, connecting to the barrel visible over her right shoulder. The brown fabric of her dress was as coarse and unkind as the sack that held the onions down in the cellar, and though Willa couldn't see the girl's features, her coiled readiness startled Willa almost as much as the girl's presence in the first place.

Willa glanced nonchalantly in the opposite direction and then turned to face the child. "This seems like an awfully strange place for a girl and her gun." She spoke loudly enough to be heard, but not so loud she might startle her. When no answer came—the girl didn't even shift from her crouch—Willa took a step forward. "I don't know if I should be afraid or feel safer with you here."

Now Silje did move, prowling on all fours, her face still hiding in its own shadow.

"You look a little like a wolf hunched down there."

Silje finally sat down, her feet straight out in front of her, looking back toward her homestead. When she spoke, her voice was surprisingly deep. "Fenrir's a wolf. And my friend."

"You're friends with a wolf?" Willa risked a few steps toward the girl. "I've never heard of that before."

Silje peeked over her shoulder, and for the first time Willa saw the cast of her eyes. It took a moment, but before the girl looked away again, Willa recognized a certain countenance: it bore the weight of a lonely future but was fettered to a child's incomprehension. Willa could, of course, not have known what expression she herself had conveyed since walking into her father's laboratory for the first time after he'd hung himself there, but somehow she knew this child was similarly vexed.

"What's your name?" Willa said.

The girl adjusted the rifle on her back and used the sleeve of her dress to wipe her nose.

"You live down on that cove, yes?" Willa pointed with her chin at the fish house below.

"With my uncle now."

"Now? What about your mother and father?"

The girl spun on her bottom and crossed her legs so that she faced Willa directly. For a long moment Silje looked at Willa before she finally said, "Silje Lindvik."

Willa could as well have swallowed the moon for all the sadness in the girl's voice.

"Silje *Sigrid* Lindvik. But I'm just called Silje. Mamma and Pappa drowned."

Willa thought of the weight of the girl's expression a moment before; she thought of the fisherman towing a second skiff some half hour ago and risked a look back down at the little harbor below. Both boats were up onshore now. "When did this happen?"

"Mamma had a toothache and was out of her medicine. So, they left when ice-out came. That was last week. They drowned yesterday, on the way back."

Willa crossed half the distance between them and sat cross-legged before Silje.

"I knew it even before Uncle Mats came back from setting the nets this morning." She unshouldered the rifle and lay it across her lap. "You're the keeper's wife?"

"How rude of me! Yes, Willa Brandt. Pleased to make your acquaintance."

"Keeper Frog's name is Frog *Sauer*."

"Keeper Frog?"

"Your husband."

Willa looked at her dumbfoundedly.

"You *are* his wife, yes?"

Willa found herself completely disarmed by this girl. As if their conversation were happening on different frequencies, and Silje were in control of the dials. "Your parents—"

"You're too pretty to be married to that man," Silje said. "And too young."

That retrogression was familiar, too. For years now, Willa had always gone back to the easier question. In fact, that might explain why she found herself here at all—on the cliff's edge, fifteen hundred miles from Radcliffe, married to Theodulf. She felt protective of this girl, she couldn't say why except that to lose your father was the worst thing that could happen to a girl. "How old are you?"

"How old are *you*? Not half that man's age, I bet. Barely older than me. I'm thirteen."

"You're an impertinent young lady, aren't you?" Willa said. Then, tilting her voice to a greater sweetness, "Tell me about your parents first, then you can ask me anything you want."

"What's to tell? They'll have to come up in the nets if we ever want to see them again." Silje raised the rifle to her shoulder and aimed again out at the lake.

"Why are you carrying that gun around?" Willa said.

"Uncle Mats is taking me hunting."

"Today?"

"You ask questions. Like a mother."

"Where's your uncle now? Was that him just rowing in?"

Silje looked at Willa, shook her head as if a mother herself, beseeching a child to cease with her inquiry, and then stood and slung the rifle back over her shoulder.

"Where are you going?" Only in asking did Willa recognize how much she wanted the girl to stay. "Come inside? You can have a drink of something and tell me more."

"Tell you more of what?"

"Well, I don't know."

Silje looked over at the houses—the three identical houses—and then down at the fish house. "Do you have cake?"

"Cake?" Willa completed a quick inventory of her pantry. "No cake, but I do have some dried peaches and apples. They're practically as sweet."

"Can you make a cake with them?"

"I could no sooner make a cake than I could swim across the lake," Willa said. She realized she wanted the girl to like her. Maybe a quip at her own expense would endear the child?

"What *can* you do?"

They were a long way from talking about Silje's parents, but Willa found herself under some sort of spell. Even the girl's eyes beguiled. "That's a hard question to answer."

"Can you hunt?"

"I've never hunted. Not an animal."

"What else would you hunt?"

Willa thought to say *numbers, comets, nebulae, the moon, musical notes*. But already knowing this girl was not wont to use symbolic language, she merely said, "Well, I guess you have a fine point on that account. Tell me, what are you and your uncle going to hunt?"

"Moose. Up on Gininwabiko Creek."

"*Alces alces.* Family *Cervidae*," Willa said, more to herself than her audience, who appeared made curious by Willa's voicing the Latin name and family designation of moose. Instead of elaborating, Willa said, "Is the Gininwabiko Creek the same as the river?"

"A creek is less than a river. You should know that, living here."

"You are *delightful*! Come, let's have a cup of tea."

Willa didn't wait for Silje to answer, only turned, trusting she'd follow. When she reached the porch, she waited for the girl to catch up. Silje paused at the bottom of the steps and looked up without tilting her head.

"You can leave that here," she said, nodding at the rifle. "And we'll have to talk quietly. Theodulf is no doubt still sleeping. We won't want him for company." She smiled, but again the girl remained somber and silent even as she unshouldered the gun and leaned it against the house beside the door.

When they got inside and passed the staircase, Willa turned her head and put a finger to her lips. In the kitchen she pulled one of the chairs out from under the table and went to the stove to see if the water in the kettle was still warm.

Whispering, Silje said, "All the windows have glass in them. And there're so many."

Willa stepped to the window above the table and pulled the lace curtain aside.

Still whispering, Silje said, "Why are they dressed like ghosts?"

"I thought the same thing when I first saw them." Willa reached into the pantry and removed the box of tea and set it beside the drying rack. "They're curtains."

"To keep the light out? What's the point then?"

"That's another good question," Willa said, thinking of the rough-sawn board and batten shutters covering the fish house windows across the water. She took the tin of dried peaches from the pantry and set three of them on a plate. "You sit here," she said, giving the peaches to Silje. "I'll be right back."

"What's this?" Silje asked.

"It's dried fruit. Delicious, trust me."

Willa untied her brogues and set them on the floor by the stove and winked and was gone upstairs. Her stockings padding on the floor, she hoped, as quietly as the moonlight falling on the lake. In her room, she eased the door shut behind her and went to the chest that held her belongings and removed the music box. She closed the chest and opened the door and walked downstairs with as much stealth as she'd used going up.

Silje hadn't moved except that the peaches were gone and now her hands were hidden under the table. Willa set the music box in front of the child and said, "Open the lid. But be gentle."

Silje's fingernails were chewed to nubs and dirty, and as Willa stood over her, watching the girl lift the rosewood lid, she noticed also the girl's hair—shocking in its fineness, white as snow—tangled and snarled and smelling of woodsmoke.

"What is this?" she asked.

"You turn this lever here," Willa said, cranking the brass key attached to the spring housing. When she let go, the comb tines playing over the cylinder gave rise to a tinny rendition of Beethoven's "Für Elise."

Silje craned her head back. There was a look of astonishment on her face. "It's too pretty," she said. The music stopped behind the click of the wooden lid.

"Too pretty?"

"Where does the music go?"

Willa walked around her and sat down across the table. "It's always in there. Always ready. You just have to play it."

Silje lowered her face to the rosewood. So close her nose nearly rested on the lid, which she nudged open just enough for a few more notes to escape. She closed it again. "Is it still playing inside there?"

"When you close the box, the music stops."

"And when I open it . . ."

"It plays. But only if the mechanism is wound."

She opened it once more and listened as the first air finished. Next came the opening of *Pathétique*, which Silje listened to while Willa made tea. When the second air finished the smile on the girl's face was euphoric. "I've never heard a song except for at church."

"That can't be true."

"Why can't it?"

They were still speaking in hushed voices, choosing their words carefully and with purpose, so Willa simply nodded now, and led the girl into the main living quarters where the piano resided. "Do you know what this is?" she asked, her voice little more than a breath.

"Of course I do. There's one at church." Silje had stepped to the piano and struck several keys simultaneously. Willa flew to the child, held her by the shoulders and quickly enclosed the keys again, and then looked at the staircase and ceiling by turns, certain the clamor had awoken Theodulf and that his temper would soon follow him down to meet them.

The next sound came neither from the staircase nor the ceiling, but rather from a loud knocking on the door, where Willa now rushed. She pulled the curtain aside to find a man outside, unshaven and unclean and either the handsomest or the most repulsive fellow she'd ever seen. He stood with his arms crossed, the flannel shirt he wore loose around the collar, and, she saw when he turned to look up at the lighthouse, Silje's rifle now slung over his shoulder.

He turned to knock again but was instead startled by Willa's face in the glass. He didn't smile when he saw her, only stepped back as if anything less than an invitation into the house was unthinkable. So, she opened the door and in her hushed voice said, "You must be here for Silje?"

Willa turned to look for the girl, but Silje was already standing behind Willa.

"That's my uncle. Mats is his name."

This was not a man given to blushing, Willa could see that much. When he said, "I'm Mats Braaten," Willa could feel as much as see the enormous weight he carried in his shoulders, which were wide enough to blot the ever-rising sun and everything else behind him. "I hope she hasn't been a bother."

Silje bolted from Willa's shadow and stepped now beside her uncle, whose hand she took as though she were an innocent little girl. "Willa has a music box that plays chairs and a piano. I played it. There's *songs* in there."

"Well, now—"

"And peaches like candy. I ate three of them."

Mats peeked down at Willa, his eyes apologetic even as he was clearly charmed by his niece.

"But no cake," Willa said.

"The peaches were better than cake."

"She has her convictions," he said before glancing away. "I apologize for her impertinence. She doesn't spend much time with other folks."

"Is it true . . ." Willa said, not sure how to finish her question.

"I'm afraid so," Mats said, instinctively pushing Silje behind him. As though she might not be able to hear him from back there. "I found their boat this morning. Up at the mouth of the Gininwabiko River." He shook his head and peeked over his shoulder at his niece. "I don't know what happened. I can't imagine."

"We need to send up a search," Willa said.

"The only boats within a league of here are my own and the lighthouse tender."

Willa, benumbed, could only stare at the girl.

Her head bobbed between her shoulders now. She hummed. The expression on her face betrayed no sadness or fright. In fact, standing beside her uncle she might even have been described as looking relieved by the developments of that morning.

"In any case," Willa said, trying to lighten her voice and change the subject all at once, "it was no inconvenience at all for her to drop in. I rather enjoyed the company—"

Willa was warned by the shifting gaze of Mats Braaten. He who'd been so content to look at her respectfully was suddenly distracted, seemed even to shrink.

The voice that came from behind her was not familiar. Not that she'd grown in any way accustomed to her husband's temper, but what she heard when he said "Who's this now?" went beyond annoyance and into something akin to vitriol.

His hair beneath his cap was uncombed and his mustache twisted, but he wore his uniform right down to the cravat and shined boots, and what she'd heard in his voice was amplified by the impatient look on his face.

"It's Mats Braaten and his niece," Willa said, as though there might be a whole host of other possibilities.

Theodulf withdrew his pocket watch and flipped it open and closed so quickly it seemed unlikely he'd have caught the time, but he said, "It's not yet ten thirty on a Thursday morning." When no one responded, he continued, "Which is another way of saying now's not a proper time to be entertaining visitors."

"I do beg your pardon, Keeper Sauer. We've had some frightful news this morning."

"News?" Theodulf said. "Here?"

Now it was Willa who spoke up. "Silje, come over here with me. There's something I want to show you."

As they walked down the footpath to the hoist and derrick, Silje began to skip. "Silje—and Willa—and Uncle's sarsaparilla," she sang to the tune she'd just moments ago hummed. "The ides of May— and time to play—and Ma's not there to ruin the day."

Of all the feelings he loathed—and there were many—bewilderment ranked near the top. And that man standing before him, his waxed hat in his hands, was a bewildering sight indeed. Theodulf had made his acquaintance before. Even thought kindly of him, for his reticence and sobersidedness, which were nowhere in evidence that morning.

They stood on the porch, Theodulf watching the girl skipping off, singsonging some rhyme about sarsaparilla, while the fisherman prattled on about the girl's parents and their boat and his prospects, suddenly much complicated by, of all things, the Lindviks—Mister and Missus—having drowned.

"How do you know they *drowned*?" Theodulf asked. "You say it with such certainty."

Mats twisted his hat like it was wringing wet. "There's no other explanation. Their boat still held all the supplies they left for in the first place. Bente's blanket was trailing in the water. For that matter, so was one of the oars."

"I see," Theodulf said, but in fact he was watching Silje and Willa rounding the backside of the oil house, headed, he presumed, for the hoist and derrick. The girl was nigh dancing, her skirts twirling around. Her lightness was an insult. A condescending rebuttal to his anguish and exhaustion.

"What should I do?"

Theodulf straightened. He shook the soot from his sleep-starved mind. *Authority*, he reminded himself.

As though a hasp had been unlocked and unlatched, he sensed his right mind opening again. The order of his duty began with faith. The man should appeal to God. "Why, if it's true they're drowned, then we must pray for their *souls*." The simple utterance relieved the bedlam of his thoughts. He placed a hand on the fisherman's shoulder, which might as well have been a dock plank for all its firmness. "Where did Mister and Missus Lindvik stand with God?"

"It's less my sister and her husband and their standing with God I'm worried and wondering about than it is my niece."

As if the other man had not spoken, Theodulf said, "I cannot bear the thought of a soul in limbo, never mind two. Neither can the child, whether she realizes or not. We'll pray for her parents' ascension into heaven. That's the first order of business."

He made the sign of the cross and bowed his head and prayed. He prayed for the orphaned child. He prayed for her parents. He prayed for the fisherman. And, as though unable to help himself, he asked for a blessing on the light. Only in that utterance did he recognize the loss of the Lindviks coincided with the light's commission. The irony jolted him, and he might have spun off into darkness had not the fisherman said, "I thank you for your prayers, but what I'm wondering more practically is, who do I tell about their drowning? And about Silje? To what authority do I appeal?" He bit his lip. "Beyond the Redeemer, of course?"

It was a simple inquiry. And yet, Theodulf found himself flummoxed. Instead of pondering the questions—all of them reasonable, all of them pressing—he silently catalogued his complaints of that midmorning: awakened, trespassed on, inquired of, made a fool. Not yet eleven and already the full day spoiled.

"You'll need to see the sheriff at his office in Two Harbors, naturally," he finally said, and headed down the steps. "And now if you'll excuse me, I need a word with my wife."

The fisherman only nodded. "I thank you," he said. Then, turning the direction Silje and Willa had gone, "I'll fetch my niece, and tell Missus Sauer you'd like to see her."

Theodulf nodded as well. "Very good," he muttered, then crossed his arms and watched the man lumber off, his oilskin pants held up by galluses, his back broad and tapered from shoulders to waist. For all his brawn, he moved like a cat.

Back inside, waiting, Theodulf went to the kitchen in hopes of finding the pot of coffee still on the stove. What he discovered instead was a table covered in used plates and teacups, soiled napkins, and a rosewood box. He inventoried this scene as he did almost everything, which is to say as a register of grievances.

He took a cup from the shelf and poured from the kettle on the stove. Tea instead of coffee, and his temper might've set his bowels afire. He splashed the drink into the sink and slammed the cup into the mess. He could have rent the sink from the pipes in the wall for all his anger, but turned instead to the table and picked up the rosewood box. When he lifted the lid, a song he recognized chimed, played at a simpleton's tempo. He closed it and opened it again and placed the song. Beethoven's *Pathétique*. The first discordant notes of the "Adagio Cantabile," but as though from a child hammering on a tin can.

"You found my music box," Willa said.

He clapped it shut. "A miracle, given these piles of rubbish." He turned to her. "Have I not made clear your duties?"

"You'll not speak to me as though I'm one of your charges."

"How dare you—"

"What? Demand decency? Ask of you courtesy and kindness?" She puffed herself up. "I'll ask of you nothing—*nothing*—but that you give me peace and quiet."

He found no answer to her requirements, so changed the subject altogether. "You'll not invite anyone into my home without permission."

"Your Christian values don't allow charity for ragamuffins?"

"This house is no way station. I'll decide who visits us and when." His mouth was pinched. He nearly spat the words.

"What nonsense—" she began.

But before she could finish her thought, Theodulf stepped to her, raising his arm and lowering it in the same motion, and struck her across the cheek with the back of his hand. Her whole head swiveled so her chin rested on her shoulder. Redness flowered on her face before she even looked back at him, and when she did, the hatred in her eyes startled him.

But he hardly knew which to note first: the recognition of her hatred, or the slap that befell his own face, one that sent him to his hands and knees on the kitchen floor. It was from that landing place he watched her dash off, and from there he heard the door slam shut behind her.

S HE'D BEEN SLAPPED once before. By her mother, on that autumn day seven months ago, after the inglorious luncheon and tallyho ride with Georg Olaussen.

They'd met Georg and his mother at the Lester Park Hotel restaurant. He impressed her from the outset as a vainglorious man, one without wit or charms of any sort and with the complexion of a boiled potato. Over deviled eggs and pilsner, he regaled her with his opinion of Robert Peary's expedition to the North Pole; his responsibilities as an underwriter at the State Bank of Duluth; and his captaincy on the University of Minnesota club hockey team during his time there as a Delta Kappa Epsilon and scholar in the College of Liberal Arts. When she dared to challenge him on the frivolity of polar exploration, or contended that the Panic of 1907 was largely the result of the undue influence and corruption of an oligopoly of bankers and investors (she listed several offenders for effect) and that what the industry needed was a cleansing head to toe and a bevy of new regulations, and concluded that of all the sports boys played, hockey was at least the most elegant, and that the University of Minnesota, though no doubt a fine institution for learning certain subjects, did not hold up well in contrast to the more venerable institutions on the East Coast, well, suffice it to say he was less than thrilled at the prospect of the tallyho ride up Lester Park soon to follow.

But ride they did, with a party of some twenty debutantes and their suitors, some of them even unaccompanied by meddling mothers. Before the coach driver announced the first bridge over Amity Creek, Willa had also schooled Georg on his affection for President Taft, and the Republican agenda more generally. By the time they reached the second bridge, they sat with their backs to each other and a palpable scorn between them.

Two hours later, when they returned to the hotel, Georg told Willa's mother, in tones intended, at once, to be hushed and heard, that he might condemn the Brandt women to the periphery of Duluth society. He possessed connections enough to do it, and pettiness enough that he just might.

While the trolley carried them back down Superior Street, Ann Brandt spoke not at all. Willa of course knew her mother was cross, knew her expectations for the day had ended abruptly, knew, even, that those expectations were not without merit. What *did* Willa imagine she might do, now that they were penniless? Return to Boston? Finish her degree at Radcliffe? She was living in the help's quarters at the Thibert Hotel. She was mopping the public water closets and changing bed linens like a proper chambermaid. The only pleasures left to her were the hour she spent each afternoon at the piano in the hotel lobby and the walks she took up on Rogers Boulevard—either at night to observe the skies, or during the early mornings to revel with the birds. Was she under the illusion any of this might fulfill her?

Remembering the condescension in Georg's voice, she shook the thought from her head. Certainly she'd not kowtow to the likes of him. A man who pretended great wealth and sophistication but was really, in fact, a cheeseparing dullard.

"You've embarrassed me to no end this day, Willa." Her mother spoke softly, so those sitting across the trolley's aisle might not hear her.

"That's rich: me embarrassing *you*."

"A peculiar choice of words," Ann Brandt said, then folded her arms across her bosom and turned to gaze out the window.

Back at the Thibert Hotel, in their suffocating quarters, Ann changed into a less formal skirt and blouse and poured herself a copita of sherry, which she quaffed in one swallow. She let her hair down and poured and sipped another before a knock came at their door.

No sooner had its reverberation ceased than Ann set the glass down and began to put her hair back up. When Willa didn't move to answer the door, her mother nodded at it, and Willa shuffled over and turned the knob.

The hotel manager stood outside. "Fräuleins," he said, twirling his waxed mustache between his thumb and forefinger. "Good evening." He stepped in without invitation and glanced about the flat. "Your mother?" he said.

"Putting her hair up," Willa said. "I'd offer you a place to sit, but, as you well know, there isn't one."

The man's name was Murdock Alderdice, and what he lacked in discretion he made up for in bad humor. He stepped closer to Willa and held her elbow and moved his lips close to her ear. "Ah, but there's room on the bed."

She jerked her arm free and had a foot out the door before her mother called, "Willa?"

She stopped. "Yes?"

Rather than respond to her daughter, she spoke to Murdock. "Wait just a moment, Mister Alderdice. I need a word with my daughter."

Willa turned in time to see her mother accept a palmful of coins from the manager. Outside their quarters, Ann put the coins in Willa's hand and said, "Go have an early dinner, yes? I'll join you in the restaurant soon."

Willa put the coins in the waist pocket she'd sewn into the folds of her dress. "I suppose," she said, buttoning the pocket, "that marriage is just another version of the arrangement you have with the hotel manager."

It was then her mother slapped her, a sweeping hand right across her daughter's cheek under the electric lamp in the hallway. It was the first and only time her mother had raised her hand in anger, and if its intended effect was to awaken Willa to their desperate circumstances, it was at least in that way successful.

Willa put her fingertips to her cheek and then brought them down into the light, as though the stinging redness no doubt staining her face might transmute to blood. It did not, and though she wished to return the slap, she only hurried off, leaving her mother to her duty and with the conviction that if ever someone laid hands on her again, she would strike them back.

Now she was huddled in a concrete building no bigger than a trolley car, looking out the single small window at their house fifty yards across the grounds. Had she done to Theodulf what she'd often wished she'd done to her mother? Did he crumple like bed linen falling from a drying line? The thought thrilled her, and she sat back in the shadows of the oil house and looked at the drums of kerosene and gasoline and turpentine, at the teeming coal box, the shelves of other supplies she couldn't quite make out. All of it arranged in perfect order.

In the last corner she glimpsed a steel trap of some sort. Two of them, she determined as she stood up for a closer look. No, three. The toothed upper and lower trap jaws, the trigger and spring and anchor chain, all of it hearty and unstained and like a medieval torture device. She stepped closer but wouldn't touch them. On the shelf above the traps, six small wooden cartons sat in a row, and she was reminded of her music box.

Her instinct told her to go rescue it. But her better sense—and the notion she might strike Theodulf again—left her sitting in the coolness of the oil house.

WHAT A STRANGE POSTURE, that genuflection. Not in praise or obedience—unless it was some new kind of obedience—but in *thanks*. Yes, in thanks *and* obedience. He rubbed the spot on his chin. Felt a churning in his bowels. A faintness.

How long had it been since someone touched him?

He counted back. It would've been the day he met Willa. In the lobby of the Thibert Hotel. A day that began in parley with his father. A lunch at the Palm Dining Room in the Spalding Hotel to celebrate his promotion to the Gininwabiko Lighthouse station. He'd had the rest of the day free before reporting back to his post in Two Harbors the following morning. There'd been the usual braggadocio and patronizing aloofness from his father. Reports of his law firm's important cases against the state and national governments, against the unions, against disgruntled employees. After the second or third whiskey cocktail, before the beef bourguignon main course, his father's attention shifted from himself to his son and the castigation he so relished. Insinuations of an unnatural sexual proclivity unfavored by God, of idleness of mind and spirit, of a fixation on his damned pocket watch as though it might transport him back to Paris, a trip now ten years in the past. And then—and as always—the pronouncement that what Theodulf needed was a wife and children. Someone to keep him on the straight and narrow. Someone to help bolster his career, such as it was.

"Any woman would do," he'd said, before tucking his linen napkin into the collar of his shirt and foisting the first spoonful of ragoût into his sloppy mouth. "There's likely one sitting in the hotel lobby right now, waiting for a proposal."

81

The rest of their luncheon passed in unhappy, bitter silence. Outside on Superior Street, his father—another pair of whiskeys gone—gave his son a disdainful look as he rounded out his scolding for the day. "You've so far proven to be a blight on your mother and me." He raised his chin slowly in a gesture well known to Theodulf, one that announced the day's last insult.

But before Ernst Sauer could utter his final mockery, Theodulf turned away. A Sauer family sacrilege. He stood there in mortified defiance for what seemed an hour and a day, and when he risked a glance back at his father, he was met with that open hand. Even as the workaday crowd passed by.

But where his father's walloping aroused in him thoughts of retaliation and murderous antipathy, the imprint of Willa's hand still ablaze on his face had led to simple prurience. So much so that what had begun as a general swirling in his bowels was now manifest in an unmistakable erection.

And where such an occurrence would oftenest result in the collision of his shame and his otherworldly ability to *blot* that shame, and hence to spend hours in a kind of limbo he likened to purgatory, he realized there, on the floor of his kitchen, as if in epiphany, that Willa was his *wife*. These agonies? They needn't exist.

What was it Father Richter had counseled during the *Ordo Initiationis Christianae Adultorum*? That, according to Paul's epistles to the Romans, husband and wife have authority *over each other's bodies*? The good priest had even opened his bible, there in the priory at Sacred Heart, and read: "What shall we say, then? Is the law sin? God forbid. But I do not know sin, but by the law; for I had not known concupiscence, if the law did not say: *Thou shall not covet*."

He coveted nothing but what he held dominion of: his wife and what she'd given him.

At the priory, Theodulf had glanced at Willa in the ladder back chair and dreamed of a marriage *ratum sed non consummatum*. But now, with his blood like a spring freshet? He used the edge of the stove to pull himself up and pressed his groin into the rounded corner of it. Closing his eyes, he allowed himself to think their union wasn't impossible. A blank and holy whiteness attended the thought, and he didn't even feel the urge to check his timepiece as he straightened and walked out of the kitchen, as well as right fucked for the easiness of his stride.

"QUASI UNA FANTASIA"

NOVEMBER 27, 1905

There was enough wind that night to account for all manner of fates colliding, and who's to say the very gusts that pushed Willa across Superior Street had not sailed down from up London Road? For the wind most certainly blew that way. A savage nor'easter.

But that's a short blow—down London Road—and the bigger question, the fairer question, is where'd that wind begin? And when? Was it the same gusty stuff that filled the headsail of Thibert's Novantique *nearly two centuries agone? The first wind that ever filled a sail on Lake Superior, one come from the headwaters of the St. Marys River out past the Sault. Or the breeze that sent St. Lusson's ensign aflutter at the same spot fifty-some years before Thibert went sailing? Does it just keep going 'round, oblivious of time? If it quiets, where's it go then? Into the hearts of the bridled souls?*

I've felt the wind off the Greenland Sea and the Great Australian Bight and a hundred places between, and believe me when I say its longanimity was the same in one place as the other.

Of all the things that could be said of the wind that night—that it would, as William Brandt foretold, sink ships; that it carried with it the bitter water of its 350-mile provenance, which is to say all the lake's fair length; that its appetite, like Boreas himself, was insatiable—that it found Theodulf in the aura of Willa Brandt's song is perhaps the most remarkable of all.

S HE STOOD AT THE WINDOW, thinking how like the sonata the storm did rise. Adagio, allegretto, presto—dusk, snow, tempest.

Down on the water a ship headed toward the new aerial bridge, flouting the mounting swells.

Night had come as swiftly as the snow, and now she could see her reflection in the wavering glass as surely as the ship bound for the canal. She adjusted the peruke in the window. She straightened the bone-white cravat wound about her neck. Most handsome. Most handsome, *indeed*.

"Will?" her father called down from his laboratory.

She left her reflection and moved to the bottom of the spiral staircase. "Yes, Papa?"

"Come up?"

Being careful not to muss her tuxedo, she gyred up the stairs, pausing on the landing to glance at the anemometer cups spinning on the deck outside. When she turned to his desk, she saw him reading the paper ticking off the barograph. Without looking up, he said, "Fools. Who would tempt this storm? Who would defy those flags and lanterns?" He was speaking of the warning systems he'd ordered raised and lit down on the harbor. "Perhaps I'd better stay in tonight. These readings are a true fright. The weather out there?" He pointed at the window. "It will sink ships."

Willa loved her father very much. His plainspokenness, his wisdom, his kindness, his sense of duty. These were some of the qualities for which he'd be honored that night at the Ionic Lodge in a ceremony to celebrate his ascension to Grand Master. It was a role for which he seemed badly cast, given the nature of those other braggarts and barons who called themselves Masons.

As if he'd just come in from the dark, he blinked across the distance between them and smiled. It was another thing she loved about him—his smile. "Your transmutation, why, it's nearly total."

"Nearly?" she asked.

He set the graph paper down and lifted instead a tin of complexion powder. Together they moved to another window overlooking the harbor. They watched as the boat she'd spied moments earlier steamed under the bridge. He tapped the lid of the tin each time the ship's prow splashed down. It towed a barge, which trailed like an untrained dachshund.

"It happened so fast," Willa said. "The turn from fairness."

"It always does." He took her chin between his thumb and forefinger. "It always *will*."

"You can't miss the ceremony tonight, Papa," she said, turning the subject quickly. She had learned so much from him, but he was better at reading the recordings and forecasts than he was her volatile moods. Which is to say she had no patience for his self-effacement or moralizing when her own priorities were front of mind. "I'm all dressed." She adjusted the wig atop her head as if to remind him of her own part in the evening's festivities.

If her moods bewitched him, he at least knew enough to give her what she wanted, and in the spirit of that generosity, removed from his waistcoat pocket the badger-hair brush he used to suds his cheeks before shaving, dripping the bristles into the tin of powder. "You're right, my dear: the storm will come and the storm will go, but this version of you? Why, we must see it through." He took her chin again and turned her face toward the window.

The bristles dusted her cheek like the snow against the pane. "What boat is that, Papa?"

Without need of a glance, he said, "That's Dick Humble's charge. The *Mataafa*." Now he did look out the window, put his nose right on the glass. "Can't see his consort." He stood upright again and dipped the brush in the powder and asked her to turn left.

"Could the *Mataafa* sink?"

"Humble's a fine master, and the *Mataafa*'s stern and stout."

He swept her chin and forehead with four swift strokes, then tucked a wisp of stray hair under the wig. "Herr Ringen," he said, bowing. "My nephew from Virginia. It's a pleasure to see you here in our blustery outpost."

"It's a pleasure to see *you*, Uncle. Your outpost suits my wilder side."

"Wilder shores and wilder sides." He spoke like a man given to rhapsody, a thing he was not.

"It's just winter arriving," she said, parroting one of his favorite phrases. "For you, I'll play the wind away."

"You always do." He checked his pocket watch. "You're sure you don't want an escort to the lodge?"

"Half the fun of this whole ruse is playing the boy. That means some freedom on the streets." Now she reached up and adjusted his tie. "Go have your aperitif with Mother. She'll be insufferable if you don't. I'll sneak out the back and save her the grievance of seeing the boy she always wished for."

He kissed her forehead. "I'll see you in an hour, right under the awning at the temple. You'll need me to usher you into the Blue Room." Now he patted her peruke. "Hold on to your hat out there."

At quarter past five she boarded the incline. The snow came crosswise, rattling the otherwise empty tram as it juddered down the tracks. When she disembarked on Superior Street, a gust of wind nearly sheared her peruke, and she had to catch it with both hands. On a normal late-autumn night, she'd have walked the half mile from the station to the Opera Block, but the foulness of the weather invited her to duck onto an eastbound streetcar.

Her nickel fare paid, she sat behind the motorman, crossing her legs before remembering there were no skirts to flatten. Instead, she settled her heels together and let her knees flare. But this was wrong too, and she shifted uncomfortably on the wicker seat.

A girl sat across from her, holding her mother's hand. They were both cloched and scarved and stoic behind their woolens, but the girl had settled her gaze on Willa, an expression nigh coquettish. Willa felt herself blush. The girl in turn demurred, ducking her own dappled cheeks behind her scarf.

Was this what she'd wanted when she'd insisted on getting to the lodge on her own? Is this how one played the boy? Wandering the city with autonomy? And something more? Was it imperiousness? In any case, she ogled the girl until she looked back. This time, Willa smiled. The girl sighed and adjusted her seat and took her hand away from her mother. For three blocks, their dalliance gamboled along with the clacking of the trolley, the mother oblivious in her dourness.

At Second Avenue Willa rang the bell and at Third she stood and strode to the exit, making sheep's eyes at the girl as she stepped onto the street. As the trolley jerked forward, the mother cast a scolding glare out the window. Willa gave a rebellious smile in turn and hurried across Superior for the main entrance, each step aided by the wind.

THEODULF STOOD PROFOUNDLY in his own reflection in the billiard room of his parents' staunch brick mansion, the candles in the wall sconces on either side of the fireplace swealing in the uneasiness of the atmosphere. The flames in the firebox gave off their own faltering light from below.

He glared into the mirror hanging from a silk rope above the mantel, made to wait like a common guest, unable to tell if all the quavering light was a consequence of his dark humors or something more sinister. They found their way into him whenever he visited the Sauer manor, which was not often anymore, as he much preferred the relative sequestration of his post as first assistant keeper at the Two Harbors station. A post to which he was scheduled to return on the *Nocturne* the following morning. Given the turn in the weather, that prospect was very much in doubt.

His mother's absence—she'd gone to St. Paul, Theodulf understood—made his own appointment on this night at best illconsidered. But his duty won out, as it almost always did, and he found himself on the cusp of a several-hours-long engagement with his father. Of all the reasons he was happy for the twenty miles between Duluth and Two Harbors, not partaking of these meetings was top of list. Why his father had insisted on his attendance this night, he could not fathom. Yet, there he was, now studying his reflection's reflection in the tall windows overlooking the lake and storm.

For once, he felt a not unhappy man.

His father's entrance—a snifter of whiskey in one hand, his cane in the other—threatened to change that. But Theodulf straightened, resting a forearm on the mantel, intent on rising above whatever pettiness was sure to arrive on his father's first breath.

"Good evening, son. I see you wore your jodhpur boots." He tipped his drink toward the scuffed leather on Theodulf's feet, which were just then toeing the plinth in uneasy rhythm with the gusts outside.

Despite his palsy, the old man moved with a leporine quickness, and by the time Theodulf looked up, Ernst stood before him, his own garb impeccable as ever. He wore a gray tweed suit with a starched white collar and silken bow tie. The cufflinks on his shirt were the same golden hue as the handle on his cane, which was in the shape of a nymph. His shoes were a pair of black wingtips that shone like the mirror.

Theodulf looked again at his boots, then met his father's haughty grin. "A choice I'll be glad of, given the snow now falling in curtains."

"Walter knows enough to put the blankets in the carriage."

"Walter?"

"The new groom. He's readying the carriage as we speak."

"Not the Ford?"

He exchanged his cane for the fireplace poker and prodded the blaze. "We'll follow the horses instead of driving, what with the snow." He switched the poker for his cane again and turned back to his son. "Your business on the docks, everything's shipshape?"

How unlike his father to inquire after his affairs. But Theodulf coupled the question with his own ill-advised confidence and said, "Well, not the docks, but yes, quite. I'm headed back to Two Harbors in the morning. First thing."

Ernst retired to one of a pair of club chairs upholstered in calfskin leather on either side of the fireplace. He gestured to the other, but Theodulf kept his post at the mantel, buoyed again by this minor act of rebellion.

"Three years later, and still an assistant," Ernst said, swirling the snifter before taking a sip. "Three years after I took my first job I was made partner. Three years after *that* I was principal. Now . . ." he made an all-encompassing gesture.

For the briefest moment, Theodulf imagined his reflection in the mirror scolding him, so he wiped the moue from his face and said, "We all admire your industry, Father. For my own self, I find my position in the Lighthouse Service a thousand times preferable to my days as an attorney."

"Not that you had much choice in your change of careers."

Now Theodulf checked his reflection; he found the self-admonishment he expected. Dropping his chin, he said, "We should revisit my ignominy again?"

"I only think of the wasted years. Well, the wasted years and the implications for our family. A charge of moral turpitude is unambiguous." He took a tight-lipped drink. "I had to call in every political favor I possessed to make your indiscretions"—he waved his hand like a magician—"disappear."

"You're well practiced in disguising moral failings. Mine. Yours. Anyone's." This time when he looked in the mirror, he saw the windows on the opposite side of the room, and then the image cast back and forth ad infinitum. His father frequently visited that epoch in Theodulf's life. He knew all the right nerves to pinch. As if to have survived his recklessness hadn't been penance enough.

Was his father oblivious to his son's agony? Did he relish it? As though answering the questions in Theodulf's mind, Ernst pressed on. "And your poor mother—"

"My poor mother?" Theodulf hissed. "She who's never once admonished me? Never once harkened back? Your pity on the matter is one thing she doesn't need."

"Your mother's a saint." Ernst finished the last of his whiskey and stood in a single motion. "And she loves her son, make no mistake of that."

Theodulf closed his eyes and thought of his mother's forgiveness. As he did, the wind lulled outside, and the quiet startled him. When he opened his eyes, his father stood before him, looking down his nose at his own reflection in the mirror. He palmed back his hair and added, "She's blind because of that love."

They stared at each other in the mirror, the light coming up from beneath them like the fires of Gehenna. The clever expression on his father's face enraged Theodulf.

"About her saintliness, you're right," he whispered. "But about her sight, I'd offer the cautionary tale of the blind man and the Pharisees as told in John's gospel."

"*For judgment I am come into this world; that they who see not, may see.*"

"*And they who see, may become blind,*" Theodulf answered, now a fiendish grin of his own turning up half his face.

"Your hold on scripture at least remains strong." Ernst tapped his cane on the floor.

"I thought we were talking about Mother."

That grin. That wretched grin. "And I thought we were talking about your perversions."

The butler coughed from the doorway and when the two Sauer men turned in unison, he said, "The carriage is ready, sir."

Ernst nodded and turned once more to Theodulf. "All of which is to say: be true to God's plan for you, son. That means a life of faith and devotion and *penance.* Pray for your forgiveness. Pray that you stay on the path of righteousness." He turned to the mirror and snapped his lapels. "And for all that is holy, please don't embarrass me tonight."

The watch in Theodulf's pocket kept time with the trotting horses. Down London Road and through the belting snow, the wind tailing. His father looked out one window, Theodulf the opposite, the lantern hanging between them like a cauldron fire.

The carriage passed a trolley car headed east. When it was gone, Theodulf studied his father's face in the opposite window. What he saw was a man he could not escape—his hold not unlike the Lord God's—studying the speech he'd soon give. In the first years after university—first as an undergraduate at Notre Dame, then a law student at Princeton—Theodulf had tried to form himself in his father's image. His first employment as an associate at Hogg, Gray &

Thibert found him a friend of the court and member in good standing of the state bar. But he made a humdrum impression as an amicus curiae before failing to make partner. He joined the Duluth & Iron Range Railroad as a special counsel instead, a position his father arranged and so was inclined to meddle in. The year he spent with the railroad was chastening and miserable, each day passing as though a week unto itself. In an effort to right the clock of his life, Theodulf took regular comfort in the hotel saloons on Superior Street. Those nights mostly ended out of time and in Lethe, shepherded to complimentary rooms by hotel managers who took kindly to the Sauer family name and Ernst's infamy as a destroyer of reputations.

On one such night, it was not a friendly hotel manager who brought him upstairs, but a husband and wife from Detroit who'd promised—best Theodulf could remember—a bottle of champagne and the prospect of gin rummy. Hours later, in the deepest part of the night, he was cast into the hallway of the Spaulding Hotel wearing nothing but the socks on his feet and clutching the empty bottle of Veuve Clicquot in a bloodied hand. He passed out on a divan in the elevator lobby, where a chambermaid found him and summoned the Duluth Police Department.

The investigation into his indiscretions led to disbarment for behavior unbecoming, a stern repudiation from his father, and, finally, an exile in Europe with instructions to sow his oats and return sober, faithful, and obedient to God or else be forever disowned and disinherited. That conversation had taken place in the same billiard room they'd just departed.

Theodulf turned to look out on the lake. Beyond his father's reflection, he could see a ship, its deck lights barely visible. He sat forward and found his own reflection beside his father's. The ship yawed beyond their visages. It rose and fell once—twice—thrice in the watery troughs. Finally his father looked away from his notes.

Ernst ran a finger along the glass. He cupped his hands around his eyes and pressed them against the window. "Quite a row out there," he said, sitting back in his seat and folding his notes. "I suppose since you took up with the Lighthouse Service, you've become an authority on inclement weather."

"I've become an expert on keeping the beacon lit and the foghorns blowing."

Ernst put his speech in his pocket. "Sounds rather like Mother lighting the wall sconces and warming the tea kettle."

Theodulf sighed.

"The man of the evening is in fact our local weatherman. William Brandt's his name. If he hasn't already, he'll surely raise the flags. I don't know if an unlikelier man has ever ascended to Grand Master."

"How's that?"

"He's a fellow of little industry, for one. As far as I can tell, he sits in his laboratory on the hillside counting clouds. But worse still, he's unchristian."

"What explains his promotion?"

Now Ernst sighed, as though it were troublesome to explain something so simple. "There's no accounting for the rabble. Mister Brandt is kind and decent, and the men at the lodge adore him. Never mind the careful standards by which we ought to govern ourselves."

"Kindness and decency, those are excellent qualities in a man."

His father glanced at him and appeared almost to roll his eyes. "They're fine qualities in a *boy*." Now he twisted his mustache. "But I'll be happy for one fewer obligation. It will allow me more time to work on my memoirs."

Theodulf had been hearing about his father's memoirs for a half decade. What the subject of such an unkind, unremarkable life might be, he could not comprehend. So, he did what he always did when the subject arose: he removed his watch and glanced at the hour. "We'll be late."

His father flashed a knowing grin. "One of the advantages of being the current Grand Master is that the ceremony *depends* on me, and so cannot begin *without* me."

The carriage veered onto Superior Street and before long was in the canyon of downtown buildings, rising on either side in bulwarks of brick and glass. By the time they reached the Opera Block, Theodulf had renewed his own vow to remain upright, and in the spirit of that resolution cast off the tartan blanket, stepped onto the snow-sodden street, rounded the carriage, and opened his father's door, where he offered his hand.

With his cane, Ernst nudged Theodulf aside and alighted on the cobbles like a cat leaping from the windowsill. With one hand on his old beaver fur top hat—a black, chimney-like thing that had been Ernst's father's father's hat, and one that he wore with the arrogance of a politician—he leaned into Theodulf and spoke into his ear. "Mind what I said about not embarrassing me tonight. These men are my closest friends and colleagues."

Without allowing even so much as an acknowledging nod, Ernst crossed the sidewalk and entered the temple.

Theodulf, left alone outside and under the awning, gazed west up Superior Street. For a moment he imagined heading into the whorling snow, all the way to Bill Lanigan's pub, where he might sit among the stevedores and seamen, a forbidden stein of beer clenched in his fist feigning dispassion while his bile boiled up. But even in his agitated state, he knew the temptation would be too much. So, he turned and slipped into the temple, where, instead of following his father to the elevator, he stole into a dark corner and sat alone with his chagrin, the snowmelt dripping from his own hat one tear at a time.

INSTEAD OF WAITING beneath the awning in the ravening wind as one carriage after another emptied, Willa dashed up Second Street, under the wrought-iron marquee of the Opera, and into the alleyway where untrodden snow had already begun to drift. There she found the service entrance unlocked and slipped inside. This had been her true intent: to infiltrate the lodge itself—the arcane Blue Room—without escort.

It occupied the sixth floor, and when she reached that level and opened the stairwell door, she found herself beside a cable shaft and a winch and derrick. A dark passageway lined on one side by doors and transoms, and on the other a mess of pallets and hogsheads and crates of every sort unfurled before her. The first two doors on her left were locked, but the third opened into an antechamber as funereal as a chancel. Beyond the benches and tables, another door, this one ten feet in height and inlaid with carved panels, glowed beside a single gas lamp. Willa tiptoed across the parquet floor and put her hand on the bronze doorknob and her ear to the keyhole. No sound came.

She turned the knob as a thief might, opened the door an inch at a time, and, satisfied she was alone, entered the Blue Room. The ceilings soared, a checkerboard of alabaster and stained glass letting onto the night. There were chandeliers and candelabras lit all around, and the Turkish rug beneath the soles of her wet brogues was as plush as an otter pelt. Across the carpet, beyond the strange God in the middle of the room, she spied the piano.

It was a beautiful instrument. A Blumenthal as black and lustrous as patent leather. When she sat down and lifted the fallboard and laid her fingers on the silken keys, she nearly swooned. So different was this piano from the one she played at her teacher's house. Instead of striking the keys, she lifted her hands two inches above them and played the air instead. She imagined the sonata from first note to last, her body moving with the song in her head, her hands as fluid as the wind buffeting the windows behind her. As the coda vanished into the quiet of her heart, the main entrance to the Blue Room opened, and several men entered.

No sooner did the crowd begin to assemble than a cloud of cigar smoke filled the room. For fifteen minutes, from behind the piano, she witnessed the secret handshakes and looks of solemn, sanctimonious greeting. So many coats and collars and fine hats. So many waxed mustaches and monocles and enough arrogance to quell the storm outside. She'd never understood why her father was drawn to this fraternity of mountebanks and robber barons. Willa regarded her father as the only noble man among them.

He arrived at six o'clock sharp, received as though he brought with him secrets untold and unimagined. Some of the solemnity was replaced by general and genuine enthusiasm for the ascension at hand, but William's demeanor was aggrieved, and as he passed among the huff-snuffs, he alternated his glances from their congratulatory smiles to the windows behind Willa where the storm continued to rise with a wicked and baffling vengeance. For all those fleeting looks, he never once considered the piano. And when Ernst Sauer entered the Blue Room, handing his hat to the Tyler, who'd ushered him in personally, her father's attention turned all at once and completely to the Right Worshipful Master.

Ernst Sauer fairly danced to the altar at the head of the room, the cane he held a partner and pike at once. He used it to hammer the altar floor. When the assembled lodge took their seats along the north and south walls, he spoke: "Good evening, all. Good evening and thank you for your punctiliousness. Even with the barbarous weather, it appears we're a quorum." He pulled a note from his coat pocket and, thus reminded, glanced across the room to the piano, where Willa sat, unnoticed until then. "Our *official* agenda this evening is exact and will commence at precisely six-thirty." Several of those in attendance checked their watches. "But afore our ceremony to honor Dr. William Brandt and his ascension to Grand Master, our inestimable brother has requested a special performance by his nephew, here from the fair state of Virginia and ready, as far as I can tell from across the room, to perform for our pleasure."

Several of those same heads that had checked their watches now turned to see Willa sitting upright at the piano, the score of the sonata spread on the music rack before her. "The young Mister Ringen will, I believe, present to us"—here he consulted his note again—"Beethoven's Sonata number 14, colloquially known as 'The Moonlight Sonata.' A favorite of the esteemed Dr. Brandt."

Spinning on his cane, Ernst Sauer turned and sat upon the elaborate Master's chair under the baldachin.

Willa—no, William, or Will—stood and adjusted the peruke and stepped from behind the piano, where he bowed to his uncle and Ernst Sauer in turn. He returned to the piano bench and flipped the tails of his coat out from under him as he sat. He set his fingers on the keys and absorbed the hush of the hundred gathered men.

But the music wouldn't come to *him*, so he gave himself back over to Willa, who began pianissimo.

DAYS AND MONTHS and even years later, Theodulf would believe he heard the music from that dark bench in the main floor lobby. He'd believe it—and not the elevator—carried him up to the Blue Room. That it had the power to lift him. And to *return* him. "Quasi una fantasia." The same music he'd heard in a Paris café five years earlier. The one on the Île Saint-Louis. The last night he'd been happy.

Waiting for the liftman to fasten the cage shut, he caught its distant melody. The excruciating slowness of the adagio—equal parts music and memory—drew him through his reflection in the mirror and back–back–back. He could taste the sugar and anise of *la fée verte* at the zinc bar in France; could, when he closed his eyes against the mirror, see instead that pianist's ecstasy. Could see his lithe fingers touching the music from the keys. Those same hands would later trace across his ribs with a similar flourish. Those memories he kept bunkered someplace even lower than his bowels? They rose in him as the elevator did the Opera building. Between the fifth and sixth floors, the music nearly dissolved him. He felt suppliant. Ill. Aroused. But more than anything, he felt unrepentant.

The lift came to a jerking halt. The gate accordioned back, and he hurried across the hallway where the Tyler let him into the lodge. The music was now urgent through a haze of cigar smoke so dense it seemed almost to drop the tone an octave. He saw the boy playing and was for a moment stunned, but then the adagio became less a sound in his ears than a magnetic force that led him to a seat along the wall.

From there Theodulf watched him play. He sported an ill-fitting tuxedo jacket that ballooned from his slight shoulders as he moved.

101

He wore a démodé periwig, and his face, when he lifted it, rose as pale and serene as the moon, a strange, muliebral kindness catching in the candlelight from the chandeliers. Theodulf reached for his watch, but only held it in his pocket. The *tick-tock* of its movement, though, was nowhere to be found. Drowned, it was. By the music or the storm outside or the one within his rotten body, who could say?

In the windows behind the boy, the blackness of the night was frantic. He could tell not only from the way it danced along the leaded glass, but because there existed in its pith an even greater darkness wanting expression. My God, how he knew that feeling. He'd had it most of his life.

He knew also he should turn away from the night. From the song and from the boy. He should dampen it. But how *could* he? Better to try to bottle that hurricane wind.

Whenever the boy feinted left—into the darker notes—Theodulf found his own head nodding along. One measure, and another, and a third. He'd wait for the music to lift them again, which it did, over and over, and Theodulf felt not only the elegance of Beethoven's composition but that thing at the heart of it.

He supposed this was how convening with God was supposed to make him feel. In communion. Entire. Forgiven. *Saved.* So why did he feel instead the opposite? Why, when he turned his words or thoughts or deeds to God, did he feel abandoned? And why did that abandonment always attend the most precious, most divine moments of his life? Perhaps he could capture the answer to these questions while bottling the wind!

As he listened to the boy play, recalling the same melody from across time and the whole Atlantic Ocean, he squelched those questions of Providence and gave himself over instead to the holiness of the moment, turning his head up not in prayer but in devotion all the same. On the alabaster ceiling, he saw the same hue as the boy wore upon his face and tresses. Theodulf imagined the fineness of the boy's fingers. He imagined the suppleness of the boy's cheek beneath his own rough hand. The music and his musings inflamed him, and, as the adagio neared its end, he resolved to look upon the boy once more.

Now Theodulf saw he wore complexion powder and if the realization perplexed Theodulf, it also aroused him even more. When the boy lifted his hand to turn the score, Theodulf saw it first through the haze of cigar smoke and again reflected in the window. He as much as *felt* it. And *held* it. And in order to imprint it permanently in his memory, Theodulf pressed his thumbs into his eyes and held them there until the first notes of the allegretto galloped through the room, at which point he stood and hurried back through the assembled guests and out of the Blue Room. He'd been there for all of three minutes and could bear not one second more.

WILLA'S PIANO PEDAGOGUE, Herr Volk—a self-described celibate, distant and *final* living relation of Cardinal Volk, a great-great-grandnephew or some such, a designation he was exceedingly proud of, and a musician himself entrenched in anonymity, composer of the once-performed *Nördlich mit Gott,* which he considered to be a rebuttal of sorts to Beethoven's masterwork but which a critic called "cacophonous and mired in mawkishness"—often reminded her that Franz Liszt, a devout Catholic who took the four minor orders of the church before his death, described the middle movement of Sonata no. 14 in C-sharp Minor as a flower between two chasms.

For Willa, a more apt simile was that it was like a *bird* between two chasms, and when her hand rose to turn the score in the Blue Room, from the first to the second movement and the cheerful allegretto that greeted her there, she saw the wing of a gull, not her own trembling flesh. The sight of it gave her a moment's panic, and in the pause before she commenced—she held it for two beats—as her hand flew back down to the keys, she risked a third beat in anticipation of the storm outside the window.

What she sensed was less the disturbance of the atmosphere than the one in her own mind. This sometimes happened at the piano. Especially if she were playing with the score—a practice Herr Volk insisted on—instead of by ear, which she preferred and believed was how music ought to be performed. But she was doubtful. Always. And her own grievous suspicions of her gifts were as wont to possess her by way of the wind as by Herr Volk's frequent admonishments. Those came weekly, when she visited his home by Chester Creek, entered its tobacco- and coffee-soaked hallowedness, and suffered her lesson. He came from that school of instruction rooted mainly in his own failures, each suggestion carried on his rank breath and borne of his never having achieved renown, despite a lifelong effort. He formerly bred and rode dressage horses and still kept a pair of retired Westphalians in a stable up by Hunters Park, and as Ernst Sauer walked with a cane, so Herr Volk carried a black leather riding crop that he used both as metronome and pointer. When his frustration was most roused, it would tremble, poised, in his hand.

His lack of accomplishment as a player and composer did not diminish his ability as a pedagogue, though, and despite his avarice and sourness and plain lack of regard for her, he must have had *some* appreciation for her talent. After all, he'd overlooked her family's heathenism and continued to tutor her for four years now. What he hadn't yet taught her was how to *abandon* herself to the music—he blamed her lack of faith in God—and it was in such moments of awareness, of her consciousness holding forth, that he'd drum the trembling black leather on her hand. Sometimes with more force than others. That strap always brought her back to the notes.

There in the Blue Room, she felt very far from the music indeed. So far that she couldn't even hear it. Instead, she listened to the wind, which she was decidedly *not* playing away, as she'd promised her father she would.

By the time she reached the Presto agitato, she was properly shaken. What she envisioned between her eyes and the score were not her hands, but a *pair* of gull's wings, thrashing as though *caught* in the gale. The chasm was all around her. And while the wind gusted ever more wildly, the gull flapped from key to key. A tear rolled down her cheek, leaving a streak of pale flesh in the complexion powder.

Now the thews in her forearms and fingers grew taut. The gull was in gliding flight and Willa winging with it. Off! Into what unhappiness? What confusion? She could not name it. Could hardly even know it was there except by virtue of her loneliness in that moment. To regain herself, she lifted her right foot above the damper pedal and let it linger there, considering a violation of Beethoven's own wishes. This simple gesture redirected her, and she began to hear the music again.

And there! A luftpause in her mind (Herr Volk was famous for adding them to his scores). She took a gulping breath that seemed to open her ears even wider. Her fingers were no longer wings. The gull had gone into the recesses of the Blue Room or the night or her own waking dream, and suddenly she was back in the melody, back in the moment and the smoke and the men sitting all round with their cigars and their inscrutable faces.

But only her father mattered, his face not vacant at all but, like Willa's gull, caught between two chasms—the storm outside and the one in his conscience. She *must* appease him. *Now.* She would try again—and harder—to play away the wind.

She closed her eyes once more to the sheets of music before her. She closed them against the worried look on her father's face. One hundred measures. That was all she had left.

The music rose. To her ears and her ego.

She felt as if she were soaring on the crescendos. Gliding on the diminuendos. Each chord an eddy in the heart of her consciousness, but all of it perfectly controlled and predestined. It *inhabited* her.

The trills now shuddering. The hair on her arms raised as if by static electricity. A lusty stirring in her bowels. She could not breathe for the commotion.

And time, vanished! Only sound remained. And her being carried. Her carrying. The splendor. Heavenly.

Here the final adagio. If God existed, these were His whispers.

Now the quarter rests, tempo primo. Her favorite sound in all the world, these notes. If she only ever heard *them* again, if she only ever felt *them,* she would be happy. Ecstatic.

But onward! Nine measures more. Thirty seconds. Thirty years. The gull into eternity, for all it was.

The closing flourish played tempestuously. Fortissimo.

Whole rest.

Darkness.

The wind played away.

Abyss. *Chasm.*

Was it an hour before she heard the generous applause? Or a single moment? In either case, it returned her to her body. All the men, standing in front of their chairs, their cigars clenched in their teeth behind their smiling lips. Alderman Haven, the man who would one day become mayor, even wiped a tear from beneath his own eye.

Willa, fearful, looked to her father. He stood with the others. Applauding but distant. Willa stood herself, thought to curtsy, but remembered in the nick of time and bowed instead. A proper aristocrat.

"Gentlemen! Gentlemen!" This was Ernst Sauer speaking. He hammered his cane upon the altar floor as he earlier had. "Gentlemen, please! We've all been moved by young Mister Ringen's rousing performance." He spoke above the lingering applause, and saluted Will from his perch at the altar, waiting for everyone to quiet.

When they did, he continued. "You have brought the storm inside, young sir. You have done your uncle proud." He straightened his necktie and lowered his chin, and in a tone altogether changed said, "But now we must onward with the solemn and righteous occasion at hand. Bid your uncle farewell, so we might commence our evening's agenda."

Willa bowed in her father's direction, then made for the door through which she'd entered. Only a friendly hand, reaching from among the Masons, saved her from that faulty exit. Instead, she crossed the Blue Room, giving her father one more glance.

IN THE MAIN FLOOR LOBBY, Theodulf watched the boy at the revolving door, his young silhouette cut as if by a Parisian silhouettist. For several minutes he sat there, admonishing himself to keep quiet, to let the boy walk away. But the longer he regarded him, the more impossible his task. Finally, he submitted, stood, and cleared his throat loud enough for the boy to hear.

Startled, the wigged boy turned, his figuration animated now.

"I didn't mean to surprise you," Theodulf said, risking a step forward.

The boy had about him some mouselike quality. Or maybe he felt cornered, on the one side by Theodulf, and on the other the storm outside. Aware of this possibility, Theodulf took a nimble stride sideways. "I was just sitting here, wondering how many times that sonata has been played. Over the past hundred-odd years."

Was the boy listening? Look at him there!

"I saw it performed in Paris once. Some five years ago now, at Le Palais Garnier." Theodulf put his hand over his heart. "Performed by a young virtuoso not much different in mien from you, friend."

The boy buttoned the ill-fitting Crombie coat he wore.

"In any case," Theodulf continued, feigning nonchalance despite feeling nearly breathless. "It's the sort of question I almost always find myself lost in." When the boy didn't reply, Theodulf said again, "How many times has that music been performed? The impossible rumination of it? I can't say why, but it gives me some sort of peace." He crossed his arms and cocked his head at an angle, affecting an air of contemplation. "It's quite an opposite thought from the ones that usually occupy me. I'm an attorney, you see. Mostly criminal cases, so you can imagine the comfort I take not only in my wool-gathering, but in the music itself."

"Sir?"

"The Moonlight Sonata. Your performance upstairs." He looked toward the ceiling, as though he might see through the several floors above. "Poor Beethoven, the composer of that masterpiece"—now he leaned slightly toward the boy and glanced left and right, as if about to share a great secret—"*the* great masterpiece, in all of music, if you ask me. And yet, he never heard it performed himself."

The boy did not speak, so Theodulf made a wide, crossing arc to stand at the starboard side of the revolving door, while the boy backed up against the one port.

"He was deaf, you see? All of that music, it only ever lived in his mind. *Betwixt his ears*, as it were!"

"But you're not?"

What a candied voice he had!

"I'm not what?"

"Deaf, sir." The boy cleared his throat now. It sounded less sweet when he continued. "You heard me from all the way down here?"

Theodulf *giggled*. A most unnatural sound from his twisted mouth. "No," he said, putting a finger to his lips to repress that ridiculous laughter. "I was up in the Blue Room for the beginning of your performance."

"But you left?"

"Too sweet a sound," Theodulf said. "And in that den of thieves. I couldn't bear the contradiction."

"My uncle's not a thief."

Loyalty! What a noble thing for so young a man. "I believe he is not. My own father, to say nothing of the rest of them, is among the very worst of them all." He caught and righted himself mid-confession. "But we're free of them down here . . ."

Theodulf could not disguise his readiness. The boy was so simple. So naive. He felt a devilish grin rising and recognized at once how like his father he must have appeared in that instant. The thought of it filled him with disgust, and to erase it he glanced up and down Superior Street through the door. He could not see the top of the building across the street. The darkness was allayed only by the snow, which seemed possessed by a distant, strobic light. As lightning in a cloud. "No moon tonight," Theodulf said, as much to himself as the boy. "Did you know Beethoven named it the Moonlight Sonata after spending an evening with his lover along the river Seine, under a radiant *lune aux fraises*?"

The boy appeared to blush at this, but rather than demure, he took a cautious step toward Theodulf. "In Paris, who did you see perform it?"

Even this vaguest reference sent Theodulf dithering. He joined his fingertips one hand against the other, nodded to himself, and said, "She actually became a dear friend. I might have married her, if not for the great distance between us and the importance of my work here."

"What was her name, this *pianiste*?"

"Paul," he said.

"A rather strange name for a woman."

"Paulette, actually. Paul was my pet name for her." He reached for his watch, flipped its lid in his pocket, and removed his hand all in one motion. "Paulette Gouttière. Perhaps you've heard of her?"

"My pedagogue back home is named Paul."

"Virginia, yes?"

The boy seemed almost to sidle toward Theodulf. Certainly, his expression was less guarded. Even rakish. Could Theodulf dare hope?

"Yes. Richmond."

Theodulf sighed. But how he wished to speak!

It was the boy who spoke more. "You all have arranged some very peculiar weather for me."

Theodulf, hoping to quell the gale rising in himself, looked outside again. "This is exceptional even by our inconstant standards. I hope your uncle has raised the weather flags. I'm sure he has. I have it on good authority he's a fine and decent man, and a learned one at that." Theodulf wanted to ingratiate himself to this boy, but it was also a moment of unguarded truth, and those facts together seemed to unlock the smile now animating the boy's beautiful, painted face.

"I don't know one finer," he said.

"Your outfit," Theodulf said, looking for an excuse to size him up and down. "It's quite decorous. If that's the word. And quite like a *disguise*. I know I ought not say this, but I rather like a good disguise."

"Doctor Brandt, well, it was his idea. He's charming in many ways, not least in his merrymaking."

"What a delightful word! *Merrymaking*. It makes me want to dance!"

"You don't strike me as the dancing sort," the boy said.

This stung, and Theodulf felt himself losing hold, something he could not do. Instead of sulking, he bore up. "How about we catch the next trolley down to Bill Lanigan's pub? I'll show you a jig!"

"I prefer a waltz."

Did he really just speak those words? Theodulf allowed he did, the gunsel! "You've at least two hours before your uncle's ceremony is finished—"

His own fantasia was interrupted by an enormous crash against the door. Both he and the boy jumped at the sound, scurrying back from the glass. Outside, what appeared to be a ship's moonsail flapped against the glass.

"Mon dieu," Theodulf whispered, as much to himself as to the boy. "What is that?"

"I believe, sir, it's an awning unmoored."

"An awning?" Theodulf said, stepping toward the door and risking another look up. "I guess we're now prisoners of this lobby."

"I know another way out," the boy said, and before Theodulf could speak, he disappeared into a passageway beyond the elevator.

Paralyzed, beggared, heartsick, Theodulf listened to the storm wail behind him.

SEICHES

APRIL 22, 1910

If you stood on certain seashores long enough, and with unwavering eyes, you'd see the moon pulling the water. The tides. When the moon's orbit is most distant, the attending tide is called Apogean. When it's closest, Perigean. The varieties between are many and many named, but they all speak to a force subtle and beguiling.

Lake Superior is not blessed by tides. Not like the oceans and seas. But she's sometimes made to spill, and not just from her famous gales. She has seiches—is there a more beautiful word?—that come unannounced and gently and stir her sweet waters.

I once stood near the mouth of the Burnt Wood River and watched the water roll out under the moonlight. I tried to imagine a tidal force at work, but knew better—desire and longing are not lost on me!—and reconciled that hollowed shore against my wishes. What I learned is that sometimes, even oftentimes, it is better to imagine than to know.

ALL NIGHT she'd watched the sky instead of sleeping. There from the headland, in the shadows of the lighthouse, she tried to possess her thoughts. But they flitted like shooting stars—between her own melancholy and something else she couldn't name or even see, only ever catching its metaphysical ripple. To quiet her mind, she thought of the girl instead.

A lamp burned in the fish house. Occasionally she'd see his shadow pass the window, and when it did, she'd move her gaze to the firmament. It shone enormously over the calm lake. The moon making its slow arc across the night. The comet in some other part of its orbit. The lighthouse beacon keeping tempo to the impossible song of the nighttide. All of it reflecting on the water and again in her lonesome eyes.

In those few moments she gathered her thoughts, they inevitably found her father's ghost. She might have prayed to him—to give her strength, to grant her the power of forgiveness, for peace—but then she'd consider the girl, an orphan if all this was true, and reckon that even praying to someone as good as he was pointless. The realization came with a nudge, and she'd glance once more at the fish house window. Then his silhouette would pass, and to the heavens she'd turn again.

Round and round.

Now it was an hour before dawn. She could tell from where the moon hung. And the notion she'd been dreaming up since the small hours rose over her like the sun soon would. She followed her intuition down the path, past the boathouse and dock, and scampering across the rocky, crescent-shaped beach. Fifteen minutes it took, and by the time she reached his dock, he stood upon it, smoking a pipe, almost as if he'd been expecting her company. In the star-light, she could see his tired eyes. Like a pair of moons they shone, and she knew it was as much for a look at them as his niece's loss that she'd come.

"A strange time for a visitor," he said, his voice only a whisper, but carrying like the beacon that just then passed over them.

"I've been thinking about your niece. About both of you."

"I'm in a fix."

"How's that?"

"For one, I'm Silje's only family."

"I wondered."

"And I don't know what to do about her folks. Where to report it. What will happen to my niece." He took a puff from his pipe. "I asked your husband for practical advice, and he only suggested I pray."

Her response came as fast as one of those shooting stars: "Don't rely on Mr. Sauer for practical advice. Or any advice, in fact."

Mats regarded her through his pipe smoke. Through the lessening night. He puffed three times. "That's your husband you speak unwell of."

Again, like another shooting star: "I forget sometimes."

Now Mats looked behind him and turned a fish box on its side and sat and crossed his right leg over his left knee and leaned on his elbow.

"There's a man in Gunflint you should go see. Curtis Mayfair is his name. He's a magistrate."

"I know Mr. Mayfair."

"Then I don't have to tell you he's an honorable man. If you went up to Duluth to report the fate of Silje's parents, and to put to rest her place in the world with you, I expect you'd encounter no end to the bureaucracy."

The glowing tip of his pipe brought a flash to his eyes. "The larger question is just what in damnation I'm supposed to do with her."

"Why, she adores you. That much is plain to see."

"Little doubt of that. But raising a child? *Me?*"

"Who else would do it?"

He nodded, then looked over Willa's shoulder. "Speak of the devil."

Willa turned, and there was the girl, listing on the dock, her nightshirt threadbare and catching starlight. When Willa turned again, back to Mats, he already stood and was emptying his pipe bowl.

"Thank you for the counsel, Mrs. Sauer." He closed the distance between himself and his niece and scooped her sleepwalking form into his arms. Her head fell onto his shoulder. "I'd wish you a good evening, but I think the night is done."

He walked past Willa then, and there seemed to trail him a wake not only of his sweet-smelling tobacco but his niece's misshapen and half-awake dreams. Willa felt them as a chill in the air.

DISASSEMBLED, arrayed on the black silk, scintillating in the lamplight: the ninety-nine pieces of the Hamilton railroad watch. Pins and wheels and jewels and pinions and springs. All night he worked, taking it apart, fueled by a deranged resolve, employing every tool. Now he trained the loupe on one of the springs, tried to imagine it moving time, despaired. Hours of this, broken only by the winding of the lighthouse clockworks.

The clockworks! He checked his Longines, tried to place the hour on the morning, peeked out the window and saw the first inkling of light on the eastern horizon like it rose from the water itself. A man could believe it did if he lived here long enough. He wasn't so far gone himself, but strange thoughts like these were already becoming regular. Instead of trusting himself, he took the spiral staircase up to the watch room. There he found the whole apparatus running exactly as it was supposed to. He checked his pocket watch again, as though much time had passed or been lost in the minute since he last looked at it. It had not.

Dear God, he thought.

Then he thought of the thing he'd been avoiding all night. The comet. He felt inside his coat for the letter he'd not yet mailed, that he'd go deliver as soon as he extinguished the lamp.

Rather than returning to the Hamilton, he climbed into the lantern room, then out onto the parapet. He chose the dark side of the lighthouse, let the starlight fall on him slowly, and, with each eclipse of the light, risked a glance heavenward. Nothing arced. No poisonous gases rained. No blaze of apocalyptic fire streaked across his view. No raving hosannas fell on his ears. And certainly he offered none himself. It was this last that riled him now. He was always waiting for the world to align. For the want of prayer to meet the moments his fear or his shame or his longing struck him most fiercely. Instead, he felt now like he almost always did: like what remained of the night's darkness.

To the west, across the yard, a light on in his kitchen window. This brought him some satisfaction. On two counts now, maybe she wasn't worthless after all.

Was he disappointed, a half hour later, that she did not greet him there? That instead of her pretty face, he found on the kitchen table a bowl of lukewarm oats covered with a folded tea towel and a cup of coffee with the saucer atop its rim? He stopped not to ponder whether he was, but only marched upstairs and opened the door to his bedroom.

"It's past seven o'clock and here you are?" She sat on the edge of the cot, taking a pin out of her hair.

"Where else would I be?" she asked.

"My breakfast is cold. There're dirty dishes in the sink. Your boots are covered with mud and sitting in the foyer like a pair of napping cats."

"It must have been quite an inconvenience, to step around them." She stood and pinned her hair back again.

"Must you be contrary?" He crossed the room and set his holdall on the floor beneath the window.

"Is your breakfast not sitting on the table? Is your cot not ready for you?"

"This morning's not for sleeping away. Mine or yours or anyone else's."

She glared at him for a full ten seconds before he said, "You'll need a shawl and bonnet." When she did not move, he added, "You'll need them *now*."

She hurried past him and out of the room and before he could

so much as loosen his necktie she returned, standing in the doorway with a sweater draped over one arm and her hat untied atop
her head.

"I'll be down to the dock in five minutes," he said. "You can wait
there."

When she didn't move, he retraced his steps to the door, and
gently shut it in her face.

And when he opened it again a couple minutes later, she had not
moved. "Where are we going that I should meet you on the dock?"

He wedged himself past her and turned around in the hallway.
"A mail run. To Otter Bay."

"And you can't manage your correspondence without help from
me? I suppose you have sacks and sacks of mail."

He smoothed his mustache and sighed. "You'll be making the
run yourself sometimes, so you'll need to see the place. And meet
Herr Winkler and his wife, Clara. You'll need to learn how to get
the boat down the ways, and how to set the sail once it's on the
water." Then he scratched his throat and sighed again, affected an
air of slight condescension. "I can't imagine that in all your training
as a debutante, you've had many lessons in useful things. Certainly
your performance thus far hasn't indicated any."

If he meant to sting her, he appeared to have failed. She only
sneered at him and walked to the door of her own bedroom, where
she spoke again. "You're dull and overbearing." Then she closed *her*
door.

He waited ten minutes at the boathouse before he launched the
boat and raised the mast. The westerly breeze would make going
easy and returning less so. He supposed this was the way of things.
Though his wife's temper was more like relentlessly being in irons.
A cold and bitter wind, too. Here she came now, fairly saunter-
ing down the path, no bonnet atop her head, no shawl across her
shoulders.

Well, let her freeze.

When she reached the dock and then the boat and Theodulf raised his hand to help her in, she ignored him, taking a seat on the forward thwart and turning her back. He answered the only way he knew how, by untying the line and pushing them off. Not more than twenty strong strokes on the oars and he was out beyond the palisade. He feathered the oars and raised the sail and watched it fill slowly with the faint breeze. He thought to tell her never to knot the sail to the gunwale, an unsafe practice, but her stalwart silence inspired the same in him, and they sailed on that way.

Rounding Big Rock, he rose to his feet and studied the depths on the port side of his boat. There at twelve fathoms lay the ghostly hull of the *Lisbon*. A swell of virtue surfaced in him, and again he thought to impart his wisdom, to show her this sunken wreck, to impress upon her the importance of his job and rank, but he sailed on in his morbid taciturnity instead.

He'd meant to hug the shore, but in the lee of the palisade his trailing breeze hardly puffed the jib, and so he rowed out until he found that companion wind again. With it at his back, they sailed a half hour down the shore. As he steered his boat to the town dock, Willa finally turned and said, "I expect we could have arrived fifteen minutes ago if you'd rowed instead of letting that whisper push us."

Before he'd even tied the boat off, she was up and stretching on the dock, her hand shielding the sun from her eyes as she took in what lay before her. He looked himself. Up on the hillside he saw smoke and heard the saw from the whining mill. The enormous stacks of timber lay like a highway to the houses and churches. The fish houses and dockside businesses bustled this fine spring day, and it wasn't more than a minute or two before Helmut Winkler appeared from the office of the Winkler Freight Depot at the mouth of the Otter River. He must have caught sight of Theodulf, for he walked half the length of the dock to greet them.

"Mr. Sauer," he said, extending a hand toward Theodulf but keeping his eyes on Willa. "This must be your bride."

Willa turned. "I have a name."

"I'm pleased, Mrs. Sauer, to meet you." Now he extended his hand to her.

"Willa," she said, shaking his.

"Charmed," Helmut said.

"It's her first visit," Theodulf interrupted. "I'll take her around. Show her what's what."

To Willa, Helmut Winkler said, "Whatever else he shows you, know that you're always welcome at my home, as well. I live just up past the Indian cemetery. You can't miss it. Biggest house in town. I'm famous for my hospitality."

"Famous, you say?" Willa said. "How come I've never heard of you?"

Now Helmut hitched his thumbs under his suspenders and pretended to be insulted. "You see, there're families like the Sauers here"—he lifted his chin toward Theodulf—"who're interested in making reputations. And there are families like mine, who're interested in making fortunes."

Theodulf puffed himself up. "The two things are not mutually exclusive."

Helmut winked at Willa.

"You're a fortune-making family? All this lumber, it belongs to you?" she asked.

Everyone knew the Winklers were lumber barons. But to see this inventory put their business into a vivid context. The yard went a quarter mile into the hills, and a quarter mile to the south. Two hundred and fifty acres of winter-cut white pine stacked to the rooflines of the houses in the platted part of town.

"Otter Bay isn't even the tip of it. Our operation up on the Burnt Wood yielded twice as much as this. We've got mills over at the Sault and down in Ashland, too. You'd be hard-pressed to find a house in middle America that wasn't built with our lumber."

"And none of these boards would have a place to go if not for safe waters to get them there," Theodulf said.

"True, true," Helmut said. "Your lighthouse will save us on

insurance, and for that we're grateful." He patted Theodulf on the shoulder as though he were but a schoolboy answering a trifling question. To Willa he said, "I mean it sincerely when I offer our hospitality. Now that the last of our children is off to college, my wife gets lonesome up here. The pleasure of your company would do her well."

"But not you, sir?" Willa said.

"I guess we'd best be off, Willa," Theodulf interrupted, his bile rising. Whether from his wife's lack of decency or his own bruised pride, he could hardly fathom. To Helmut he said, "We appreciate your hospitality, and will keep the invitation front of mind. But now"—he gestured at the town—"we must attend our business."

Helmut doffed his hat and winked at Theodulf, as if they'd been coconspirators in this game of braggadocio, and then turned up the dock and headed toward Winkler's Dry Goods.

Theodulf watched him enter the store, then, without looking at her, addressed Willa. "You'll not behave like a common strumpet." He thought of his Hamilton watch left in pieces on the black silk in the cleaning room, wondering now how to make time go backward so that he could have avoided the exchange with Helmut altogether. Almost as soon as he thought it, he changed directions again, charging into the present moment. "It's unbecoming. And a mortal sin, no less." Now he did look at her. "What's more, what's *most*, is that behavior like that is a blight on the institution of the Lighthouse Service."

"I was merely being neighborly."

"You were being flirtatious, with a brute of a man famous for his dalliances, no less."

"That old sod?"

"This is not a lark, Willa. We are pillars of this community."

"Community? It's twenty houses and a dry goods. There're more horses here than people."

"It's growing. It's where we live. And it's where God *sees* us."

Willa made as though to speak, but Theodulf raised his hand to shush her. "We won't speak more of this, but I expect compliance."

He straightened his necktie and adjusted the cuffs of his coat as though he might realign their whole day. Their whole marriage. "Now, you see we tie up here at the town dock. If there's no cleat, just run the skiff onto the beach over there at the mouth of the river."

He walked the length of the dock. Where it met the shore, atop two flights of wooden stairs, a small hut was built into the hillside. He was halfway up that staircase before he saw his wife was not behind him, but rather strolling up the dock as though it were a Parisian quay, and the skiffs tied to the cleats were golden gondolas manned by handsome gondoliers. He waited for her there on the landing, observing her from that perch. She was shapely and tall, boyish even without her comely face to lend her femininity. Her irascible nature was the least attractive thing about her, and perhaps the most dominant, but he could admit that from afar there were reasons to be attracted to her.

When she finally reached the base of the stairs, she paused once to look back from where she'd come before ascending, holding her skirts high with one hand. At the landing, she said, "The sign says this is the post office."

"It's the main reason you'll be in Otter Bay. I've arranged so you and the other keepers' wives can collect official correspondence for the lighthouse."

"You *are* thorough."

"There's much to do, and we all must to lend a hand."

He continued up the second flight of stairs and held the door open for her. Inside was little more than a ten-foot-square room with a stove on one side and a counter on the other. Behind the counter were the mail slots, names beneath, and an old man who seemed unable even to lift his head.

"Mr. Sauer," he said, peering up over the wire rims of his spectacles.

"Mr. Holzer, how goes the parcel business?"

The old geezer swiveled around and emptied two of the

slots—one for the lighthouse, the other for Theodulf personally—and set the post on the desk.

Theodulf, in turn, reached into his pocket and withdrew the single letter addressed to Hosea Grimm.

"This'll leave with the *Nocturne* today," Mr. Holzer said, dropping the letter into a canvas sack already half-full of other mail.

"Can't get there soon enough," Theodulf said.

"What business do you have with Hosea Grimm?"

"He's a friend, is all."

Mr. Holzer turned to Willa. "This must be the Missus Sauer."

"It is. And Willa, this is Arnold Holzer. She'll be coming for the mail often enough."

"I lock the door as soon as the *Nocturne* disembarks. Don't expect me to open it for you."

Willa appeared charmed by his curmudgeonliness. "I'll expect no such thing."

"Then we'll get along just fine."

Theodulf withdrew from his coat pocket a broadside announcing the public celebration of the lighthouse. "Fine with you if I post this on the board?" he asked.

Holzer looked closely and nodded and said, "Then, if you'll excuse me, I've got other duties needing attention." He nodded. "Happy to know you, Missus Sauer."

"Likewise."

As though to usher her out of the post office, Theodulf put his hand on the small of her back. When he felt her recoil at his touch, he reached for his watch instead. The seconds ticked.

On the landing, he paused and watched her walk down the staircase. She fairly strode. He twisted his hands before him, glanced at the lighthouse tender tied among a half dozen other boats to the dock. He let the idea of paddling her with one of the oars entertain him—whether to punish her impudence or rekindle in himself the fire first stoked the previous day, he did not know. In either case, he hurried the thought from his mind.

It was then he saw it, though he could not name it: a seiche. All the boats tied to the dock bobbed as though an enormous boulder had been rolled into the lake. As quickly as the swell came, it was gone again. He glanced at the river fifty yards across the bay. It ran fresh but was not the cause of the wave. He next looked heavenward, where all he saw was another lowering sky. A rumble of spring thunder. No heavenly body. No comet or falling star.

"Willa!" he shouted down to her. "Did you see that?"

She turned back, shielded her eyes against the white sky. "See what?"

"That wave. That singular wave. It upset all the boats here." He gestured at the dock.

She did not respond, only descended the last few steps and turned toward the dry goods at the end of the dock.

Theodulf stood there on the landing, watching the boats, feeling unnerved. By this strange phenomenon and his wife both.

When he made his way down the second half of the staircase, the wave came again. He was alone on the dock, so no one else saw the boats rise or heard them knock together. Basso castanets. He hurried toward the boats, reached them in time to hear the water sieving through the pilings beneath the deck.

He looked around again, as though a curtain might be pulled back to reveal a grand farce.

By the time he reached the dry goods, rain spat against the windows overlooking the bay and mouth of the river. The shelves were well supplied now that the *Nocturne* was making the first spring runs. There were even bunches of bananas sitting in a countertop basket. The shelves of canned goods fairly bowed under the weight of them, jars of honey and preserves stood in pyramids on the counter alongside bowls of licorice and horehound and butterscotch but also the foil-wrapped chocolates Theodulf fancied. Crates of candles and crockery and fine tinware sat around each of the four columns supporting the coved ceiling, and bolts of denim, gingham, and canvas hung above the crates from those same columns. There was a wall of Red Wing workboots, and another with a rack of Winchester rifles, and below them a glass case of ammunition and hunting knives. In the back of the store hung a wall of tools of every sort, as well as shelves with cans of paint and turpentine along with boxes of nails and nuts and bolts. And the purveyor of all this: Patrick Dreiss, whose potbelly strained against his apron as he stood behind the counter, writing a receipt for none other than Mats Braaten, the fisherman, who was distracted by his niece and Willa, consorting on a bench beneath one of the windows. The child had a whip of black licorice, and she was dressed as if for church.

Theodulf ambled across the store, affecting an air of influence he did not naturally possess, and greeted Dreiss as though Mats were a common ghost. "Mr. Dreiss, you might have postponed this cold rain until my wife and I were safely back up the shore." He laid another of the broadsides on the counter and slid it across. "You'll post this?"

Dreiss glanced at it and nodded and changed the subject back to the original question. "Mr. Sauer, if I had that sort of power, you can bet your last nickel I'd not use it to stop the rain."

Mats Braaten flipped a silver dollar from his thumb, caught it, and set it on the counter. "What would you use it for, Patrick?"

To this Dreiss looked up and said, "I'd start with finding that girl's folks." He turned around and opened a drawer and removed two tickets for the *Nocturne*. "It's due at eleven."

By instinct, Theodulf flipped open his watch.

"Mr. Sauer," Mats said, placing the tickets in his coat pocket, "I owe your wife thanks."

"Thanks for what, Mr. Braaten?"

"She suggested I head up to see Curtis Mayfair about Silje's parents."

This simple announcement vexed Theodulf completely, and it

was all he could do not to march over to Willa and confront her yet again. Instead, he said, "Mr. Mayfair is a good fellow." He bit his lip. "But why go so far when surely there's a friend to your situation in Duluth, if not Two Harbors?"

"Mrs. Sauer thought Mayfair might be the friendliest."

Theodulf finally removed his hat. He took his kerchief from his pocket and buffed the visor. "I wish you a safe trip." With that he donned his hat again, stuffed his kerchief into his pocket, and strode toward Willa and the girl.

As he approached, Silje quieted, lacing the licorice around her fingers and leaning toward Willa.

"Now you're advising the fisherman on family matters?" He spoke with his teeth clenched, barely above a whisper. "Girl"—this to Silje—"go to your uncle. He wishes to speak with you."

Willa took the girl's hand, spread her fingers, and dropped more confections into her palm. "We'll see you when you return, I hope."

Silje nodded, held the candy with both hands, and looked up at Theodulf. "Your wife is very pretty," she said. "She's very pretty and she doesn't like frogs."

Theodulf watched her over his shoulder. He watched her walk to her uncle and put the candy in her pocket. He watched her skip to the door and out and disappear on the dock. Only then did he turn back to Willa. "That child is witchlike and queer. There's something infernal about her. What she needs is schooling from the nuns. Is she possessed?"

"Only by a sharp wit and exceeding powers of observation."

Theodulf wasn't listening. "And what about frogs? Has Beelzebub got her tongue?"

Willa removed her own whip of licorice from her dress pocket and took a bite.

"What's this?" Theodulf asked. "Did you buy this? Did the fisherman buy it for you?"

Willa chewed the candy. She said, "I bought my own licorice."

"Charged it to our account?"

"Paid with my own coin, of course."

"What coin have you? What coin that's not mine first?"

He witnessed the rising of her ire—it was becoming the most regular thing about her. Rather than say anything, he removed from his pocket a piece of lighthouse stationery upon which a list of provisions had been written. "You'll fetch these items from the store here." He called to Patrick Dreiss behind the counter, "Add Mrs. Sauer to the account, Mr. Dreiss. She'll be here often enough now."

"The lighthouse account or your own?" Dreiss asked.

"Either, but today's go on the personal ledger." He turned back to Willa. "Only what's on the list. Luxuries forbidden."

"Luxuries forbidden?"

"Chapter 5 in the *Instructions to Light-Keepers*. Regulation number 186, I believe."

Willa made a great show of filling her mouth with the length of licorice. She took the list as though she were receiving a used handkerchief and went about finding the items from the shelves. Canned goods and a quart of paint and tea towels. Theodulf announced that he would meet her at the boat in twenty minutes, whether the rain quit or not. She ignored him, attending to the list instead. Five pounds of sugar, mousetraps, baking soda, and white vinegar.

He left the dry goods, heading in the direction of the lumberyard. Once there, he walked the edge of it up to the first bend in the river, where he sat on a boulder and folded his hands as though about to pray. What he thought of instead were the watch parts sitting in the cleaning room at the lighthouse.

Bᴀᴄᴋ ᴀᴛ ᴛʜᴇ sᴛᴀᴛɪᴏɴ, Willa bustled about. She stowed the provender in the pantry, put the tea towels on the shelf above the kitchen sink. She made Theodulf a pilot bread and cheese sandwich for lunch, cut an apple and served it as though it were a piece of rhubarb pie. She made a pot of tea and poured them each a cup, and as she sat down across the table, he rose and said he'd take a rest. They were the first words either had spoken since they departed Otter Bay.

"Mind this mess," he added. "And take this can of paint out to the lighthouse cleaning room. Set it beneath my desk."

He didn't wait for her to respond, only shuffled out of the kitchen. But he returned almost as quickly as he left and said, "We'll need a full accounting of your capital. That belongs to both of us now, and we mustn't keep secrets." He left again and went upstairs, his footfalls like the grumble of distant thunder.

She washed and dried the dishes and put them on the shelf. After another cup of lukewarm tea, she hefted the can of paint and carried it across the grounds.

For the first time, she entered the lighthouse building. At this noon hour it was well lit and cold and gave her the strange sensation of being in a crypt. She set the paint beneath the desk. There was the log with its two- and three-word entries—general duties, cleaning plate glass, general work/painting—and beside it what appeared to be a disassembled timepiece. She crossed through the passageway and turned her head up the lighthouse tower and felt a wash of dizziness as her eyes followed the spiral staircase bolted to the wall. For the briefest moment, she remembered her father's laboratory and the deck up there. But the unkind memory of his favorite place was too much to bear, so she went back through the passageway.

The minuscule watch parts spread on the black silk like shards of shattered glass caught her attention again. She went to them, bent at the waist for a closer look. They were arranged in a meticulous if puzzling order, like rows of stars against the black night.

It occurred to her to wonder why Theodulf checked his watch so often. A nervous habit, certainly. But something more, too. Always when he appeared most vexed, most addled. But this watch in pieces? It wasn't the same one he kept in his pocket. That one he'd checked just fifteen minutes ago, after he'd scolded her about her money.

Her money! As though it were a subject of any real concern.

She picked up the watch face from the cloth and held it between the tips of her thumb and forefinger. Flipping it over, she noticed how moonlike it was. Silver and hollowed like the myriad seas where the wheels and levers and springs fit into the stainless steel.

She stood upright and looked out the window and when she set the moon back down, she lifted one of the smaller wheels from among the parts and put it under her tongue. It fit there like a cold, thinly sliced grape.

On the lakeside of the lighthouse, she kicked a rock over the cliff's edge. Seconds later, the water cockled. She walked nearer the edge of the cliff, found another rock, and threw this one. Four stones later, and she glanced back at the house. At the bedroom window on the second floor.

Was that her husband's silhouette in the glass, ghosted by those lace curtains? Was it only her imagination?

In either case, she pinched the watch part from beneath her tongue and flipped it over the edge. She took a step in its direction and watched for a splash.

None rose. Or none that she could see.

FOR ALL SILJE KNEW, the Lighthouse Road could have been the Champs-Élysées, given the hubbub in the town of Gunflint. This despite the weather, which had followed them down the shore. The sky hung dull and ambiguous and caught between seasons.

Longshoremen lugged the *Nocturne*'s hawsers to cleats, their broad backs fuzzed with whatever fell from the sky. Snow and drizzle and brume all at once. She watched from the gangway, holding her uncle's hand and eager to disembark. She distrusted the big passenger ferry. Believed a fishing skiff a superior and more sensible conveyance under any circumstances. When she announced that someday the ship would sink, her uncle told her that to row from their cabin to Gunflint would take two days each way—and this only if the wind and weather were right—and that he'd gladly take his chances.

She'd kept her eyes clenched shut the whole six-hour voyage, and not for sleeping. Every time the ferry yawed or caught a gust of infrequent wind, it foundered behind her eyes. Now that it was moored, she danced foot to foot, needing a loo as much as she did the solid ground beneath her feet. She tapped her uncle's palm to an iambic beat. *This ship did sink, thrice methinks . . .*

Finally, the gangway lowered. Her uncle hefted his duffle over his shoulder, and they crossed onto the dock.

Horses pulling wagons, wandering dogs sniffing around the fish barrels, a thousand gulls melding with the sky. Their cacophony an anti-rhythm to Silje's song. It was all she could do not to curse their bluster, to reach into the sky and catch them by their wings. She even made to stomp on one, but a dog's sharp bark drove it off before her foot landed.

"Leave the birds," her uncle said.

"The birds've killed my song." Still she tapped his palm. Just the tip of her index finger.

"Your song's not been *killed*. You'll find it again soon enough." He paused at the freight house mid-dock. Inside was dark. "What do you have of it so far?"

"This ship did sink, thrice methinks," she crooned.

"The ship didn't sink, Silje. Much less three times." He pulled her along.

"Not yet, it didn't."

He looked down at her, shook her hand loose, and put his arm across her shoulder. "We'll go straightaway to Mr. Mayfair's office. I doubt he's in, but it's worth checking."

"Is Mr. Mayfair a priest?"

"A priest? Not at all. Mr. Mayfair is a magistrate."

"What's a magistrate?"

"Someone who keeps the civic books, methinks."

As if she'd not asked, nor him answered, Silje stopped walking and looked up into town. There were dozens of buildings, dozens more homes, a lumberyard like in Otter Bay but even more expansive. She turned to look out at the harbor. At the end of the road, beyond the clamor, after the dock turned into a breakwater and the breakwater surrounded the harbor, a lighthouse guarded the safe water. Much smaller than the new one above their cabin and fish house. A dozen boats rested at their moorings on the other side of the harbor, and half a dozen fish houses very like their own met the water on gravel beaches.

As suddenly as she'd shaken her hand free, she reached for her uncle again. "Is this a *city*?"

He switched the duffle from one shoulder to the other. "These are good folks, Silje. Folks like us. It's a little bigger than we're used to. A little louder. But you needn't fret."

They passed a neighing horse, a white dog that looked about the muzzle an awful lot like Fenrir; it trailed them to the end of the dock before bounding into an alleyway. A shiver shook through her body.

At the end of the Lighthouse Road, they stopped at a two-story frame building that matched the address in his pocket. For all its import in his mind, the courthouse appeared as ramshackle as the fish houses on the other side of the harbor. He removed from his pocket the scrap of paper on which Patrick Dreiss had written the address and held it up to the numbers nailed above the door.

"Are we going to someone's house?" Silje asked. "Are they poor as us?"

Her uncle checked the slip of paper again before answering her. "This is the Arrowhead County courthouse." He glanced at the buildings on either side of it—the Traveler's Hotel and a watering hole called the Devil's Maw Saloon—and climbed the six wooden steps up to the porch. The county seal was stenciled in gold letters on the glass, and when her uncle cupped his hands around his eyes and looked in, the door opened. Her uncle startled back.

"Can I help you?"

"I'm looking for the county magistrate."

"You've found him." He extended his hand. "Curtis Mayfair. You caught me on my way home."

"Mats Braaten," her uncle said. "I was afraid I'd not catch you at all given the lateness of the hour."

Curtis checked his pocket watch. "Time does move, no? I see I didn't even beat the *Nocturne*."

"We just arrived on her."

Mayfair made an expansive gesture of looking around Mats's broad chest. When he locked eyes with Silje, he pretended surprise. "I don't mean to alarm you, Mr. Braaten, but it appears there's an urchin behind you. This town's rotten with them."

"Sir?" Mats said.

He put his hand on her uncle's tense shoulder and said, "I jest, friend." Then he turned to open the door of the courthouse again. "Let's step inside and you can tell me why you're here."

"I won't keep you from your family, Mr. Mayfair. Only wished to make an appointment at your convenience."

Silje listened to the men exchanging formalities, but her attention was mostly on two boys sitting on the steps outside the building kitty-corner. They leaned back on their elbows, flipping stones onto the wooden boardwalk. One had a bandage wrapped around his head and covering one eye, the other a ruffian's jacket worn through at the elbows and a necktie bound at his throat in a fist-sized knot.

"Silje?" her uncle said. "We're going to step inside with Mr. Mayfair."

She took one last glance across the intersection and then turned with the two grown men and went inside.

"Have a seat," Mr. Mayfair said, motioning to a bench facing the window overlooking the harbor. "And tell me what brings you down the shore?"

For the second time that day, Silje felt her powers of prophecy abounding. The first was on the ferry, where even her closed eyes couldn't hide the ship's fate. Here in the courthouse, instead of closing her eyes, she opened them wide and looked around. The unswept floor and windows gauzy with dust gave the sitting room a dull air, but somewhere beneath the haziness, Silje sensed a magnificent pull. As a tide or a loss of breath. For a moment, it seemed unkind, but just as quickly gave her pleasure. One that tugged at her tummy the way jumping from the dock into the cold lake did on hot midsummer days.

Her uncle was in midsentence. ". . . and so now I'm wondering just what in God's name I do?"

"I can help you on the matter of filing their death certificates, but allow me to ask again: You're certain they've passed? Your sister and her husband? What's to say they won't wander out of the woods with a travois full of fresh venison?"

"My sister wouldn't go out back of the cabin, never mind into the woods. And besides, Bente would sooner leave Silje alone up the shore than her medicines unattended."

"Bente, that's your sister."

Mats nodded.

"What medicines?"

"She's nervous. I can't recall the names of her potions, but she takes them morning and night."

Curtis Mayfair stood up and removed from his pocket a nickel, which he pinched between his thumb and forefinger. "Over at the apothecary there"—he pointed out the window and across the street—"Rebekah will help you choose some candy. Why don't you go see what she's got while your uncle and I finish talking?"

Silje took the offered coin.

"I'll come find you when we're done," Mats said.

She put the coin in her pocket. Before she left, she said, "Mother's medicine was called laudanum" and bounded out the door.

Knowing her uncle would be watching, she made a show of heading across the street. Midway, she glanced over her shoulder and saw only the back of his head through the smudged window, so she turned around and skipped to the back of the courthouse and into the alleyway, hiding under the window to eavesdrop on the rest of their conversation.

Again, she joined them midsentence, but this time the magistrate was speaking. ". . . the sisters at St. Michael the Archangel run an orphanage, if that's what you mean."

An orphanage?

"I don't know," her uncle said, his voice slow and unclear. Like it had been infected by the atmosphere of the room in which he sat.

"You could adopt her yourself. The state would surely look upon that kindlier if you had a wife, but I've arranged other such accommodations. In fact, our man who runs the apothecary just yonder adopted one of our orphans not more than twelve or thirteen years ago. He's got no wife, though he does have a daughter. A grown one."

A pile of dirty snow still clung to the shade of the porch. Silje packed three snowballs from it, each a little bigger than the next, and built a miniature snowman. This would be her uncle.

"Oh, there are lots of places to find a wife," Mr. Mayfair said.

This, of course, roused Silje, and she almost announced herself so she might declare the lighthouse keeper's wife as a good and likely candidate, never mind the fact of her being already married. But instead she made another snowman, this one half the size of the first.

"It's also true a wife brings virtue and order to a man's life. A good wife does, in any case." The magistrate spoke now more like a preacher than a man of the court, but still Silje approved of his tone. "Of course, you can sleep on it, Mr. Braaten. Whatever you decide, we can draw it up here and put the whole ship in motion in less than an hour."

Silje, hearing their conversation winding down, tapped each of her snowmen on the head, then bounded around the building again, heading for the apothecary.

She found the two boys inside when she got there. The one with the bandage sat at a stool before the counter while a woman with a stern but beautiful mien slowly removed it. Silje couldn't help but stare at the two of them. Such tenderness she'd never seen.

Silje made a slow parade around the store shelves, pretending to consider all manner of goods but actually studying the boy and that woman. She stood now between Silje and him, the cut of her dress like something from a newspaper advertisement. No coarse gingham there, rather something akin to silk. She stood upright, the woman did, as though she had a spine made of a shovel handle. The ringlets of her downy hair fell like still more silk. When she stepped to the side, the boy stood facing Silje.

A quarter of his face seemed to be missing. Where his eye should have been, only a sack of soft-looking flesh hung. Like a fish's belly.

He closed his good eye and smiled, and when he opened it again he said, "Hi, you."

Silje ducked as though they were playing hide-and-seek, but

then stood as quickly, feeling the fool. She walked over to him, the woman turning to greet her. "I'm Rebekah. I don't know you," she said, her voice matching her countenance exactly.

Silje did not respond, only looked at the boy, who said, "I just winked at you, but you couldn't tell, could you?"

From the stool beside him, the other boy spoke. "Odd's a goblin, ain't he?"

"Did you have an accident?" Silje asked, ignoring both of the others and taking another step closer to the boy with one eye.

"An accident?" the boy with the jacket and tie guffawed. "More like he picked a fight with the wrong bear." He took a bite from a piece of jerky.

"You hush, Danny," the woman said, straightening the knot of his tie and then laying a gentle hand on his cheek. "And you," she continued, talking now to Silje, "look like you could use a sip of water. Or anyway *something* to cool you. What's your name?"

Still Silje kept her gaze on the one-eyed boy. "Did a bear really do this? We have them around the cabin all the time. Wolves and bears both. One wolf is like to curl up on our hearth, he comes around so much."

"Where's your cabin?" he asked.

"And I repeat, what's your name?" the woman rejoined.

Finally, Silje turned and offered her hand in the manner her uncle had to the magistrate some fifteen minutes before. "I'm Silje Lindvik. My parents drowned and now my uncle is putting me up for adoption, or becoming my new papa himself. I'm not sure. We came on the *Nocturne* from Otter Bay. She'll sink, the ferry will. Three times if I heard rightly."

"Heard from who?" the be-tied boy asked, his tone scoffing.

"You wouldn't understand."

"It's funny," the one-eyed boy said. "I often have dreams about the *Nocturne*. She's always running aground in them."

To this, the woman said, "But you also dream about waltzing with the same bear that did this." She dipped her finger in a small canister of ointment and applied it to the crease where the boy's eye should have been.

"I'm getting a glass eye when this heals."

"A glass eye?" Silje said.

Just then a man walked into the apothecary. Silje had seen him collecting the mail sacks on the dock while she stood in the shadow of the courthouse making snowmen. He seemed bigger out there.

"Who's this?" he fairly bellowed.

"This is Silje Lindvik, our new friend. Silje, this is Hosea."

He set the mail sacks beside her on the counter and stood with his thumbs hooked in his suspenders.

If the woman's face betrayed solemnity and reserve, this man's ruddiness and practiced smile gave the impression of a harlequin just demasked. She distrusted him instantly. The way he ogled her. The way he leaned toward her. The sourness of his breath, which reeked of pickled herring.

"Silje has recently lost her parents, if what she says is true." This was Rebekah again.

"Why would she lie about that?" Odd asked.

"I'm not lying." Silje slithered out from between the counter and Hosea. She felt in her pocket for the nickel Mr. Mayfair had given her and stepped down to the end of the counter with confections piled upon it. She chose a chocolate bar and came back to Rebekah and offered her the coin.

Rebekah had already started to wrap Odd's eye again, paying strict attention. "Just put the coin on the counter. And tell me, where is your uncle now?"

"Do we know her uncle?" Hosea asked. His voice possessed a lascivious register, one that warned Silje even as she couldn't quite shake his grasp.

"My uncle is meeting Mr. Mayfair, and I doubt you know him. His name's Mats Braaten."

"You're Mr. Braaten's niece? Mr. Braaten the sawyer? From up at the Burnt Wood Timber Camp?"

"Two winters he's been up there," Silje said, still doubtful of the man.

"I know him, indeed! He's a springtime customer. In fact, he wasn't much more than a week ago here, headed back down to *you*." A wide smile filled his clownish face. "But you say his sister and her husband have drowned? Your *mother* and *father* have?"

Silje, tired already of the story of her loss, merely nodded.

Odd, his head now wrapped, stood. "Shall Danny and I walk you back to the courthouse?"

"Count me out," Danny said. "My mother told me I had to be home for supper." He ran for the exit like the building had gone up in flames, and he was gone from view before the screen door slammed shut.

"You can walk this young lady back to the courthouse, but hurry back for supper yourself." Hosea spoke from behind the counter, where he'd gone to commence sorting the mail.

Rebekah seemed perturbed that Odd had offered the girl an escort. Her expression, which had changed as easily as the spring sky, now bore a certain crossness.

"Thank you for your hospitality," Silje tried, playing bashful, hoping to regain Rebekah's kindness.

"You know, Silje Lindvik, our boy Odd is an orphan, too. You have that in common. But about Curtis Mayfair, know that he's only an authority on these matters where the state is concerned," she said.

"What other authority is there?" Silje asked.

"There's no end to men with power." The thought seemed to sober Rebekah. Or soften her. And she walked Silje to the door where she as much as whispered in her ear, "Be mindful of that. As you and your uncle sort things out, yes, but also as you grow up. Every single boy and man you meet will want *something*." She turned and called for Odd to take Silje across the street.

* * *

Silje tore the paper wrapper from her chocolate bar. They stood on the corner and waited for a wagon pulled by a single horse to cross, then continued on, quiet, in lockstep, Silje feeling quite peculiar.

Before they reached the Traveler's Hotel, she turned to look back and see if Rebekah still watched them. At first she was gone, but as soon as Silje felt relief, Rebekah's visage appeared in the second-story window. Her eyes from up there could have bowled her over. Indeed, they might have, had Silje not turned back to Odd.

"When were you orphaned?" she asked.

"I never knew my mother. There's only a single photograph of her and me. Hosea took it when I was just a few days old. She got an infection after a surgery. Died a couple days later."

Silje fell silent again for a few paces. "Rebekah . . ." her voice trailed.

"She's like my sister and mother both. And other things besides, a good friend included."

When they got to the steps of the courthouse, he asked, "What was that about the *Nocturne* sinking? Are you a witch or something?"

Silje looked inside. Her uncle stood with his hat in his hands. Mr. Mayfair held a pipe in his own hand and twice brought it to his lips for a puff. Silje took another bite of the chocolate bar. She offered the second half to Odd, who took it greedily.

"Why is it that whenever a girl knows things, people think she's spooky?"

Odd looked at the last bite of chocolate. He let the hand holding it fall to his side. "I've just heard of witches before. I don't even know where, and I don't know what I meant by asking."

Silje climbed the first step and turned so she was eye to eye with him. "And I don't know how I know things, but I do. As soon as I had words to put to thoughts, it started happening."

"Did you know she's already been aground twice? The *Nocturne* has. Ice and another boat, the culprits. Every time I look at it, I think it's cursed."

"I didn't know that." She closed her eyes for a moment. Closed them tight. Whether trying to conjure those groundings or some auguring about this boy she hardly even knew. Whatever the case, she discovered nothing. This might have upset her, but when she opened her eyes she found him smiling instead of mulling over any haunting thoughts.

"Someday I'll build my own boat, then I'll never have to step foot aboard it again."

"You'll make a fine boat, I expect."

"I hope your uncle makes a good decision. My great-uncle could have adopted me back when Hosea did, but he was touched. It all worked out for the best. I expect it will for you, too."

She looked into the courthouse sitting room. Her uncle made one of his elvish faces at her, and she felt righted again. Her psychic balance restored. "I expect so, too."

Odd smiled. He nodded and walked slowly back to the apothecary. Silje didn't take her eyes from him until the door closed behind him. The thrill of not knowing brought other warmth. So much that when her uncle finally came out and put his hand on her nape, he immediately removed it and felt her forehead and asked her if she felt feverish.

She did not. She felt, rather, as if she'd run her own keel aground. But safely. On a sandy bar. The *Nocturne* sent up one long whistle, followed by three short, and the smoke from her stack rose at the same time. Slowly the boat drifted from the quay. Ungainly, it seemed.

Her right forefinger found the palm of her left hand and she tapped her meter. *This ship will sink, once more methinks, but I'm a bird above the brink.* The song complete, she took her uncle's hand and they headed for the Traveler's Hotel.

STELLAR ABERRATION

APRIL 26, 1910

I am the night and the dark it brings.

I am the child and her howling mind; the keeper and his insomnia; his attendants and their toil; their wives and their everlasting patience.

I am the laughter and tears; the sighs and the whines.

I am the hound and the comet's tail.

I have come from the farthest reaches of the known sky.

I am also the laws of the physical universe and the human ignorance that misunderstands it.

I am all misunderstanding.

I am the stars and the force that moves them.

I am the light—the light!—and the reason it's warped.

I am not God.

I can hardly imagine believing in such a force.

LESS THAN A WEEK, and already Willa felt herself to be a distant, celestial object viewed crossly by her husband's untrained eye. A stellar aberration on this mound of earthly granite. Certainly she knew less of him now than she had a week before. He was as mercurial as the weather, which on this day brought ill-timed snow. For a half hour at dawn, she watched the lighthouse vessel steaming from the west, likely bound for their dock. It trudged like the Pleiades across a night sky, seven deck lights coming in and out of the fitful snowfall.

Already Theodulf had extinguished the lamp, a morning ritual she'd somehow become to feel a part of—as if the imminence of his presence snuffed the light in her, too. Sometimes he returned with nary a word. Others with a simmering rage. This morning, with the other keepers arriving, likely on the approaching vessel, she didn't know what to expect. The fact she'd not even finished making the coffee did not improve the likelihood of his arriving with good humor. Another woman might have hurried to the kitchen, but Willa only watched the boat.

She heard the door open downstairs. Heard him enter. Then stop. Presumably at the banjo clock, which he wound each morning upon entering. Then she heard the resumption of his passing through the house and into the kitchen. She waited. But not long. Soon after he filled the pot and set it angrily on the fire, he came bounding up the staircase. This, too, had become a regular part of their routine. His castigation. Her silent rebuttal. Then Theodulf would go down and make his own coffee and oats while she loitered in her bedroom.

This morning was different, though. He opened the door to her still mostly empty chamber and stared at her from the threshold. He didn't speak. His breathing did not betray him, nor did the scolding stare. For a full minute they merely glared at each other before finally he said, "It's a husband's solemn duty to covet his wife. To honor her and to protect her and to see her on a path to righteousness." He shifted his weight from one foot to the other and wiped the exhaustion from his eyes. "But, Willa, in order for me to honor our union, I need you to participate in it."

"You don't understand the first thing about your duty to me, much less to our marriage, which is as dark and misshapen as your very *soul*."

His eyes widened and his nostrils flared. Through clenched teeth, he said, "I made vows before God. I have upheld them—"

"Why don't you take me into your bedroom and fuck me like you're supposed to?"

"Your vile tongue!" he boomed. "Let me never hear that word uttered in this house again!"

Willa pushed her sleeves up. First her left, then her right. She took a combative stance. "You come in out of the night with your practiced words! A speech you've been rehearsing all night!" She swooped to the window, pushed the curtains aside. "I'd rather hear Father Richter proselytize. For that matter, I'd rather hear the Lindvik girl!"

Now he joined his hands before him and brought them to his lips. "I do not believe a man should strike his wife—"

"And yet you've struck me! Your convictions are as your nature: weak weak weak."

He now appeared stunned. As though she had landed a mighty blow. Still he persisted. "But if you leave me no choice, if you persist in your vulgarities and intractability, if you continue to treat your role in this house as child might, then you'll leave me no choice but to ensure your obedience, however I might." He risked a look back at her.

Her response? She *laughed*. As though his threat had been a great joke. Once she gathered herself, she sat on the windowsill and wiped tears from her eyes. "Not only would I rather hear the fisherman's daughter preach, I'd more fear her wrath." She shook her head as though she'd just scolded him and hated to do so. "I likewise guess that the only reason you've not yet cuffed me again is you fear a similar reprisal as the last time."

She stood. "You should go meet whatever vessel is about to land at our dock."

He flinched. "What vessel?"

"All morning, it's come from the west."

He hurried himself to the window now, as if they hadn't been about to injure each other, and pulled the curtain aside as she so recently had. "Today is the twenty-sixth." It was not a question, though it sounded like one. "Oh my." He looked again out the window. "That's the lighthouse vessel. That's Misters Wilson and Axelsson. Surely it is." Now he glanced down at his uniform, still creased despite his night on watch.

"You're inept at everything you do, aren't you? Is it because your mind is constantly tangled with itself?" she whispered.

"What?"

"Do you know what a stellar aberration is?"

He looked about the room as though it were burning. "You must put on a dress! Presently! You must meet them *with* me."

She only shook her head.

"*Presently,*" he begged, and was gone again.

Willa went to the window and watched him lope across the yard. She saw him disappear down the path to the dock.

She'd certainly not wear a *dress*. Instead, she removed from her closet a short-sleeved blouse and the pair of bloomers she figured were most likely to offend. She took her time changing. After lacing her brogues, she fetched last her parasol. She would walk slowly. Ladylike, if not ladylike at all.

Willa discerned from a glance that the two women disembarking from the lighthouse vessel—one twice the age of the other—were matronly and stern. They indeed wore dresses. The younger of them a woolen thing with a mock neck and gathered sleeves and not a single flourish; the other a petticoat beneath her hoop skirts and already an apron cinched beneath her ample bosom, as though even to travel were to serve. Both had shawls likely crocheted by their own hands draped over their shoulders, and by the time they took their bearings—sweeping views of the Lindvik place, the hill-side, the lighthouse atop the cliff—their eyes settled on Willa with dismay if not outright contempt.

Theodulf stood mid-dock, his hands clenched behind his back like a soldier at ease, a posture of both passiveness and aloofness, one that sought approval even as it aspired to mastery. It was, Willa realized as she approached him, the only sort of demeanor he was capable of, a man of near-constant agitation, one never *actually* at ease, one always being rent.

Willa reached him the same moment the wives did. He ignored her, giving all his attention to the new arrivals instead. "Mrs. Wilson," he gave a slight bow to the elder, but kept his hands knotted behind his back. "Mrs. Axelsson, welcome." Now he did remove a hand, not to salute the approaching Misters Wilson and Axelsson, but to check his watch.

Willa, finding his uncouth manner intolerable, stepped forward, donned her brightest smile, and said, "I'm Willa Brandt, pleased to make your—"

"Sauer," Theodulf said.

The two wives looked affrighted.

Willa, her smile persevering, said, "Excuse me?"

Through clenched teeth, he said, "Willa *Sauer.* Née Brandt."

Willa put her fingers to her lips and snickered. To the women she said, "I guess it's taking me some time to get accustomed to my . . . new . . . state. My condition. I mean, that I'm a married woman."

For the first time, Mrs. Wilson spoke. "Whoever heard of such a thing?"

Willa already saw the sport in this. "Oh, please don't misunderstand, I love my sweet Teddy, and couldn't be happier." She pretended an adoring look at him as the other lightkeepers joined the coterie there on the dock, noted his still rising choler, and concluded, "But it's a strange place, this rock. I find myself not unlike the ship's compass."

Mrs. Wilson looked at Theodulf, as if he might decode his wife's riddling.

"Which is sent dithering here, given the iron ore deposits in the earth. It's all around us," Willa explained.

"Well!" It was Mrs. Wilson who spoke now, she in the apron. She with the impossibly long braid—like a rope—hanging down her back. "I'm not certain I understand what you mean, Mrs. Sauer."

"Please, call me Willa."

The looks of despair on the faces all around! She may as well have profaned again, for the impropriety she'd apparently uttered.

"Until the terms of our friendship are consummated, I'll do no such thing," Mrs. Wilson scolded. Now she gave Theodulf an admonishing glare. That his wife should be so irreverent and unpolished was unpardonable. "Surely we'll learn our roles here at the station, and posthaste. Mr. Sauer, you know our husbands."

"Indeed. Gentlemen," Theodulf said, doing his best to gather his composure and his standing as Master Keeper. Hands were shaken all around. "Welcome to your post." He nodded at Willa. "You've already heard from my wife, Mrs. Sauer."

"You're newlyweds, yes?" This was Mr. Axelsson, a bearish man with a full, dark beard and small eyes. His uniform ill fit him, and his voice betrayed a certain jocularity. Indeed, he might have appeared merely oafish, but there was also something crooked about the way he glanced at Willa from beneath his unruly brow, which grew in a single great line across his forehead.

"We are," Theodulf answered. Had he expected Willa to answer him? Willa who, upon receiving that glance, took a step back?

Mrs. Wilson spoke next. "There will be time enough for pleasantries once we unload this boat."

Willa couldn't help but wonder if Mrs. Wilson had intervened in the conversation so as to spare Willa Mr. Axelsson's underhanded lewdness. She even gave the other woman a silent acknowledgment, which of course went unresponded to. An air of apprehension befell the group, and for a moment they all six stood silently.

The captain of the lighthouse vessel interrupted their silence as he walked toward them. "Are we celebrating the posting of these keepers, or making prayers here on the dock?"

Now here, Willa thought, *was a man with gumption.* He outranked them all, a fact that alone would have bestowed on him the confidence of his action. But he also possessed charm, plainly, and this Willa welcomed.

"Hello," she said, perhaps too eagerly, for Theodulf stepped forward, giving her still another silent reprimand.

"Captain Voigt," Theodulf said. "Welcome. We've just made introductions." Now he turned and summoned Willa with a quick wave of his hand. "This is my wife, Mrs. Sauer."

"Charmed," the captain said, but he was quick to move the party along. "I'll bring the boat over to the eastern edge of the cliff. At least we've got a fine morning for unloading. You three sirs should get to the top of the cliff and ready the hoist and derrick. We've got a long day ahead of us." Now he gave his attention to the women. "Mrs. Sauer, I expect you'll amuse these fine ladies while we unload your furnishings."

Without waiting for a reply, he turned back for the boat, and the keepers and their wives moved like a group of reprimanded schoolchildren. Slowly. Heads bowed. With a solemn purpose.

Willa watched them for a moment. She could not say why, but the sight of them kindled the memory of her Radcliffe classmates leaving Bertram Hall on exam day, facing questions they could not master. Willa herself never left Bertram with that look about her, and as she followed the Axelssons and Wilsons and Theodulf himself, she had another familiar feeling: brashness. She'd never left Bertram Hall with anything but full confidence.

* * *

Once inside, sitting in the kitchen, the kettle boiled empty and nearly scorched after a half hour over the flame, dirty dishes piled in the sink, the last cheese rind a coiled centerpiece on the table, Willa suspected that whatever hope she had of befriending the other keepers' wives vanished the moment they witnessed her slovenliness. Still, she tried to be gracious, emulating the memory of her mother from those long-ago nights she and her father hosted friends or colleagues.

Willa brewed tea for her new neighbors; she offered them the only food from the pantry that seemed appropriate—the last of the pilot bread and a bowl full of dried apples and peaches—and advised them they could use the water closet after their journey from Duluth. And if their comportment changed—as if proximity to a kitchen, even one as messy and unkempt as Willa's, softened them—they remained aloof.

"How long have your husbands been in the Lighthouse Service?" she asked, and their answers could not have been more concise or simultaneous: "Twenty-two years," said Mrs. Wilson, "Three years," Mrs. Axelsson said. When Willa inquired of children, Mrs. Wilson said, "Both my daughters and both my sons are married," and Mrs. Axelsson said, "We hope to have children soon." Willa also asked them where they were from, to which both replied, Detroit, Michigan.

Then passed another awkward silence, one spent nibbling the pilot bread and pretending grave contemplation.

Mrs. Wilson finally broke their stalemate. "You've been married for how long, then?"

Willa, unaccustomed to fielding questions about her marriage, looked to Mrs. Axelsson. When, after a moment, the younger woman did not answer, Willa let out a yelp, and then covered her blushing cheeks. "I'm not used to being a wife," she said. "Perhaps that's obvious. But let's see, Theodulf and I married March the sixth. So, not quite two months."

"Thirty years for me," Mrs. Wilson announced.

"And just three for me and John." Mrs. Axelsson caught and

corrected herself. "Mr. Axelsson, I mean." She looked away, as if she'd committed a terrific gaffe.

Mrs. Wilson harrumphed, then drummed her fingers on the tabletop. "Brandt, you said before? Your maiden name?"

Willa nodded.

"A bohunk, then?"

"My father, yes."

"Bohunks are, what, mostly Catholic?"

"My father was raised Protestant but didn't practice any religion by the time I was born."

Mrs. Wilson nodded knowingly. "So, you converted to Catholicism before your nuptials?"

"I beg your pardon?"

Now the dowager spread her hands across the table and leaned toward Willa. "This is what I meant about consummating our friendship." She appeared exhausted by the prospect but persisted. "I reckon Mr. Sauer will want a passel of kids. Catholic men usually do. Same with Catholic women, for that matter."

Mrs. Axelsson leaned in and whispered, "He seems unsuited for you, from the vantage of age. He's old to enough to be your father."

So obvious was the younger woman's faux pas that Mrs. Wilson stepped in immediately. "You were married in the Church, then?"

Willa took a moment to collect herself. "Sacred Heart. Theodulf and the Sauer family are fast friends with Father Richter—"

"Bishop Richter, you mean?"

Willa nodded. "He presided."

Mrs. Wilson was gaining confidence. She pressed on. "Your father left the church . . . why?"

"He was a scientist. A meteorologist."

"A man can't be a meteorologist and a man of God at the same time?"

"In my experience, the two vocations aren't especially compatible."

"You're a scientist, too, then?" Mrs. Wilson asked this condescendingly, even solicited Mrs. Axelsson to join in her mocking chuckle.

"In fact, I am. I studied astronomy at Radcliffe College."

"And that makes you Leonardo da Vinci?" At this, Mrs. Wilson apparently had had enough. She reached into her reticule and removed from it a small copper flask, which she uncapped and drank from, lifting the hem of her apron to wipe her lips after.

Willa wouldn't have been more surprised if she'd pulled a pet monkey from that purse, and her expression must have betrayed this. Mrs. Axelsson was less surprised—perhaps she'd seen it before?—but still sat up straighter.

"Here's the truth, Mrs. Sauer: We've only the three of us to entertain each other. This sip of brandy? It makes me a more tolerable person. For that matter, it makes the two of *you* more tolerable."

"Theodulf will not allow it," Willa whispered.

At this, Mrs. Wilson chortled. "He might have a say about what happens in *his* house, at this table. But after that?" She took another sip but did not offer it around. "Why, after that, Theodulf has about as much providence over me as I do over him." She put the flask back in the bottom of her reticule.

Mrs. Axelsson appeared delighted, which in turn brought some joy to Willa, who couldn't help but smile.

Well satisfied, Mrs. Wilson said, "You seem a sweet girl, Willa Sauer. We'll get along just fine, provided you resist that holier-than-thou attitude about your days at Radcliffe College."

Willa blushed.

"There's no need of embarrassment. It's simply true we're all three equal here. That's important. Agreed?"

Willa nodded. So did Mrs. Axelsson.

"Good. Now, tell me, how's your marriage bed?"

If, on the dock, Willa believed the other wives would be her adversaries, and if she brought that belief into her own kitchen and sat through the first frosty moments of their togetherness, and if

the first hour of knowing them left Willa with a wider chasm between herself and happiness, then the next hour proved a bridge
spanning it.

The three women continued at Willa's kitchen table, their teacups full and steaming with a second brew, discussing all manner of
intimacies. On the subject of her new marriage, Willa discovered
herself baffled to be considering it seriously for the first time, much
less articulating her feelings aloud. She stopped short of avowing
her husband's duplicity, but did admit, without much prompting,
that he had so far demonstrated no desire for her. That he had, in
fact, not so much as touched her hand except to help her onto and
out of the lighthouse tender—she omitted the story of their striking
each other—never mind even once kissing her goodnight.

To this, Mrs. Axelsson said, "If only my John would kiss me less"
but then brought her fingers to her lips and pretended to button
them shut.

This provoked Mrs. Wilson to fetch her flask a second time.
She took a long drink from the tea, uncapped her flask, and used it
to top up the cup before settling in for a long explanation about a
woman's responsibility to her husband.

"Given your recent conversion—to wedlock, that is—and your
apparent befuddlement as to the duties therein, I hope you'll let me
share some of my own hard-won wisdom on the subject." She took
another long drink from her cup. "Ainsley—that's Mr. Wilson"—she
winked at Willa—"he's a gentle man. Always has been. Unlike most
louts I've heard of, he even considers my *pleasures.* I suspect part
of the reason that's true is because I've always been a giving wife."
She glanced at each of them, raising her eyebrows in turn. "And I'm
not *just* talking about scrumping." She paused again, finished her
tea, and let out a small burp.

"A wife need be many things. Friend. Mother. Companion. Suppliant. Yes, of course, all these. But also: Housekeeper—nurse—
seamstress—laundress—*chef de cuisine,* as they say in old France."
She contemplated the ceiling, as though writ up there was the
list from which she read. The next qualities she ticked off on her

fingers. "Don't forget: Extoller of her husband's virtues. Purveyor of his moods. Defender of his righteousness. Guardian of his dignity. Champion of his intelligence." Her speech accelerated, still she kept score on her fingers, now switching hands. "Admirer of his wit. Keeper of his stores. Partner in prayer. Attendant in faith!" Again she paused, on the ninth finger, taking a deep breath before smiling coyly. "And general sorceress." She looked in her teacup and appeared saddened that it was empty. But still she continued.

"What's more, she must do all of this without being *noticed*. Without offending him in any way, lest he be devastated by his own lack of prominence in their union."

Willa, on hearing things so plainly listed, determined not to be broken by the news of her duties, but rather inspired to *demolish* them. The prospect brought her hands together in a moment's applause. A gleeful smile puckered her face. It would be no easy thing, of course. She would not be able to rely on lessons learned at Radcliffe or from her own mother's counsel on the subject, but still she knew—even with some certainty—that she'd prevail. She simply could not—indeed, *would* not—suffer the indignity Mrs. Wilson had taken pains to articulate.

For the first time since Mrs. Wilson had begun her explanation, Willa looked at Mrs. Axelsson, expecting to find a partner in mischief and shared purpose. Instead, she found tears—bulbous, unmistakable—streaking down the fair girl's cheeks. Rather than console her, as her instincts advised, Willa looked to Mrs. Wilson.

"She cries," the elder said, "because she's lived for three years under the weight of the expectations I just took pains to describe. Even if she hasn't put her finger on it quite so simply, she's lived it. You can be sure she has."

"Never mind me," Mrs. Axelsson whispered, as though she hadn't heard a word of Mrs. Wilson's explanation. "I sometimes get this way. I guess with the move and all. And the cruise down the shore this morning—so early!—I've just lost my bearings." Now she removed from her sleeve a handkerchief to blot the tears.

Mrs. Wilson peered suggestively at Willa and nodded her head, as though Mrs. Axelsson's self-deprecation were inevitable. Were in fact proof of her whole project thus far.

As if to put an exclamation point on Mrs. Wilson's thesis, Mrs. Axelsson removed from her own reticule not a flask of liqueur but her needlepoint, which she promptly took up. She hummed, sweetly, and found a brave face

But it was a project Mrs. Wilson had not finished, and after she excused herself to use the loo—the brandy, she said, had cleared her pipes—she returned to her spot at the table and recommenced her discourse.

"We've covered the general principles of marriage," she began, very much in the tenor of a Radcliffe professor. "Let's now visit *womanhood*."

"Oh," Mrs. Axelsson said, her voice rising like she'd just pricked her finger. "I wonder if we might *not*." She set her needlepoint on the table and stood, casting her eyes about the kitchen. "We should bring the men a pitcher of water."

"We'll bring them no such thing," Mrs. Wilson said.

Mrs. Axelsson stopped her searching and looked once at Mrs. Wilson then once at Willa and sat down again, taking up her needlepoint as she crashed into the chair.

Willa couldn't help but pity the poor girl. It was becoming clearer with each passing moment that what gripped her was as much fear as bewilderment. If the last half hour had taught Willa anything, it was to marvel at her having arrived in a situation almost exactly like Mrs. Axelsson's. The only difference between them, really, was Willa's resolve. Which, she realized as soon as she thought it, had hardly been tested yet. Or at least not tested with the advantage of the new perspective Mrs. Wilson had bestowed upon her. And despite her pity for Mrs. Axelsson, Willa was eager for more tutelage.

"Of all the things that are true in our lives," Mrs. Wilson continued, "the lives of women, of wives, I mean, none is more so than that we must buttress each other. Even if it needs to be sly, we must help each other and be kind to each other."

This, too, met Willa's ignorance. How could a notion so simple have evaded her until this moment? "I've never thought of that," she said. "I never once considered another girl my ally. Not even my mother. Especially not my mother."

Mrs. Wilson smiled broadly. "We'll cover our mothers another day, Mrs. Sauer."

"Please don't call me that," Willa insisted. "I simply can't bear it. Call me by my given name."

Again Mrs. Wilson smiled. "Very well, young Willa.

"As I say, we'll talk about mothers another time, but on the subject of *ourselves*, let me say at least a few things."

When Mrs. Axelsson did not protest, Mrs. Wilson settled back into her chair, crossing one leg over the other and adjusting her skirts. "Let's start with our dress. Our husbands have strict ideas about how we look best. *Wear this, not that,* they say. *You look dowdy, or like a common strumpet,* they say. *Your corset is bound too tight, or not tight enough,* they say. And as for our bosom, the very life source of the children they demand! Well, on these"—she made a show of hoisting her own bosom—"they are regular old philosophers!"

All three of them tittered at that. But those humors were quickly lost, given over to pensiveness as the truths amassed.

"As though we have any control over our bodies, especially after we've had their children." Mrs. Wilson looked now at Mrs. Axelsson. "Do you even understand what happens to your body? How or when a child might be conceived?" Now she turned to Willa. "Do you?"

"My mother told me it was God's will decided when a child takes to a womb," Mrs. Axelsson replied. "She says the reason John and I haven't had a baby yet is because God has a plan."

"God might very well have a plan," Mrs. Wilson said, "but do you honestly believe it involves your progeny? In the whole scheme of life, of all the faithful folks on this planet, you think He took some time to line your husband up for this particular disappointment? With some broader implication as to His will? I guess I just don't believe that."

Mrs. Wilson sat up and reached over to hold Mrs. Axelsson's

hand. "Child," she continued, "tell me how you and Mr. Axelsson try? Tell me about your monthlies?"

"I couldn't possibly!"

Mrs. Wilson lifted her hand and turned now to Willa. "You see?" She sat back again. "Here I am, a wasted old hag full of wisdom, offering it freely—and this lass, just a babe, blind as Bartimaeus, being offered *sight*, and what does she do? Shrieks at the prospect of it." She sighed. "I don't blame you, child. I truly don't. You've been taught to embrace your ignorance just like you've been taught to serve your man. But that service gets harder the longer you suffer it. Mr. Axelsson might be patient and understanding about his lack of offspring now, but another year, or two, or three down the road and what happens? You'll meet his meaner side. Or you'll fall altogether out of his favor and end up where? Begging the Sisters of Mercy, who'll shun you for having failed your husband. Your ignorance might slay you then."

"It's not always as bad as that," Willa said doubtfully. Hopefully.

"Perhaps not. Perhaps Mr. Axelsson is an exceptional man. Decent and upstanding and more enlightened than just about every other one." Again Mrs. Wilson sighed, this time adding a determined shake of her head. "But I doubt it. He's with the Lighthouse Service, after all!"

They found each other's laughter again, let it linger for a moment longer than the last.

"I'll tell you a personal story. One day, about a month after Ainsley and I were married, he chanced upon me in the bath. I didn't know he was in the doorway. Didn't know he was watching me. Now, believe me when I say I would have delighted at his being there, the blush still being very much *on* the rose back then. Why, I might even have put on a show for him someways. But I didn't know he was there, and instead I only scrubbed myself. This included betwixt my legs, it being my moon time and all. When Ainsley saw me washing there, he nearly shrieked, and *I* nearly jumped out of the tub for how it startled me. My goodness, I can still feel the fright of it!

"The thing is, he understood my washing myself to be a perversion. He thought I was *masturbating*, if you can believe that, and when he saw the menses on my leg, he understood *that* to be my punishment. If I recall, he told me I'd be lucky not to suffer a plague of warts on my hand. Well, as I've told you both twice now, I'm a lucky woman. Mr. Wilson is not above learning, whether from me or his superiors or from Father Jerome, doesn't matter, and I took the opportunity to explain to him where the blood came from, and how it only meant we hadn't succeeded in making a child our first month of wedded bliss."

Poor Mrs. Axelsson. She might as well have been in the operating theater, watching a disemboweled patient for how uncomfortable this conversation made her. But there was also a part of her on high alert, taking it in, sorting it, filing away this alien wisdom. At least that's what Willa believed was happening.

"Point being," Mrs. Wilson continued, "men are as unwise on the subject of womanhood more broadly than they are about our bodies and how we make children. Even the doctors and surgeons, some of them. The only person to trust once you're pregnant is a midwife. My sister delivered my children, and if everything goes according to plan, she'll deliver *their* children someday, too."

"My goodness, Mrs. Wilson, you've painted quite a picture of our earthly fate!" Willa said.

"There's no such thing as fate. Not in my experience." This Mrs. Wilson said soberly, but with an air of finality.

"You've given me an awful lot to think about, Ruth," Mrs. Axelsson said. If her given name slipped, neither woman let on.

Willa felt challenged and aroused, even giddy, for the first time since she'd left Radcliffe. She stood and started to clear the dishes from the table, setting them in the sink and returning the tin of pilot bread to the pantry. When she rejoined them, she said, "I guess the only question left to answer is why we marry them in the first place." She meant it as a playful jest among friends, not necessarily as a question to answer.

But Mrs. Wilson answered spontaneously. "I won't speak for the two of you, but I married Ainsley because I loved him. I still do."

"I love my John, too," Mrs. Axelsson said, her voice quavering, again on the verge of tears.

"Sure you do," Mrs. Wilson said. "Sure you do."

Willa could not fathom a world in which she might love her husband, though she did let an image of Theodulf flit across her mind. There in the doorway just this morning, his anger as plain on his face as his pallid complexion. If such a thing were possible, she disliked him more for the memory. Not for the first time, she contemplated a lifetime in his servitude.

"Of course," Mrs. Wilson said, "not all women marry for love, or ever grow to love their husbands." She spoke for Willa's benefit, divining what must have been unmistakably written on her face.

"The arranged marriage, or marriage of some other convenience, is not always without benefit. In fact, most of the people I know who married *conveniently* are happier than us lucky saps."

"What is there to be happy for in such an arrangement?" Mrs. Axelsson asked.

"For one, those marriages aren't always embroiled in emotions. Indeed, they rarely are. Especially jealousy, which is the ruin of most of us. And then of course there're financial concerns, and social ones, too."

If Willa had so far aligned with all of Mrs. Wilson's thinking, this last found her breaking from it. In the experience of her brief and unhappy marriage, she could not yet see any financial benefit. On the contrary: her purse, she had just learned, was not her own. And jealousy? Theodulf was jealous of the comet, for all the sense that made. And society? Willa turned and glanced once at each of the women, accounting for all the society she'd know. Then she remembered Silje and Mats, which made four whole souls. Unless that girl had two, which would then make five.

Again Mrs. Wilson spoke as though she had a portal to Willa's every thought. "Of course, some marriages—many, in fact—are simply doomed. Which doesn't mean those wed need also be doomed."

She stood now, Mrs. Wilson did, with some effort and again adjusting her skirts. As she retied her apron, she said, "Somewhere in your pantry, you must have that pitcher? So we can bring the men some water? I reckon by now they've worked up a thirst." This last she directed at Mrs. Axelsson, who had also stood but appeared ready to collapse again.

Willa fetched the pitcher from the shelf above the stove and handed it to Mrs. Wilson, who filled it from the faucet while Willa cleared the teacups from the table.

With the pitcher in hand, Mrs. Wilson asked Mrs. Axelsson to bring three glasses, then told Willa she should lead the way to the hoist and derrick. As soon as they were outside, Mrs. Wilson said, "Thank you, Willa, for your hospitality. I'll look forward to many more such conversations around the board."

Not to be outdone, Mrs. Axelsson said, "Yes, thank you."

Mrs. Wilson smiled back. "A last thought for the day, if you'll both allow it?" When the women leaned toward her, she continued. "Our little sorority will get us through plenty of hard and long days. Let's not forget that. And from here on, we call each other our given names. All that down at the dock? That was for your husband's benefit, Willa. Whatever else you feel about him, you'd do well to remember that sometimes giving him little things—especially things that mean and cost nothing—will be worth the price."

Finally the older woman arched her back and retrieved her handbag from the back of the chair. "You'd do well to keep this kitchen tidy, as well. If only to keep the mice at bay."

EVEN AS SILJE GOUGED THE WOLF'S EYES she saw the boy's face instead. Odd's. The fish's belly. The scar. The watery looseness of flesh. The absence of something more than a second eye, like all of his loss and privation were epitomized by what the bear had taken. By what the bear had left behind.

For two days she'd hardly stopped thinking about him. Not for the rest of her stay in Gunflint. Not while the *Nocturne* ferried them back to Otter Bay, and not while her uncle rowed them back home while it snowed at twilight. Not until she picked up Fenrir and her finest gouge and even then only for a moment. As she bore through Fenrir's wooden skull—narrow, narrow, narrow as a mole's burrowing place, almost through to his ear—she puzzled over their likeness to each other. Him and her.

Orphans both, that was the main thing. But something more, too. She didn't know why, but she kept thinking about the sound the gun made when she shot it over the water. That reverberation, for all it might have brought to mind, delivered her to a storm some years ago.

She would one day learn it was her mother's third miscarriage. *The three sisters,* she'd come to think of them. Like her father described the wickedest, most roguish seas.

This particular storm brought whole civilizations of sisters at once. She could remember her father down on the dock, battening what he could. He might as well have been a thousand miles away for all she could behold of him.

She'd left him there an hour earlier, as the winds advanced and darkness with them. Before he'd shooed her away, she'd stood on the dock beside him, watching a pair of freighters steaming by.

162

Eastbound, one a mile before the other. The feeling of community that usually accompanied their passing was nowhere in her, replaced instead with a premonition of the ships' doom. This hunch did not alarm her, only settled like some ancient grief she bore for others. And felt born to bear.

But *whose* grief?

"Back you go to Mamma," her father had ordered, his voice high above the wind. "Keep her warm and put the curtains up, eh? We'll get a fair spray off the tops of what waves is coming."

So, she'd put the sailcloth up, dragging the stepladder from porthole to porthole, tying it afore the shutters.

As for keeping her mother warm? Well, the sweat sopping her cheeks gave Silje to believe no work was needed in that department. Still, she stoked the fire in the stove. She put her doll, named Bunny, to bed early, lamenting the truth that it was not a real sister.

She wished her mother would herself go to bed, instead of trailing blood all over the place. Willa followed her around, mopping it up and then rinsing the rag in the wooden bucket she dragged beside her. It was a fine mess. A considerable one. The hem of Silje's own threadbare skirts were wet and cold now, furbelowed with blood and water both. The half-moons under her fingertips were stained the color of beets.

And her mamma, keening like the wind. Her unwelcome song keeping time with the sailcloth flapping against the shutters. Her father had been right about the water. The seas broke onshore, and the gale carried its spray a full six rods into the woods.

Her mother went to the barrel and set the dipper in. She brought it up and drank and set the dipper down. "Dear God," she said. "*For-bannelse*. Mine. *Mine*."

Whether in Norwegian or in English, those lamentations and damnations fell idly on Silje's ears. So young, and already hardened against her mother's suffering. Silje wedged the door open, was blown around the side of the cabin where she dumped the slurry of blood and water, and pressed herself back inside.

From the door, she could see her mother's face as ashen as the snow hoarding the night outside. Pappa was in the fish house, if the glow from the landward window was any indication. Doing what, Silje could not imagine. Certainly he was not following Mamma, who made another round of the puncheon floor, a trail of blood like from a gut-shot deer.

"*Forbannelse! Forbannelse! Gud ta meg!*" she crooned.

Silje went to check on her doll. She nestled her lips right up to Bunny's ear and whispered, "Don't worry, sister. I won't ever be like that. I promise."

As Silje tucked Bunny under the eiderdown, the cabin door whooshed open, her father blown in behind it, soaked to the bone and looking as if he'd just wrestled a bear. He pushed the door shut and lowered the extra latch, and before he was out of his coat he had one arm around Bente's waist and the other holding her hand.

"Aye, Bente, you've got to go to bed. You're as limp as an un-baited line."

"Fix me a cup of pennyroyal?" she said, her voice as raspy as her complexion was white.

Without answering, Arvid helped her to the rocker beside the stove. He eased her into the chair and hurried to the board, where he dippered the kettle full of water and set it on to heat. Then he wet a cloth and wrung it and folded it onto her forehead.

"You're cooking alive, Bente."

"But shivering, too. This one's like to kill me." Something seized her and she doubled over. When it passed, she hissed, "*Forbanellse . . . Gud ta meg . . .*"

Arvid fetched the afghan and laid it across her shoulders. He went to the jars lining the shelf and opened one and pinched some of the dried pennyroyal into the tea egg. When he replaced the jar, he saw on the same shelf a bottle of pills.

"Will this medicine help, Bente?" He held the bottle in her direction.

In answer, she only groaned again.

Silje, meanwhile, sat with her knees up, petting Bunny's tresses.

They were made of woolen yarn, and stubbled with cockleburs and slivers from all manner of boards. The doll's belly was stuffed with excelsior. She hummed, Silje did, a little tune in alexandrine time, based on some nursery rhyme or another. Her uncle Mats brought them at Christmastime or on her birthday in June, and she carried, if not the words, at least the meter.

In truth, she hummed for the same reason she'd hung the sail-cloth, but to keep her bitterness, and not the spindrift, at bay. She loathed her father's attention on anyone but herself, and even believed a part of her mother's antics were to garner it.

When the water was warm, Arvid made the tea and delivered it to his wife. He knelt before her, a hand on hers. "Bente, you're to be strong. You're to be strong so that Silje keeps her mamma and I keep my wife. Don't worry and fret about the baby gone." He wiped his still-wet hair off his forehead and took her hand again. "The baby's gone, I know. But we still need our missus to help us along. Who'll keep us in bread and butter? Who'll keep us in trousers and skirts?"

"Quiet," she said. "Quiet now." She took a sip of her tea. "Dip this cloth again. And bring me another one dry, and the other night-shirt. I think the bleeding's stopped."

He dashed to their corner of the cabin, where he found what she asked for and returned. He helped her to stand and remove the bloody garment. Except for the dark patches of hair beneath her arms and between her legs, her entire body was contracted and sallow. She swayed as though the cabin were a boat out on those waters.

"Let's to bed with you," Arvid said gently. He scooped her up like he sometimes still did Silje, her drenched hair in the crook of his elbow, her legs hanging there like two caught fish on a stringer.

Silje, still awake and watching all this, twisted Bunny's legs into a knot. She could feel the cabin quaking under hold of the wind, so relentless now the sailcloth no longer flapped. Kicking her legs out, she slithered under the eiderdown, her shield against whatever else the night might bring. She could see her mother's naked backside while her father laced her arms through the clean nightshirt. She watched as it fell like a curtain down her back. And she watched as he lowered her into bed.

Silje's last thought, as she turned away from her parents and gathered Bunny into her arms, was to wonder if the fish house would still be there in the morning. Or if the cabin would.

What she didn't see, but still somehow knew, was that as soon as her father put a fresh, cool cloth on her mother's head, and pulled their eiderdown up over her shivering body, he came over to rest his hand on Silje's head. As though the abortion might be contagious, and his daughter now infected. He stood beside her bunk for a long time, until he was sure she was sleeping, humming the same melody and in the same time that Silje so often did. She had no other prophecies that night.

This boy she knew now, she couldn't prophesy anything about him, either.

She flipped the carving of Fenrir in her hands and chiseled from the opposite side of his skull. A few minutes later, the two holes met, and she had a tunnel all the way through the wolf's head. She held him up to the window, closed one eye, and peered through the channel. She stood up and hurried out onto the dock and turned her face toward the sun and again held the wolf up like a telescope, switching it from eye to eye and studying the sun as though the only answer to be found might reside in its brilliance.

What she saw came not from the heavens but from the light she knew within her, suddenly as luminous as the sun above. She followed it. Into the fish house. Fenrir found his place among the other animals she'd carved. A bear. A fish. Moose antlers. A misshapen gull.

From the little box she kept under the counter, she rooted around for the right chunk of birchwood. She held it cupped in her hands as though it were a wounded bird and closed her eyes to see it right. He emerged as a young man, taciturn at twenty years old, but steady. Disciplined like her uncle, hungry like her uncle was not, and not nearly as broad of shoulder or as tall. He was lonely, but not alone, and not embittered. Handsome as the day is long, even with the glass eye and the scar that would hold it like a frame.

That's where she started, with the same gouge she'd used on Fenrir's head, but delicate this time. First a marking up from what would become his jawline, then into the hollow of what would become his upper cheek. She spent an hour on this alone, each curl of wood falling to the floor and leaving in its place something she desired.

EXHAUSTION PLAGUED HIM. Unable to sleep, his lower back aflame after the day's long labor moving three households off the derrick, across the grounds, and into their homes, he missed the overnight toil of operating the light. He missed, too, consorting with the disassembled watch. Two nights of trying to put it back together had left him frustrated, but also excited. Almost charmed by his own failure.

He sat up on an elbow both to stretch his back and to check for the holdall beneath the window. His back spasmed. The holdall was there.

Wilson sat watch tonight. The old gasbag. Theodulf knew him from a month at Devil's Island, where Wilson had come to substitute for one of the keepers who'd gone off injured—a broken neck, suffered in a fall down the rocky shore, almost drowned, Theodulf recalled. He didn't like Wilson then and already suspected he wouldn't like him now. All day Theodulf had felt his authority challenged. If Wilson were anywhere nearly as competent as he thought himself, he'd be commissioner of the whole Lighthouse Service, not second keeper here.

Worse even than his bluster on the subject of their occupation was his sermonizing about former president Roosevelt, whom Wilson revered and whose replacement, William Howard Taft, bore no likeness whatever. Not that Theodulf had strong opinions on matters of national politics, but to listen to a man regurgitate newspaper headlines and call himself civically involved—which was a point Wilson made more than a few times—well, it irritated Theodulf. It reminded him of conversations with his father. And Wilson's wife!

She seemed a shrewish hag. He'd need to find a way to keep the two of them in their place.

To make matters worse, only one of the two beds he'd requested had been delivered. He'd of course moved it into Willa's chambers with Axelsson's help, Wilson being too feeble to carry furniture up the staircases. Theodulf was left now, still on his cot. A situation that no doubt exacerbated the pain winging up his spine, which seemed now to be bleeding down into his legs. This new sensation spurred him out of the cot, and in his stockinged feet he padded in circles around his own dark room.

Now, Axelsson. There was a man who kept his own counsel. After the garrulous show he'd made on the dock, a show, Theodulf admitted reluctantly there in the dark, that did not originally draw him to his second keeper. In fact, it repelled him. But once the women were gone, he proved himself altogether changed. A man's man. And a veritable Hercules. Able to lift whole hogsheads off the derrick and set them aside as though they were loaves of bread. When they'd moved the furnishings—beds, yes, but also chests of drawers, armoires, gilded mirrors—Theodulf felt not as if he were helping on the other end of whatever item they hefted, but as if he himself were carried upon it. And while Theodulf labored for breath and poured sweat, Axelsson appeared to exert himself not at all. Appeared, even, to think of the labor as sport.

He smiled constantly, a quality that did not normally appeal to Theodulf, but in Axelsson he found charming. Even the vaguely lecherous way he presented himself to Willa? Why, Theodulf found a not unpleasant disturbance around the thought of it. One that alerted those fallow desires he tried so hard to keep buried.

As if to redouble his effort, Theodulf pressed his eyes with the pads of this thumbs. When this did not work, he bent at the waist and clenched his whole body in hopes of inflaming his back again. But this, too, failed. So, he paused at the window overlooking the lake, put his hands around his neck, and squeezed. He kept himself thus until he grew lightheaded, and then released his grip.

My cursed fate, he thought, regaining his equipoise. *And nothing to do but bear it.*

The reminder only wearied him more, and the new depth of exhaustion—which was now spiritual as well as physical—gave him to push the lace curtains aside. He set his arms upon the top window rail and gently rested his forehead against the cool pane. Every ten seconds—and he counted them each—the blaze from the lighthouse lamp would come back around, bearing right for him, nearly at eye level, before it disappeared, leaving, for the next sixth of a minute, the light of the stars instead. Oh, how he loathed that expanse! So much so that the intervals between the light's gleam began to feel like a taunt.

His fatigue, too, mocked him. Now that his body had come all ways alive, the prospect of sleep was only more remote. He reached over for his watch, which sat atop the chest of drawers, opened it, and held it toward the oncoming beam of light. Exactly midnight. If he'd been the cursing kind, surely he'd have let loose. Instead, he set his watch back down, returned to his cot, and enfolded himself in the woolen blanket, counting the flashes of light like a child counts sheep.

The numeration brought him close to sleep, so close he couldn't have known if he dreamt the music, or heard it rising from the sitting room below, though the tinlike tune suggested fantasy. Never was the song more aptly titled. Suspended there on the precipice of his night's slumber—at last!—he let the far-off sound carry him. Back to Paris. Back to the Île Saint-Louis. Back to Paul. Back to the moment of his enlightenment. And his truest happiness.

How he loved the opening movement. How it harmonized with his prevailing psyche. Melancholy. Languishing. Ardent. Devout.

Paul seemed to know all those things about him from the moment they first spoke at the zinc bar. He certainly understood the music, which he'd performed as though conducted by Beethoven himself. Confident without a whit of arrogance. Of all the things Theodulf admired about him, foremost was his own self-possession, which guided all. The way he performed. The way he introduced himself and made himself known. The way his intentions were never in doubt. The way he was ever mindful of Theodulf's own reticence. Paul might have been the only person alive—outside Theodulf's mother, of course—who looked at him with that depth of comprehension.

And not just comprehension, but humor and kindness and exhilaration, too. And, of course, desire.

Paul was happiness. That night was, too. An evening nonpareil, one that only lived here now. In the abscesses of his defective slumber.

Distant. Distant like the stars, and as cold.

For all the wisdom Curtis Mayfair imparted, none struck home like the last pair of sentences he'd uttered, spoken with a gentle hand on Mats's shoulder the morning after he and Silje had arrived in Gunflint. "One thing's sure, Mr. Braaten: that child over there"—he'd lifted his chin at Silje, now cavorting with one of the wild dogs on the dock—"will depend on you for just about everything. Don't let her down."

Now they were home. She asleep in his arms as he carried her from the fish house up to the cabin. The night above was brilliant even through the boughs of the white cedar straining toward the heavens. He'd never imagined this weight but carried it with ease. Up the trail. In his heart.

Inside the cabin he lowered her onto her bed and covered her with the eiderdown. The stove fire he'd started upon their arrival had only just begun to take the chill out of the air.

Silje curled onto her side and pulled the quilt to her chin. How she slept so easily, Mats could not understand. A man given to spontaneous and profound slumber, he'd had little of it since he'd found the empty boat. This night at least held promise, given his exhaustion.

From the pocket of his coat, he withdrew the three documents Mayfair had drawn up for him. Two death certificates and one amended birth certificate for Silje, showing him the adoptive parent. He deposited them in the tin box that held all their important papers, then replaced it on the shelf above his sister's bed. Well, his bed now.

From the other pocket, he withdrew the carving Silje'd been

working on as she dozed off. Only just begun, it appeared to be the beginning of a face. An eye, it seemed. He set it on the bedside table. He took off his coat and hung it on a peg. He sat down and removed his boots and slid them just under the bed, peeled off his socks one at a time and laid them flat on the puncheon floor. He could have lain back right then but thought it better to stoke the fire once more.

Then he did go back and lie down. Through the window he watched the lighthouse beam careen in its arc. He watched it disappear just before it reached them, then reappear out on the water.

He'd never been much for grand ideas, but he had one now. Or the fulfillment of it had anyway arrived. Something kindled by Mayfair's parting words, grown into an inferno. Unpracticed in the art of contemplation, he hardly knew how to articulate the commotion in his mind, but lord, did he take pleasure in it. Some combination of love and responsibility and *prospects*. For all the difficulty now upon him, his had never seemed brighter.

There again the lighthouse beam.

Brighter days, but harder, too. With no one to help fish or hunt or cut wood. And certainly he'd not be able to work at the lumber camp next winter. He'd be busy taking Silje to school in Otter Bay. Busy making sure the dinner table was clean, the pots scrubbed after meals. The slope here was slippery, so he turned away from it, and thought instead about what the recent turn of events meant for his niece.

As much as he admonished Bente and Arvid, as much as his sister's mind had gotten in the way of her mothering, as often as her husband's lackadaisical work ethic had gotten in the way of their trade, as much as they both made him crazy sometimes, he could nonetheless see how their loss would render Silje somehow changed. His job was to temper the loss. To stand in for them and improve her lot the best he could. It was this notion that brought so much of the pleasure he was this night experiencing.

Of course, he'd always loved Silje. Loved her very much. But she'd been something like a prize. Something he could look upon and cherish, but not be responsible for. He'd never thought of it like that before.

Now, though, he was what Mayfair called her guardian. He liked that word. The duty it implied. He would do right by her. As right as he could.

He glanced across the cabin, saw her face in the distant flash of the lighthouse beam. She possessed such innocence. Such cleverness. Maybe too much cleverness, in fact. He remembered her foretelling their death. Not her first such clairvoyance. He'd dismissed her, not taken seriously her arcane wisdom. And he'd certainly not thought of what those powers might be doing to the same innocence he gazed upon now.

It was only then he thought to wonder what she knew about him. What she could foresee. Would he want to know? The fact he'd never thought to ask led him to conclude that he probably didn't know the answer to his own question.

Instead, he just watched the arc of light. A hundred or a thousand passes he watched, each one pulling him closer and closer to the man he'd have to be now.

FINALLY, proper bed linens to sleep under. No more wool blanket coarse as sandpaper, better suited for a woodshop than a newlywed's bed. And a proper bedside table with a lamp upon it. She'd even set her music box there. An arm's length away.

She'd had the men stage her bedstead under the window, pulled the curtains aside, and made the bed so that she looked up the shore instead of down: west, toward the fishing family's cabin. Toward Sirius and her companions and, if she awoke early enough, the possibility of Venus and Jupiter. The mere thought of all those heavenly bodies brought peace. The most she'd felt since her arrival.

And speaking of arrivals, there was Mrs. Wilson. After one visit, Willa already thought of her as a mentor. Not on the subject of marriage, though she supposed that, too, but of how to navigate a world of cold men. The prospect of the imminent years brightened just because of her. For all Willa had learned at Radcliffe, not one bit of it had so far translated to married life. Now she had her professor. Her marriage pedagogue.

The thought pleased her so much, she chanced the music box, opening it and holding it under the quilt to muffle the sound. The fourth air tinkled in her hands.

Why had she asked Theodulf if he understood stellar aberrations? A taunt, she supposed, but if she really thought about it, perhaps for another reason as well. Maybe she wanted to offer a portal to herself. To be better known. And understood.

His flippancy and arrogance would, of course, never allow that. Nor would his trifling intelligence. And his blind Catholic faith? Thinking of it reminded her of a lecture on the heliocentric theory given by Annie Jump Cannon at the Harvard Observatory, during

175

which she mocked Catholics for being the last to believe the largest and most incontrovertible fact of life on this planet, for clinging to the geocentric theory instead. Theodulf had a geocentric theory of *himself.*

She brought the music box out from under the covers and set it on her tummy.

The lighthouse beam, constant as a metronome, beat up the shore. Its light lessened heaven's, but not so much that she couldn't observe it with some awe. As the music chimed, she visited the skepticism she'd carried with her from the time she first understood how to equate the distance to a star, or its size, or its context in its constellation, the one that held some regard for the *impossibility* of knowing, even as she worked so hard to do just that. Probably it made her insufferable, and certainly many of her professors understood her position as a child's tantrumming. Indeed, her marks sometimes proved it. But even for all the certitude in those hallowed Harvard classrooms, she couldn't help but notice the universal quality of skepticism that every man at the head of the classroom let slip. True, any good scientist needed to possess it. But these men, among the very brightest in the world, they held within them what Willa understood as a kind of surrender.

Theodulf would never surrender, and she feared she might.

As the music box switched airs—now to the fifth, the first movement of "Quasi una fantasia"—she saw it coming over the tree line. She set the music box on the bedstand, bolted upright, and pulled open the sash, as though she might call the comet to her. Cold air rushed in, and whether that or her own excitement, the flesh of her arms and bare legs sizzled. It moved slowly, like a bird in flight a thousand feet high. Its vaporous tail trailed like the exhaust from a steamship stack. She watched, so intently she leaned into the window glass. And for the first time she saw herself from the comet's point of view. That lump of matter that traveled beyond the most distant planets, into a part of the galaxy unstudied, even unimagined, and then back again every seventy-five or -six years.

What did it see, passing over the earth? Passing over this station?

Did it hear the music box's feeble melody? Did it see the lake lit first by the astral plane, then by the vertiginous lighthouse beam? Did it see the orbiting minds of people like her, their swirl like a reflection of the luminaries above? Did it see the man on watch? Or the dreams of the sleeping child? Or the wife in her bedchamber, perplexed by having no dream at all?

A LONG SHADOW BEHIND

MAY 9, 1910

I've heard said that the eyes are the window to the soul. I reply: nonsense. The eyes deceive the soul, which comes in shadow if it comes at all. In fact, a man's whole face might conceal what he brings with him.

Take Hosea Grimm there. I've known him from the day he came to be. Even at first glance—and despite his kindly aspect—I knew what trailed him was an ambiguous, even poisonous, shadow. The first time I saw him, it showed a satyr's horn and cloven foot. This despite his fine brogues and belled top hat. What's more, he knew it himself.

Then there's a bloke like Theodulf Sauer, a man with little shadow to speak of. A man whose soul is waiting for discovery, because so is his self. It's as if he can dodge light, and so have no shadow at all. It's as if he does.

Or Mats Braaten, him with a blotting shadow. It's borne partly from his bearish size, but mostly because he brings so much goodness with him.

I don't mean to repeat myself about the virtues and iniquities of these gentlemen, but only to say I know them down to their ethereal parts. You might trust me.

THE GARDENS PLANTED, the shorebirds returned, the hills greening, spring had finally beset the station. Theodulf took it as an accomplishment of his own that the season turned, that even in the highest hills and deepest forest, the snow had melted and the scent of the earth did rise.

Mornings after a watch, he stood in the window of the cleaning room, his night's duties behind him, and considered the wives as they met over the clotheslines or on the front porches, whispering their confidences, smiling in the wisdom of them. If he begrudged Willa her contentedness, the company of the other women at least spurred his wife to take up her own responsibilities more rigorously. His breakfast was ready each morning, the coffee hot, the kitchen sink uncluttered. She likewise tidied the rest of the house and went to get the mail on her appointed days. And if her performance as a hausfrau was only passable, certainly it was better than the alternative. This and the fact that she was also less inclined to confront him meant they hardly spoke at all.

His primary concerns on this particular morning numbered two: Why hadn't he been able to put the Hamilton railroad watch back together? And why hadn't Hosea Grimm replied to his missive? The former he spent watch nights trying to solve, disassembling and putting back together again the timepiece, always with some part missing.

On the question of the unanswered letter, he was less easily pacified. Why would a man in his standing be ignored? Especially on such pressing matters? Twice, while he struggled to right his railroad watch, he paused to pen angry follow-ups. But twice he threw them in the coal stove and let his thoughts sizzle with the burning letterhead. The whole business had the reek of a slight.

That petty thought accompanied him across the grounds, his holdall tight in his grip. When he reached his house, Willa stood on the porch, her back to him, her gaze cast down the shore. She turned when he cleared his throat behind her.

"Your breakfast is on the table," she said.

He nodded, meaning thanks, and said, "What's yonder?"

She glanced again behind her. "My eyes might deceive me, but I believe there's a boat on the horizon."

"Probably the first of the Lighthouse Service vessels we'll see today." He walked to the edge of the cliff and strained to see the oncoming boat. It was but a glint in the distance. When he turned back to her, he added, "Everything is shipshape, I hope."

"I believe so."

"Good. I'll eat my breakfast and ready for their arrival."

"Mrs. Wilson and I will set the picnic tables."

He nodded his approval.

"And Mr. Braaten said he'll deliver two barrels of sarsaparilla sometime this morning."

"We'll drink well."

"And Mrs. Axelsson has baked three cakes."

"Eat and drink both, then."

Theodulf climbed the stairs and opened the door, holding it for her to enter behind him. Inside, he set his holdall down and took off his peacoat and said, "I appreciate your help readying for today, Willa."

She curtsied, if slightly, and he could not tell if that simple gesture was meant as a taunt or an acknowledgment of his gratitude. As though answering his thoughts, she added, "I've put the mail I collected yesterday on the kitchen table."

At this news, he hurried there.

And sure enough, a dispatch from Hosea Grimm. It appeared to have crossed a hundred years—and the equator twice—on its way to him, so puckered and water stained was the envelope. His name in ink was smeared, and the envelope's glue barely held, as though it had been steamed open and closed again.

Theodulf set the letter down, poured a cup of coffee, and spooned his oats with one hand while the other held the letter. Perhaps the interminable waiting had granted it a deceptive weight—both literal and figurative—but the prospect of opening it was now portentous. He set his spoon down and turned in his chair and held the letter up to the kitchen window. For all its apparent antiquity and even with the benefit of the sun shining through, the paper stock of the envelope hid the letter inside.

He took out the small pocketknife he carried and opened the blade. As he slid it under the top crease of the envelope and started to cut, the flap popped up. He paused to consider the flimsiness of it one more time before blowing into the open envelope and pinching the letter out with his nervous fingers.

Mr. Grimm's penmanship appeared typeset, and for a moment Theodulf recollected the myriad legal briefs he came upon as an attorney. It was with that niggling feeling he read.

April 28, 1910

Dear Master Keeper Sauer,

I've heard reports from no few travelers that the light from your station is already much in service to their vessels steering a straighter course. My compliments to you for its timely and much needed commission. I recall, with much disquiet, the great storm of 1905 which set into motion its necessity. We harbored any number of boats those grim November days. My only wish is that the Lighthouse Service would consider another such beacon on Gunflint's own craggy shore.

As I'm sure you well know, there's more ore on the Mesabi Range than in all of Europe. In order to capitalize on this bounteous resource, we'll need the infrastructure to carry it offshore. The Gunflint harbor is most suitable for this endeavor. It has long been my contention that we're positioned for worldly renown, and in order to reach it, our first step must be the replacement of our present lighthouse with one akin to the Gininwabiko Light you so rightly and proudly superintend. Perhaps you might put me in contact with the commander of the Lighthouse Service, with an eye on furthering these prospects. I would, indeed, be most indebted to you.

Now, to your inquiries regarding Halley's Comet I answer with zeal. Though my professional training is in the medical arts, I've nonetheless spent ample time studying physics and astronomy, both formally and as a hobbyist. In fact, while I undertook my degrees at the Sorbonne, I was fortunate to have been a colleague of Camille Flammarion, who most consider the foremost authority on said comet. I even had the pleasure of visiting with him personally at his private observatory at Juvisy-sur-Orge. Mssr. Flammarion is the founder and president of the *Société astronomique de France*, and the author of some dozen books on the subject at hand. In 1907, while delivering a lecture at the Radcliffe Observatory in Oxford, he announced with certainty that a 'Seven Tailed' comet would indeed orbit the earth, and soon. That very comet now infects our atmosphere, and his prediction of it has cemented his place in the pantheon of great astronomers, right alongside Da Vinci, Galileo, Copernicus, and Ptolemy.

All of which is to say that what I now vouchsafe comes on good authority, as Mssr. Flammarion and I have conducted a rather extensive correspondence since that lecture in Oxford. He on the subject of his considerable cosmic expertise—and myself on the subject of how we might survive as a species in the comet's wake, from a medical perspective. If this last observation reads as melodrama, I assure you it is not.

You see, Mssr. Flammarion's hypothesis is that one of two outcomes from the comet's passing is inevitable. One, the thousand-miles-long tail of the comet possesses enough cyanogen—that is, poisonous gas—to infect and kill the unprotected populace. Or two, when the unfathomable, unquantifiable amount of hydrogen in said tail is combined with the oxygen in the earth's atmosphere, the very air we breathe will suffocate us, vanquishing all sentient life on earth in an instant. There is, of course, no defense for the latter potentiality.

Luckily for you, and for the many thousands of other inquiring customers I've served this year, I've been working tirelessly on an antidote to the cyanogen gas problem. It's quite ingenious, really, my tincture of colloidal silver and several other choice components, and if administered prior to exposure, a fail-safe preventative. And strikingly affordable, too. I will gladly send the recommended dosage to you and your wife for the nominal cost of two dollars, one for each pill.

But you had best declare your interest presently. For, according to Mssr. Flammarion, the most likely date of cataclysm is fast approaching. On May 18 or 19, the earth will cross with the vaporous tail of the comet. That leaves only some few days for me to ship the prescription to you. I ask you please advise me on your intentions.

Sincerely,
Hosea Grimm
Medicinæ Doctor
Philosophiæ Doctor
Apothecary

Postscript: As to the question of my faith, I align here again with Mssr. Flammarion, and am so avowed to a cosmic force beyond our capacity to understand, but not to search for.

Post-postscript: Enclosed please find a clipping from a recent issue of *Revue Philosophique de la France et de l'étranger,* an image commonly known as "Flammarion's Engraving," which, as much as anything, might put an image to my first postscript above.

Post-post-postscript: As to the scourge of wolves, we have lately not suffered them much this far north. Should you be able to trap any, especially the bitches in estrus, I would gladly remunerate you handsomely.

Post-post-post-postscript: As to your query regarding a Bullarium issuance by Pope Pius, I claim no knowledge, though my friend, the good Bishop Richter, confers he has only heard rumblings.

He read the letter twice. First with a sense of incomprehension, then with impending doom. How to even begin considering the end of humanity? He was not a man equipped for such profundity.

Rather than grappling with it, he folded the letter and put it in his pocket and finished his breakfast. The oats were cold now. The coffee tepid. Outside, Willa and the other wives busily and merrily set the picnic tables. The sight of them—so frivolous! so inattentive!—stirred him to a full-throated panic.

He bounded up the stairs and into his bedroom, closed the door, and went to the window, looking up at the bright spring sky. So blue and untroubled. So *heavenly.* He knelt. Put his forehead gently against the window glass and closed his eyes against the calm.

Dear God, he began. *I beg of You, answer: why have You abandoned me? Is it because I have been unfaithful to Your vision of me? Because I have strayed from who You wish me to be? Because it has been so long a lull between my last believing and now?*

Unwittingly, he pressed his forehead still harder to the glass. His hands clasped at his waist, wringing from each other the despair of his whole body.

I would gladly—even joyously!—accept this fate, but You promised angels and have sent instead a gaggle of succubi! I cannot die like this! I will not die like this!

The piercing of the soft flesh of his hands nearly roused him from his agony, but the visions simply would not relent. He saw himself choking on the floor of the lighthouse cleaning room, sputum dribbling from the corner of his mouth, eyes bleeding. He saw the other keepers likewise suffering, and their wives—and his—in confabulation with the other fiends descended from the comet's tail. He saw his father, twisted inside out. And his mother—his mother!—convulsed to death, her hair torn out with her own hands. How strange his people died!

You've asked me to suffer, and suffer I have! For you I have! For you I have forsaken myself!

He saw Paul now, in his pied-à-terre off the Boulevard Saint-Michel, near the Sorbonne of all places. The easiness and readiness of his laughter always caught Theodulf off guard, but of all the things he remembered about that night, none was so immediate as the sound of it.

In all my life, one episode of happiness. One!

The door opened behind him, and he swiveled on his knees to look. Willa? Bitter, blithe Willa?

"Are you all right?" she asked.

"What?" he demanded.

"I heard ranting in here."

"There's been no ranting."

"You were screaming as though the house was on fire."

Theodulf stood. He straightened his pants. "I was praying, something you'd do well to emulate."

She crossed the room and stood before him, a look of smug satisfaction on her otherwise blank face.

"That boat is drawing nearer. Almost certainly it's the Lighthouse Service."

His whole body tensed. His eyes fell shut.

"The picnic tables are set. Mrs. Wilson and I have seen to that."

She put her hand on his arm, which startled his eyes open.

"You look unwell," she said, unexpectedly moving her hand from his arm to his cheek, which blazed under her touch.

He recoiled, rubbed viciously the spot on his face she'd just grazed with her fingertips, and stepped around her, his back now facing the door through which she'd moments ago entered. "I'm not unwell," he mumbled, backing away.

But she closed fast upon him, another clever look on her face.

As though she alone would survive the apocalypse soon to befall the rest of mankind.

"I'm fine," he said, backing away.

She stood in the doorway now. He halfway between her and the staircase landing, the bathroom on his left. He felt cornered, even though he had the whole world to run to.

"Your face," she said, shaking her head. "Why, it's completely blanched."

He reached again for his cheek, felt this time his stubbly whiskers after his long night of work. And then he did what he always did: pulled his watch from his pocket. Flipped it open. Pocketed it again.

"I'll just freshen up," he said, more to himself than to her. And into the bathroom he ducked, closing the door between them.

Poppy? Who would so name a ship? Well, not a ship exactly, but rather a two-masted, single-stacked tender, bearing then upon the lighthouse dock. It sidled coyly, the scourge of coalsmoke spouting from its stack the only blemish on an otherwise peerless morning.

Misters Wilson and Axelsson stood with their wives beside them, the exertion of hustling down the cliffside brightening their faces. Willa must have exhibited a similar flush. But where the other wives were tuckered, Willa merely buzzed. Nearly giddy, she was. Between the arrival of the tender, the celebration it announced, and the stagger she'd caused in Theodulf by finally delivering Hosea Grimm's letter—that bunch of bombastic drivel!—she felt a thrill for the first time since she could not remember when.

She looked at her comrades. First the keepers in full uniform, then their wives in the same garb they'd worn the day of their arrival. Beneath their fatigue, she noticed something else. Was it dread? Boredom? Ambivalence? Some call to duty among the men? Whatever the case, they stood in a row. First the keepers, then their wives. Even John, the genial dunderhead, had traded his constant smile for a quizzical expression, one that didn't change even

as he moved past her to the outermost piling to receive the landing hawser. Mr. Wilson stepped to the piling mid-dock, his hands
joined behind his back as though even landing a boat required zest-
ful protocol.

Willa sidled up to the women and said, "Why the funereal air?"

"Where's your husband?" Mrs. Axelsson nearly hissed. "It's his
duty to first greet the superintendent."

"Why, he's just off watch," Willa said, satisfied that her own rank
as the master keeper's wife might suffice in his stead. Certainly, she
felt cunning enough to stand in.

She turned again to the arriving boat. Not only were the deck-
hands readying the landing lines, but a retinue of officer types,
five of them, stood on the starboard side of the poop deck. Some
looked up at the lighthouse, but the man in the middle—the superintendent, she presumed—studied the group waiting on the dock.

Willa leaned toward Mrs. Wilson. "He looks a wet bird."

Mrs. Wilson smiled and whispered, "You keep that sharp tongue
firmly in cheek. The superintendent is the utmost stickler. The
men all despise him."

Willa looked him over again. She could see here his sunken
cheeks and scant hair beneath his cap. He held his chin in one
cupped hand, and what appeared to be a whistle, which he swung
on a piece of string, in the other. For all his narrowness, he yet possessed an innate superiority. One that found its best evidence in
the men on either side of him. They stood regimentally, and as the
Poppy reversed her thrust and settled light as a gull on the dockside fenders, the crew of officers did not so much as sway with the
motion of the boat. Before Willa removed her eyes from the superintendent, the gangway had been lowered.

The parade of officers down from the poop deck struck Willa
as overly mannered. As if the superintendent were in fact the rear
admiral of the Atlantic Fleet and not the supervisor of the Elev-
enth Lighthouse District. He let his officers disembark before him,
and waited until they formed a line opposite the keepers, who
had hustled back to stand ready by the gangway. When finally the

superintendent stepped off the *Poppy*, he put his whistle in his pocket and walked first to Mr. Wilson.

"Keeper Wilson," the superintendent said. "I see it was too much trouble for you to properly tie your cravat this morning." Without waiting for a response, he moved on to Mr. Axelsson. "You're the second assistant keeper?"

When Axelsson nodded ascent, the superintendent took a step closer and put his ear right under Axelsson's bushy beard. When the bear still did not speak, the superintendent stomped his boot on the dock and said, "I'll not have mumblers and bumblers. State your name."

"I'm John Axelsson, sir."

"Tell me, Mr. Axelsson, where's Master Keeper Sauer?"

"He's just off watch, sir."

The superintendent made a dramatic show of checking his own pocket watch. "Sunrise was some forty minutes ago. Surely he saw the tender coming down the shore?"

Mr. Axelsson looked helplessly to Mr. Wilson, as though the question had been some great conundrum and not as easy enough to answer with a simple nod. When the elder keeper didn't offer a tether, Mr. Axelsson turned back to the superintendent and said, "Sir, I do not know."

"You're a lighthouse keeper and not in possession of the time the sun rises?"

"Sir, I mean I do not know whether Keeper Sauer saw the tender approaching."

"Is it a keeper's duty to be advised of incoming vessels?"

"Sir, I believe so."

To Mr. Wilson the superintendent said, "You're what, Ainsley, twenty, twenty-five years into your service?"

"Twenty-two years, sir. The last four at Pointe aux Barques."

"I know your history of service. What I'm asking, since you're too daft to catch my drift, is why you haven't trained young Mr. Axelsson on some of the finer points of his job?"

To see Mr. Wilson stunned into silence moved Willa into action.

She approached the superintendent and introduced herself. Then she said, "Keeper Sauer was held up in the lighthouse. Something about the watchworks, he said. He asked that I escort you up to our quarters, where he'll meet you presently. He's been looking forward to your arrival."

This speech, such as it was, enlivened her almost as much as handing Theodulf the letter had just a short half hour ago. And whether the superintendent warmed to her confidence or prettiness didn't matter. That he looked scoldingly at Misters Wilson and Axelsson, and then followed Willa up the dock as the rest of his retinue disembarked and got in line behind him, that was all she cared about. The superintendent couldn't see her expression—the belittling one she wore at his expense—but then, for all his powers of judgment, he likely saved very few for himself.

Theodulf met the parade coming up off the dock midway to the station. He'd shaved around his mustache and changed his shirt and cravat, and his hair was combed behind his ears under his hat. Despite his preparations, he still appeared disheveled and flustered. This of course pleased Willa—was in fact precisely her intended effect—but she couldn't help feeling sorry for him. That a man should so easily be made the fool, why, it was unbecoming.

"Theodulf," she said before he could mumble his apology, "I explained to the superintendent about the watchworks. I'm sure you were able to make the repair?"

She may as well have kissed him softly on the mouth for all the surprise his expression betrayed. Before he could question her, she said. "Was it the ball bearings, as you suspected?"

Instead of answering her directly, Theodulf turned his attention to the superintendent, who stood again as he had on the dock, with his hands clenched behind his back and his chin thrust into the air. "Welcome, Superintendent Thomas. My apologies for having missed your arrival. I was, in fact, tending to an issue with the clockworks in the lighthouse. But that situation is rectified. So, allow me to escort you up to the station. We're all looking forward to a most celebratory day."

"Indeed, Master Sauer. A most celebratory day. But first, an inspection." He looked over his shoulder at his men. "Jackson, you'll observe the quarters. I'll see to the station itself."

Another aspect befell Theodulf. One of near panic, no doubt thinking of his own quarters and the lackluster job Willa had been doing keeping them up to snuff.

To Jackson, one of the men in his retinue, the superintendent added, "Begin with the Axelsson abode."

Jackson nodded stern approval, and the procession continued up the hill to the station, led by a staggering Theodulf.

"How is it less than a month into service, there should already be markings etched here?" The superintendent kicked the toe of his boot at the floor beneath the desk in the cleaning room. They were the first words he'd spoken since he'd conveyed his few orders on the hillside five minutes ago. "There should be pads on the bottom of these chair legs."

Without waiting for explanation, he continued, surveying the room. "There's an unreasonable mess there by the hod box. That needs to be swept every morning." He walked to the stove, lifted the kettle atop it. "And this needs to be emptied." At this he removed from his back pocket a notebook bound in leather and began jotting notes. When his first entry was complete, he returned to the desk and opened the log. He read through the entries and closed the ledger and made another notation. Again, he looked around the room. "The window here is smudged." He removed from his other back pocket a handkerchief and wiped at the fingerprints. "As if a child's been at play."

Now he headed through the passageway and into the watch room, where he paused to take in the tower looming above, bisected only by the column holding the clockworks cables. When he brought his gaze back down, it settled on Theodulf. "You're a very lucky man to have earned command of a station like this. It's the grandest in the whole Service." He walked slowly to the center column and gripped it and twirled around, keeping his eyes aloft. "And I don't mean only on the Great Lakes, but in the whole blessed country. A man should relish the honor of an assignment like this."

For the first time since they'd arrived in the lighthouse, Theodulf spoke. "I do, Mr. Thomas. Both relish the assignment and agree that the station is a marvel. I'm trying to get the crew into the spirit of excellence. I believe they should approach their commission as a man of faith would his devotion to God."

"Less devout, I should hope, than diligent. That's the thing." He stopped circling the column. "Tell me about your watch last night. What happened with the clockworks?"

It took no effort at all to fabricate a story. "It was nothing. I thought I noticed a problem in the watchworks when last I wound them this morning. As soon as I extinguished the lamp, I checked the gears and ball bearings, erring on the side of caution."

"And what did you discover?"

"Everything is in fine fettle."

"As it should be."

"Indeed."

Nonetheless, Thomas went to the foot of the caracole and started climbing. Thirty-two steps snaked up the wall. A walk Theodulf made six or seven times a night when on watch. One that never so much as taxed him. So why, this morning, was he winded when he reached the watch room on Thomas's heels? Why did his collar feel as though it were a hand clenching his throat? Why was he certain the sheen on his face was cold sweat, and not the blush of embarrassment?

Thomas fiddled with one of the brass vents at the foot of the wall. "The lamp is drawing well?"

"Very."

"Any trouble with vapors?"

"None."

"Do I need to make a special scrutiny of the clockworks?"

"As I say, everything is shipshape." Theodulf felt another anger rising, this one directed at Willa for her meddling in the superintendent's arrival. For her suggestion that the clockworks had somehow malfunctioned. The very mention of it had cast a pall over Thomas's inspection. *Dust under the hod box? Smudged windows?*

Triflings, these. The station, especially the lighthouse itself, was in pristine condition. These nits, they were personal.

"Do you see this?" Thomas had his finger on the lid of the mercury float. What, swiping at a layer of fine dust?

"I do."

He sniffed his finger, glowered at Theodulf, then lowered himself at the waist and began a pass around it. When he finished circumnavigating the apparatus, he shook his head solemnly and removed his notebook. After he scribbled his observation, he said, "This is a grave infraction, Keeper Sauer. Not only is there a dearth of mineral oil to seal the bath, but the lid has not been properly or adequately affixed."

How had Theodulf missed this truth, which was, as soon as Thomas declared it, as obvious as the green-tinted flower of glass above them.

"Is there an issue with the float? A leak?" Thomas hurried a look around the floor of the watch room. "Why was the lid removed in the first place?"

"I don't know. Certainly, it wasn't myself who tampered with it. There's been no need."

"Are you suggesting your assistants might have tinkered with it?"

"No. Axelsson and Wilson are both fine keepers." Theodulf bent himself, scrutinizing the heavy steel lid. It appeared to be dented. As though someone had lifted one edge of the container to have a peek. "Must be residual of its installation."

"I doubt that very much. I supervised the assembly of the lamp myself."

After another moment's study, Theodulf said, "Well, I'll gather the toolbox and put this right."

"You'll need to check the mercury level first. And, of course, use the mineral oil to seal the container. This needs to be done immediately." He took another cursory look around the watch room. "In the meantime, I'll inspect the oil house and fog signal." With that he descended the spiral staircase.

TWO HOURS. That's how long it took Theodulf to investigate the case of the mercury vessel. Two hours of laborious toil conducted alongside his growing paranoia, the turning of each bolt like a loosening of his own fate. When he got the lid removed, he discovered the mercury level was indeed low. Another conundrum he could not fathom.

After he'd stowed the tools, he returned to his house to find Thomas, the lighthouse tender Captain Voigt, and two other officers he didn't recognize and hadn't yet met sitting around his kitchen table, eating a proper cake. Their joviality gave the impression of brothers long separated finally reuniting. And on the periphery of that party, flitting about like a hummingbird, laughing at their joshing, refilling a coffee cup, her hair unplaited and following her around like a perfumed banner, Willa.

Willa, who had never once perfumed herself in his presence, who had yet to bake him a cake. That she even knew how was unthinkable. So he stood there feeling very much like he had after reading the letter from Hosea Grimm: determined that the end of times was upon them, and that his only companion through the end of these last days would be his bewilderment.

Willa, in another flourish of sorcery, turned the officers' attention to Theodulf's arrival. "Here's the master keeper himself, looking altogether knackered. Captain Voigt, perhaps you could let Theodulf sit for a piece of cake? He'll need a boost before we start our picnic."

Voigt rose and held the chairback for Theodulf. He tightened his tie knot, noticing the streak of grease on his shirt, and buttoned his coat to cover it. Willa set before him a cup of lukewarm coffee. She leaned across the table and wedged the last piece of cake from the pan and served it upon a bread-and-butter plate. Theodulf reached for a fork and a napkin, cut a piece of cake, and ate it.

Willa put her hand on his shoulder. "It's delicious, yes?"

Theodulf dabbed the corner of his mouth. Her touch did not alarm him—as it would have under normal circumstances—but rather roused in him again the morning's dread. It was interminable.

Captain Voigt, standing behind Theodulf, said, "You're a lucky man, to find yourself at this fair station with so handsome a wife."

Voigt appeared inebriated, but was perhaps only flush with the excitement of Willa's company. For her part, Willa's duplicity was never more pronounced. At once she commanded the room and was nowhere in it; she aroused the men at the table and was one of them; she spoke soothing words—as now, when she said: "You look a ghost, Teddy"—and appeared ready to crucify him.

Was Mr. Thomas who spoke next, "Less a ghost than colored by mercury. The float, what discoveries found you up there?" He sat with one leg crossed over the other, his long arms enfolded across the upper knee, his knuckles bulbous and knobby, like whatever meat had once resided in his shoulders had melted into his hands. "Keeper Sauer?"

Theodulf took an unconscious survey of those faces around the table. So many pompous leers, such faithless aspects, such churlish smirks. He stopped on Thomas. "The float is fine. The whole lighthouse is." Now he turned his disconsolate gaze on his wife. Did he see quicksilver in her eyes? "Fetch me my bible from the desk in the front room?"

She turned as though on a breeze. Before the scent of her dissolved, she called from the front room, "Why, our guests are approaching!" in a tone of voice at once giddy and wry. "Sailboats and a few fishing boats. Even the *Nocturne* if I judge her stack right."

As she came hurrying in with Theodulf's bible, Mr. Thomas said, "We've a party to ready for." He rose himself and donned his cap. "Now's the time for celebration, not sanctimony." As though he were an orchestra conductor—or a priest—he summoned those sitting around the table by raising his hands. He made a show of looking out the window. "The good Lord *has* blessed us with a lovely day. Let's partake of it."

The officers filed out, leaving the master keeper with only his wife and good book. She sat in the chair recently vacated by Mr. Thomas and crossed her legs as he had. She folded her hands as he had. For a long moment she only gazed at Theodulf, expressionless herself. But then her eyes brightened and she leaned toward him and tapped the cover of his bible. "You appear troubled. Is something wrong with the lighthouse? What was that about mercury?"

Theodulf clenched his eyes shut.

"There's something more, yes?" Willa continued. "Is it the burden of today's fête? Are you worried it won't be a success?"

Now he moved his gaze slowly to her. He blinked.

Answering that hollow man, Willa said, "It must be something bigger? Something more all-encompassing?" She tapped his bible again and then stood and went to the doorway.

But before she left, she said, "It's the Book of Revelation, isn't it? That describes the apocalypse? That is, the end of days? Maybe visit those old verses?" Again she turned to leave, but again paused. This time she spoke over her shoulder, "I'll be your *best* wife today."

SILJE HAD NEVER BEEN TO A PROPER PARTY. Outside of her schoolhouse and church, she'd never seen so many people gathered anywhere before. From her perch astride the pony wall surrounding the lighthouse, she'd watched the *Nocturne's* tender ferry the first arrivals to shore. Dozens of dignitaries—including the mayors of Duluth and Two Harbors and their wives, Senator Nelson and his, and that rangy priest she'd seen so many times since the lighthouse was built—had gathered under the canvas tent erected on the middle of the grounds, sipping sarsaparilla her uncle had provided. Out on the lake, there were still other boats anchoring in the cove between her fish house and the dock, and groups of two and four beaching their dinghies on the rocky beach, parasols raised against the warm midday sun.

Her uncle in his mackinaw would be among those coming ashore soon. After delivering the kegs of sarsaparilla, he'd gone back out to set his nets again. She hated when he left. A hollow feeling filled her in his wake, one that deepened at the sight of her father's skiff, resting nowadays on ways up the beach. From her perch by the lighthouse, she saw the boat now, hidden in piney woods. She missed her father for countless reasons, but perhaps mostly because his absence had changed her uncle. He was always tired now, and Silje spent most of her time alone. When the hours found him at home, he veered mostly into pensiveness. He would scold her for things he used to tease about, or ask her to do chores that had once been considered too rigorous for her mother. Splitting wood. Gathering it. Mending nets. Baking bread. Next day she would plant their gardens. The thought of it all made *her* pensive and tired.

Today she would play, though. She'd finished carving the boy's face, and he sat in her pocket. She'd yet to see Frog or Willa, but there were other men in uniform. And other wives. They came from their brick houses, bearing plates of ham and jars of mustard, cakes, salads. The tables under the tent fairly burst with the smorgasbord.

Out on the water, the *Nocturne* rendezvoused with her tender again. Another dozen travelers with half a dozen more sunshades veered toward the lighthouse dock. It landed as a brass band appeared from the first house. Trombone, cornet, flugelhorn, tuba. Four men in red hats and black pants with garters on their sleeves and red laces on their patent leather shoes. Before they reached the picnic they started to play.

As if the band had summoned Frog, he came limping up to the party. Willa, in trousers and a chambray blouse, followed him as though she herself danced before a flutter of butterflies, so light and flitting were her steps. Silje swiveled where she sat, emulating the ballerina-esque movements of Willa's shoulders, which moved to the music. She wanted to go to her, Silje did. Down the knoll of granite the lighthouse stood upon, across the grounds, and into the woman's shadow. She wanted to be so graceful and so resolute. But each of these thoughts only turned the girl more inward until finally she was peering at her hands held tight on her lap.

By the time the brass band finished its first number, Silje was ready to risk another look at the party. But a swath of periwinkle blue cotton blocked her view.

"If it isn't Miss Silje Lindvik," Willa said. She knelt and put her hand on the girl's shoulder. "I hope you brought your friend. What's his name again?"

Silje felt the dumb, quizzical look come across her face.

"The wolf. The one who stole my ham."

Now Silje wiped the sun from her eyes and pointed down on the lawn. "It looks like the whole pack is here."

Willa turned her attention to the assembled guests and laughed. It was the first laughter Silje'd heard in weeks. Maybe since the last time she'd sat beside the lighthouse keeper's wife.

"I expect there're more lambs than wolves down there. Would you like to meet the mayor of Duluth?"

Silje turned a cockeyed glare.

"Of course not!" They both looked over the swelling crowd as still others paraded up from the dock. "Well, would you like a piece of chocolate cake? Or a sandwich?"

"I'll wait for my uncle."

"He's not here?"

"Out setting nets."

Willa looked over the lake as though she might spot him.

"He's down around the Bunchberry," Silje said. "You can't see there from here."

"I have just the thing." She offered her hand to Silje, who took it as she stood.

Together they walked down the slope, through the crowd, and along the pathway to the third brick house. They went inside where Willa said to wait a moment. She rushed up the narrow staircase while Silje made a nosey walkabout through the main floor. Fully furnished, the house still felt queer. Like church. It did smell lovely, though. Clean and without the burden of woodsmoke spiriting the air.

At the piano, Silje wedged the fallboard open and then looked over her shoulder to find Willa standing under the arch.

"You don't need to worry. If Theodulf's not here, you can poke your nose anywhere you like."

Silje doubted this. She set the fallboard back down.

"This," Willa said, holding up a brass wand, "is what I wanted to show you. Come!"

Willa ushered her back across the grounds to the edge of the cliff. She hopped onto the quarter wall, where Silje had recently been perched, and signaled the girl to stand beside her. Willa gripped the wand with one hand on either end and extended it magically. Three times its original length now, Willa removed the caps from both ends and handed it to Silje.

"This is a telescope. It makes what's far away near."

Silje held the mechanism, its weight surprising, and stared at it suspiciously.

Willa took it back and demonstrated its function, explaining as she did how the glass lenses inside the brass housing tricked distant objects into hurtling toward the viewer. "Here," she said, offering it again, then helping the eyepiece to rest on the bridge of Silje's nose.

The world rushed forward in a watery blur, and she pushed the telescope away as a wave of dizziness washed over her. For a moment, she felt she might stumble over the cliff's edge. Her legs went limp, and she sat.

"At night, it brings the moon close enough you can see the shadows in the craters," Willa said.

Cautiously, Silje raised the telescope to her eye again and trained it out on the water.

"This knob focuses the lens." Willa set Silje's forefinger and thumb on the ribbed dial and helped her twist it. "Adjust it until what you're looking on comes clear."

Silje lowered the telescope briefly, surveyed the view, decided on her house across the cove, then brought the telescope to her eye again. There was the dock, the boxes upturned upon it, the net roller, the shingles of the fish house, her father's skiff beneath the pines, the front door of the cabin farther ashore. All of it so close she could touch it. She even reached her hand in front of the lens to effort at doing so.

"It's an illusion," Willa said. "Everything is exactly as far away as it was before you set the telescope to your eye."

Silje did not answer, but moved the lens out over the water, up past Gininwabiko Point and then farther offshore. She spied a boat not her uncle's. The water, which in plain sight appeared placid, was agitated up close. So much so that the ketch trailing the breeze rose and slapped the waves. It would be a rough row home for her uncle, wherever he was. Swiveling the telescope to the distant hillside trees, their green came brightly and blurred, until she again adjusted the lens and found the black veins of the trees' limbs webbed against each other.

"It's like my own sight," Silje said. "How I can bring the faraway to hand." At this she lowered the telescope and held her hand out as though a bird should alight there.

"What do you mean?" Willa said, her own eyes widening.

Silje turned the spyglass onto the *Nocturne*. She rested the glass on the railing where she'd stood on the way to Gunflint those days ago. Thinking of that town brought her the boy, which caused her to shiver and demure. "Oh, it's nothing," she said.

"Tell me, sweet girl. What can you bring to hand?"

"Things that were. Things still to come." She thought of the boy again. Of his eye. Her own eye she buried in the telescope once more and turned it this time to the lighthouse grounds below. Two twists of the focuser brought the priest's face several times larger than life, a vision she could not behold. So she moved across the crowd, to the edge of it nearest the first house.

That's where she found him. Sitting cross-legged against the slats of the barn. The sandwich in his outheld hand appeared as large as his head, which itself was grotesquely magnified. Silje let out a laugh and was off the wall and down the hill and across the grounds before she heard Willa calling, "My telescope, Miss Lindvik!"

As she slowed before him, Silje thought perhaps her summonsing powers hadn't been lost after all.

"I wondered if I might see you," Odd said.

"But you didn't come looking for me?"

"I went over to your cabin before I came up here. That's your father's boat up on the ways?"

"It is."

"A fine boat, if not a little prickly about the gunwale and stern sheets. You or your uncle ought to get a coat of varnish across her boards." He took a bite of his sandwich and looked up at her with his good eye. "What've you got there?"

She held the telescope up as though surprised to find it in her hand. "This makes what's faraway near."

"Is it a telescope? Hosea has a whole carton of those things up in his office."

She felt desperate. As if what this brass mechanism had brought was not the faraway, but her own simpleness. She glanced over her shoulder, in the direction of her home, beyond these stately brick abodes and the brilliant light. In her mind, she could see the cabin tucked down on the lakeshore. Could see the wolf tracks in the mud out back. Could see, too, that for all the sorrow of that place, it was nothing more than a few small rooms and their poverty—nothing more. The realization embarrassed her.

She turned to leave, but he called out, "Where're you headed? You think you'll have a better conversation with the priest?" He nodded to the edge of the gathered crowd. "Or the gentry?" Now he nodded at the statesmen huddled around a special table for dignitaries. "Or the band?" which were just then starting another tune. The clever smile upon his half face warmed her.

Certainly he was right. She'd be best off in his company. "Why'd you come here?" she said, sitting beside him in the tender grass.

"Hosea wanted to see the lamp"—he nodded up at the lighthouse. "Says he knew the inventor of the lens, from when he lived in Paris."

She felt again the world spinning away. Like Paris was as distant from this shore as the moon, and that she was as likely to step foot in one place as the other.

"Of course, Hosea's known to tell a lie now and again."

"Why does he lie?"

Odd shrugged and took the last bite of his sandwich. A dollop of brown mustard dripped on his chin. "I don't even think he knows he does it." He wiped his chin with the cuff of his sleeve. "Maybe the story in his mind is better with a few fibs along the way."

"Where is he?"

Odd scanned the crowd, spotted him, and pointed.

"That's Frog he's talking to," Silje said. "The head lighthouse keeper. Frog is married to Willa." Saying her name sent Silje's eyes back up to the granite knoll, where Willa no longer stood.

"Frog?" Odd said. "That's a peculiar name."

"He looks like one."

He smiled and craned his neck for a better look. "I can see it. And Willa?"

"I don't know where she is. We're friends. She gave me this." Silje held up the telescope. "Does it seem like Hosea is your father? Does he act like one?"

Odd studied him, so Silje did, too. He wore woolen trousers and a vest and coat that matched, but no necktie. She couldn't tell if his paunch protruded above his belt, or if his suit was merely ill-fitting, but in either case the illusion of heft gave him the appearance of a laboring man. He seemed affable, too, and smiled and even guffawed as passersby in the crowd stopped to say hello and shake his hand. Frog, meanwhile, was hunched and pale and meek. He appeared, frankly, unwell. As though he were at the end of a long illness and his next step might trip him into the grave. Twice he lifted his arm and pointed at the barn on which Silje and Odd leaned.

"Like a father? Not hardly. Try headmaster."

"But he takes care of you?"

"Rebekah takes care of me." Now he stood. "Let's have some cake."

Together they worked through the crowd, arriving at the picnic table as the band dropped their horns and sang a shanty instead, their voices in spellbinding harmony. It put Silje in mind of one of her own songs, but as happened with her sight in Odd's company, so too did her voice remain elusive.

She collapsed the telescope, holstered it in the waist of her skirt, and joined the whorl of partygoers circling the banquet. She forgot about waiting for her uncle and heaped cake and gherkins and two slabs of ham onto her plate. Together, they returned to the spot beneath the lighthouse she'd recently been with Willa and ate in peace. Silje her whole plateful. Odd his sliver of chocolate cake with butter cream frosting.

She'd not had pork since Christmas, and the saltiness rewarded her in a way a full belly alone wouldn't have. Sinking into a contented stupor, she gazed easily onto the lake, listening to the brass band down on the lawn, until she saw her uncle rowing back up the shore. At the sight of him, she removed the telescope and trained it on his broad shoulders, confirming by the tilt of his head that exhaustion was returning with him.

"There's Uncle," she said.

"He's well known, Mats Braaten is."

"Well known for what?"

"Decency. Diligence. C'est un homme qui travaille dur, as Hosea might say."

"I probably don't have to tell you I don't speak French. That is French, yes? Certainly it sounds songy enough."

"It means he's a hardworking man. That's his reputation. And sober." He appeared embarrassed by his own flash of showiness. "Sorry for prattling on in French. He's been teaching me since I was five years old." He brushed the hair off his forehead. "I'm always trying to be less like him."

Silje looked at her uncle again. "I should be more like *him*."

After the wives cleared the platters, while the men had second sarsaparillas and congratulated each other on the grand achievement of the new lighthouse station, Silje found herself suddenly and without explanation in the company of Hosea Grimm. Like an expert hunter, he'd cornered her near the oil house the moment Odd had excused himself for the loo, and now, as Hosea spoke, was herding her away from the crowd. He'd exhausted the subject of Odd—whom he called his dear boy—and described presently his many enterprises.

"Mostly I'm an apothecary—do you know what that is?"

She felt something between a song and a premonition burbling up in her. But discordant and unmeasured and cloaked in blackness.

"The natural world is full of curatives! In these northern wilds alone there's a virtual panacea." He gazed around as though lost in the wonder of it. "You didn't tell me how old you were."

The change in subject reminded Silje of her mother who, when frustrated by her daughter's lapses in attention, would turn the subject to Silje herself in an effort to regain favor. It was something her uncle never did. *Where was he?* she wondered. "I'm sixteen," she lied.

He looked doubtful, but then nodded and turned a glance over his shoulder. Now Silje couldn't even hear the chatter of the guests.

"You'll be finding a husband soon, then," he said. He looked over his shoulder again. "Tell me, does your uncle keep you elbows-deep in fish guts? I imagine that since the tragic loss of your parents—my condolences, yes . . . my most sincere condolences to be sure, I heard of your situation from my own sweet daughter. I believe you met her when you and your uncle came to Gunflint for Mayfair's fair counsel? I was saying, I imagine that since then, your uncle has required your collaboration about his business? Which is why I ask about the fish guts." He paused and raised his hands and extended his arms, framing her face with his forefingers and thumbs.

What peered back at her through that frame was a fiend disguised as a man, one who kept talking.

"My advice is to wait until *just* the right suitor comes along. My daughter has deflected dozens of proposals so she might be free to live her own life." He finally lowered his hands and took a step toward her, raised his hands again, and set them on her shoulders. "You're quite strong indeed." He slid his hands down the length of her arms. "But fresh, too. Like springtime itself."

Silje's whole body had clenched at his touch, and she was unable to speak, much less move. And yet, as he turned away from her, she took several steps backward. Almost stumbling. She immediately felt the error of her progress—now she was farther than ever from the gathered guests.

He must have sensed her uneasiness, because he stood upright and straightened his waistcoat, affecting an air of indifference as he did. "Your uncle, I've not seen him all day?"

"He's here," she lied.

"Is he?" Again, the contrived aloofness. And yet more bluster, "You'd make an excellent subject, do you know that? I'm a portraitist as well as an apothecary. I take photographs, you see? Some might even call me an artist. Some *do*. I've made my daughter nigh famous the world over!"

"Famous?" It was a word she didn't exactly know. Many of his words baffled her.

Now he locked his hands behind his back and straightened like Silje so often saw Frog do. He nodded vehemently, as though that one-word question gave him a new kind of access to her naïveté. "She's a beautiful young woman, my daughter. You've seen her. American ladies are much revered for their shadow selves, and in Paris, where most of my work is traded, Rebekah is as renowned as Sarah Bernhardt." He lifted his nose and smiled. "At least her pictures are as ubiquitous!"

The thought of his daughter's portraits in Paris must have delighted him, for the smile that seeped across his buttery face told Silje to run. Everything about this man suggested impurity. She'd sooner be in Fenrir's company.

As though thinking of the wolf alone might summon him, something like his bellows boomed through the air, its source so near and loud as to injure her ears, which she covered with her hands as she knelt for fear.

Hosea Grimm merely turned to the noise. Three times the cannonades roared, then a rueful silence. She watched him gaze back upon the lighthouse, a reverent look on his face. He began to speak, but she leapt from her crouch and flew up the trail with the cleverness of a hare outfoxing the wolf.

Only a hundred strides had separated her from the crowd, but for the relief she felt being back in their comfort, it could have been a hundred miles. The priest stood on a dais, blessing the gathering and commending the Lighthouse Service while the officers looked approvingly at each other. Silje slipped into the throng, weaving a path among them meant to make her invisible, searching for no one.

How had that man done this? Made her want to disappear? Fold herself a thousand times until she fit into her uncle's pocket?

"Consider the foghorn you just heard a call from on high! His glory is everywhere for us to see! Look! Look!"

How could his voice carry across the grounds like that? She was back at the barn wall, sitting in the grass. From there, she could see his garb. The cassock and collar, the wooden cross hanging from a cord around his fat neck.

"Rejoice!"

She put her head between her knees and pressed against her ears. The better to be alone. She put her hand in her own pocket. There was Odd. Where had he gone? Where was Willa? Or her uncle?

One of the officers now commanded the crowd. He was less vociferous than the priest, and Silje could hardly hear his speech, though his solemn intentions were clear from the cast of his eye. Better company was the boy in her pocket, which she removed and set upon her knee. Next she removed the telescope from her belt and placed it to the boy's tunneled eye so he was staring back at her. She couldn't imagine what he saw.

When next she looked up there were her uncle and Willa, smiling down upon her, their conspiratorial humors plain as the late afternoon sun now righteous in the western sky.

"Your friend, what does he see?" Uncle asked.

She handed the telescope back to Willa, who said to Mats, "That's a girl scared witless by *something*." She squatted beside Silje. "Whatever it was, *who*ever it was, you're okay now. Your uncle's here. He's found you."

"It took you long enough getting the nets out." Silje feathered his hair back.

"Wasn't getting the nets out that stole my day, but the breeze that came up to thwart my getting back. What say we find your tired old uncle a piece of cake before we head home?"

Silje risked a glance. His hair was plastered to his head as though he'd rowed home in a downpour. "There's probably none left," Silje said. "But we can look." She rose, whispered something into the boy's wooden ear, then took her uncle's hand.

The warmth of his calloused flesh as they wound back through the dwindling crowd gave her to song. Before they'd taken ten steps across the lawn, she was drumming a new beat on the palm of his hand. The rhymes came easily: Some cake he'll eat, and then we'll meet, Fenrir my friend, upon the peat. He'll growl and howl and then he'll wink, and be gone in the dark, he'll take his stink.

There was indeed still cake. What's more, Odd was sneaking another piece himself. "There you are," he said, offering his spoils without guile.

"I can get my own," Silje said. Where was the boy's keeper? That cad?

"Are you angry?"

"I think she's tired out. What with all the fun," Mats said.

"I'm not tired." She scooped a piece of cake onto a napkin and wrapped it like a gift to herself. "And this party's for creeps."

Merely saying the word summoned the worst of them, for no sooner did she utter it than Hosea appeared on the edge of the straggling crowd, his bent leer settled on her like a January midnight. A chill ran down her arms and through her hands and fingers. Willa put a comforting hand on the girl's shoulder.

"I'm not a creep," Odd said.

Rather than respond, she stepped away from Willa and turned her whole attention to Hosea. When she did, Odd and her uncle did, too. Hosea waved, as though he were a sought friend.

It was Willa who spoke next: "Silje Lindvik, I have another thing to show you. Would you like to see?"

"Yes," Silje said, keeping her gaze on Hosea.

Willa started to usher her away, but Silje again dodged her hold. This time she stepped to Odd, who appeared flummoxed by the turn in her mood.

"You're not a creep. I didn't mean it like that." She removed from her pocket the boy she'd carved. "Here." She handed it to him. "I carved this. You should have it."

He held it before him. A mirror likeness. A birch boy.

S HE HELD THE TELESCOPE up to her knee, as if that knobby thing had sight, the lens pointed toward her. He thought, *How like a child.* He thought, *How like a nincompoop.*

If he held the telescope, he'd search for Mr. Grimm, whose company had evaded Theodulf all day. Apparently his counsel was much sought. More even than his own, which among this crowd made little sense at all, and filled Theodulf with a tempestuous jealousy.

Ah! There he was now, standing on the edge of the gathering, adjusting his waistcoat as though he'd just rolled down a hill. He had a queer look about him. Flushed and excited and guilty. Mr. Grimm ran a hand across his face and surveyed the yard. In profile, Theodulf recognized something he hadn't at first. Something frightening.

How could a man so worldly as Hosea Grimm, a man who'd strode among Parisian belles, who'd likely even cavorted with them, a man who knew the world's great scientists and philosophers, who *corresponded* with them, if what he said was true, look upon that Lindvik girl with such depravity? He'd no need of a telescope, that much was certain. Even from across the grounds Theodulf witnessed a gaze that beheld not God's creation but Mr. Grimm's own lecherous intentions. A *bogresse.* That word he'd heard twice in his life. Once from his father the morning he collected Theodulf at the Duluth city jail. And then again when Paul whispered it to him on the balcony in Val-de-Grâce.

Now was not the time for such a visitation. To dispel it, Theodulf looked back at the Lindvik girl. She handed Willa the telescope. A moment later, the four of them—Willa and Mats and the Lindvik girl and Hosea Grimm's boy—looked in unison at Grimm, who waved at them. Now Willa took the girl's hand, and they walked down the path toward his house.

If the fate of these souls were as decided as his letter implied, why did Grimm wear that expression of felicity upon his smiling face? Why had he wandered among the assembled as though it were a right cause for celebration, not a wake for all the living? Why—and this question settled on Theodulf with the weight of an anvil—had his prayers gone unanswered? Why had God not smiled upon him?

Theodulf crossed the hundred paces between him and Mr. Grimm. As he stepped before him, Hosea Grimm swiped his hand across his face again.

"Mr. Sauer! I doubted I'd get an audience with you, sir!"

"I've—"

"You're in much demand. *Much* demand. And I understand why. This kingdom"—he made a broad gesture at the lighthouse and grounds—"why, it's a proper testament to American industry. You must feel a grave and great responsibility."

"Indeed," Theodulf nearly whispered. In fact, he wanted to scream. He wanted to take this man by his lapels and ask him how these platitudes weren't condolences.

"And this soiree! Why, I've not had such a lovely time since I can't remember when!"

"Sir, if I may, I'm only just in receipt of your letter."

"My letter?"

"Sir, your letter dated April the twenty-eighth."

Mr. Grimm stuck out his lower lip and tilted his head like a dupe.

"Regarding the comet. And your antidote?"

Now he smacked his forehead. "Of course," he said, glancing around like a thief. "My colloidal silver concoction." He patted his breast pocket. "I never received your reply."

"As I say, I've only just this day received *yours*."

"That's peculiar. I sent it promptly. I wonder what accounts for its delay?"

"I wonder the same."

"Well, wonders never do cease, as they say. But the good news is, I had the foresight to bring along doses aplenty." He reached into the breast pocket he'd earlier touched and removed a bottle of white pills. He presented the bottle on the palm of his hand.

"It says aspirin, sir."

Mr. Grimm made a show of inspecting the label. He smiled. "As I said in my letter, this is an invention of my own device. I simply used the aspirin bottle as a vessel. I assure you this is the remedy for you."

Theodulf lifted the bottle from Hosea Grimm's hand. He turned his back to the crowd and inspected it.

"We're a mere week and a day from our fate, Keeper Sauer. So the scientific authorities insist. What's in that bottle is your salvation."

Theodulf glanced at him.

"I grant you the cost is prohibitive for many, but surely a man of your employ, well . . ."

"I'd like to buy one dose," Theodulf whispered.

"I beg your pardon, you said one dose?"

Theodulf nodded.

"But what about your wife?"

Theodulf removed from his pocket a two-dollar note. He handed it to Hosea Grimm. "I presume you can make change for this?"

Grimm took a step back, and a knowing, deviant smile crept across his face. Without saying anything, he removed four quarters from his trouser pocket and handed them to Theodulf. Then he took the bottle, uncapped it, and let one pill fall onto his own palm. "Take it immediately. Drink as much water as your stomach will allow, then drink more." He capped the bottle, put it back in his breast pocket, and concluded, "There's no such thing as too much water, do you understand, Keeper Sauer? You could drink the lake, and it wouldn't hurt you." Now he handed Theodulf the single, chalky placebo. "Godspeed. For you and for all of us. May the good Lord have mercy on us all."

"Bless you," Theodulf said as he walked away.

SHE'D FELT IT BEFORE, sitting in front of certain pianos—the Mason & Hamlin at Fay House in Cambridge, the Steinway grand in the lobby of the Thibert Hotel. A volcanic urgency; the need to make sound. So it was with her hand on Silje's shoulder, ushering her up to the second floor.

As they passed the landing window, Willa noted a string of guests marching back down to the dock. She could still hear the brass band playing a waltz, but it was melancholy and distant. Their final song of the afternoon. She hadn't been revived by the party, as she thought she might. Rather, it felt like the rest of her summer would suffer for the absence of these guests.

The girl stomped a gauntlet. A rousing of anger and fear and fortitude. The lithe but firm muscles under her dress quivered as they entered Willa's room. Silje immediately went to the window and cast the curtain aside.

"Looking for Mr. Grimm?" Willa said.

Though she couldn't see Silje's face, she did notice the way her shoulders hunched and flexed. She might even have heard a hiss.

"Men like him, they're under every stone. You've got an instinct for detecting them. That's the good news."

Silje spun around to face her. "Frog's just like him."

"Frog acts like he has the world on a string, but that string is just the tightrope he walks. Mr. Sauer is nothing at all like Hosea Grimm, who would use my husband's string to strangle you."

This assessment did nothing to ease Silje's ire. She crossed her arms and could hardly gain control of her breath.

Her posture gave Willa courage. "What I say's true, but I'm glad you won't hear it. I'm glad you know better."

214

She opened her closet and pulled out the steamer trunk and glanced at her small friend, whose interest was piqued, no doubt recalling the music box she'd been introduced to last time the trunk appeared in her life.

"I see you're embroiled in your own mulligrubs, but I want to tell you a few things."

"What're mulligrubs?"

"My father loved that word. It means you're in a foul mood." She slid the trunk around and unlatched the top. "He was a very good man, my father was. The best. He taught me a few lessons I'll never forget," Willa said. She knelt by the trunk. "You already know most of what he taught me, that much is clear. But on one subject I want to make sure you've heard it plainly, and from a friend." She got to the false bottom and removed the Smith & Wesson, rising and holding it behind her back before Silje might see.

"My father told me there are three types of men in this world. First, the good-hearted. People like your uncle. Like my father himself. Though of course he'd never have classified himself so. These are the folks who put the welfare of others above their own. Folks whose first instinct is to goodness and kindness. There aren't many men like this, and fewer all the time. Their rarity is a consequence of this nation. So my father always said."

Silje must have recognized something in Willa's speech, because she took a few tentative steps across room and sat down on the edge of the bed. She clenched her hands before her as if she had a miracle to pray for.

"The majority of men, he thought, are weak-hearted. These folks suffer for want of conviction, but not because they lack morality and not because they're cruel. They're wayward, is all."

Now Willa swung the pistol from behind her back and sighted it on the wall sconce. "The worst are the rotten-hearted," she continued, closing one eye and resting the heel of her right hand in the palm of her left. She took two deep breaths and then feigned a shot. "These are corrupted men like Hosea Grimm. They're without morals or scruples, they abhor weakness and see it as something to conquer. Which is why that man made *you* feel corruptible." She lowered the gun and looked thoughtfully at Silje, whose attention was whole now. "He plays the learned citizen. Probably he goes to church and attends town meetings. He can't fathom a world that doesn't orbit around him. Often the world *does*. And yet, in his soul is a vile impulse. One that commands his true nature. He is depraved and libidinous. Naturally he is. But he's also charitable, though when he gives alms or offers shelter, it's never without thought of remuneration. All of this is bad enough, but worst still—worst of *all*—is that he doesn't see any of this. He truly believes his position is ordained. He believes God chose him. Even if he doesn't actually believe in God himself."

Silje unclenched her hands and turned them palms up and gazed upon them as if written there was further explanation.

Willa crossed to her, stood just out of reach.

"That's your Mr. Grimm. To be sure, there are others like him. Many others. But of all the rotten-hearted men I've met, he's the most warped and the most malignant."

"Why?"

"He will risk everything, that's why. He will risk everything and not believe he's risking anything at all."

Silje shifted, gave Willa her full attention. "How do you know about Hosea Grimm? Have you met him before?"

"He's the sort of man who thinks he's above judgment, so he knows no bounds."

"What should I do the next time someone like Hosea Grimm stalks me?"

Willa stepped across the room and handed her the pistol, mother-of-pearl stock first. "Do you know how to use one of these?" she asked.

SEVENTH SUNDAY

MAY 15, 1900

At the Paris Universal Exposition of 1900, one of the preeminent attractions was the great telescope. Dreamed up by François Deloncle, a diplomat whose vision was inspired by fame, to be sure, but also, as was then reported, by a desire to "Bring the celestial bodies almost to our doors."

The telescope was built by the L'Optique Company over the span of some eight years, and, when finished, was housed in the Palais de l'Optique on the Champ de Mars. The interchangeable lenses were more than four feet in diameter, the scope itself some 190 feet long and encased in a two-hundred-foot steel tube. The greatest and most famous glassmaker in all the world performed the nine-months-long task of creating the mirror. It would be two meters wide, by far the largest of its sort ever constructed. It was said of such a grand telescope that it would capture *la lune à un mètre.*

Alas, the moon cannot be captured. Especially by a telescope that had no practical functionality. True, a few scant images were captured by the telescope before the L'Optique Company filed for bankruptcy in 1909 and dismantled their creation. Among those images are three photogravures taken by Charles Le Morvan, who is sometimes considered the third author of Loewy and Puiseux's *Atlas of the Moon.*

Some years ago, I saw those photogravures at the Met. If they didn't bring the moon within a meter, they're certainly among the most evocative images I've ever beheld. Especially plate 7, the image of Mare Crisium. On clearest nights, I can sometimes still see it.

Pentecost—the ides of May.

Only the day before he'd disembarked at Le Havre and taken the train to Gare d'Orsay, and already he found himself in penitent silence, shadowed by the arches in Notre-Dame cathedral for the second time. Last evening, unable to rest and not hungry, he'd attended vespers. Now it was Whitsunday, and he gazed out the midday rose as the priest in his sanguine vestments preached from the high altar. "Deus, a quo bona cuncta procédunt largíre supplícibus tuis: ut cogítemus, te inspírante, quæ relta sunt; et, te gubernánte, eádem faciámus . . ." These masses he knew by rote if not by heart. He could as much as envisage his father's casuistry at Sacred Heart under *its* stained glass and Latin mass, praying not for the deliverance of his son's soul, but for his own ascension. In this life and the next.

Theodulf had no prayers himself. Only an overwhelming gratitude for being so far from the familial clutch, and the vestigial guilt that had trailed him across the Atlantic. He'd not pray for forgiveness because he needed none. He'd not pray for his father's because he deserved none. His mother required no prayer herself. Her salvation was predestined.

Trumpets blared. The epistle was read. Theodulf cast a curious gaze at the congregation. The women wore divine dresses, the men bowties and pointed collars. He was cravat-less himself, opting instead for a loose-fitting tailcoat, a silken paisley scarf, and an edelweiss boutonnière in his lapel.

All those people, and none of them familiar. They only welcomed him by virtue of his faith and his fine clothes. Father Richter had as much as commanded him to attend service while abroad, imploring him to use those days to find two things: purity of soul and calmness of mind. On the matter of his soul, Theodulf had no expectations. But as for calmness of mind, certainly the image of the last judgment in stained glass hanging above him helped. It was a gorgeous kaleidoscope of suffering and vindication, backlit by the cold Parisian sun, and it helped him believe the sublime was not only possible but all around him.

Surrounded by his acolytes, the priest sang the greater alleluia. The congregation sang back, and all was further well. Theodulf felt the kindness of the Lord just then. Felt love for his mother and even contemplated forgiveness for his father. Really, what choice had he had than to send him away? To ask him, his only son, to search his soul. The whole history of salvation was predicated on God the father sacrificing *His* only son, so oughtn't Theodulf accept his earthly fate with as much contrition?

What was it his father had said, as he put Theodulf on the eastbound train in St. Paul just a fortnight ago? "You've deceived yourself, Theodulf. Into believing your unnatural urges are more powerful than your *true* nature. Than the one God has in mind for you. Than the one I've instilled in you. Go find that true nature in Paris. Bring it back home with you, and you can start over as my son."

The whole train ride to New York, then the first half of the ocean voyage, Theodulf had pondered his own rebirth. But since a rainy night in the North Atlantic, unable to sleep for the tumultuous seas and hopelessness of becoming someone new, he'd given up the idea of returning as anyone other than the man perched in that ocean liner's berth. Each moment since, he'd become more and more right with himself. Or so he thought. What remained was the irreconcilability of life with his father.

The priest was now reading from the gospel of John. "Amen, amen, dico vobis: si quid petiéritis Patrem in nómine meo, dabit vobis. Usque modo non petístis quicquam in nómine meo: Pétite, et accipiétis, ut gáudium vestrum sit plenum . . ."

Theodulf had been raised on the Latin mass, and what Latin

he'd once known was residual of those endless readings from the good book. Those sermons Father Richter spoke from the pulpit at Sacred Heart. But here in the grand cathedral, the newly inflected words found him differently. And barely. What had the priest just read of the gospel? "If you ask the Father anything in My name, He will give it to you"?

What had his own father ever gifted to him? Of all the things Theodulf had asked for—love, kindness, acceptance, autonomy— Ernst had given none. It had never occurred to him to ask the Lord God for anything, not even for as often as he'd been implored to pray. Would *He* grant love or kindness?

Theodulf folded his hands and relegated the priest's voice to the background of his thoughts. He turned again to the midday rose and tried to believe the kaleidoscopic light shining through was holy indeed. He sought the questions he might ask of the blueness, and found only one: "Is there such a thing as happiness for me?"

It stunned him, his query did. Not because he'd never wondered it before, but because he'd never done so here in the House of God. Had he *ever* been happy? Days of boyhood innocence? Abiding friendships? Romantic liaisons that he could recall fondly? That weren't, in fact, torturous for one reason or another? Were there moments of great intuition or inspiration at Notre Dame or Princeton? Moments when the rigor of his studies led to a kind of happiness for the knowledge it came with? Or, before that, summer days spent romping through fair breezes with his chums? Fishing or hunting or playing ice polo? What of his early childhood on the Detroit River, galivanting through the pear orchard or the shipyards with his grandfather as his guide? He supposed those days were as close as he'd ever come to happiness

What about further back? His childhood proper? Before his twisted nature awoke? He could smile recalling whist and checkers games against his mother at their house in Agate Bay. There was a vestige of happiness in the recollection of rolling out the bread dough with her. Her sweet voice commending him for his gentle touch. They sang together, but what songs, he could not now recall.

The priest was singing the communion psalm. The midday rose darkened, and Theodulf closed his eyes. He was back on the Agate Bay docks. Thirteen years old. An uncommon nightfall of shooting stars and sweltering heat. A fever dark. Two men. One in stevedore's garb, the other dressed like his father in a cutaway frock suit, passed a jug. Their banter was foul and drunken and when they reached the lee of a freighter they found a resting place among a stash of hogsheads.

How could it be that what Theodulf saw next arose in him *here*, in the cathedral, while he tried to recall happiness? The thought of those men—undressing, their tongues wagging, coalescing—disgusted him. So much he nearly wretched. Now, not then. Then, he was happy. Simply.

Rather than joining the communion line, he turned for the exit. He rushed up the main aisle, crossed the labyrinth carved in stone, then out the main entrance. Crossing the courtyard before the cathedral, he turned his closed eyes heavenward. Should he open them to the blinding sun? Would he be sounder of mind if he went purblind? Would those memories disappear with his sight?

Crossing the Petit Pont, he looked back at the cathedral. Shielding against the sun with his hand, he thought, *nothing is sacred.*

He followed the plowing barges on the Seine. At a boulangerie on Quai Voltaire, he stopped for a croissant and coffee, as though filling his stomach might empty his mind. He carried his breakfast back across the river and sat beneath a bur oak in the Jardin des Tuileries. And it did have some effect, his petit dejeuner. The garden also began to fill. Those same Parisians who'd knelt beside him in the cathedral were now taking their Sunday constitutionals. So many parasols. So many bonnets and nacre-handled walking canes. He wished desperately to be among them and, equally, to be apart.

So, he crossed back over the river a third time, pausing on the Pont de la Concorde. From that vantage he caught his first sight of the famed tower. Erect against the distant plains, soaring. It fairly astounded him for its beauty. Better, it removed every other thought from his mind.

He hurried now toward the fairgrounds. Toward that clearness. Past Les Invalides. Past the apartments and hotels and the Gare d'Orsay, from where he'd first entered the city. Then onto an esplanade with a quarter mile, unimpeded view of the Eiffel Tower. People rode past him on bicycles and in hansom cabs. Droves of them. Their laughter and calls on the late morning air like so many cheerful birds. He was anonymous again, which was a relief unto itself. But even more, he had vacated the rotten chambers of his mind and found himself back in a world of possibility and peace.

Soon he was standing beneath the tower itself, staring up at the filigree of steel that scintillated in the sun. Like a crystal. Like a portal, it seemed. And not to Heaven, but rather—and staunchly—to earth itself. To something very much like happiness indeed!

The crowds passed with yet more gaiety. Children held their parents' hands; a jester danced by, juggling lit torches; a troupe of mimes performed for a circle of onlookers; and beyond that crowd, another, watching an acrobat perform a tumbling routine. Buskers put their music on the air. Clarinets and flutes and the *tap-tap-tap* of a snare drum. Tambourines. Moving onto the Champs du Mars, he saw a man on a penny-farthing riding alongside a monkey on a leash. He saw two regal borzois, also on leashes, walking like show horses across the grounds. Their master wore gold epaulettes that rained silk down the shoulders of his hussar jacket. He marched as though leading a regiment, and when one of the dogs stopped to shit, the commandant turned his nose back to the Eiffel Tower and waited on the hound. They left the steaming pile of dung in the middle of the path.

Theodulf hurried past it, and into a tunnel of food vendors. The air was soaked with sweet and savory smells. Onion and garlic from a creperie. Skewered poulet grilling on an open fire. The sweet, hot smell of beignets boiling in oil. It was almost enough to make him hungry again.

It had been his intention to visit first the Palais de l'Optique, but how to discern which of the myriad edifices was it? Lining both sides of the Champs de Mars were castle-like buildings. Opposite the Eiffel Tower, the Château d'Eau loomed behind its fountains. The opulence appealed to him, even if he was bewildered by the scope of it all.

He'd come full circle, orbiting the grounds for a half hour before arriving back where he'd started, but facing the opposite direction. The Palais de l'Optique beckoned from his left in the shadow of the tower, perhaps the grandest of all the architecture. The stonework appeared carved from Languedoc limestone, and it was capped with latticework as intricate as the queen's diadem. Dozens of columns ran the length of the palace, which must have measured a full thirty roods.

Theodulf joined the queue. Hundreds of people, each as unsuspecting and guileless as the next. Every moment among them relieved him further of the morning's dark thoughts. So much so that by the time he'd crossed the cordoned hall, the day's earlier searching seemed never to have occurred at all.

As he reached the entrance, an attendant handed him a brochure with an image of the Palais de l'Optique printed on it. Inside were several drawings and a description of what wonders awaited in the exhibition. He read absentmindedly as he entered. The midday sun shone luminously through the skylights in the domed ceiling above, each of the twelve signs of the zodiac occupying a different panel. To the left, the Hall of Mirrors called. On the right, the Grand Lunette Room. But running the length of the hall, protected by a wrought-iron railing, the foremost attraction: Le Grand Télescope de l'Exposition de Paris. This is what he'd read about in *Harper's*. That article had provided the main statistics regarding the telescope: that it was considerably more powerful than any telescope that had ever been created previously; that the tube was in excess of two hundred feet long; that the movable plane mirror was nigh seven feet in diameter; that it had taken nine months simply to grind the glass for the siderostat mirror; and that, most intriguingly, it was practically useless as an astronomical instrument given its location in the Palais.

He waited for the telescope line to move forward, peering around those before him. With no view yet in sight, he turned his attention back to the brochure and read about the telescope. Something about the moon and meteorology and earthly affairs, his French had lain mostly dormant since he'd read George Sand in a literature course at college. He persisted, though, the line still little moving. Something about the globe and the tides and Greenwich. He looked about, hoping to find a more complete translation in the air!

With redoubled attention, he turned again to the page: Mais la plus importante raison que nous ayons de nous intéresser à la lune, c'est que l'observation de cet aster mort nous aide à reconstituer la genèse de notre globe et à conjecturer ses destinées. *Conjecture its destiny*? Whose destiny? Was destiny in fact a thing to consider?

He looked at his hands—the hands of a thirty-year-old man—and saw them soft as a child's, his nails newly filed. For all his anguish, his labored thought, his capricious fealty to God, to say nothing of his own earthly father, he'd hardly ever considered his *destiny*. Was it a thing to manifest oneself? Or was it something the moon—that dead star!—served?

The line moved. He stood now at the ocular lens end of the scope, staring down the length of the tube. Not naturally predisposed to understand how an instrument like this worked, he dwelled instead on the new question that had taken root. But what if he could turn the telescope on his own destiny? Gazing into the future, he thought: What would happiness look like? Freedom from indignity and self-doubt, for one. Freedom from his father's wretched hold another. Simple and unadulterated faith in God. Prayers that came as easily as the self-recrimination did. A contented city life. Meaningful friendships. Love.

This last startled him. On what basis did he think he'd one day *love*? He hardly knew what it was. Surely the night that set his fall in motion, he'd been hounding it. *Love.* Or at least its gnarled cousin *desire.* The two had always confused him for their likeness. That husband and wife in the Thibert Hotel, feeding each other smoked whitefish and sturgeon roe, inviting him to join their repast. They'd looked at him as though he were a toy. And he'd relished it. Was excited by it and desirous of their company. By the time they convinced him to adjourn to their room, he'd convinced himself they were many things, not least fond of him. Or even more. Their expressions promised something more, certainly. Something he mistook for fondness. Which, he hoped, could grow into friendship. And then love. So eager was Theodulf for this cascade of eventualities, he offered to pay for dinner. He'd ordered another bottle of champagne for the occasion of midnight. He'd even given the man his own cufflinks.

How pathetic, that he didn't know enough to see their delusive intentions. No. It was worse even than that. He'd understood them very well, in fact, and *still* his wishful thinking prevailed. Talk about dead stars!

And *destiny*? Even in Paris—even among the conviviality of the fairgoers—even given his ease—even given the freedom of his thoughts and the world of possibility here at the exposition—even despite all this he could hardly comprehend it. Was it preordained? His future? His earthly fate?

Certainly, he could never have imagined how things would unfold. How, a decade hence, he'd be stationed at a remote lighthouse station, married to a petulant bundle of incorrigibility and arrogance, surrounded by nincompoops, still under the thumb of his implacable father, chewing on a pill most surely provided by a charlatan, fearful of the end-times, studying a young girl holding his wife's own telescope, without any better vantage on a future and with a further past only more obscured by failure and faithlessness.

Would he be able to see, then, in the night, with benefit of the light, overlooking the lake, something like the destiny he spent the rest of that seventh Sunday in Paris pondering? Or would what unfolded in the following twelve hours be his blinding curse?

THE SERPENT'S TAIL

MAY 19, 1910

"Comets are vile stars," the seventh-century astronomer Li Ch'un Feng wrote in his treatise, Record of the World's Change. He believed they foretold doom.

What philosopher—from Eratosthenes to Azophi to Copernicus to Galileo or a hundred others, a thousand—has not studied some celestial object with an eye on its vileness? And how have their studies not brought us closer to wisdom? Is there none to be found? Is all of the ever after just a void?

Was it Job, patient and wise and humble all, who said, "He stretcheth out the north over empty space and hangeth the earth upon nothing"?

It was. And was he not as right as any of our great stargazing philosophers?

Do I abhor them? Those celebrated cosmologists? Of course not. There's beauty in what they see, and what they pretend to know. I feel a great affection for them, in fact. How many times have I tried to trace the ellipse of some consciousness, only to find myself on the dark side of the moon? Too many to count. In this way we're not unalike. I'm sure they took as much pleasure in the exploration as I ever did.

And anyways, it's not those who seek wisdom that we ought to worry about, but men who, like the ancient priests of Greece and Egypt and China, hold their certainty with righteous zeal. They are the true foils of an enlightened age.

S HE LEFT THE HOUSE at four o'clock in the morning and walked up the scorched hillside. A mile from the station she roamed, so she could stand in the peace of darkness on this momentous night. The sun would rise in two hours, but already it threatened the horizon beneath the lake. The stars, they fell like snow.

A stagnant silence greeted her up there. With no trees to stir, it was just the night and a faint breeze that met her. All the darkness hung the same. It could have been the desert but for the ferns just softening with springtime. They tickled her ankles, kept her company in the night.

According to her calculations, the comet would appear in the east, before the moonset, through the constellation of Virgo. She carried only the telescope and a piece of lighthouse stationery and pencil. The pencil was stuck in her hair, which was in a bun.

A mile below her now, the swoosh of the lighthouse beam skimmed the lake ten seconds at a time. It was all enough to make a young woman dizzy.

Theodulf crossed her mind. On watch that night. Oblivious of everything but the fear she'd invoked for him—privately, wishfully— and which that quack Hosea Grimm had corroborated. If she felt guilty about it, it was a feeling as short in lasting as the last gentle breeze. And it made as little impression.

There were other feelings short in lasting, too. Ones less easy to identify. Feelings that seemed at once to be orbiting her as the comet did the earth, and emanating from her with each breath she took. She kept reaching for it and catching nothing. Another breath. And another.

Her breathing leveled there on the hilltop. A chill sent a shiver through her. And then a yawn. Behind her, inland, the wilderness ran into profane umbras. Welcoming. She'd never gone out in the woods alone. Not at night. But if she hadn't the comet to hold her on the ferny hill, she'd have run farther. Or liked to think she would.

Even that simple thought—that boastful urge—aroused in her another ache. She freed one hand, pressed it against her belly. The effect was like throwing a bole onto a fire. She reached lower, pressed again. Infernal. Lower still.

There. The font of that elusive fervor she'd soon know as desire.

But first she sat, hoping to collect herself. She lay her telescope in the ferns, pulled her knees up to her chest, and rested her chin atop her folded hands. The next two things happened almost at once. First, the howling of wolves, which came from the woods behind her. She felt their grumble in the soles of her feet even before she recognized what that baleful sound augured. They sang beautifully. Musically. And she kept her eyes tightly shut until they paused. When they did, she looked up. The comet had appeared precisely where she predicted it would. Rising before the rest of star-bright horizon.

It dawned first as a minor moon. Bright, unwieldy, and zipping like a misfit at a party, already cockeyed on champagne. But as she watched, the light of its nucleus sharpened. The tail, too, became less wild the longer it got. Like champagne being poured under a chandelier, it caught and held the light above it.

She watched it for a long time, marveling at how far away it had been. And yet still was! What a thing to know. And to witness.

Its arc lasted longer than the rest of the night. She watched it until it disappeared in the light of dawn, then hurried back down the hillside, headed for the station.

Sweat trickled down her neck as she stood above the cutting board chopping onions and carrots and parsnips. She already had a pot of steaming water on the stove. The fish Mats had delivered just a half hour earlier lay in cutlets on the table behind her, ready for the soup. He'd brought them as offering. Payment for the haircut he'd arranged with Theodulf.

She'd found less pleasure than she anticipated leading up to this supposedly fateful night. Theodulf's mood—which she expected to be hysterical—was stoical. Even calm. Standing above Mats out on the lawn, his shears in his fingers, she might have mistaken his expression as one of surrender.

He'd draped pieces of cheesecloth over each of the fisherman's shoulders and stood behind him, one hand resting upon Mats's left shoulder while the other combed his hair. That hair—it had followed him onto the lawn like the mane of a horse.

Willa had to look away. She wasn't sure why, but now there was warmth exuding from her belly as well as the stifling kitchen air.

A knock at the door surprised her, and she dabbed her cheeks with her apron as she went to open it. There stood Mrs. Wilson—Ruth, Willa reminded herself—her braid slung over her shoulder and hanging across her breast, holding a pouch before her.

"What's this?" Willa asked, stepping aside and holding the screen door open. The elder woman's belly strained against her ubiquitous apron, rubbing the back of Willa's hand as she slid past.

"I saw that Mats Braaten bringing his box of fish up here. Knew that meant a kettle of chowder, and what's better in chowder than a passel of sliced mushrooms." She held the pouch up as a child might their favorite amusement.

Willa accepted the pouch, loosened the string, and reached inside for a sample. "Why, these mushrooms are all shriveled up. They'd be tougher than a strip of jerky."

Ruth let out a great laugh. "Bring that pouch in here."

When they stepped into the kitchen, Ruth fairly took over. She took a bowl from the pantry, filled it with water from a pitcher on the board, and emptied the mushrooms into the water. "This is called reconstituting them, young Willa. Soak them for an hour and they'll be ready to julienne." She stirred them with a wooden spoon, pushing the top mushrooms to the bottom. "These were dried last year. They keep this way, rather than going rotten."

Willa stirred the mushroom bath herself now.

"What's more, you'll have yourself a delicious broth from that water there. You put that up in the pantry after the chanterelles are done soaking, and you'll be halfway to pot of beef stew."

"I suppose they'll be all mushy when they come out of the water?"

"And I suppose how soggy they are won't matter much once you add them to the chowder."

Now Ruth went to the window and pushed the curtain aside. "I see your man's no slouch with those barber shears." She motioned for Willa to take a peek. "He's turned our herring choker into a regular old dandy."

It was true, the oft bedraggled Mats Braaten suddenly appeared smart. Almost dapper. The lines of his jaw appeared squarer without his bangs hanging down over his ears. His crown appeared golden, now, too.

"You look out there much longer and we'll have to leash you, young lady."

Ruth let the curtain drop and turned back to the board. "I see you've got your onions and parsnips chopped. Now the mushrooms are soaking." She put a finger to her lip. "Tell me, how do you intend to season this vat of chowder? I hope with more than salt and pepper, yes?"

"I suppose your pantry is plum full of fresh lemon and dill," Willa said, surprised by her own defensiveness. "But unless vinegar or molasses would add something"—she risked a glance at her matron's face—"would molasses or vinegar help?"

"I'm impressed you'd even know to mix lemon and dill and fish!"

"I'm not a cretin! I've eaten at fine restaurants before."

The two women smiled at their easiness together.

Ruth said, "My pantry's as bare as yours or Ida's in the department of fresh herbs. The trick is to make do. It's to be creative. You'd sooner pour a cup of skunk's piss in that soup than a cup of vinegar. But I suspect you have a bit of bacon left in your stores?"

"I'm sure I do."

Ruth waddled around the table and sat so she could see out the window. "This heat, it's enough to drain a woman dry. And in May?"

For a moment Willa panicked at the thought her kitchen tutorial was over, but as soon as she thought it, Ruth began again.

"Bacon'll give it a little smokiness. Another dimension of flavor. And if there's a single thing bacon doesn't make better, I've not met it yet."

"Theodulf's a great fan of it."

"Well, there you have it." She looked at Theodulf and Mats out on the lawn, considering them for a moment. "Here's something true, young Willa: a pot of good soup can change a whole day. A whole week, even. If you change your days and weeks for the better, enough of them, leastways, all of a sudden you've made a good season. If you change enough seasons, well, you get the idea." She spotted something out the window and paused to move the curtain aside. She shook her head. "But it's also true that a good pot of soup is better'n a bad one. As much as for you as for him."

"In Boston, you should have tasted the clam soup."

"Never mind about Boston. You live here at the station now."

Whereas a month ago Ruth's comment might've felt like a judgment, Willa found it now a simple truth.

"And tell me, young Willa, how is life suiting you?"

She joined Ruth at the table, folded her hands across her lap, and sighed. "I'm a long way from where I thought I'd be, but I'll speak true: I believe things are possible here. Mind you, this is no thanks to Theodulf, who remains the churl. But I've struck up a strange friendship with the Lindvik girl, I have a resplendent view on the sky at night, and for as many hours as I've spent regarding the horizon, I'm relieved to find it never gets any closer. And now I'll have bacon in my broth!" At the thought, she realized she'd not yet added it. "I'm so easily distracted here in the kitchen! Escort me down to the dock to fetch some?"

"What a lovely idea." Ruth wedged herself up, but took one more look out the window before they left.

"Maybe it's you who need a leash," Willa ventured.

Without turning around, Ruth said, "I'm just wondering if part of your contentedness here has to do with the man whose hair your husband just trimmed."

It hadn't occurred to Willa that Mats Braaten was anything more than the girl's uncle, but she spent the rest of that sultry spring day thinking as much about his face framed in the window as she did the promise of the comet's final pass coming later that night. That the latter had almost completely slipped her mind troubled her more than the former.

After they'd been down to the dock for the bacon, and after she'd returned to the kitchen and fried it up, and after she'd put the rest of the fixings into the pot and written Theodulf a note saying the soup would be ready by noon, and that he should put the leftovers in the cellar, Willa saw Ruth out, went up to her trunk to fetch her copy of *The Moon* (the one masquerading as a Douay-Rheims bible), and changed into her chambray shirt, thinking she'd go down to the lake and spend an hour reading while the soup simmered and she waited for the girl. Silje would accompany Willa to Otter Bay after lunch.

Once down there, she sat on a stool outside the boathouse and paged through her book, looking specifically for the chapter that dealt with the topography of the moon's surface. As she recalled from previous studies, it was the authors' contention that most of the features of that topography were the consequence of volcanic activity, a theory Willa refuted more and more as this season of watching the comet neared its end. How many hours had she spent in the early mornings since she arrived here, shifting her gaze between the moon and the comet, imagining them colliding? Too many to count. But a hypothesis had formed, one she hadn't been aware of until Ruth mentioned Mats Braaten's fairness.

She blushed to realize it. But even as she did, she felt that once regular thrill of discovery take hold. She'd only just opened the book to chapter VIII when she heard a whistle and looked up to see him coming down the path, his own chambray shirt unbuttoned at the neck, the fishbox empty and hanging from his left hand.

He startled to see her. "Why, hello there, Mrs. Sauer."

"Mr. Braaten," she said, shielding the warm sun with her book.

"You've picked a fine spot to study the good book."

She lowered the bible, embarrassed what he saw. "Oh!" she said quickly. "This is all a part of my ruse." She stood and took a step closer to him, thought for a flitting moment about whether or not she should divulge her secret, then decided she simply couldn't have him believing she was the sort of woman who'd waste a lovely day reading the gospels. "You see, Theodulf isn't one for . . . what, *learning,* I guess. But I am. I don't say that to sound uppity, but it's true I've a natural inclination to the sciences. And this"—she opened the book to one of the images printed in the book—"is no bible at all, but one of my college textbooks *impersonating* the good book."

He tilted his head up and looked down on the page before him. "College, you say?"

"Likely you've never a met a woman who attended?"

"I most certainly have not."

"You sound as if you're rather frightened by the mere notion of it."

"No, ma'am. On the contrary, I'm intrigued."

Had he meant to sound so arch? Had the look on his newly un-framed and longer-now jawline actually bitten down on his own words? Had the thought stirred in her an altogether brand-new feeling? One that reached down to the very bottom of her belly? She couldn't wait for the answers to this litany of spontaneous questions. She must talk! "Radcliffe. In Cambridge. Near Boston."

"You're a long way from there, Mrs. Sauer."

"I said the same thing to Ruth less than an hour ago."

"I imagine it sometimes feels impossibly far away."

This turn to wistfulness, it suited him. "Sometimes," she admitted.

Now Mats kicked at the stones beneath his boots. A moment of silence passed before they spoke simultaneously. Mats said, "I understand you're taking Silje to Otter Bay" while Willa said, "Mr. Sauer did a fine job with your trim."

They laughed at once, too, then both fell silent for a moment.

"It's okay I take her? She asked to join me."

"She thinks the sun rises on you."

"Well, the feeling's mutual."

Mats ran his hand through his hair. "I reckon I'll go find Silje. Let her know you're ready to row." His teeth shimmered in sunlight when he smiled.

"Before you go, tell me how she's doing? From what you see, I mean."

He moved his hand from his hair to his nape and held it there. "Silje's about as temperamental as this doggone lake. And I'm nearly as daft. But she's holding her own. And helping out in the fish house like she never did before." He finally took his hand off his neck and put it in his pocket instead. "I take her wanting to go to Otter Bay with you as a good sign."

Willa stood and said, "Speak of the devil."

Mats turned around to see his niece. "You could stalk a ghost, the way you quiet around."

Silje came up and stood beside him. "You don't hear the kettle whistling at dawn," she said. Then to Willa, "Shall we?"

"We shall." Willa stepped inside the boathouse to stash her book, then faced Mats once more. "Thank you for the fish."

"Fish is one thing I've plenty of," he said, then walked away with his hat in his back pocket.

STANDING IN THE LANTERN ROOM, tying the linen apron behind his back, Theodulf feared the heat was from the comet's poisonous tail. He'd been imagining it arriving like smoke from a fire or fog off the lake, but maybe, as with all the great mysteries, it had come without any form at all.

Something trickled down his neck, under the collar of his shirt. It startled him for a moment—as though the poison were aqueous— before he realized he was sweating. And not only on his neck but from his whole body. Even the buff-skin in his hand was damp. He set it on one of the lens prisms, unknotted his tie and unbuttoned his collar, and rolled up his sleeves. He took the buff-skin back up and began cleaning the lens. One panel of glass at a time.

That suppleness in his hand! He rubbed absently between each prism, the softness delivering him to a half hour earlier, Mats Braaten's flaxen hair between his fingers. The tines of his comb pressed into the flesh of his palm had done the job of keeping him alert to the task at hand. But without their bite, who could say what ghastly slip he might have made? That softness—it carried him as far away as Paris. As far away as Paul. Paul, whose shoulders were no match for the fisherman's, upon which Theodulf had laid cheesecloth to catch the clippings.

There he was now. Mr. Braaten. Down by the boathouse talking to Willa, who would soon be making the mail run.

Her impropriety knew no limits, and if he were honest with himself, standing there, buffing the lens, he would admit that he as much as wanted her dead. Not because he hated her or thought her deserving of such an unkind fate, but because the absence of her would put his mind considerably more at ease.

He turned his gaze to the horizon above the hills, expecting any moment the annihilating vapors. He abhorred the indignity of anticipation.

What were they discussing, anyway? It'd be one thing to say a hello in passing, quite another to spend a full five minutes on the shore like they were old friends. Was it possible she desired him? Or him her? The mere notion stoked a bitter resentment, as though the heat of the day had found a kiln in his bowels and was being rekindled there. But that heat was duplicitous, he realized as soon his guts began simmering. He hated them; and he wanted to fuck.

He put his hand to his sweaty throat and watched them down there. He tried to imagine them falling over dead. Just toppling. Them and everyone while he rode the antidote prescribed by Hosea Grimm.

Would the world be a better place without the lot of them? Would he be a happier man? He turned away grudgingly, knowing he'd sooner satisfy his desire than answer the impossible question. The water spreading to the horizon fractured the blazing sun. He stared upon it, intent to blind himself. Alas, he did not, and before another ten minutes passed, what sailed into his view was the lighthouse tender, his damned wife on the oars. A Thursday mail run.

Now he felt something even deeper than the cauldron in his gut. A simple question. Was he a fool?

Silje lay across the stern sheets, her head resting on the gunwale, trailing her hand in the water. Occasionally she brought her fingers up to her face to let cold droplets fall on her lips.

"You'll be sun-kissed red if you don't put that bonnet on," Willa said.

"It's too hot."

"Better to be warm out here on the water than to cook all night in bed."

Silje sat up and put her feet on the burden boards and dipped her tin cup into the lake, bringing it out and taking a long draught before dipping it again and offering it to Willa, who paused in her rowing, drank it down, and handed it back.

"That was thoughtful," Willa said.

Silje shrugged, remembering how her mother had trained her to help when she could. Her mother would also have demanded she wear her bonnet. So, Silje removed it from her pocket and donned it and tied it beneath her chin.

"You'll be glad of that choice," Willa said.

Silje shrugged again.

"What's troubling you?"

"I saw Fenrir again this morning. That makes twice in the last week."

"I'd be right shaken if I thought a wolf was following me around."

Silje thought to say, "There are wolves all around," but didn't. Instead, she said, "I wish we were going to Two Harbors or Gunflint instead of Otter Bay."

"Oh?"

Willa had an even, almost elegant stroke at the oars. Her narrow

239

shoulders and thin arms belied a strength that revealed itself as the boat scudded across the flat water.

When she didn't offer more, Silje added, "I would like to eat in a café."

This apparently delighted Willa, who smiled mischievously. "I made a pot of soup today and all I thought the whole time I was at it is that I wished to be at the Palm, eating beef bourguignon with my father."

"What's beef bourguignon?"

"Oh, it's a delectable dish. A stew, more or less. But not the kind you're used to. Beef bourguignon has wine and mushrooms. It simmers with a bouquet garni. There are onions galore. And bacon. My mouth waters just thinking about it."

"What's the Palm?"

"The Palm Dining Room in the Spalding Hotel. My father would take me there sometimes. Just the two of us."

"Your father, he's kind?"

"My father's like yours, Silje."

"Gone?"

"Gone."

Silje dipped the tin cup into the lake again, but sipped it this time as if it were a hot cup of tea. "When did he go?"

She could see Willa counting back, the expression of astonishment that it didn't take long. "It's been less than a year. Eight months only."

"Eight months seems like a long time," Silje said.

"Yes. It certainly does."

By the time they rounded the headland Silje called Lisbon Rock, she'd fallen back into her own thoughts. Of the wolf, mostly, whose pawprints she'd seen so many of lately in the peat behind their cabin. That day, while she stood on the back stoop tossing out the dishwater after breakfast, she noticed a shift in the shadowy trees. A twitch, really. Down in the deadfall and just-greening forest floor. He sat as was becoming his custom: his teeth pointing from his black lips, on his haunches, his back toward her, his tail twitching, looking over his left shoulder through the birch-colored fur of his coat. His black eye could have been a knot in the tree he sat beside, so still was he.

Her feeling about the wolf had changed since her encounter with Hosea Grimm just more than a week ago. Whereas before Fenrir had seemed like an aloof, occasional pet, she now saw his teeth as weapons. When she daydreamed about him, his claws always arrived first, leaping into her consciousness out of nowhere.

That morning, behind the cabin, he made no movement at all. Not even when Silje banged on the pot and shouted at him. So, she left instead. Turned back into the kitchen and finished her chores, and when she cracked the door and checked for him again ten minutes later, he was gone. Even if that spot among the base of the birch trees seemed darker for his having been there.

"What do you think's a wolf's favorite thing to eat is?"

"Well, not beef bourguignon," Willa said, smiling at her cleverness.

"Moose, is what I think."

"I've heard that. Why do you ask?"

Silje took a drink from the tin cup. "Just wondering."

Willa sculled on. They passed the Black Granite Brook, halfway to Otter Bay, and Silje could see the smoke now from the mill in town. What she didn't tell her friend is that ever since she'd been cornered by Hosea on the day of the grand opening jubilee, ever since that dread feeling had swamped her, she'd declared that she would trap Fenrir. She would trap him and train him and use him as a weapon. This trip to Otter Bay was the first step toward that outcome. It was also her chance to fire a salvo at that sinister old apothecary, in the form of the letter she felt for in her dress pocket.

She'd written it that morning, after her uncle went out fishing. Calling up all her scant learning, she'd taken pencil to paper in the fish house. So carefully had she considered and planned the missive, staying up most of the night before thinking about it, she'd committed it to memory.

To mister Grim, I am an expert with knifes. I can carve chain links from a birch log. I can gouge a wolfs teeth so you'd see each one like you were in its mouth. I tell you this because you should know if you ever come near me again.

I should also tell you I know a wolf. A wild one. I will sic him on you if you ever come close to me again. Fenrir can kill you with his mean stare alone.

Also if you ever do anything awful to my friend Odd, or to Rebeca, I will bring Fenrir to Gunflint even if I have to walk all the way there.

So do not ever come here again. Do not ever touch my shoulder again.

~Silje Lindvik

"You look mad enough to spit, Silje. Did I say something wrong?"

Silje looked at Willa, still rowing, sweat dampening the hair which earlier had hung in gossamer curls around her eyes. "You didn't say anything wrong. I'm not mad. Not at you."

"Well, good." She feathered the oars, removed her own bonnet, used a kerchief to wipe the sweat from her brow. The tender came to rest in the calm waters, just fifty yards offshore. "It's not supposed to be this hot."

Silje filled the cup again and handed it to Willa.

"You're a regular saloonkeeper. Thank you." She drank the water and rolled her sleeves past her elbows. She put the oars back in the water and steered them for Otter Bay. "Would you tell me something?" Willa ventured.

Silje looked up from beneath her bonnet.

"Why doesn't your uncle have a wife?"

Now Silje felt her unwilling smile. "Why do you want to know?"

"It's such an improper and impertinent question. I'm sorry."

"My mother wondered the same thing. I think he knew he had to take care of us. It was as good as being married, having her for a sister."

They rowed the rest of the way in easy silence. Willa brought the boat ashore and, after Silje stepped out, hauled it up the gravel beach.

"We should tend to our letters first," Willa said, shielding the sun with her hand and checking the post office hut on the hillside. "Mr. Holzer keeps scant hours."

Together they walked across the beach and up onto the quay. Inside, Arnold Holzer sat behind his counter, reading a folded newspaper that sat in a square of sunlight.

"Here's an unnatural pair of birds," he said.

"Not so unnatural," Willa said. "And certainly not birds."

Without rejoinder, Mr. Holzer reached into the box designated for the lighthouse and removed the letters, which Willa accepted and stashed in her handbag. The slots designated for Silje's family and her uncle were empty.

"Nothing for you, Miss Lindvik."

She removed from her pocket the letter she'd scribed. "I need to send this to the apothecary in Gunflint," she said, laying the folded piece of paper on the counter.

Mr. Holzer opened a drawer beneath the counter and removed an envelope. He dipped his pen in an inkwell and handed it to Silje. "Address here," he pointed to the center of the envelope, "and return address here," he pointed to the upper left-hand corner.

Silje carefully addressed the envelope and stuffed the letter inside.

"Two cents to send," he said.

Silje reached into her pocket, beneath the folded dollar bills, and removed a handful of coins. She pinched two copper pennies onto the counter. "When will the letter arrive?"

"Next boat's tomorrow," Mr. Holzer said. To Willa he added, "Anything else, Mrs. Sauer?"

"Not today."

"Well, then." He returned to his newspaper and concluded, "Give my regards to your husband."

* * *

After leaving the post office, they walked up and over the bridge and to Winkler's Dry Goods. If such a thing were possible, Silje noted that his round belly had grown even from her last visit a month ago. His joviality seemed to have grown with it.

"If it's not my favorite fisher girl," he said, stepping from his ladder and reaching into a canister of licorice and handing Silje a string.

She thanked him but remained serious, scanning the store for what she wanted.

Mr. Winkler, picking up on her intentions, turned to Willa and said, winking, "She's all business today." He stepped out from behind the counter and wiped his hands on his apron. "What can I help you with today, Mrs. Sauer?"

"Bacon," she said. "Do you have any?"

"As luck would have it, Swanny—that's Mr. Mikael Swanstrom, lives up 'round the logging camp—he just butchered a couple of his hogs and set me up with some. I've got it in the icebox over here." He was already moving toward the oak icebox in the back corner of the store. "One pound? Two?" he said.

"Two, I think."

He unlevered the handle on the icebox and pulled out two packs of bacon, each labeled with a grease pencil. He brought them back to the counter and started a receipt.

"That," Silje said, her voice barely above the scribble on the paper. She stood just a few paces off, pointing up at the wall of traps and riffles. "And I'll take a pound of bacon, too."

Mr. Dreiss paused in his work, stepped around to the counter before Silje, and said, "Now here I thought you were a fisher girl. What in damnation are you going to do with a number 14 wolf trap? Is this for your uncle?"

She chewed on her licorice by way of answering, but somehow Mr. Dreiss understood she wasn't joking. He removed the trap from the wall and brought it to the counter where he laid it before Silje, who had followed him over. He looked skeptically to Willa, who merely shrugged.

"Do you know how one of these works?" Mr. Dreiss asked.

"Of course I do," Silje replied.

"What do you need this much trap for, anyway?"

She stared at him deadpan. "A friend."

"A friend, you say?" He looked again at Willa, as befuddled as if Silje had asked for his hand in marriage. Next Mr. Dreiss placed the trap in a gunnysack for carrying and laid it on the counter. "It'd be a strange creature who'd want to be friends after getting his leg clamped in this."

"I'll worry about that, so you don't have to."

"Fair enough. But I must say, Miss Lindvik, I don't feel right putting an item of this extravagance on your uncle's account. Not without his direct permission."

Silje removed the dollar bills from her pocket—five of them—and spread them on the counter.

Now he smiled as if an elaborate joke had finally been given its punchline. He rang the till and punched the drawer open and deposited the bills. "I'll be curious to hear how your hunting goes."

Silje took the gunnysack off the counter and hefted it over her shoulder, the steel jaws biting into her flesh. "You'll know when I come back with Fenrir on a leash. Don't forget the pound of bacon."

"Fenrir?"

"My soon-to-be friend."

He could only nod, fetch another pound of bacon from the icebox, and wish them a good day as they left.

The afternoon had settled beneath a rampart of suffocating clouds, a day evermore like August than mid-May. Silje's thoughts were up in them for most of the row back to the station.

It wasn't until they rounded Big Rock again that either of them spoke.

"Did you see the comet last night?" Willa said

Silje lay again on the stern sheets, resting her cheek on the gunwale and staring down into the limpid depths. "It looked like spindrift off a November storm wave. One that rolled for half an hour."

Willa smiled and nodded agreement. "That's a beautiful description. They've been calling it 'The Serpent's Tail.'"

"The comet? Who has?"

"The comet's tail. The newspapers and scientists."

Silje sat up suddenly. The waters stood calm enough she could see her face in the flat surface, but below it, the *Lisbon*. "There it is."

"There's what?"

"Stop rowing," Silje demanded. "Look."

Willa again feathered the oars. She came beside Silje and looked down into the water.

"Do you see it?" Silje asked.

"The ship that sank here five years ago."

Silje nodded, calling up the draugar of her memory, those men who came ashore the night of the storm five years ago as though descended of the enormous waves.

Willa, as if sharing the girl's thoughts, said, "It's hard to believe the same lake as this"—she gestured at the calm waters all around—"sank that." She nodded at the inverted hull nine fathoms down.

"Is it?" Silje asked.

THE STORM

NOVEMBER 28, 1905

Are souls like ships, plying godless seas?

What child ever saw one and didn't feel the affinity, even if they couldn't name it?

I've never believed in souls or divine seas, but I've known plenty who have. Some because they lack imagination, others because they have too much. Some are less a ship on a godless sea than a godless sea unto themselves.

THEY WERE SHELTERED in the trees on the trail the mail carriers used in winter, but still the storm found them. The wind screamed up their backs. The snow fell crosswise. And if not for the darkness of the lake water coming in and out of view as they marched, delineating the snowscape, they'd have had no compass to mark them. Silje had never seen her father frightened before, but he was now. He carried her like he had when she was a toddler, guiding them through the deep snow, sometimes falling to his knees as the trail dipped and rose.

They'd left the boardinghouse in Otter Bay at first light, her father eager to return to his wife even as the storm intensified. Her mother was no doubt climbing the walls like a spider. But he was concerned for his fish house, too. Not only did it hold his livelihood, but he could find refuge nowhere else. He hadn't shuttered it. Hadn't tied his boat to a tree.

That's what he'd told her, at least, tying a scarf around her neck and hefting the rucksack over his shoulders. "We've walked in worse," he said, though she was certain that wasn't the case.

"I doubt this is a good idea, Pappa," she'd said. "My boots." She lifted her left foot. Showed him the crack in the sole.

He flashed an unconvincing smile and said, "I might have cobbled that a month ago. I'm sorry, sweet girl. But don't worry, I'll carry you if I have to."

And he had, for the second mile. Now they were crossing the small bridge at Black Granite Brook, the one Samuel Riverfish built on the mail route, and he had to set her down. She sank into snow up to her waist.

Two steps she took before he brought her back up onto his shoulders. "You keep me warm, anyway," he said.

"I'll do my best, Pappa."

"You reach back and pull that hood up, eh? Is your scarf still tied?"

She pulled on her hood and tightened the knot in her scarf.

Her whole life she'd remember that haul. More than anything, she'd remember the snow, which fell in such abundance that it enveloped the forest around and above them so that the trees became mere shadows of the storm itself. Became monuments to it. Many moments found them in a blur of whiteness so complete Silje felt as if she were upside down. But then they would come again to a part of the trail overlooking the lake and again the contrast of that black water put them upright.

They trekked all morning and at noon reached the junction on the Wabun River, where he set her down to rest. His toque had disappeared under snow and Silje reached up to knock it clear. He was exhausted, but still he smiled and said, "Almost home, sweet girl. Can you walk from here? I'll break the trail?"

"My boot," she reminded him.

"Ah, that's right. Well, hop back on."

As she did, the wind lulled and in its absence they heard a brontide in the near distance.

"Pappa?"

He put his finger to his lips and canted his head as though to hear better, but the wind moaned again and for a moment the sound disappeared. But then in another respite the peculiar grating sound returned.

It came from the direction of the lake. Silje thought for a moment it was perhaps a new kind of wind, one cleaving granite from the cliffside. A notion bolstered by the fact that she believed she could feel it through the sole of her broken boot. And though she was terrified of the possibilities, she was also compelled to slide off her father's back and trudge her own path between the trees on the point.

With each step both the sound and vibration grew. Louder and more unnatural. Despite the hour of the day the quality of dusk held all around, and so it wasn't until they were practically on the edge of Big Rock Cliff that they saw the orchestra of this cacophony: a ship coming apart on the shoal. Its three masts pointing in different directions. One east, one north, one west. Its hull had split, and the fore and aft ends of the steel boat listed in opposite directions. That sound, they learned standing there watching the wreck, came whenever a wave big enough to toss the ship into the face of the cliff rose out of the lake. When that happened, it felt like the whole shore would collapse, and Silje had to muffle her ears.

She knew enough to be awestruck, but the look of sheer wonder on her father's face confirmed it. They stood there long enough for the ship to be lifted onto the cliff face three or four times before he finally said, "The men . . ."

It hadn't occurred to her to think of those aboard the ship, but her father's mentioning them beckoned a new reaction to accompany her awe: fear. And not just for the men aboard the ship, but for her mother, alone, not a whole mile up the shore. Now she felt like the masts on the ship, rent and pointing in different directions. They should rescue the men onboard. They needed to return to her mother and save their fish house.

"What do we do, Pappa?"

Her question seemed to answer whatever beguiled him, and he simply offered his back so that she might climb on it again.

As they crossed the shoreline of the cove, she could see their cabin in the woods. Their fish house, too, which was fanged in ice but still whole. The boat, which they'd left upturned on the beach, had blown to the first trees off their forest, but it appeared undamaged as they passed and made for the front door. Before they went inside, Silje could hear the voices. Subdued but certain and as unnatural coming from their cabin as the ship had been beating against Big Rock cliff.

No sooner did she hear it than did she convince herself it was a hallucination. That as sure as they'd just spent the better part of that day walking through the storm, she would go inside and settle into a fever dream that was then, on the threshold, already announcing itself. But if the sounds coming from inside were dreamed, what accounted for the nine men huddled on the floor around the stove, holding bowls of hot stew in one hand, and crusts of bread to scoop it up in the other?

As if the sight of them weren't enough, Silje next saw her mother hanging heavy coats from a clothesline she'd rigged behind the stove, whistling while she did. Of all the things Silje witnessed that day, her mother's mastery of the situation was perhaps the most surprising. That woman, given always to melodrama and hesitancy, to idleness and fatigue, busied herself with that crew as if she were the steward and porter both.

"Arvid," she said matter-of-factly. "You're all right? Silje? You too?"

"We are," her father said.

"We've some unexpected company, as you can see. This is the crew of the *Lisbon*, which has gone aground against Big Rock."

"We saw the wreckage," her father said.

One of the men stood, reluctantly leaving his bowl on the floor behind him. He stepped to her father and offered his hand. "I'm Captain Durand, of the schooner barge *Lisbon*."

"You're . . . whole? Your crew, I mean."

"We are, sir. Improbably we are, thank the Lord."

The captain's voice brought a kind of equilibrium to the scene, and Silje's father removed his coat and hung it on its pegs by the door. He helped Silje out of her boots and coat and untied the scarf he'd several hours ago wrapped around her neck at the trailhead in Otter Bay. From his rucksack, he removed his wife's medicine and offered it to her. She accepted it, but only put the bottle on the table and continued her ministrations to the crew. She filled their coffee cups, she cut them more bread. She rearranged the blanket over the shoulders of one man and offered one of Arvid's old toques to another.

Her father removed the one he wore, knocked the snow from it, and hung it beside his coat. "Tell me, how'd you come to be here? What else can we do for you gentlemen?"

"Missus Lindvik 'as been most generous already. She fixed us up this moose stew and we're on our fourth pot of coffee. Likely we'd 'ave frozen to death were it not for 'er warmth." He raised his coffee cup and said cheers. The men seated around the stove all lifted their cups as well. "As for coming to be 'ere, our Mr. Saturday there, our first mate, 'e remembered seeing the fish 'ouse yonder from trips down the shore afore. When we all got off that barge, 'e reckoned it was the closest place to us. 'E weren't wrong."

"Captain Durand, you ought to come back here and sit down," Silje's mother said, sliding her father's rocking chair closer to the stove. "Finish your supper before it gets cold."

The captain went to the chair and sat and took the bowl from one of his mates.

"You say that boat wrecked on the shore was a barge?" her father asked.

"A schooner barge, yes sir. We were towed behind the SS *Philadelphia*. Come across from the Sault but a couple days ago. When the storm come up we tried to outlast it in the lee of the Apostles. In fact, the last light we seen before this warm fire was over at Devil's Island sometime around midnight last. I don't know if we could 'ave steamed across the lake any faster than that wretched storm blew us."

"And what happened to the *Philadelphia*?" her father asked.

"Never saw her after we blew off course. Not even when we were triced up to her. She's either out there still, or made Duluth, or she's on the next rock one way or 'nother."

Now her father came over and put his arm around Silje, who hadn't moved from the spot where she'd landed inside the door. He picked her up and held her like a toddler. He carried her to the bench along the landward side of the house and sat down, keeping Silje on his knee. She could feel the enormous tension and strength in his shoulders.

Her mother said, "I heard the distress calls at daybreak. I heard them and somehow knew I ought to put on a pot of stew. Enough to feed all these fellows."

He shifted Silje on his lap. "You got that sense," he said.

"This stew's good enough to serve in the Palm Room," Captain Durand said.

Silje had never once thought to compliment her mother's cooking. Nor had she ever heard anyone else make a similar claim. Of course, these nine men were the first guests they'd had since Christmas and her uncle's last visit.

Silje could see the bewildered expression on her father's face, notable mainly because it so rarely appeared. As if to lighten his load, Silje uttered her first words since they'd arrived not ten minutes before. "Sir, I wonder how you all got off your boat."

"Well now, young lass, we've got Mr. Saturday to thank for the answer there. Simon, I believe you've been called on."

Simon Saturday was not nearly as loquacious as his captain. In fact, for Silje, it was almost incomprehensible how a man of such imposing physical stature could have such a diminutive voice. "Wasn't much, Cap'n," he began. "I climbed up the mizzenmast, hoping to get above the water and onto the rock. When that didn't work, I grabbed a line and made a jump for it. Lucky I found a ledge, I reckon. I got up that cliff like a goat, tied off the line, then lowered it down for the rest of you." He used the last crust of bread to wipe the bowl of stew clean. "Next thing you know we're sitting here supping on this fine fare."

Captain Durand was not satisfied. He turned from Saturday to Silje and added, "A greater feat of daring and strength you 'adn't seen before, I'll tell you that much, lass. Mr. Saturday cleared ten feet from deck to rock, could as easily 'ave fallen into that lake and never been seen again.

"Even without falling into the soup, we got a land soaked to our socks, I tell you. I didn't think we'd live to see 'nother moment's warmth, never mind a right feast like this one."

The coats closest to the stove began to steam, sending up a not unpleasant odor. Before long, the whole cabin grew sauna-like, and the crew of the *Lisbon* leaned back against the walls or curled into themselves and fell asleep on the floor like a litter of pups, one on top of the next. Silje's mother tiptoed among the men, fetching their empty bowls and coffee mugs and bringing them to the counter.

Only Captain Durand remained awake, and lest he be thought a poor guest, he got up and helped Bente with the dirty dishes, chattering all the while about the wickedness of the storm as though it were a personal adversary. But he also charmed Silje's mother by asking about her family, and where she came from, and complimenting Silje herself, who'd hardly taken her eyes off the man since she walked in from the cold.

Silje, emboldened by his observation, dared another question. "Captain, I wonder if the line that held you and the other boat— the *Philadelphia*, I think you said it was called—well, I wonder if the storm broke it?"

"I've been wondering much the same myself, lass. I 'ave indeed."

It was her father who spoke next, his voice deep and thoughtful in Silje's ear. "I wonder, sir, if it might have been the prudent thing. To sever the tie, I mean." The peculiar quality of his voice gave Silje to crane her neck so she might read his eyes. He looked guilty. But of what? "*And* if that's what the captain of your consort did. Sever the tie."

"Yes, naturally," Captain Durand said. "I wouldn't poison 'is name even if he 'ad to cut the line. Better some survive than none at all."

"What recourse do you have, in that situation?" her father pressed. "I mean to ask: what did you do after the line was cut?"

"We dropped anchors, a course. Both of 'em. Nine hundred foot a chain each." He returned to his seat in the rocking chair, navigating the bunched-up men as if the puncheon floor between them was stones across a creek. "We laid 'em out and we 'oped to Jesus and Mary both we kept water under 'er. A course, we couldn't see one

end of the barge from the other, never mind the shoals or shores."
He changed subjects in his mind as though the storm had blown it.
"I beg your pardon, Mister Lindvik, Missus Lindvik, but would it
be terrible imprudent if I removed my boots? There's a gall in 'ere
about to catch fire."

Her mother hurried across the room and knelt before the captain and began unlacing his boots. Here was another posture Silje
had never witnessed before. The day would not stop surprising her.

His boots removed, Bente returned to a chair at the table. She
appeared embarrassed in much the same way Silje's father had a moment before, but neither of them so much as glanced at the other.

The captain rested his head on the back of the chair. When his
boots were off, he lifted his right foot and held it in his hand, the relief on his face as plain as the charm in his voice while he continued
with the story. "It weren't long—not two hours even—before we run
aground. Another hour after that Mr. Saturday saved our bacon."

Bente took the bottle of medicine from the tabletop and read the
label as though it were an unknown cure. What exactly the medicine was meant for, Silje could hardly guess. Curmudgeonliness?
Meanness? Sleepiness? More than anything, unhappiness?

She was surprised when her father spoke again. "I imagine your
ordeal won't soon be forgotten, Captain Durand."

"No, I suppose not." The captain let out a cavernous yawn. "This
floorful of stew-fed chums 'ave got me thinking 'bout a moment a
rest myself."

"Captain Durand, why don't you rest on Silje's bunk. It's just
here." Her mother was already across the cabin, in Silje's dark corner,
arranging the ticking as though she might next sing him a lullaby.

It was the captain who sang instead, as he elbowed himself up
off the rocking chair and started a song. "We come across the water
blue, blown about like kites, 'tis true, and dashed upon a rocky
shore, now we'll dream of depths galore . . ." He sat on the edge of
Silje's bunk, whistling like a hermit thrush harkening to the melody he'd just sung. So sweet and pure and out of proportion with

his physique, which, though not on the level of Mr. Saturday's, was nonetheless quite imposing.

Silje felt his sweet voice on her warm face. On her hands and in the lobes of her ears most of all. She hardly knew where her echo came from, but when she sang back, "I'll sing like him forevermore," Captain Durand looked up from rubbing his eyes. His smile suggested that coming through their horror was worth it just for her sweet answer.

For her own part, that verse escaping from her mouth seemed to have been dislodged from a part of her she'd not previously known existed, and on her lips felt like melted butter. On another day— probably *any* other day—she would have been embarrassed or surprised by her singing out, but instead, she felt like the whole cabin was brighter because of it. She might even have imagined it finding the ears of the sleeping men and sweetening their dreams.

"Zounds, Mrs. Lindvik! I do believe your daughter is a regular minstrel. Careful this one doesn't sing 'erself all the way to Broadway." He batted a playful eye at both mother and daughter.

"I don't believe we need worry about this one flying the coop."

"Perchance," he said, now laying his body down. "Perchance."

"Good rest, Captain Durand," Silje said.

THEODULF STAYED at the Spalding Hotel the first night of the storm. After his encounter with the pianist in the lobby of the Masonic Lodge, he'd braved the killing gale. The trolleys had stopped running because of the snow and ice on the tracks, so he trudged up Superior Street to the hotel, thankful the wind came behind him, and resigned himself once there to a corner table in the billiard room. He ordered a brandy and used it to settle his guts. A second sent him into a pleasant stupor. At midnight, he adjourned to his room on the fifth floor having not eaten dinner. He went straight to the window, cast the curtain aside, and startled at the unwavering darkness. The only thing he made out in the glass was his own sorry reflection, and even that shone vaguely and ghostlike.

But now it was a new day, and what greeted him at the window nearly blinded him: a whiteness as absolute as the blackness had been the night before. He checked his watch. It was past nine. He bathed and changed into his uniform and went up to the Palm Room for a late breakfast. Already lingerers had gathered at the windows overlooking the harbor. The blizzard lightened at intervals, and in those lulls he'd catch glimpses of the waterfront landmarks. The aerial bridge. The breakwaters. The ore docks. The spidering train tracks.

He asked the waiter to bring him the morning *Herald* and read it while he ate. A bowl of oatmeal. A hardboiled egg. Coffee. One thing was abundantly clear: he would not be returning to the Two Harbors station. Not only was the *Nocturne* laid up, but according to a headline, there'd be no train service in or out of Duluth that day or the next. And perhaps even longer. So be it, he thought, raising a hand for the waiter and asking for another cup of coffee.

When he finished, he signed for his bill, folded the newspaper under this arm, and went down to the lobby to arrange another night's stay. At the reception, he also sent a telegraph to the lighthouse station in Two Harbors announcing the delay in his return. His responsibilities satisfied, another night of lodging procured, he found himself standing in the lobby looking at his watch again. It was only eleven o'clock. He had twenty-four unfettered hours before him. Twenty-four at least. And for the first time since he joined the Lighthouse Service, he was without duty or responsibility on a Tuesday in November.

After he changed again—this time out of his uniform—and had a shave at the hotel barber, after he played a few games of billiards with an insurance salesman from Buffalo who was also stranded by the storm, after he had his shoes shined while imbibing another cup of coffee, Theodulf found himself back at the Palm Room, which was by then packed with oglers watching the storm from the sixth-floor windows overlooking the harbor.

An uncertain and uneasy murmur rose from the crowd, and for some minutes Theodulf chalked it up to the spent wine and beer bottles scattered about the tabletops. But eventually he recognized an urgency that belied his impressions, so he got up and joined the many guests at the window. The snow had lightened and now, in the drab afternoon light, what he saw out on the lake nearly poleaxed him. Three freighters foundered in plain sight. Out on Park Point, one had fully come aground. Down the shore, near what must have been the shoreline outside his father's house, another took massive, broadside seas. Before him, just beyond the canal jetties, the *Mataafa* appeared split in two. Waves washed over her with such voluminous hatred that he could not believe the good ship hadn't been broken into a dozen pieces. What's more, the whole lakeshore was aflame. For a moment, he thought some great conflagration had broken out among the warehouses and waterfront shanties. But upon closer inspection, he realized the blazes were in fact twenty or more bonfires raging against the nor'easter. In all his years living upon the water, he'd never seen anything like it. Never seen anything vaguely like it.

"I rounded Cape Horn in July," a man standing next to Theodulf said unexpectedly. "In a tempest, no less." Now he checked to see Theodulf was listening. "I don't think those seas had anything on this." He nodded out at the lake.

"I was just thinking something similar," Theodulf responded. "I've lived on the lake my whole life, and never seen the likes of this."

"They've already called it the worst hurricane on record."

From the corner of his eye, Theodulf glanced at the garrulous fellow, who turned forty-five degrees and flashed a practiced, politic smile.

"I'm H. H. Edwards, my good sir. To whom do I have the pleasure of speaking?"

Theodulf took his offered hand. They shook. "I'm Theodulf Sauer."

"Of course, Ernst Sauer's son." This he spoke with something like caution, almost as if he hoped it were otherwise.

Theodulf blushed, realizing he wished it were otherwise himself. "I don't know that either of us proclaim the relation much these days."

H. H. Edwards lifted his chin and nodded sagely. "Fathers and sons, the Russians write novels about them." He took a sly look around, pulled a flask from inside his coat, and uncapped and sipped from it. He offered it to Theodulf, who raised an abstaining hand.

"Speaking of people writing books, I understand your father will attempt his memoirs, now that he's retiring."

"I'm sorry, Mr. Edwards, I should have asked how you and my father are acquainted."

"Of course! We oversaw the merger of the Superior Steamship Company and American Steel. From opposite sides of the table, mind you. But all the same. Since then, we've become quite friendly. We go dove hunting together."

Certainly, this was not a fact that recommended H. H. Edwards.

But two points prevailed. One: he had a charming, even rakish countenance, something that endeared him. And two: the prospect of a whole evening alone held no appeal to Theodulf. So a moment later, when H. H. Edwards again proffered his flask, Theodulf accepted. Before long, the two men took chairs at a table overlooking the harbor and ordered proper refreshments.

They conversed for an hour, regaling each other with their dubious exploits and exaggerating their accomplishments in the way of men of a certain class. Theodulf especially inflated his position in the Lighthouse Service, which he tried to make sound as if he were part spy and part naval officer. H. H. was an attorney, naturally, whose rise to prominence even he admitted was thanks to his own father's influence. He'd been born and raised in Cleveland, and after a distinguished run at Yale—where he'd played baseball as an undergraduate and edited the law review while studying for the bar—spent a few years working in New York, a stint cut short by an offer to return home and work in-house at American Steel, where his father oversaw mergers and acquisitions. The rest of his rise, he said, was a foregone conclusion.

"And now you're stuck in Duluth, waiting out a gale," Theodulf said.

H. H. took a tight-lipped drink.

"Tell me," Theodulf said, "what occasion found you rounding Cape Horn?"

The other man's expression turned, and he looked again out the window. For a considerable few moments he regarded the storm and the heavy afternoon light. When he returned his attention, he said, "One of my mates from law school, a Brooklyn boy whose family once raced for the America's Cup, wanted to sail around the horn to Chile. He had an old-fashioned notion he'd be a better man if he did. And he wanted to find a South American wife. Someone with influence in that part of the world. I don't know why this was true, but every man tells himself a story, eh? In any case, I agreed to crew with him, having had some experience sailing out of New York myself."

"It must have made quite an impression, making that westward turn?"

H. H. took another drink and nodded. He appeared as Theodulf often imagined he himself did whenever that singular night in Paris crossed his mind. It was no great curiosity why that occasion should seize him now, but he pushed it down, remembering the uniform that hung starched and ready in his hotel room just one floor below.

"It was," H. H. continued, a smile slowly rising, "like seeing God." He checked himself as if coming out of a dream. "I mean no blasphemy, and hope I've not offended."

Theodulf raised a forgiving hand.

"There is such *power* in this world, is all. On this *earth*, I mean. And I knew, as we battled that bitter ocean, one monumental swell after the next, that I would one day possess a power *like* it. That I was simply *made* to." He swirled his whiskey glass, watching the eddy. "I suppose that's why a storm like this"—he pointed his glass at the window—"entertains me more than anything."

They turned in unison, watched a few minutes of the gale. All this time, the wind circling the hotel made a whistling sound at odds with the impending night. Almost as if it were making light of the violence. In one of the lulls of that whistling, Theodulf leaned forward. He craned his neck and squinted. He couldn't quite believe what he saw, so asked a woman at the table next to theirs if he might borrow her opera glasses.

Now he could confirm what it: the *Mataafa* no longer smoked from its stack.

"Do you see that, Mr. Edwards?" Theodulf asked, handing him the woman's opera glasses.

H. H. sat up dutifully and scanned the harbor.

"Train them on the *Mataafa*. She's lost her steam. She's doomed."

H. H. studied the ship for a moment, confirming Theodulf's assertion or relishing it, who could say? But when he stood and returned the glasses to the impatient woman, he said, "This calls for another round of drinks. To toast the brave men aboard that broadsided boat."

The woman who'd lent them the glasses said, "Here, here" and went back to her own afternoon cocktail.

For his part, Theodulf felt swept up in the impromptu spree, and so agreed to another whiskey. Before long, three other men from his firm joined H. H. and the spree became a proper fête. Theodulf excused himself and went to the other end of the dining room, where he watched the throng of citizens gathering on the waterfront. The crowd in the Palm Room grumbled about whether to join the hayseeds out in the weather, but for the most part they stayed where they were, feasting on early suppers of whitefish and roast duck under candlelit chandeliers.

What had begun as a restive mood was by then rowdy, and at six o'clock sharp—Theodulf had just checked his watch—H. H. Edwards and his band of cronies passed him on their way out of the dining room.

"We're headed down to the waterfront," H. H. said, his breath boozy but warm. "Come with us, Mr. Sauer." He paused for a moment, caught between Theodulf's deliberations on his partners' exodus. To hasten Theodulf's decision, he added, "We'll no doubt end up in the Bowery before the night's up."

This settled it for Theodulf, who buttoned his coat and followed the others to the elevator.

Down on the lakeshore, the crowds impressed. It was as if the entire city had gathered on the boardwalk to witness the distress of the *Mataafa*, which, he could see as plain as day now, was indeed doomed. The lifesaving crew had set up their Lyle gun and bombarded the foundering ship with breeches buoys. The first several shots caught in the still-bellowing wind, blowing off course by several degrees. This despite the fact that the ship lurched less than a quarter mile into the lake.

Set against the inviolable night, the *Mataafa* was visible first as an animate creature lit by the bonfires onshore, bucking against gargantuan seas. But the pilot house on her forward deck was also lit from within, adding a kind of signal that rose and fell in the furrows of storm surge. Standing on the forward decks, her captain—Dick Humble, it was whispered and murmured about on the beach—used a megaphone to beseech the lifesaving crew. Demanding they not give up. His voice sailed on the wind. Theodulf had never heard a more desperate man.

For an hour they watched, H. H. Edwards and his cronies and Theodulf, moving among the onlookers as if they were distinguished guests, or at least presumed themselves to be. Theodulf was in awe of the damage the storm had done already. The docks on the lakeward side of the harbor peninsula had all been splintered to kindling. The shanties and no few storefronts that as recently as the day before had unrolled their awnings against the morning sun were gone now. Disappeared as fleeting thoughts. The road running out to the aerial bridge was flooded with a slurry of lake water and ice chunks and the flotsam of the battered boardwalk and decimated buildings. In toto, the ruination kindled in him a sense of awe he'd never felt before.

The fires yet burned. And somewhere in the confluence of all that heat and the colossal winter storm, all that snow and ice and raging lake and towering flame, he recognized the forces in his own psyche bartering with each other. Filling him with uncommon doubt. That's when he saw the girl. A child, really, standing with her mother beside one of the soaring blazes. Her expression conveyed the kind of genuine terror and worry Theodulf knew he should have felt himself but found nowhere in his being.

Edwards put his arm around Theodulf, offering his flask, which had been replenished with rum. Theodulf took a long drink against his feelings of guilt, noting as he wiped his lips on his coat that the girl studied him again. Something between a scowl and an expression of sympathy showed on her face in the firelight, a look she did nothing to suppress. He turned away quickly, but just as soon ventured another glimpse. She'd given her attention back to the yawing ship, and in profile her uncanny countenance struck him as suddenly familiar. Like maybe they'd known each other in a different lifetime. Such a thought disturbed him even more than the moribund *Mataafa.*

He wished he could step over to her and ask for forgiveness. He wished he could explain how he'd fallen so low. Could explain how this fraternity of fools and hustlers now surrounding him was not a fair representation of the company he normally kept. Indeed, he despised men like this. Men like his father. Men who saw misfortune—even calamity—as a means to opportunity. To profit. Indeed, men who saw a ship and her crew drowning in plain sight, and thought not of the water drenching their lungs, but of the legal claims they might make against the shipping companies or the weather bureau, or even against the storm itself. He wanted to say—to *explain,* even—that he was in the business of *saving* lives. Not unlike the rescue crews still busy with their Lyle gun and breeches buoys. Finally, he wanted to say that he believed in God and that His wrath, surely the source of this storm, could not be satisfied. Not even if Theodulf gave himself over to his faith.

Instead, he took one more look at the girl, shouldered up to his fugacious cronies, and decided against any virtue at all, taking instead his longest drink of rum yet.

They did indeed find their way to the Bowery. Later that night, after the fires died and the gawkers started their slow parade back up to hillside homes now buried in eighteen inches of snow, Theodulf and H. H. Edwards and half a dozen other drunken galoots H. H. called chums blundered back up to Superior Street and headed west for LaRue's.

Despite all his carousing, all his indiscretions, Theodulf had, until then, known that bawdy house only by reputation. He couldn't help but think how happy, even proud, his father would have been to know he was consorting with this crowd, at this house of ill repute, even despite his drunkenness.

What greeted him in that dimly lit, smoke-ensconced bagnio was as misaligned with his desires as the flames and the churning

water had been on the waterfront. The women decorating the staircase heading up to the second-floor rooms flaunted their offerings
with all the enthusiasm of dozing cats. Whether because of the late
hour or the lack of johns, Theodulf couldn't know, but he found
their lack of cunning a relief as he went to the bar and removed his
hat and ordered a whiskey.

Whereas Theodulf dodged the molls and their uninspiring se-
ductions, H. H. and his pals dispersed among them like shot among
doves. By the time Theodulf's drink was delivered, the rest of his
coterie had matched up, some of them already traipsing upstairs for
their desserts. Glad to be rid of them, Theodulf finally sat down
with the glass pressed between his thumb and forefinger.

No sooner had he unbuttoned his coat and loosened his collar
than did one of the molls sit down next to him. She had a boy's haircut and a black silken shawl over her shoulders. When she spoke,
her voice came cracked, as if it was the first time she'd spoken in
days. "You're the first group of johns to visit all night," she said. "We
were all about to turn in."

Theodulf looked at her dumbly.

"What's the matter? Did the storm button your lip?"

"It wasn't my idea to come here," Theodulf said.

"Well, you're here now, aren't you, John?"

He drank the rest of his whiskey and signaled for another.

"I'll have one, too, mister." She stood and leaned her elbows on
the bar, letting the shawl slide down her arms.

Theodulf nodded his approval to the bartender, who set another
glass on the bar and filled two while Theodulf looked at the woman's supple shoulders in the mirror behind the bar. She turned to
him when he reached for the drinks, exposing her collarbones and
the downward slope of her breasts.

"You don't like my hair?" she said.

Theodulf sighed. "There's nothing wrong with your hair."

She twirled around and primped it while studying herself in the
mirror. "You like a lady with long blonde tresses, I'll bet."

For the first time since she joined him, he felt a bit of intrigue. It was the huskiness of her voice. The boldness and self-possession. Now he looked her up and down.

"Maybe you don't care at all about a girl's hair," she said, smirking into the mirror where he met her gaze.

"I most certainly do not," he said.

Her shoulders flushed and she waved a fan that had been hidden in the folds of her shawl. Something registered and she shook her head knowingly, keeping her eyes on him in the mirror. After a minute, another mischievous smile rose from her lips. She tilted her head without taking her eyes off him in the mirror. As the bartender sauntered to the other end of the bar, she whispered, "Are you fond of my hair because it's like a boy's?"

"I beg your pardon!" he protested.

"Honey, it's okay," she whispered, hefting the shawl back up over her shoulders and holding it at her throat. She kissed him on the ear and said, "You close your eyes, and I can be whoever you want."

When she pressed into him, he faltered from his drunkenness but didn't recoil. Only held on to the bar as if the floor of this dive suffered its own swells from the storm.

"What's your name?" he asked her.

"I'm Dove." Her wet lips were touching the lobe of his ear. "But you can call me anything." Now her whole body aligned with his, and her left hand reached under the bar. "Something got your attention, didn't it?"

He grabbed her wandering hand and tried to push her away. But she was like water in the way she enveloped him. She kissed his neck and nobbled more wicked endearments in his drumming ears, and it wasn't long before he was following her upstairs. Pulled as the moon does the seas.

She worked with incredible efficiency. Getting him on the bed, collecting her fee, washing herself with water from a bedside pot, her seductive powers having abandoned her—or been forsaken—now that he was prisoner to her chamber. He looked around. Two candle sconces hanging on either side of the bed, the bed itself covered in a threadbare blanket, a stove in the corner, a small chest of drawers on which she laid her black shawl.

Now she stood before him unlacing her corset. Younger, she seemed. Positively bored. Not boyish at all. He sat up, his vision sloshing like water in a bowl. "Please, put your clothes back on."

She sat down on the edge of the bed and reached for the buttons of his trousers.

"I mean it."

Chastened, she folded her hands on her lap.

"Keep the money," he said, clutching the sides of the bed. "Can I get a drink in here?"

Dove stood up and went to the chest of drawers and removed a pint of rum. "I have this, but you have to pay."

Theodulf struggled getting his billfold from the pocket inside his coat. He fumbled a single dollar bill from it and handed it to her. She gave him the bottle in turn, which he uncorked and took a drink from. He put the cork back in and handed it to her. His last drink. Tonight and always. He fell back on her bed.

"You can't sleep here, John."

"Come over here," he said.

Her expression betrayed annoyance, but she did. Again she reached for the buttons on his trousers, but again he took her hand away. This time he held it, making room for her on the bed. He put his arm around her and pulled her gently toward him. With her lying beside him, Theodulf realized how warm it was in the room. Sweat slicked his brow. His feet in the boots hung off the end of the bed, wet with snow all the way to the felt liners. Outside, the storm still rang.

His head, too. No more drinking. He opened his eyes, saw her looking back.

"You can close your eyes for a spell," she said, putting her fingers to his eyelids. She let them linger in his hair, folding it behind his ear.

That he couldn't conjure the memory of Paul had less to do with his drunkenness than the peace of that moment. The pirouetting of his thoughts slowed. His drunken spinning, too. Her hair smelled like anise. Or marigold. Her fingertips were soft as sweet cream.

At two in the morning, as battered and bent as the waterfront, Theodulf discovered himself back at the Spalding Hotel. Unable to find his room, he returned to the Palm Room and stumbled to the same corner table at which he'd met H. H. Edwards. He slid a chair closer to the window and rested his face on the frigid glass. Yet a half dozen fires burned on the waterfront. Like six houses ablaze. And the *Mataafa* held her place in the surge, enduring her crucible. From this vantage he could see her whole, even through the night. Cracked amidships. The unrelenting waves bashing her starboard hull. The nearly constant expression of those waves born again as spray above her coamings. The faltering light in a window on one of the forward decks.

From shore, the good ship had disappeared with each rising swell, giving the whole scene an intermittent quality. But up here, she never went out of sight and the remorselessness of her ordeal was magnified. Even from this great distance.

Theodulf felt the swells of his bile rising in profound syncopation. The last of the storm's snow spit against the glass. Its coldness bracing and welcome. He watched the ship.

The last light aboard the *Mataafa* went out sometime around then. Just after two o'clock. Around the same time Theodulf fell asleep against the cold embrace of the glass.

ANIMA

NOVEMBER 29, 1905

When I say I've held dying hands, I tell the truth. When I wonder whether Saint Thomas Aquinas or Aristotle—those great prophets on the subject of the soul—ever held one, I mean no disrespect. They had their jobs and I have mine.

It strikes me, though, that while I've spent my days cradling the dying, they spent theirs in abstract thought. I suppose the world is no worse for their ruminations. Indeed, from what I've heard and read of those thoughts—and heard of them I have!—many are quite beautiful. And profound. And no doubt in the service of their Gods.

I should say, I don't doubt the existence of God. But neither do I believe in—much less worship—Him. I offer the contrast merely as an example of the vagaries of belief. It's important to say this plainly. About the soul I'd hardly have a thought if it weren't for the conversations I've overheard, and which are pressing in the moment of this tragedy.

I mentioned overhearing them. Let me use an example from some half century ago. There was a priest—a good one, honest and devout as ever lived—who preached on these very shores. Father Volk was his name. Later Bishop and finally Cardinal Volk, I might add for emphasis. He was a student of Saint Thomas Aquinas, and he'd measure his paddle strokes with his preaching. They made a surprisingly good harmony, his paddling and preaching did. And if I wasn't convinced by his talk of death and salvation and eternal life of the anima, it's only because of my own experience, which I must acknowledge has the benefit of many thousands of years of experience that Volk—never mind Saint

Thomas Aquinas or Aristotle—was not lucky enough to possess. I promise: I'm not being braggadocious, only stating plainly what, by any definition of truth those great philosophers and theologians might conjure, is unassailable.

Volk had it, as most true believers do, that God judged the lives of the dead and dying, measuring their readiness for the after-life—and where they might end up in it—against their mortal days on earth. In that moment of reckoning, the soul, which was—which is still, if you align with this sort of poetry—either ascended into eternal happiness in heaven or descended into eternal damnation in hell. It would leave the body and, though immaterial, make its flight. I might ask, who wouldn't behold a notion so beautiful as that, and wish it true?

But I know how grotesque the human body is. How fragile and prone to illness and disfigurement. How quickly, even willingly, it can die. But it's also beautiful, and capable of elegance and health and longevity, to say nothing of conditions of love and loneliness, happiness and sadness. Sin abounds in all of this, of course. The good and the bad, both. The healthy and the un.

Aquinas believed that sin damages the soul, and that might well be true. But one beast's sin is another's virtue, on that I think we can agree. And so I suspect the inverse is true as well. That is, that the soul is like a muscle, and virtue its exercise. Whether through prayer or contemplation or kindness, who can know?

Father Volk would have had us believe that sin is as inevitable as death, and that the best we can do is atone for it. Is ask for forgiveness and try truly to live with purer intentions. But I ask, who's keeping score? I am, I can tell you that much. And if I haven't bought the Christian doctrine whole, it's for good reason.

Read on. See the body lost and then found. Behold the eyes that rescue it from the battering waves—I am the waves! I delivered that suffering body!—and understand that that man is as much the body's savior as any God might be, and it's only in his memory and subconsciousness that the drowned man's anima resides.

Is my contention as elegant and reasoned as Aristotle's? Is it as measured and sure as Saint Thomas Aquinas's? Of course it's not. But as I say, I am the author of his death and was his usher in it, and the only thing I saw take flight was another lashing of spindrift, wet upon our hero's face. And as he carried that drowned man's frozen body, all the elegance and reason and measured certainty appeared to me as weak and wicked as Theodulf's resolve.

A T DAWN Theodulf watched the lifesaving boat steer from the sea fog, a dozen or so weary pilgrims from the night before framed in her gunwales. Rising behind them, the mast of the *Mataafa* rose in the hoary morning, coated with ice that had frozen perpendicular to the main deck of the ship. The lake rolled now, exhausted. There came before that boat a mournful sound, as if the lake itself between them and the shore were humming a hymn.

The crowd, though less considerable, watched in solemn silence as the surf boat slipped on, its oars like spider legs. If Theodulf felt anything at the sight of them—and with each minute they came nearer, revealing their shocked and bruised faces, their shoulders sloped and weak—it was *conviction*. That he might also emerge from the storm of his own life. He vaguely remembered the drink of rum the night before. At LaRue's. In that dove's private chamber. Remembered that he'd decided it would be his last. He even felt an urge to pray. To go up to Sacred Heart and commune with God as this new and better version of himself.

That mournful sound grew louder and more urgent until one of the voices on the surf boat overawed it, calling across the water, "Make way! Make way! We're coming ashore!"

The crowd parted as the men forward in the surf boat jumped into the shallows. With hauling lines crossed over the shoulders, they ran the boat up the rocky shore, sliding in the ice and snow but landing it all the same. As if the scene had been choreographed, countless denizens came rushing forward with blankets and offerings of food and rum and hot coffee. The source of that unholy keening had been from the ranks of the *Mataafa*'s crew all along.

So haunting was it Theodulf backed away, toward the canal. Finally he turned, vomited, and palmed a handful of snow to wipe his lips.

It was there, on his knees, and looking upon the lake again, that he saw it. What he at first mistook to be the cap of a wave, and then believed merely to be another item in an unending procession of flotsam, before realizing it was much more than that. A human body. Was it swimming? Its arms surging with the water? No. Not at all. With each swell it came closer. A rigid human body, stiff as a piece of driftwood. Theodulf used the same cold and wet hand he'd wiped his mouth with to rub his eyes now, whether for greater clarity or to wash away what he saw he hardly knew. But the fact remained, and in another minute the body washed ashore not more than ten feet from where he knelt.

It arrived face down, arms spread as if it'd been crucified, its peacoat spread like a cape. Twice the waves pushed the body farther up the beach before a third flipped it over. A pallor so white it could hardly be distinguished from the snow save for the black hair plastered over one eye.

Theodulf tried to call out but only mustered a faint choking sound. And anyway, the entire citizenry had gathered a hundred yards down the beach, where now a cortege of ambulances stood ready to ferry the crew of the *Mataafa* off to the hospital as they disembarked the lifesaving boat.

He crossed the distance to the body, kept looking between it and the ship tilting offshore. It seemed he could reach out and touch it, the *Mataafa*. And except for the list, seemed like it could have been at anchor, not run aground. And yet . . . here was this corpse in the standard-issue peacoat. A member of her crew. Washed to shore.

As if a wire had been tripped in him, Theodulf unbuttoned his coat and shrugged it from his shoulders. He knelt and covered the body. He pushed the wet hair off the man's face. He felt for a pulse in his neck. All of this he did quickly. With a sense of urgency. Like maybe he could revive this . . . Theodulf stopped his ministrations. He fell back in the snow. Sat there in every kind of disbelief. Behind him he could hear the bustle of the lifesaving crews and the neighing of horses as the survivors were carted off. Cheers went up for each departure. For each man spared the fate of the corpse resting on the snow in front of him.

Theodulf lifted his coat. He put it back on. He reached under the dead man's arms and hefted his stiff body and began dragging him toward the rabble.

Later, at Sacred Heart, Theodulf sat in the back pew, his uniform freshly pressed, the ache in his head announcing itself with each beat of his heart. The church was full of stunned parishioners, eager in that Wednesday noon hour for an explanation about all that had transpired the previous forty-eight hours.

Father Richter made a slow walk in front of the altar. He'd already read from the gospels and lamented the tragedy of storm. Now he reached the pulpit again and used one hand to steady himself while he turned to look at the stained glass looming behind him.

He stood motionless for some full minute before he began to speak. "We have gathered here on this day of reckoning to stand together in the house of God." He glanced at the window again. "Behold this heavenly light. Behold its beauty. And remember what darkness it *follows*." He shook his head, as if he'd found the thread of his own thoughts. "Already we've heard news of nine souls lost. Nine of God's children"—he looked yet again to the stained glass— "born again in eternity."

An almost inaudible hush came from the parishioners, who glanced uneasily at their fellows in Christ. Father Richter had their attention. That much was sure.

"As sinners, we may be tempted to wrest from God reasons for our trials. We may be tempted to beseech of Him an explanation for events such as the one we've just endured. But, lo! Let me remind you that the men lost in the storm, if they've kept their faith in order, are not asking the same. Indeed, they're relishing their ascension into heaven! They have undergone their last trial and are now seated at His table. If they could speak to us, if they could howl down from their lofty perches, they would not ask for pity but would rather pity *us*"—he made an all-encompassing gesture—"left here on earth, awaiting *our* admission into heaven." Still again Father Richter paused, this time surveying the packed church. It seemed he paused on each of the hundred faces. Or anyway, Theodulf felt signaled out.

"I think of their trial. Those men aboard the *Mataafa*. The nine that did not survive. I can well picture them in the bowels of that ship. The bitter cold. The fear and loneliness of it. The *doubt*." He shook his head, more animated now. "Those men, they could look out their porthole and see the fires we set for them! They could see their God-fearing brethren upon the shore! They could no doubt hear our cries across the water! 'We are with you!' we shouted. 'We are here in your hour of need!' "

He removed from a hidden pocket beneath his chasuble a handkerchief and wiped his face with it. As his homily mounted, he'd become more animate, and now he was riled to the point of perspiring. He held the handkerchief at arm's length, inspecting it as though it were the Shroud of Turin. As though written in his perspiration was the divine truth. He nodded. He closed his eyes and lifted his face heavenward and continued his homily. "But what could we do? Standing in the teeth of that storm. Naked before God. Calling out in brotherhood, but powerless.

"*That*, my fellow believers, is the lesson God has laid before us these last days." Now he nearly whispered, but still his voice carried through the church. "We are brothers, and we are powerless. That storm"—he pointed to the window behind him—"was a manifestation of God's wrath and His love at once. It was a reminder—a *reminder*, I repeat—that we should be ready at any moment to face His judgment. Were their souls in order, those nine men aboard the *Mataafa*? Were they ready to face their final judgment?" Again, he wiped his brow, this time putting the handkerchief back in the folds of his vestments. He nodded. He put both of his hands on the pulpit and seemed to meet the gaze of the entire laity. "Are *you*?"

Theodulf stood with the congregation. He too was fevered and perspiry, as much from the overwarm church as from his answer to Father Richter's final question. Before the priest had regained the altar, before he began the Liturgy of the Eucharist, Theodulf went back out into the cold afternoon to search for his answer.

As he walked back to the Spalding Hotel to collect his trunk before making the afternoon train to Two Harbors, Theodulf thought of the man he'd pulled up the shore earlier that day. The weight of him, all sodden and drowned. That man whose name he'd never know, surely his trial and death *alone* would have prepared him for God's judgment, would it not? But what of it? That man had lost his place on this mortal coil. Theodulf was yet left to tend his.

And surely his singular good act—bringing the victim to the gathered crowd, where a coroner met them—did not make his *own* soul right. What's more, he knew the affinity he felt with the drowned man was an afront to his tribulation and death, to say nothing of God's will. What's *still* more, he suspected he'd never earn God's love and forgiveness. Not living as he did, a reprobate to the marrow.

HER FATHER HADN'T SLEPT the night before. She knew this because neither had she, though she suspected the causes of their insomnia did not pair. Not exactly.

It had been a night of egregious wind and munificent snow. But their brick house on the hill hardly squeaked in the gale. The furnace hummed all night, keeping them warm. Her mother had left a fresh loaf of bread on the rack in the kitchen, and so Willa had a chunk of it with butter and raspberry preserves when she got home from the ceremony. And a glass of milk. And a cup of tea brought to her room. And when her father returned sometime around ten o'clock, and closed the door behind him, and made his way up to the weather station on the third level of their house, all was right. This despite his not stopping to say goodnight. Nor to commend her for her performance. Twice before midnight Willa snuck to the bottom of the spiral staircase and listened intently, and twice she heard him sigh while the graphs ticked and shuffled his papers.

But after midnight Willa lay in bed, still dressed except for the peruke, which she'd cast off, aware of the storm and her father's consternation filling the house like the radiated heat, but focused instead on who she'd been that night. The boy who rode the trolley to the temple, who'd flirted with the girl as the car clacked along the tracks, who'd performed her song in the Blue Room, and who'd met that unhappy, lost soul in the shadowy lobby. Any of those things in and of themselves might have been noteworthy. But that confluence of events taken altogether? She couldn't escape the feeling that something sincerely significant *had* happened. Something life altering, even. And what was worse, something she was ill equipped to understand.

Now she stood before the bathroom mirror, scrubbing the complexion powder from her cheeks, staring back at herself. She was exhausted, yes, but also vexed by the incomprehensibility of the night that had just passed. The surety of change hadn't abated at all. If anything, it had grown stronger.

She rinsed the cloth and rubbed another swath of her cheek clear. From downstairs, she heard the clock chime seven. Felt the need to hasten her getting ready. It would be a slog getting to the Maynard School two miles past the temple on East Superior Street, but she'd never missed a day and couldn't imagine doing so.

Again she rinsed the cloth. The complexion powder was entirely more difficult to remove than it had been to apply, and as she scrubbed with more vigor, a new thought entered her mind. Or, perhaps it was more like a new thought had entered the mind of her reflection, so out of body did it feel: this sensation of erasing herself. She stopped at the thought of it.

"Willa!" her mother called from the other side of the closed bathroom door. Her knuckles wrapped quietly. "Willa, can you hear me?"

"What is it, Mother?"

"There will be no school today. The storm has caused the trolleys to cancel their routes. Apparently, some eighteen inches have already fallen. With more promised and winds to blow it all around. Beastly weather. Just beastly."

Willa opened the door and stood face-to-face with her mother.

"Oh!" the latter said, taking in her daughter's divided visage. "You look a ghoul!" She retreated to arm's length. "It's the complexion powder, yes?"

"What else would it be?"

"With you and your moods, it could be anything."

"Is there a secret to removing it?"

"Of course there is." Now her mother joined her in the bathroom, ran the tap until the water warmed again, and let the sink fill. She put the toilet seat down and told Willa to sit and put her head back against the wall. When she did, her mother covered Willa's whole face with a hot, drenched cloth.

"We might take the opportunity of there being no school to join your father down at the harbor. I understand half the town has gathered to witness the *Mataafa,* which has run aground right off the canal pier."

"That seems a bit macabre, does it not?" Willa asked, even as she admitted to herself that the prospect *did* sound gripping.

"So young, and already as righteous as an anchorite."

Willa started to lift the cloth, but her mother swatted her hand away. "And besides, your father is going down to the lifesaving station. We can make it a family affair." She replaced one compress with another, and gently massaged it into Willa's face, starting at her hairline.

Willa wanted to protest—by instinct, she did—but took pleasure in the hypnotic effect of her mother's caress. How long had it been since she'd felt it?

As if extending a conversation she'd been having in her mind, her mother said, "Honestly, what use does your father think he'll be?"

"Perhaps the telegraph lines are down, and he needs to make a report," Willa said, her voice muffled.

"I suppose. But it occurs to me that his reports are part of what's caused this mess."

Willa sat up. The compress fell onto her lap. "You can't honestly think the storm is Papa's fault? He ordered the weather flags raised almost twenty-four hours ago."

"Your father orders the weather flags whenever the wind blows." She picked the cloth up and laid it back across Willa's face and recommenced her work.

Almost instantly Willa sank back into the comfort of it.

Five minutes later her mother folded the damp, loose strands of her daughter's hair behind her ears and lifted her chin to check if she missed any powder. "How was your performance? I didn't get the chance to ask last night."

Willa stood and looked in the mirror above the sink. Her mother had been asleep on the divan when Willa returned last night. A decanter of brandy sat on the table before her, alongside an empty snifter. "It was fine. Papa was *very* distracted. So was I, if I'm telling the truth. I saw the gulls again."

"The gulls! Did they fly away?"

"Soon enough, yes. Thank goodness."

Her mother touched Willa's hair, this time bringing it back out from behind her ear and straightening it with the pads of her thumb and forefinger. "You're growing up so fast," she said. "I hardly recognize you anymore."

Willa almost said, "That's because you hardly look at me anymore" but thought better of it and just twisted out of her mother's gaze.

"We could have lunch at the Palm Room? Or better yet at the Thibert Hotel. How does that sound?"

"I still think it's strange we should go watch a ship sink."

"Ships sink all the time, my dear daughter. You'd do well to remember that." She turned to go up the spiral staircase but stopped short. "The secret to life is to avoid the ones that do."

Even dressed as she was—silk stockings and wool pantalets, corset and flannel petticoat, dress, tall boots, cape, fox fur muff—the gale pierced through. Such a sharp wind and snow. The three of them left their house at noon only to discover that the incline, like the trolleys, had canceled service. This meant a long walk down the treacherous Seventh Avenue boardwalk that ran parallel to the tracks. Willa thought it strange that in the throes of a storm as epic as this, so many footprints would have preceded theirs. The snow was trodden, as if a migration of some sort had already passed.

And there was more proof of just such a notion when they reached Superior Street. The Incline Saloon was full to bursting, the big window out front bleary with condensation. Hordes of people—more even than the annual Fourth of July parade—moved toward the waterfront. Snowballs crisscrossed the street as boys hid behind lampposts and mailboxes. A few brave horse-drawn carriages burrowed through. One carrying kegs of beer. Another the daily milk run. And coursing through it all, the breath of the storm. That wind that would not relent. Not even long enough for their voices to be heard.

Willa wanted to implore them to turn back. The snow hit her teeth like sand off the beach. She kept one hand up to block it but had to alternate every few seconds for how quickly the exposed flesh nearly froze. It was foolishness to be out in this. Perhaps not for her father, who had a purpose. But for her and her mother? Why hadn't they stayed home, with their feet by the fireplace and clutching cups of tea?

But on they went. Block by block, each an endeavor, each more crowded than the next. At Lake Avenue, her father huddled them together and told them to be careful and that he'd see them at home when his business was finished. He left with hardly a glance in his daughter's direction, though what glimpse she caught foretold myriad dooms. He kissed neither of them.

Fifteen minutes later found them in the lobby of the Thibert Hotel, knocking the snow from their capes and fixing their hats, which had been blown to pieces in the storm. All those clothes Willa wore, they now held the cold as if she'd brought the weather in with her. She couldn't stop shivering, not even when Mr. Murdock Alderdice, the maître d'hôtel, ushered them to a table by the fireplace and snapped his fingers for a pot of hot tea.

"How is it you ravish even on a day like this?" he asked, bowing before Mrs. Brandt.

"Mr. Alderdice, this is my daughter, Willa."

"Charmed, I'm certain," he said, lifting Willa's hand to his lips and kissing the middle knuckle. "You're every bit as lovely as your mother said."

He smelled of cinnamon or coriander and his hair and dress were impeccable, both of them slick as sealskin, and as black. He

wore a handlebar mustache that she might have hung her cape from.
But despite his refinement, Willa sensed about him some flagitious
quality. As if he possessed dark and magical qualities. She wouldn't
have been surprised if he tilted his chin up and withdrew a sword
from his throat.

"Say thank you, Willa Brandt," her mother said, tapping her
daughter's hand with the tip of her long fingernail.

"Thank you," Willa said.

"My pleasure." His words were like melted wax.

"Look there," her mother said. "It's Mrs. Cobb and Mrs. Walbank. I should say hello." She tapped Willa's hand once more and
added, "I'll be back in just one moment." To Mr. Alderdice she said,
"We'll start with the creamed artichokes and a glass of champagne
for me. Bring Willa a glass of milk." She was up and straightening
her skirts before Willa registered that she was about to be alone
with Murdock Alderdice.

No sooner did the realization arrive than he leaned closer and
put his hairy hand on her shoulder. "The last time I saw you I might
have mistaken you for a boy," he said.

His breath reeked of anchovies and garlic, and now that he was
so near she could see dried spittle in the corners of his mouth and
nose hairs wiry and blackest of all his fleece.

"But now?" He stood ramrod straight and pretended to swoon,
his eyeballs rolling in their sockets. "No longer." He fixed her in a
monstrous gaze. "You're as buxom as your mother. And I can see
from the mischief in your eyes, you're as devilish, too."

Now he looked across the dining room at Willa's mother, who
stood in conference with Mesdames Cobb and Walbank but kept
one eye on Murdock, who just then began to walk away. But not
before he brushed the loose strands of Willa's hair off her neck with
the back of his mitt. "We should spend some time together. Come
see me." He finally clicked his heels together, bowed, and twirled
his mustache. The last thing he said before he left was, "Let's not
tell your mother we spoke of this. She'd be jealous."

* * *

Willa and her mother ate the creamed artichokes and then had roast duck and spinach for their main course. Ann Brandt ordered a glass of wine with each course, and by the time they awaited their dessert—a pot de crème to share and coffee for Willa—she was gossiping about her friends from the Rotary Club as though they were at the Palm Room, and not sitting across the Thibert Hotel dining room and as likely to hear her as not. Willa was of course not surprised. Her father always said that wine on his wife's lips was like wind on a chime. No, what bothered Willa on this occasion of her mother's logorrhea was not the sheer vapidity, but more the fact that it came as it did while so many other important matters were neglected. There was the storm, of course, the severity of which grew with each hostile moment. But there was also the fact of her mother's slatternly behavior, a quality Willa had never witnessed before. Each time Murdock Alderdice passed their table—something he did with unnatural frequency—her mother would ogle him or chirp some flirtation in his direction.

"You're embarrassing me, Mother," Willa said after one of his passes.

"Oh?"

"Why are you being so flirtatious with that waiter?"

"He's the maître d'hôtel, not a waiter."

"Would it matter if he was the mayor?"

Her mother picked up her empty wine glass and drank from it. "Our mayor is a gnome."

The waiter delivered dessert, and when he asked if there'd be anything else, Ann tipped her wineglass.

Willa took only one bite of the chocolate crème, deciding on her coffee instead. Her mother likewise neglected the chocolate, using the opportunity of its sitting dormant on their table to remind Willa that too many confections would widen her hips.

"You ordered it," Willa said.

"Hoping you might show a little happiness. Honestly, how could you be any dourer?"

"My mother *is* fine company, especially soused on a school day."

"I'm not soused. Merely making merry like the rest of this city."

"I don't know if merry is what people are—"

"You're insolent," her mother interrupted. "Excuse me." She stood and hurried out of the restaurant.

Left alone, Willa sipped her coffee and stirred the pot de crème around like it was a bowl of too hot soup. When the waiter delivered her mother's third glass of wine, Willa thanked him and waited for him to leave and then poured the wine in the saucer under the potted weeping fig. She finished her cup of coffee and had another, and eventually she ate the rest of the chocolate, one bite at a time, as though she had to ration it out. Which in a sense was true, for how else was she meant to pass the hour she sat alone in that bustling dining room?

Just as she was about to get up and make her way home, the hotel concierge came to her table. He wore his starched uniform and kepi, appearing for all the world as if he'd just marched in with other members of the French Foreign Legion to deliver some grave message.

Indeed, he leaned close and said, "Mademoiselle Brandt, yes? Our maître d'hôtel has asked me to request you wait in one of our meeting rooms. Your mother has been indisposed on a matter urgent to the Rotary Club. Allow me to escort you, please." He stood upright, almost at attention, again not unlike a soldier.

"The Rotary Club?" Willa said. "A matter urgent to the Rotary Club?"

"I believe so, yes. I understand she'll be done presently. And that she'd rather you not be out in the storm until she can attend you."

"You're to escort me to a meeting room? Why not let me wait here, where I can at least enjoy my coffee?"

"I'll be happy to arrange for a fresh cup of coffee in the meeting room. And anything else you like. But you see, there are so many people waiting to dine here. Even at this strange hour." He checked his watch. "Yes, you see, it's past two and there's a line out to Superior Street. It seems everyone in Duluth has come down to be a part of, well, *whatever* this day's become . . ."

Willa couldn't say whether her mother had responsibilities in the Rotary Club. She couldn't figure out why she'd stormed off and left her in the dining room. She didn't know what her mother meant about sinking ships and not finding yourself on one. All of this lent to an already ambiguous day an air of impossibility. She felt, Willa did, as though she might count every second of the rest of that afternoon. That if she didn't, time would lose its hold. So, as she stood and set her napkin on the table, as she straightened her skirts and her hat and followed the concierge out of the dining room and through the lobby, she ticked the seconds off. One to fifty to one hundred to two. At two hundred and thirty-eight, the door of the meeting room closed behind her, and she sat alone at a mahogany table lit by an electric banker's lamp.

Seven thousand. She had counted past seven thousand before the door of the meeting room opened and her mother walked in. She was disheveled and her mood had turned again. She was nearly jolly now. Her expression flushed and as if she'd drunk a whole bottle of champagne while attending her meeting.

"There you are," she said.

"Who would leave their daughter like that? For more than two hours?"

"I had business I had to attend to."

"Today? By happenstance? At the Thibert Hotel?" Willa stood and squared her mother in a righteous gaze. "Are you inebriated?"

"Of course I'm not. And if you must know, yes: *today, by happenstance,* and *at the Thibert Hotel.*" She straightened her skirts and pulled her sleeves down her wrists. "Your father isn't the only industrious one. You'd do well to take a lesson in that. If you're the modern young woman you aspire to be."

Willa stared at her with mistrust and ire, not certain of the underlying reasons for her strong feelings until her mother crossed her arms under the lace bertha of her dress and surreptitiously adjusted her bosom. It was in that instant she knew her mother had cuckolded her father. While Willa herself had been made to wait. She wouldn't have been more surprised at the realization than if the *Mataafa* had been lifted by a wave and stove into the lobby of the hotel. It was scandalous, yes. But more to the point, it was unimaginable. Her dour mother? Taking a lover? Murdock Alderdice, no less? A slick, uninteresting fool? Pondering these questions, Willa found herself uncharacteristically speechless.

Her mother, intuiting her daughter's thoughts, said, "Remember about the sinking ship. Speaking of which, we'll go see that one now. For emphasis if not for entertainment."

And then, as though she had the power not only to intuit but also to summon, their cloaks and muffs were brought into the meeting room by the same concierge who had delivered her two hours ago. Before they left, Ann Brandt took her daughter's arm, removed from an inner pocket a palm full of hair pins, and used them to secure her daughter's hat on her head. She stood so close, Willa could smell the souring champagne on her breath.

When her mother finished, she kept her daughter at arm's length and said, "Someday you'll understand. I know you find that hard to believe, but I'd stake my life on it. In fact, I have."

What could a child already so addled by the previous twenty-four hours of her life take from such a lesson? The answer to that question would elude her for half a decade. But on that afternoon, she walked with it. Down to the waterfront, the storm still rowdy but also as if it were anticipating its own sentimentality. Even as she thought it, Willa was ready to admit the thought might as easily describe her own state of mind.

Of course, that didn't make it better or easier to walk among the throngs with her mother, who treated the occasion of those monumental fires and the nearby horror aboard the *Mataafa* as an occasion to celebrate her own revelation, if that's what she'd had—and then preached to her daughter—in the meeting room of the Thibert Hotel not a half hour before. No, for Willa, the storm and the fires and the foundering ship . . . all of it was like a fulfillment of the night before. Or at least it felt like one. The gulls laboring against the gale intimated a kind of proof of this theory. And though she'd sooner have been able to reach up and grab one of those birds than reason out the string of connections that began with her father applying the complexion powder the afternoon previous and her standing on the shore now, the snow blasting a new paleness into her cheeks, she nonetheless believed it was inviable—that string—and that someday, as her mother suggested, she would indeed understand.

And if it was grandiose thinking—surely it was—it was also the truest thing she'd ever known. And the smartest. Another new feeling welled in her. It compelled her to look up, heavenward, where a break in the clouds gave a glimpse of the moon, as pallid as the clouds and snow, and as callous. She would come to know it. Yes, she would.

It was then, finally, that she took in the faces of the crowd. Had any of them seen the moon? Had any of them taken their eyes off the hobbled ship in that instant of parting clouds? Of parting storm? None seemed to have. Not the children cavorting in the snow. Not the women with their hands at their mouths. Not the men stoking the fires, as though the flames from shore might warm the men on the *Mataafa*. Not even the dogs, who chased at the waves coming ashore until they crashed with power enough to shake the earth.

She gave the crowd one more chance. That's when she saw him, also looking out on the eastern sky. The man from the lobby of the temple the night before. Did he, too, espy the moon? The man who would become her husband?

FOG

JULY 3, 1910

In his epistle, chapter 4, verse 14, the apostle James, after imploring his readers to shun their concupiscence and to live humbly and in God's service, writes: For what is your life? It is a vapour which appeareth for a little while, and afterwards shall vanish away.

I don't agree much with James—or with any of the authors of the old book—but on this notion of life as a fog that vanishes in death, we find some common ground. Which is not to say that I doubt the possibility of a soul. Indeed, I've seen them leave the dead! But what becomes of them, of the souls of the departed? On that I'm less experienced.

Still and all, I often think about James and stammer at his wisdom. How did he know what dark forces would govern the minds of those many, would lead them to confliction? This man— these men—who wrote on parchment and on stone millennia ago, in deserts and in tents! They knew the human heart, even if they couldn't imagine another side of the globe, where the fog was so temperamental.

J UNE HAD NOT YET RELENTED to July. On the calendar, yes. But not in the spirit of the days, which continued to sulk and stack like the banks of fog that rolled in each night. The birds did call. The ferns did green. The rivers drained the hills. But the balm of summer could not be summoned even with the air horns, which every night beseeched a new season that would not come.

As though to further confuse the natural order of things, those same air horns sent the wolves into a nightly pother. Their howls echoed. They cried all the black hours. And their lamentations found their way into Theodulf's mood, which was as bleak as the weather. Saturdays, Sundays, and Mondays he took the overnight watch. They were shorter now with the lengthening days, but still he found plenty of darkness to attend his thoughts, which fought constantly between his duty to the Lighthouse Service and the Hamilton railroad watch which for more than a month now had bedeviled him.

At the top of each hour, he'd check the light and the air horns. He'd adjust the vents and note the gasoline levels in the compressors and wind the clockworks. And on the quarter hour he'd return to the watch room and sit at the desk and for the umpteenth time, try to put the watch back together again. The fog signal accompanied him most nights, every twenty seconds like an alarm announcing his incompetence.

One night he'd even left his Longines on the bedside table in order that the failure of reassembling the Hamilton would have graver consequences. But even that motivation failed, and when he'd put the screws in the caseback and turned the Hamilton over in his palm and the hands still didn't move, well, he'd merely turned his eyes to the ceiling and admonished himself in one breath and God with the next. He hadn't gone anywhere since without the Longines in his waistcoat pocket.

On this drab morning, he checked it despite the fact he'd just extinguished the light, which meant, in early July and accounting for the fog, the hour was six. An infamous hour in his family. The one his opa Hrolf died. This would have been in the summer of 1882, before Theodulf turned eight years old and before his father moved the family to Two Harbors—then called Agate Bay—in order that he might make his own, unaffiliated fortune.

Theodulf had never forgotten the details of that morning, or the countless others he'd spent with his opa while the old man declined. Hrolf had made his fortune with his brothers—Willi and Walther—building ships on the Detroit River, a career that had left his hands knotted and bent, but strong as vices. In his dotage, which Theodulf attended near daily, he used those hands for two purposes: to press his pears into schnapps, and to carve the fallen branches from the pear tree into clocks.

Two dozen pear trees lined the bank of the river between the Sauer estate and the shipyard. Each was harvested yearly. So much in abundance were those pears that the brothers often joked they could have been gentleman farmers by their yield alone. It was the sort of joke, Theodulf now understood, that only affluent people made. Still, the trees were legendary. French Jesuit pears, they were rightly called. Though not by his opa, whose allegiance to his German roots were as deep as his orchard's. He referred to the trees collectively as Hamburg pears, except for the grandest of them all, which he named Saint Mary in honor of the great cathedral of his birthplace. Every couple of years, a storm would come down the river and knock a limb or two from the giantess. It was from that windfall that he carved his *Kuckucksuhr*, his English bulldog (named Brick, because he so resembled one) bundled beside his hobnail boots.

His opa proselytized. About God, yes, often, but also about his hobbies. And because Theodulf accompanied him so often, he absorbed, at a very young age, much of his opa's wisdom. Such as it was. By those later days, he was a man given to rambling speech. Whether it didn't make sense to the boy because of its wandering, or because of the boy's inexperience with sophistry all together, he would never know. But regardless, he loved following Opa around the estate. From barn to workshop to sitting room. Listening to his incessant banter.

Opa's favorite subject was clocks. Well, clocks and church. So, naturally, they sometimes found each other in confluence.

"Clocks are like cathedrals, Schatzi," he might say, standing over his workbench, chisel in one hand, mallet in the other. "The housing, that's what we're carving now, is like the church itself. The edifice, that is. Ornate, you see? Decorative. Pretty. It's meant to capture one's imagination. The reason it's beautiful? Because it needs to seduce the skeptic. Needs to draw the wayward into God's kingdom." He'd chisel a few more curls of wood. "And let me ask you: would a man with a wayward soul rather occupy a castle or a shanty?" He paused, thinking for a moment. "In fact, which would most any man?"

Oh! How was a child, one as guileless as Theodulf, supposed to know the answer to this? Theodulf, who, finding no solace in the contemplation of it, felt instead simpleness as Opa's hand tousled his hair.

"Of course, what good is a clock that doesn't tell time?" He'd blow the shavings away, run the pad of his thumb up a particular curve in the wood. "Which is why we pay even more attention to the *movement*. To that part of the clock that *keeps* time."

He'd take a sip of his pear schnapps. Wipe his lips on his knobby hand. "This is also like a cathedral. There's the edifice"—he'd tap the housing of the clock—"and there's what happens inside. Community, prayer, ceremony, devotion, constancy. All of this, yes. But more than anything: *faith*." He'd finish the schnapps. "The movement could also be understood to possess these qualities. What's more, if the soul is organized by the Church, then time is organized by the movement. It's a machine that orders the whole world. The whole universe, even. And on something so grand as that, we need faith. A clock is a faith machine."

He'd hoist young Theodulf onto the stool that sat ready beside the workbench. Gave him a small gouge and set him to work on a limb from the pear tree. "So the clockmaker, like the priest, has a sacred duty. In the same way a congregant ought to pray, and be constant, so too should a clock. Every spring and wheel, every gear and pendulum, every chime and hook and lug and screw ought to be accounted for. Ought to be treated with devotion and reverence. Maybe even awe and joy."

He'd built any number of clocks, Opa had. But his grandest horological accomplishment was the one that still hung on the wall of his father's billiard room. Some two feet tall and another foot wide, it depicted the tree of its origin in minute detail. At the top of each hour, twelve carved doves ascended from the crown of the tree, each with a distinct *cuckoo* attending its flight. The numerals on the face were hand stamped brass brought home from the shipyard. The pendulum was also brass, molded into the shape of a cross. How many times had Theodulf heard the Kuckucksuhr chime? A dozen times each day, for all eight years of his life until then.

That is, until six o'clock in the morning on the day of his Opa's death. The night before, one of the storms had come up the river. Instead of knocking a limb from the tree, it uprooted the whole thing. As if a sinkhole had opened there on the bank of the Detroit. Opa, observing it from the sitting room window the night before he died, said, "As goes Saint Mary, so goes my soul."

The next morning, just before six, after breakfasting with Theodulf and leading him into the sitting room, where he lit a fire in the hearth, Opa stepped to the sideboard and poured himself an ounce of pear schnapps. He took one snort from his snuff board, downed the schnapps, and stepped to the Kuckucksuhr, reached into the housing and stopped the pendulum from swinging. Finally, he went to his rocking chair, sat down, and asked Theodulf to bring the afghan from the back of the divan.

When he delivered it, Opa took his hand. "Remember, Schatzi: what good is a clock that doesn't keep time?"

Theodulf realized then that the Kuckucksuhr in the sitting room hadn't chimed. He looked desperately between it and his opa, who only smiled and settled into his chair. He studied the fire in the hearth for a spell and said, "Time is surer than God. I wish I'd known that fifty years ago. Tell your uncle Willi there's four hundred board feet of pear tree down on the bank." He lifted the afghan up to his chin. "I guess I'll go see if I can find Rebekah." And then he closed his eyes and died. The stopped clock recorded the hour.

For all its sadness, the memory gave Theodulf respite. It brought clarity. He turned back to the fog signal building. The blast was muted inside, a relief he'd not realized he needed. He checked the fuel in the compressor despite knowing it was adequate for the morning, however long it might last. Next he returned to the cleaning room, where he carefully slid the log book to one side of his desk, and the silk cloth covered in watch parts to the other.

On a piece of letterhead, he wrote first to his mother:

July the 3rd, Year of Our Lord 1910

Dearest mother,

Is it possible Opa Sauer had a crisis of faith as he passed into everlasting life? That man of stalwart and unconquerable faith? Do I remember correctly that his clock never ticked again after he deceased? Is it still stuck on the hour of six?

I guess you might say the interminable fog has me pensive and reflecting.

God be with you.

Your loving son,
Theodulf

As if this simple missive broke a dam within, he took another piece of letterhead from the drawer and wrote a second.

July the 3rd, Year of Our Lord 1910

Dear Mr. Grimm,

I thought of you this morning as the day broke again in fog. It reminded me of our last correspondence around the time of the comet's passing. What I mean to say is, the fog itself reminds me of the comet's vaporous tail. It could be residual! At any rate and as I say, you crossed my mind because of it. I never thanked you for your advisement. Though we all appear to have weathered its advance, I'd be remiss if I didn't say I'm glad I won't live long enough to witness the next orbit. My, how that comet did disturb me.

So, I send my thanks.

Sincerely,
Theodulf Sauer
The Gininwabiko lighthouse station

After reading both letters, he stuffed them in envelopes and addressed them. He made the day's recording in the logbook. For a long time he looked at the disassembled watch on the black kerchief, waiting. Finally he sat down and pulled the lamp close and began to put the Hamilton back together. For almost an hour he persisted, the foghorn blowing, it seemed, with each piece he added to the assembly. By the time he screwed the caseback into place, his mind had gone fully clear, and he packed his tools and placed them in his holdall. Last he extinguished the lamp on the table and checked that the cleaning room was sewn up for the morning.

Rather than returning to the house, he made a right turn out the door and stood on the cliff's edge between the lighthouse and the fog signal building, the Hamilton in the palm of his hand. He closed his eyes. It would have been a good moment to pray, but he was well past that. Instead, he tried to wind the watch one more

time. He counted to ten waiting for the second hand to begin ticking, and when it did not, he smirked, thought passingly of his opa,
and threw the railroad watch into the fog over the lake.

The sensation that followed was akin to what he imagined jumping from the cliff would feel like. First one, then two, then three
four five seconds passed, his belly dropping and his knees wob-
bling. When no splash came, nor any other sound for that matter,
he opened his eyes. The foghorn blasted again. Then it did before
finally he turned toward home.

Willa would have breakfast on the table. He would thank her.
Tomorrow he would deliver the letters, tucked now in the pocket
of his shirt. The foghorn sounded behind him. It did three times
more before he stepped under the portico of his house, where he
checked his Longines.

L ATE MORNING and still the foghorns moaned. For the better part of twelve hours they'd been grieving. Now that Theodulf had breakfasted, the kitchen cleaned, even the herb pots watered, Willa discovered she needed to get away from that sound. So she checked the schedule she'd written, saw it was pork and potatoes for supper, and decided to make her way down to the dock. The errand would accomplish two things at once. She could fetch their fare, and it would put a quarter mile between her ears and the foghorns.

If she were generous with herself—and with Theodulf—she might admit that in the last month the rhythm of life at the station had become, what, endurable? The blackflies had come and gone. The bitterly cold nights, too. Thanks to Mrs. Wilson, she had learned to make seven edible dishes. She'd also learned to keep the house tidy. She was sleeping well. And if the weather was foggy (there was the blasted air horn again), it was also easy. Weeks like these, it was easy to forget about the light's purpose altogether.

And Silje. That sweet child. That determined young woman. Between her and the other keepers' wives, Willa had a burgeoning community of people she cared about for perhaps the first time in her life. She had to check the realization whenever it dawned on her. Not because it didn't delight her—of course it did—but because it seemed so unlikely.

These murky days, the improbability was even more pronounced. She walked down the hill, the fog stacking the closer she got to the lake so that by the time she reached the dock, she couldn't see the pilings at the other end. The foghorn sounded. Muffled down here on the shore, a hundred feet below the station and halfway to Silje's cabin. She walked out to the end of the dock, where the foghorn had a still different intonation. She wondered how it might sound to a ship a mile out. In the time it took her to think that thought, the bellow from above and behind came again. She put her hands over her ears and heard in the whoosh and tailing from the foghorn something like the sound from inside a seashell.

At the barrel—what a brilliant solution to the problem of keeping their perishables fresh—she took a pound of wrapped porkchops from the supply. By the time she reattached the lid and brushed her hands and knees and looked up again, the fog had all but lifted. The first thing her eyes alighted on was the Lindvik dock. Or the Braaten dock, she supposed. The boat was tied up, and Silje herself came from the fish house laboring over a loaded wooden box. When she got to the cabin, she walked around the outside of it and disappeared in the trees. The foghorn sounded twice during her short journey.

Willa thought about paying a visit, but as soon as the possibility entered her mind, something changed it. To be more precise, Mats did. Stepping out the fish house door, he sat on an upturned box and unlaced his boots. He held his pipe in his lips, and with each movement he made—his arms, shoulders, lifting one foot and then the next—puffs of smoke rose from his pipe and then his bowl, one right after the next. Once his boots were off, he slid his galluses over his shoulders, then untucked his shirt and took that off, too. Next he unbuttoned and removed his trousers and socks and standing there in the cool late morning, he finished his pipe, the bowl of which he tapped empty and lay atop the pile of clothes. Finally, he removed his skivvies and went bare naked to the edge of the dock, and dove in.

The mere thought of that cold water made Willa's body seize. So much that she lost her breath for a moment, finding it again only by gulping. The foghorn gave a final call from above, and in the middle of it, Mats reemerged from the water. Like an otter, his hair all slicked back, he swam toward her with his nose just above the water. For a moment she thought he might swim all the way to the lighthouse dock, but as soon as the thought filled her, he dove again, his feet coming up behind him. When he reappeared, it was back at the ladder on the end of his dock. He climbed out, shook his hair like an animal might, used his shirt to dry his face and hands, then gathered the rest of his clothes, slid his feet back into his boots, and walked to his cabin still naked from the ankles up.

It took a few moments for Willa to gather herself. As if she'd just had a strange dream and needed to get reacquainted with the waking world. The seizing she'd felt vicariously when he'd first dove had not yet left her body. In fact, it found her center. The only way to halt that strange, eager sensation was to walk. Which is what she did. Back across the dock and up the hill.

"THE TRAP IS SET too close to the cabin," her uncle said.

"But he comes around all the time. Sometimes right up to our door."

He slid the box of fish guts out from under the counter and put it on top. "He's a smart boy. When he comes around, you can believe he's paying attention." He lifted a second box of fish guts up onto the countertop. "He's watching where he steps, is what I mean. And that trap you have cocked just out the door? Not only would he see it, but he'd smell it, too. He could smell *you* from the ridge top."

"How do I catch him?"

"That's another thing, kiddo. The trap's not going to catch him, it's going to kill him."

"I know that."

The air inside the fish house was close and rotten with the stench of fish and salt. Enough that he might have boxed the smell right alongside the guts. It had been a good season so far, and despite his fatigue—he did the job of three, day in and day out—her uncle's mood had warmed with the onset of summer. This morning, though, the relentless foghorns from the station above had worked him into impatience.

He wiped sweat from his face with the sleeve of his shirt, hammered the lid onto one of the barrels of salted fish. "What'll you do with him?"

"I'll sell his pelt."

"It's not the season for that."

"No one will buy it?"

"Sure, someone will buy it, but if you get caught, you'll pay all your proceeds to the fine." He stacked the boxes of guts and carried them outside. When he came back in, he said, "I thought this wolf was a friend of yours."

Silje finished cleaning the knives, wiping them dry with a cheese cloth they kept for the job specifically. She put the knives back in the block. "He's a trickster, not a friend." She thought of saying more, then thought better. Why did her uncle need to know her every fear and inhibition? Her every thought about danger? She wouldn't tell him. She *couldn't*. Not really. She only knew that Fenrir had started scaring her as soon as she met Hosea Grimm. And the longer that coward went without answering her letter, the more scared she was of the wolf.

"It's child's play, Silje. Trying to trap this wolf."

"I'm not a child?"

He packed his pipe, considered his answer, and said, "I don't know whether you are or not." He nodded at the final box of offal on the counter. "Regardless, I'd take that out into the woods. All the way over to Odegaard Creek. Spread it along the shore. Leading up to a standing pool in the creek. Set your trap near that." He took a match from a box on the windowsill and lit his pipe. "I'm going to see about scrubbing some of this stink off me."

Silje hefted the box and led her uncle out the door. "I'll be back in an hour," she said, heading toward the woods.

"This fog," he said as though he were speaking to the weather itself.

"It's been here for weeks," Silje said, speaking very much to him.

In the woods, the fog hung in the treetops. The ground was boggy. Exhaling. She stumbled over the roots and fallen tree branches, the reeking box of fish as much as slapping her while she went. Her hands were wet with slime oozing from the bottom. For as often as she ventured back here—among the ferns, among the deadfall, under the quiet canopy—it never ceased being otherworldly. A whole different ecosystem than the one a hundred yards back on the rocky shore of the lake. Here, in the woods, the world inverted. Instead of the lake to orient her, she had the hill, which rose slowly the foggier it got. She hardly blinked for fear she'd lose her way.

Despite her caution, it wasn't long before the strain in her strong young legs was the only indication she moved in the right direction. When she paused—to rest, yes, but also to sense her whereabouts— she'd have sworn she heard voices. Whispers. Whether the voice of the wolf or her parents or the weather itself, she couldn't say. But between their presence and the fact she could no longer see the trees before her, never mind the trap splayed across the top of the fish box or her own hands that held it, she started to cry. Not from fear, but because this moment seemed the culmination of so much confusion and spiritual disarray. As if the instant she realized her parents had drowned finally had its end here, up on the hill, in blinding fog and with a box of offal and a wolf trap.

The weeping was solace, though, and she squatted and set the box among the ferns and lifted a shoulder to each eye one at a time to wipe her tears. She wiped her hands, too, on the knees of her skirt, and then put her hands to her ears to block the distant fog-horn, and clenched her eyes shut. In this particular darkness, a no-tion took root. She could no sooner describe it to herself than she might the blackness that attended it, but its realness and certainty were as absolute as the pulsing of her heart, or the blood it sent coursing. She might have called it an awakening if it didn't seem so like a dream, but regardless, her world grew enormously as she stood there. As if a whole season of rain and sun had nourished her maturation.

When she opened her eyes, not only could she see the trees and ferns and fish box again, but the fog had vanished altogether. Even up in the heady canopy of the pines, daylight reigned. She checked behind her. Was the still-throbbing sound of the foghorns mocking her? Warning her? Serenading her? And which did she hope was true? She looked at her hands, sticky and speckled with blood. By some association she could hardly fathom but was aware of all the same, the sight of her hands led her to the image of her parents sunk a half mile offshore, a quarter mile down in the depths, spotless. Resting. At peace in a way they'd never been in life. Almost happy.

It wasn't long before she reached Odegaard Creek, where she stood on a fallen tree spanning the brook. Several trees bridged the water, which trilled with the hope of two recent rainstorms. She saw the riffles settle into a pool at a bend a hundred feet downstream. A copse of cedar trees shaded the pool, and for a moment she imagined herself bathing in that spot. But just as soon as she saw the box of fish guts and the trap, the frivolity of the idea left her in a gust.

She made her way down the bank and set the trap and fish box on a rock. For a long moment she stood there, the sun warming her back and shimmering off the water. When clouds passed, she could see into the pool, where fish schooled, their tailfins curved with the current. As soon as her shadow crossed their backs, they darted as one into deeper water.

Always, there was deeper water.

Uncle Mats had cooked the bacon—which she'd relished even as she feigned injury—but the truth was, the offal would be better bait. Especially here along the creek. She slung it along the shoreline rocks fifty feet in either direction and by the time she stood again beside the pool, ravens and their caws filled the now cloudless sky, their hollering filling the void left by the foghorns.

She lowered the trap in flowing water and looped the drag around one of the trees, leaving the ten feet of chain underwater. The trap she arranged between rocks half-submerged in the creek until it was firm and level. She stood up and looked at the ravens and the trail of carrion and guts and then tried to imagine the wolf coming up the creek bed at the beckoning of these birds. Likely he was already on his way. He and his whole pack. They'd move carefully, pulled along by the stink of the dead fish, alert to every sound but the cawing birds. Likely they'd sample the fish skin, they'd slurp the bowels, they'd develop a taste for it. Here at the pool, they'd pause to drink, their paws finding purchase on the larger rocks, the rocks as much as cemented in place. There were a couple of dozen such rocks surrounding the pool.

She double-checked the trap between the rocks. As she spread the jaws, the teeth drawing flat on either side of the triggering plate, some feeling in her own guts spread, too. It broadened her, left her feeling empty and wanting and dangerous and like she'd not known herself until this morning.

What might possibly have accounted for this? She couldn't know. But as she laid the last of the dead fish on and around the trap, as she washed the slime and blood from her fingers in the creek water, as she stood upright and felt the warmth of the sun this time on her face, she imagined the trap snapping shut and saw not a wolf in its hold, but a man.

INHERITANCE

JULY 5, 1910

We speak often of the separation of the soul and body after death, but what of the soul before a body is born? Do we inherit our souls as we do our toes and thumbs, our spleens and bones, our blood and marrow?

I've sometimes pondered the possibility of our lives having been foreordained, as though we are but stars streaking across the cosmos, flaring and fading and dying. Who sees to it we're illuminated? And snuffed? Before we arrive and after we've gone, are we but essence? Possibility? What force sets us in motion?

Most people would name it God and would endow Him with these and infinite powers. A lovely, simple notion. For it answers all questions. Indeed, it is written, in the 138th Psalm, that Thy eyes did see my imperfect being, and in thy book all shall be written: days shall be formed, and no one in them. Thy, here, of course being God. It sounds as plausible to me as anything else.

But whoever declares the answer is a charlatan, even if I can't blame them for wondering. Myself? I tend to think we are like a forest of trees, ready to be made into shanties by the boards that come of us. Or better, an alphabet, soon to be made into words.

FOR THE BETTER PART of thirty-six hours Theodulf had sulked and stomped around the grounds, fretting about the fact that the post office wouldn't be open due to the Independence Day holiday. His incorrigibility since Mrs. Wilson mentioned it was out of proportion even for him.

But now he rowed the lighthouse tender, hoping to beat the *Nocturne* down the shore. If she were on schedule, he'd have half an hour to spare when he got to the dock in Otter Bay. But she'd not come up out of the lake even after he'd rounded Big Rock. Not even the steam from her stack. He feathered the oars and checked his watch, fretful that perhaps he'd mislaid the time again.

Eight o'clock on Tuesday morning. That much was certain according to his Longines. Except that when he took the oars again and sliced them into the still water, the lake answered with its own yawn against the hour. He'd noticed other phenomena of this sort since he'd thrown the Hamilton into the fog. As if the lake kept its own time. Cosmic. Godly. Interminable. And he at its mercy.

Madness, he thought, digging harder with the oars.

Fifteen minutes later the whine of the mill shrieked across the water. Still no *Nocturne*—not in either direction—though a freighter made several knots against the horizon. Of course, the first hot summer day would arrive just in time for him to sweat under its burden. Perspiration fairly poured from his body, soaking the back of his shirt. He stretched his shoulders, glancing up to see a scavenging of gulls mistaking the lighthouse tender for a fishing boat. Their riotous calls set him on edge.

It was not yet nine when he tied up on the dock in Otter Bay. He'd rolled his sleeves up past his elbows by then. Unbuttoned his collar. Left his cap on the thwart still damp with sweat. If he'd been back at the lighthouse, with the privacy of the dock there, he'd have stripped down to his skivvies and jumped in the lake. Instead, he walked up the dock and onto the beach and stepped to the water and splashed his face with it. He ran his wet hands through his hair. He rinsed his forearms.

A summer day wasn't the worst thing, surely, but as he stood there, he'd have been hard pressed to think of something worse. No sooner did the thought cross his mind than a swarm of flies descended upon him. Normally he'd use his hat to swipe them away, but he'd removed it in the boat. So instead, he slapped at his neck and bare arms and ears, hurrying from the cloud of whirring bugs out to the end of the dock. But there was no breeze, and the flies followed him like his own dark thoughts. One flew into his ear canal, bit him, and tickled its way back out. The itch flared immediately, and while he was busy waving the flies away with one hand, he stuck the pinky of his other into his ear to scratch the bite. But he couldn't reach it, not even by twisting his head around like a horse and plunging each of his fingers in turn. He might have screamed at the indignity, but just then he saw the *Nocturne* in the distance. The sight of it calmed him, and he went back up the dock to the post office.

Mr. Holzer already had the door wedged open. Inside, the darkness had kept the warm morning at bay. But now the humidity came in like smoke from a fire. His back ran like a freshet again. Standing behind the counter, old Holzer didn't even answer when Theodulf helloed, leaving him standing there instead, feeling like he was melting.

After another minute, Theodulf touched the bell on the counter and cleared his throat. Mr. Holzer turned around slowly, as though he were on a rotating pedestal that had a chink in its gears. "Ah, Keeper Sauer." He lifted his eyes but not his face when he spoke. "A locomotive could sneak up on me these days. Feels like the Missus Holzer poured her tea honey in my ears."

"I'm sorry to hear that, Mr. Holzer."

He waved the sympathy away.

"I've a couple of letters to send," Theodulf said, reaching into his pocket to retrieve them.

"Did you go for a swim with these in your pocket, Mr. Sauer?" Holzer held the limp letters at arm's length.

"It's like a sauna out there. No summer at all until this morning, and then it rises like Lazarus of Bethany."

"I reckon some of your pious friends and associates would liken that comparison to blasphemy."

"Oh, let them," Theodulf said.

Mr. Holzer raised a suspecting eyebrow.

"I only meant it as a figure of speech." He wiped his brow. "I'm agitated, Mr. Holzer. Soaked through with sweat and eager to get these letters sent."

Holzer shifted his gaze out to the dock. "Here's the *Nocturne* now."

Sure as he said it, the good ship slid up to the dock. Stevedores stood ready to catch the hawsers from over the railing before she even touched the fenders. When Theodulf looked the other way, streams of townsfolk headed toward her, ready for whatever she brought. There might be friends and family, cows and kerosene, flour and apples, boots and gingham, Winchesters and violins. For certain there'd be mail. He only cared about the mail.

Which was delivered not five minutes later. A sack each of letters and packages, both dropped on the counter. In the same motion, the man from the *Nocturne* picked up the sack Mr. Holzer had set in the outgoing box atop the counter. Not a word passed between any of the three men.

Despite his aged tilt and ponderous belly, Mr. Holzer filed the letters as though it were his singular purpose in life. The lighthouse had a larger postbox. Into it went the official correspondence. Each of the families had their own postboxes. By the time Mr. Holzer had finished sorting—not five minutes after the sacks had been laid on his counter—there was mail in each. Finished, Holzer resumed his listless posture and returned his attention to Theodulf.

"Now," he said, as though picking up in the middle of their conversation, "your agitation doesn't much interest me. But getting you what you came for does. So . . ." He turned to the very postboxes he'd just slotted the mail into and removed the lighthouse station's official correspondence—there was but a single parcel—and a letter from his family box. "This here's for you."

Theodulf inspected the return address which announced the Sauer estate on London Road. It was written in his mother's hand. For a moment he was baffled. How could she have replied so quickly? But as soon as he thought it, he realized mere chance left him with the letter in his hand. He stepped onto the deck outside the post office and slid his finger under the seal of the envelope. What news greeted him there:

July 3, 1910

My dear son,
    Your father passed away this morning. Peacefully and without apparent cause as he slept. Please come home.
    Your loving mother

What news indeed. How was it that not a single emotion coursed through him save a slight peevishness at needing to leave his post? And imminently.

He looked up. The same stevedores who had caught the hawsers were now untying them. Black steam sputtered from the *Nocturne*'s stack. Before the fact of his father's death settled on him, the ship was sailing off. Theodulf looked at his watch. He followed the ship's slow reverse passage, and its turn east, down the shore. The day's soddenness redoubled. The itch in his ear flared again. Still his pinky could not reach it. He knocked his ear with the heel of his hand. Rubbed it with the pad of his thumb.

The *Nocturne* would return in twenty-four hours, headed back up to Duluth.

S HE'D WEEKS AGO quit trying to understand his moods or the vacancy of his expression. But this one? The shroud of sincere bafflement? Of absolute defeat? Well, this one at least intrigued her. She stood in the kitchen with a paring knife in one hand and a peeled potato in the other, waiting for him to say something. When, after another moment passed and he didn't, she spoke softly, "Do you have heat stroke?"

He swabbed his face with the loose cuff of his shirtsleeve.

"Sit down," she said, pulling a chair from under the table and then turning to fetch a glass of water and a tea cloth from the pantry. She imagined wiping his brow but handed him the cloth instead.

He wiped his face again, drank half the water. After he set the glass on the table, he said, "I had a letter from my mother today." He took the letter from his shirt pocket and laid it beside the glass of water. Outside, Ruth and Ida crossed the grounds. Theodulf watched them, his eyes as distant as the noontime sun.

"What did your mother's letter say?"

He answered without turning back. "My father is dead. He passed in his sleep."

"Oh my," she said and sat across from him. She set the knife and potato on the tabletop and wiped her hands on her apron. "My condolences, Theodulf." They might well have been the first genuine and kind words she'd spoken to him since the day she arrived at the station.

"Yes, well."

"You'll leave on tomorrow's boat?"

He nodded.

"Shall I join you? Is that the custom?"

Now he turned to her. "No." He tapped the letter with his finger-tip. "She asked me to come alone." He drank the rest of the water. "I imagine her shock is matched only by her confusion. She needs my private counsel, I think. My calming presence."

Willa's sympathy vanished. She looked between Theodulf's complexion and the potato. They could have been mistaken one for the other. The waxen color. The sheen. Even the expression.

"Yes," he said, as though to confirm his thinking. "That's what she needs. That's why she's asked me to come alone."

Willa's lip quivered. She stood and turned to the pot on the stove. She quartered the potato, letting each chunk drop into the water.

After dinner, Theodulf visited Keepers Wilson and Axelsson to inform them of his impending absence. Willa circled the house, watching from different windows as he searched them out and spoke with them. He moved like a thief. A wolf. Quickly and with purpose. He found Mr. Axelsson at the oil house and Mr. Wilson under the portico on his house next door. The sun was still brazen at eight o'clock when he returned. At his desk he composed several letters. He asked for a cup of tea.

All this while Willa moved anxiously about the house. As if a party would soon begin. He hardly spoke to her but to ask for the tea.

At ten o'clock he found her in the sitting room.

"I'll be turning in," he said.

Willa set her book down.

"I'll need you to bring me to Otter Bay in the morning."

"That's fine."

"At sunrise."

She nodded.

"Mother will be expecting a note of condolence."

"I already wrote one. I'll put it on your desk."

He appeared to take some satisfaction in this. As though his civilizing influence were the reason for her having written, not her inherent good manners and general kindness.

"Well, then. Goodnight." He hesitated.

"Theodulf," Willa said. She sat up on the edge of her chair, set her book down. "When my own father passed—"

"Your father's death and my father's death have little in common." He turned up the stairs.

Two months ago, she'd have fumed. Now she was only glad for his absence. She picked her book back up and held it toward the lamplight. *Of these similitudes,* she read, *the one which has the best pretensions to a rude accuracy is that first mentioned; for the resemblance of the full moon to a human countenance, wearing a painful or lugubrious expression, is very striking.* Indeed, she thought, remembering her husband's pallid, ugly face as he ascended the stairs.

She clapped the book shut. Put it on the table. Realized that the moon shone now in the bright summer sky. Better to behold it than to read about it.

When a child, Willa used to sit in her father's office on the top floor of their house and listen to him work. She loved the sounds of the graphs ticking out their information, her father's pencil tapping some code as he took his readings, his own mumbling as he riddled the forecast. He often described the weather as being predictable until it arrived. She understood that better now.

Standing in the shadow of the lighthouse tower, the beam from the lamp aligning every ten seconds with the moon's steady rays and shining on the Lindvik place across the bay, she saw a bridge of light. She couldn't help the thought. Uncrossable, true, that distance, even with the light to carry her. She turned back to the moon itself. Wished more than ever she could get there.

It occurred to her, the pale moonglow carrying her thoughts across the water, that the memory of her father grew fainter and fuzzier. As the time after his death grew longer, she found her feelings about him growing more complicated. Wasn't he the reason, after all, she had been exiled to this place? With this man? And the future that bore down on her with greater urgency each day? As bad, or even worse, was the fact that his final, decisive act had not only ended his life, but also provoked in Willa herself a latent knowledge that she, too, might be capable of such an action. She despised her father for this and found herself conflicted and arguing with what she presumed was true about herself—that she would never end her own life—and what his actions had kindled. Namely, the possibility that she might.

And what else had he left her? Besides destitution? The music box for one. Her mother's total authority over her another.

She turned away from the thought. Tried to find comfort in the fact that her mother lived fifty miles up the shore. She'd not heard from her since a letter in April. One Willa hadn't responded to. Maybe she had some autonomy after all.

The mere possibility enlivened her. She walked through the darkness, past the houses, to the top of the path that led down to the dock. She was fifty yards closer to the Lindvik cabin. The beam from the lighthouse ceased just a few degrees to her left. She loved this spot. Felt, standing here, like a spy.

IN A BOX under her parents' bed, Silje found a dress. It was a miracle there were any discoveries to be made in that cabin, but she held one in her hands. A sagging skirt, a bodice cut for housework, the only things to distinguish it from the house frocks her mother wore were the brush train sewn with pink thread and the silk bow of the same color around the waist, lost now in the folds of rough cotton. She could no sooner imagine her mother wearing it than she could herself. Except she knew its provenance. She knew her mother had indeed worn it. Even knew that on the day she did, she expected it to lead to happiness.

Certainly, she never found it. Nor anything like it. No. What she gained instead was a husband who displeased her. Who didn't hold up his end of the bargain. He toiled endlessly, Silje's father did, but never seemed to finish the job. He couldn't find the right fishing grounds. Couldn't hammer a nail without also mugging his thumb. Around the house, he shuffled from one unfinished task to the next as if he had all the time in the world. Laying in wood, he'd split it wrong and stack it wrong and leave it uncovered against the snow and rain. Any of these shortcomings might have been forgivable, but according to her mother, he was also a loveless, ambitionless bore.

Silje laid the dress on the bed like she was putting it to sleep, the bateau resting on the lumpy pillow, the sleeves folded across the bodice and resting at the pink belt. It was easier to see her mother here. To imagine her resting. Silje placed the left sleeve of the dress over the pillow instead. Where her mother's head would have rested. Then she went to the doorway and stood with her hip against the frame. Oh, the moaning and complaining. The lamentations up and down her life. *Where was God and His grace?*

Where was her husband's gentleness and diligence and ability? Where was the weather's warmth? Winter's retreat? The coffee's bitterness? Where was the son she never had? The thankless daughter who only complained like her father, unless her head was in the clouds? Why wouldn't she quit humming those silly songs?

Her mother had an objection for every hour of the day. The severest of which she doled out whenever Silje was alone in the house with her.

Silje shook her head at those vestigial grievances. She went into the main room of the cabin and took her seat in the window. Her teacup from earlier sat on the ledge, a fly floating belly up in the dregs.

How did she know some part of her parents' life was missing? That there ought to have been nights where she lay up in the loft herself, listening to their bodies moving under the quilt and the muffled gasps of their breath in the room below. She'd never once heard the sighs that would've attended their lovemaking, only the ones that announced its absence. Sometimes she'd hear her father roll out of bed again in the middle of those nights, step back into his trousers, and head out to the fish house to do God only knew what.

For the first time in a long time, she tried to imagine what happened on the day they drowned. Maybe they argued. Maybe the night before, in a hotel room in Two Harbors, he'd made a husband's overture and been rebuffed again. Maybe he scolded her as they rowed home, and her mother, in a fit and as she often did, lunged at him and battered him about the shoulders and neck. Maybe, as they tussled, they fell into the lake, and instead of trying to save each other, gave themselves up to the depths because it was easier than surviving.

Did they even look at each other as they gasped their last breaths? As they sank?

Less and less could she stand to be in the cabin, but as soon as she stepped outside, the heat sapped her anger. It had been her intention to go check the trap again, but instead she just stumbled to the water, pulled off her shoes, gathered her skirt, and waded in. She supposed it was strange that the water didn't frighten or haunt her, but as she lifted her skirt fully above her waist and went in up to her bloomers, all she felt about it was the coldness. Days like these seldom fell upon the shore, and though she hated the bitterness of winter, this opposite was no better. In many ways it was worse.

She waded back ashore. Satisfied that no one watched from the trees, she pulled her dress altogether over her head and returned to the lake. When the water reached her waist, she dove in like her uncle often did. The coldness of the water riveted her to breathlessness even after she lifted her head into the air. She tried to scream but only gasped, and though her feet found the rocky bottom and the water only rose to her breasts, the shore seemed a mile away. Her arms swimming, feet stumbling over the rocks, she managed to get there. The flesh on her legs tingled, shone pink, and she laughed at the folly of it all, dabbing her face and neck with the dress.

Twenty minutes later she walked out of the cabin, the Winchester slung over her shoulder. She wore the same dirty dress. It still held the dampness from her toweling off with it, and the cooling breeze along the lakeshore came through it. Here was this strip of rocky land that defied the heat. She loved it for that.

It was short in lasting, though. As soon as she turned into the woods the air closed in. Her brow flushed and sweated and by the time she reached the trail along Odegaard Creek, she had to hitch up her skirt. The first mosquitoes of the summer descended on her en masse, stinging her ankles and knees. She stopped every twelfth step to swat at them, her hand coming away smeared with her own blood. The air vibrated with their buzzing, the whir of their wings susurrating from the ferns and wildflowers even above the trilling stream.

The fish guts looked like dried scabs on the rocks. Had they done their job? She stopped to toe an eyeless head into the water.

It caught a riffle and swam downstream, disappearing behind one of the larger boulders. A mosquito bit the lobe of her ear, and as she slapped it, she knocked the barrel of the gun into her cheek. She cursed the day.

A couple of minutes later, reaching the oxbow before the trap, she looked up onto the lip of the gully ahead of her. The wolf observed her without passion. Almost as if they had an appointment and she'd arrived early. Of course she froze, meeting his nonchalance with what must have seemed like clumsiness, for she stumbled into the water, nearly dropping the gun. When she regained her balance and looked back up, the wolf had stood. Perhaps startled himself.

"I guess I know the answer to the first question," she said aloud.

The wolf cocked its head, its ears flaring forward.

"If you want to know the truth, I'm not proud of setting the trap. I hardly slept worrying you might have found your paw in there." She glanced around the bend, relieved at the unsprung trap.

"You're probably wondering why I set it then?" She realized she was pointing the barrel of the Winchester at Fenrir, lowered it, and shook her head. "I'm wondering the same thing myself." She sat on a piece of driftwood. The wolf sat, too.

"I think I wanted to blame you for something that happened awhile back. This horrible man . . ."

The wolf stepped down the bank opposite her.

Silje stiffened and cocked the gun, but she left it laid across her lap.

He uncurled his long tongue and drank from the creek, not fifty feet from where she sat.

"It's hot enough, isn't it? And you with all that fur." She studied him then, his coat lustrous, silver, with shedding clumps on his rump and shoulders. "But I see you're taking off your winter coat." She smiled, thinking of her swim just an hour ago.

"Do you ever jump in the lake? That'll cool you off."

Now the wolf lay on its belly, its eyes and ears still alert.

"Why are you always alone?" she asked, the hypocrisy of the question dawning on her as soon as it escaped her mouth. "You could ask the same thing, I know." She decocked the gun. "I have a good excuse. Do you?"

She watched a swarm of mosquitoes materialize as if from the wolf's mouth. They flew at Silje, ten of them alighting on each arm. The suddenness of her swiping at them put Fenrir back on alert. He rose to his haunches but didn't stand.

"Stupid mosquitoes." She snapped her fingers. "Not one all summer long, then *whoosh,* they cover me like my own fur."

As if acknowledging her, Fenrir lifted a front paw and dragged it across his nose.

"I'm going to spring the trap. Will you let me?"

Now she stood and put the Winchester where she'd just sat. At the edge of the woods, a long and sturdy stick lay wedged between two rocks. She pointed at it, shook her head as though Fenrir had given her permission, and retrieved it. All the while, the wolf just watched her, his eyes vigilant but his body unmoving.

"This is going to startle you," she said. "It's going to make a loud noise." She stepped to the trap, keeping her eye on Fenrir. She was just about to swing the stick at the pan when a bird landed on it, pecking at the fish guts. Silje flinched, sure that at any moment the bird would be flattened, but a full minute passed while it flitted about and the trap didn't spring.

When, finally, the bird lifted off and disappeared into the woods, Silje looked at Fenrir and laughed. "Can you believe that? What a lucky bird. What a dumb bird." She took another step and turned again to Fenrir. "Remember, this is going to make a loud noise. No need to startle."

She swung the tip of the stick at the pan. Before the clamping sound of it reached her ears, the stick was ripped from her hand and trembled in the teeth of the trap. Fenrir stood on all four paws now, his ears back, his tail between his legs, but still his expression held steady. Silje doubted the same was true of her.

When the stick ceased quivering, she stood astride the trap and pulled it from its grip. Next she went to the tree around which the drag was looped. It took a minute, but she set the chain free and dropped it beside the trap, which she unwedged from the rocks that had held it.

Hoisting the chain over her shoulders like a shawl, she spoke again to the wolf. "Don't hold it against me. I was upset. I won't set this trap again. No, sir."

Fenrir had come even closer. His ears twitching as the mosquitoes bombarded him. Silje held the trap in one hand and picked up the Winchester with the other. "I'm going home. I hope you come visit again."

She turned to go, started down the creek's edge. A couple of minutes later she risked a look back. Fenrir loped along behind her, not thirty paces back.

By TEATIME the next day, Theodulf walked into his mother's house, called her name up the grand staircase, and followed the servant girl into the drawing room. He drew the heavy curtains and waited at the window. Outside, the lawn going down to the lake needed cutting. At the boathouse, window boxes bursting with purple verbena and impatiens hanging in planters from each of the three corners he could see gave the impression of a Parisian garden. Years had passed since he noticed flowers. Perhaps a whole decade.

He turned and took in the drawing room. Of course, everything sat in its place. In a cleanliness beyond measure, no less. A bowl of potpourri in the center of the coffee table reeked of anise and cinnamon, and Theodulf took one of the throw pillows and covered it. He sat on the chaise longue and closed his eyes against the cloying sensation that never failed to descend on him here.

"Would the mister require anything?"

Theodulf hadn't even noticed her still standing there, sheepish in the doorway. He removed his watch and checked the time.

"I'll bring the missus tea, of course. But perhaps you'd like something more? A sandwich or some such after your day of travel?"

"Remind me your name?" Theodulf asked.

"I'm Rosemarie Haas, sir. Only six months in your family's service."

"Miss Haas, did my father still keep brandy in the house?"

"Yes, sir."

Theodulf sat forward and loosened his necktie. "Would you bring me one?"

She curtsied and turned to leave. As she did, Theodulf's mother appeared in her stead. She wore a black dress and black veil but appeared as an actress on a stage in her mourning costume.

"You're drinking again?" she asked, whirling into the room and closing the same curtain Theodulf had opened only a moment before.

"I'm remembering my father."

She smirked. An invitation to him.

He crossed the room and lifted her veil and kissed her once on each cheek.

"I'll join you in remembrance, then."

He made a small ceremony of escorting her back to the chaise. She sat and removed the veil and from a pocket in her dress withdrew her brisé fan. It had been a gift from Theodulf himself. The sight of it made him smile.

"This heat's enough, maybe *it* killed him," she said, waving the fan before her face.

He sat across from her. "How are you bearing up, Mother?"

" 'Bearing up' . . . that's one of your father's phrases. A vulgar one, if you ask me."

"Very well, how are you holding up, Mother?"

She folded the fan and tapped her skirt with it. "The truth is, I don't know. I've spent a considerable part of the last two days feeling almost jaunty." She whipped open the fan again, fluttered it before her flushed cheeks. "Perhaps it hasn't sunk in."

The servant girl brought a tray and set it on the table between them. She made a move to lift the decanter, but Theodulf waved her off, thanking her as she curtsied and left. He watched her until she closed the French doors.

"I wonder if Willa would approve of you ogling the help."

"Please, Mother. Miss Haas is young enough to be my daughter."

She nodded. "Then again, so is your wife."

He nodded in turn, a gesture that practically mirrored his mother's. Certainly he'd inherited it from her. He poured two cut glasses with a finger each of brandy, handing one to his mother and raising his in a toast. "To Father."

She sipped her drink without returning the cheer. "How is your wife?"

He glanced back at the door again. "She's fine. About as interested in our marriage as the servant girl is in her job."

"Yes, well, marriage is its own course in endurance."

"I should have known that," he said.

She took another sip of her brandy. "You did, son."

"Maybe once."

"In any case, she decided not to join you on this solemn occasion?"

"The only prospect worse than laying him to rest is laying him to rest with her petulance an audience to it."

Now his mother quaffed the second half of the brandy. "It can't be that bad."

"Willa—"

She waved the fan, this time in the direction of his open mouth. "Enough about all that." She nodded at the brandy. "Pour me another."

Theodulf did. And one for himself.

"We'll have a funeral mass tomorrow at Sacred Heart. Father Richter will preside over the liturgy. Your father will be laid to rest right here at the Scandia Cemetery."

"So close?"

"Any farther away and he'd philander even from the grave."

"He was an unkind and inglorious man."

"He was also industrious and important."

Theodulf couldn't help but roll his eyes.

"Speaking of the kind of man he was . . ." Mrs. Sauer went to a sideboard between the windows and retrieved one of the folders her husband had used for his casework.

"His will?" Theodulf ventured.

"It's in probate, you know that. Your share is in trust until I pass, then everything will be yours."

"Please don't ever die, Mother."

She smiled kindly.

"This," she said, holding up the file, which filled both her hands, "isn't accounted for in his will. In fact, I only found out about it the morning after he passed."

"What is it?"

She handed it across the table. "It's his memoirs."

As though she'd given him a roasting pan right out of the oven, Theodulf set it down. He wiped his hands on his trousers. "I'd rather it were his cold, bloody heart."

"Your own marriage hasn't softened you."

"It's all the same, Mother. My animus, my unhappiness, my indolence. And my resolve. Why would I give one minute to his self-perception?"

"Shall we burn it?" She picked it off the table and took it to the fireplace.

"There was never any question about the origin of my dramatic flair."

She pulled the wire curtain open and tossed the file on the grate. "If it weren't so uncommonly hot, we could set it alight now."

He didn't retrieve the file, but neither did he rest, watching it from the corner of his eye. As though it might spontaneously combust. When his mother got back to her seat on the chaise, she resumed fanning herself.

"You're not mistaken about him. Him and his rotten brothers. At best, they were double-dealing robbers. But if your father convinced me of one thing in our years together, it was that our nation required men like him and his brothers. Men whose ambition and fortitude saw us out of the darkness that once covered this whole, unholy continent."

Theodulf felt the dread he associated with the billiard room and his father's verbosity. Knowing better than to press back, he did anyway. "What darkness did he and my uncles save us from?"

She lifted her hand and counted off on her fingers: "Heathenism, crime, immorality, liberalism"—she closed her fist around those four then raised her thumb—"the untamed land most of all."

His resolve stiffened. "I've come to know the man who runs the mail up and down the shore." Already exhausted from contemplating his father's supposed virtues, he pressed on. "He's a Chippewa. The name of Riverfish. Samuel Riverfish. I doubt he'd agree on the subject of the blotted darkness. The one that formerly enveloped this nation."

"Is it true he delivers the mail by dogsled?"

"In the winter, yes. In summer by skiff. But often as not we fetch it ourselves in Otter Bay. Speaking of Otter Bay, I've crossed paths with Helmut Winkler no few times."

"Can you imagine living in such a place? I can't imagine his wife is much for it."

"His wife I've not yet seen."

His mother scrunched her nose. "By skiff and by dogsled," she said, as if the mere prospect of it put up a stink.

"By my own accounting, or rather by the deduction of inalienable facts, there's simply no other means of delivery. There's nary a road between Two Harbors and Canada." He straightened his lapels. "Perhaps Father's lightness project hasn't been brought to completion."

"And perhaps *you* should pick up where he left off."

He could not fathom what she meant, but neither did he care. He hadn't the inclination to take one step in his father's image. That ship, as the old man often chided, had sailed when Theodulf was disbarred.

"I think I'll let his dereliction in the department of human progress stand for itself. Though my own mark is less pronounced, it's also less vile."

"Vile is a strong word, Theodulf." She glanced at the manuscript in the fireplace. "But I suppose there's no need to argue semantics."

"Indeed, there's not."

She noticed then the pillow sitting atop her bowl of potpourri, removed it at once, and scolded him with wide-open eyes.

"It puts off such a wretched smell," Theodulf said.

"You and your delicate constitution. Will it never cease?" She stood and carried the dish across the room, then returned and poured herself a third finger of brandy.

"Speaking of picking up where he left off . . ." Theodulf said. Next he spoke loudly over his shoulder, "Miss Haas!"

She appeared almost immediately, her hands behind her back.

"Bring a carafe of water?"

She nodded and disappeared as quickly as she'd come.

"She's expedient," Theodulf said.

"Her mother worked for us in the laundry."

"She could teach Willa a thing or two."

His mother sat back on the chaise, holding the glass in both hands. "Willa. I expect she's overmatched by just about all of her duties, not least as wife to you."

Theodulf reflected honestly for a moment. He almost admitted he was no easy man. Instead, he smiled at Miss Haas as she returned with the water and poured two glasses full. "You're delightful," he said. "Don't let my mother sour you."

"Sir," she said, blushing, "your mother is herself delightful. Her kindness is a daily blessing." Again she bowed and left.

His mother set the brandy down and picked up the glass of water instead. "Tell me, Theodulf, when I might expect a grandchild?"

Later that night, after his mother retired for the evening, properly drunk and untidy in her arrogance, Theodulf wandered first down to the lake where he spent some time smelling the flowers and noting their colors in the moonlight. The world felt more beautiful without his father in it, he believed that. But it also felt strangely less exigent, especially on the subject of Theodulf's own prospect for children.

Instead of making him uneasy, his mother's question had sent him back to his own childhood. From a very young age, he'd been made to understand that he'd one day become the Sauer paterfamilias. And since they were a family of renowned importance, eventually siring children was more than expected—it was, in fact, a solemn duty.

As he crossed the lawn from the lake back to the house, he wondered when that expectation had vanished. A long time ago. Probably longer ago for his father than for him, a fact that no longer mattered.

But what of his mother? Did she really want—or even expect—that Theodulf and his wife would have children? Did she not know him better than that? Had she merely fallen into a certain type of melancholy, brought on by the death of her own husband?

Theodulf looked up at the lighted window on the third story of the house, the room his mother had made her own almost as soon as they'd moved into the manse. She chose the room on the top floor so she wouldn't be bothered by her husband's coming and going. That, and she'd be closer to the servants, something she preferred.

From his spot in the middle of the yard, he saw his mother at the window. She opened it to the breeze off the lake and as she studied the night air, Theodulf moved into the shadow of one of the half dozen elm trees towering above the grounds. Her robe caught the breeze and flared behind her, fluttering and then landing on her back again. She looked right at the spot he stood, her shoulders and head outside the window. She bent at the waist, farther out the window, and appeared to reach for the branches of the closest elm. For a moment it appeared she might tumble from the window altogether, but as though she were a gymnast she righted herself, reached down to her side, then stood again, lighting a cigarette in a long holder. He'd never seen her smoke before now. Her face clouded with smoke as she exhaled. When it cleared, she was gone.

Back in the house, he went straight for the drawing room. Each step on the hardwood floors echoed like a drumbeat. His father's memoirs still lay on the fireplace grate, and the tray of brandy had been removed. The memory of it brought a thirst, and he took the manuscript from the fireplace and headed for the billiard room, where his father kept what amounted to a dramshop. He opened the mirror-fronted cabinet that held the bottles, took an unopened cognac from the uppermost shelf, and removed the cork. He poured a finger into a crystal snifter and lit the electric lamp beside his father's favorite chair, where he unbuttoned and loosened his collar, intent on spending the rest of that night with the comedy on his lap.

He read into the small hours of the night—only pausing to refill his snifter with cognac—and fell asleep at the end of the manuscript. Sometime before dawn, Miss Haas awakened him from a terrible dream. She stood over him, shaking his knee with one hand while she held a candle in the other.

"Mr. Sauer, Mr. Sauer," she repeated.

As he sat up, the guttering flame made him dizzy. Roused but still disoriented, he said, "Please, set the candle down. Over there." He pointed at the table

"I heard screaming, sir," she said, setting the candle where he asked. As she turned back to him, the profile of her body showed through her shift.

This, too, dizzied him.

"I came running, I don't know why."

She stood before him again. Ghost-like, her hand back on his knee.

He took an accounting of the room—the bottle of cognac and snifter on the table beside him, the manuscript pages spread on the ottoman, his grandfather's clock hanging in the corner. It all came back to him at once.

"Are you all right, Mr. Sauer? You look like you climbed up out of a doozy. What can I do for you?"

He felt the pressure of her hand. Felt the warmth. He didn't understand.

The room closed in, both lit and warmed by the candle's flame. He craned his neck to look around her, which she understood as an invitation. She sat on his lap, her arm around his neck.

"I thought so," she whispered. "The way you eyed me . . ."

Now she kissed him, her mouth wet and hot and impossibly soft.

Her whole body pressed into him now, writhing. She moaned. Her hand moved up his thigh, held steady just below his groin. The rush of it all. Waking. The dream. The headiness of her body.

She paused her kissing and put her mouth to his ear. "Your mother will sleep until noon. The rest of the staff won't be up for an hour or more." She took his hand, which had been sitting on the arm of the chair and brought it to her breast. She tongued his ear, then licked a line from his lobe to his shoulder blade.

His entire body stiffened against the pleasure, and he couldn't help but moan himself. He closed his eyes and put his mouth on hers and kissed her this time, lifting her up and seating her where he'd been himself only a moment before. She reached for the buttons of his trousers, undid them in a single motion, and before he could fathom any of this, she spread her legs and pulled him toward her with her feet. He was no longer chaste.

Whether his mother slept until noon that day, he couldn't say. Five minutes after Miss Haas found him in the billiard room, she left with her candle. For just a moment he sat on the chair bare-assed, then pulled his trousers back up, wishing he could undo his transgression. His remorse, though, took a moment to classify. He stepped through the rooms of his conscience as he did the night before the rooms of this very house. First, he visited the chamber of his faith, then his marriage, then his family name. He found no guilt in any of them. Or none, at least, he cared a whit about. It was only in dishonoring himself that he felt any culpability.

His dammed busy mind! He leaned forward and ordered his father's manuscript and placed it back in the file. He took the cognac bottle from the table beside the chair and stowed it again in the cupboard. Even from the short distance across the room, the stain of obscenity on that chair appeared diminished. Appeared already to be fading. He took some comfort in this. Outside, the first light of day cracked the horizon. Here was another invitation to move on. To let the wheel of time do its bidding.

He removed his watch and opened it as the second hand announced a new hour. Five. Lauds, his father might have commented. If the clock on the wall still worked, it would be pealing.

The clock. He turned to see it, hanging on the wall opposite the fireplace. So peculiar that it should recently have been front of mind. In fact, his mother would likely receive his letter inquiring of it today. The novelty of that appeased him yet more. Avoiding the chair, he crossed to the clock. It was an hour ahead of him. Or eleven hours behind, if looked at another way. The carved tree was somewhat less intricate than his memory of it, but the brass cross hanging where the roots might have been was larger. Why did his father never have it repaired?

In his memoirs Ernst wrote at length about the influence of his father. As a young boy and as a man. He also described him as single-mindedly exacting. His devotion to austerity matched only by his devotion to God. These qualities his father found desirous in a virtuous man, but if Theodulf read the tone of his description properly, repellent in a father.

Did his father hang the clock here as a way of keeping his own father close? Of reveling in his death? Or was it simpler than that? Perhaps Ernst merely admired the craft of it. Maybe he liked looking upon it because it was beautiful.

A captain's chair rested against the wall directly beneath the clock. Theodulf took a tentative step on the seat of that chair—first one foot, then the other—and stood tall upon it. He reached up and held the clock by the trunk, lifting it from the hook on the wall.

"Pray tell, why are you standing on that chair?"

Theodulf turned. Caught like a thief.

"The sun's not even up yet, and the house stirs like a party's started." His mother stood in the doorway, the same robe that had flailed behind her in the window last night now cinched at the waist. She withdrew from its pocket another cigarette and lit it. This time without the holder.

"Since when do you smoke?"

"Your father thought it unladylike." She looked around the room as though seeing it for the first time. "You haven't answered my question."

Theodulf held the clock up as though it were explanation enough.

Now she walked in and circled the billiard table and paused near the chair and ottoman. She took a long drag from the cigarette and shook her head ever so slightly.

"It doesn't become you," he said, stepping down. "The smoking."

"I'll no longer conform to anyone's version of propriety but my own. Forty years of subjugation is long enough."

"Subjugation?"

She picked the file holding the memoirs off the ottoman. She looked at the snifter still half-full of cognac on the table beside the chair. "Are you really such a masochist?"

Theodulf finally stepped off the captain's chair and carried the clock to the billiard table, where he laid it down.

She took another long drag. "Did you actually read it?"

"Most of it. Halfway drunk and fully loathing myself."

"I was tempted myself, but then I remembered his stern admonitions to be steady and forthright. For once I listened to him." She dropped the cigarette butt in the snifter. "Anything worthy of note?"

"Oh, it mostly aligns with his version of himself. Childhood on the Detroit River, illustrious Ivy League academic life, a career conquering and crusading, political aspirations never pursued lest they interrupt his fortune-making. Plenty of ho-hummery on the subject of God and virtuous living. Very little about his wife. Nothing at all about his only son."

She sat on the ottoman, the file holding her husband's life on her lap. "His egoism and shallowness were always the most notable things about him."

"Neither account for his total lack of regard for us."

"Your father understood the world in much simpler terms than either of us do. He was never once troubled by an existential thought. You and I are plagued by them."

"The funeral mass is today."

"Tonight. Before vespers. Father Richter is due to arrive on the one o'clock train from St. Paul."

"Another scabrous fake, him."

"But a harmless one."

"Father wasn't harmless, was he?"

"I suppose it depends who you ask."

He looked at her intently.

"Your father is dead now."

"That ought to settle it."

"More than ought." She lit another cigarette. "It's delightful, smoking these."

Theodulf only smiled.

"Why the clock?" she asked.

"It's strange, you'll receive a letter from me today or tomorrow asking about it. I can't remember what provoked me to write it."

"Your grandfather built that clock."

"I remember."

"He was a good man, Hrolf. Kind, at least."

"That pairs with my memory."

"You were often with him as a boy."

"That also pairs."

"You're the last man to carry their name."

"A burden, really."

"Not that you have a choice in the matter, son."

He nodded.

"It's okay if it ends."

He nodded again.

"You stand to inherit a great deal of money."

"Anything I want, money can't buy."

"You could go back to Paris," she said. "I believe you found what you wanted there?"

Now he sighed. "I still wonder if that's what I found."

DEAD STARS

MAY 15, 1900

Every star in every galaxy will one day darken and die.
All septillion of them.

Think of the darkness on offer.

O N THE RECOMMENDATION of his Baedeker's guide, Theodulf decided on a bistro in the second arrondissement for dinner. After a full day at the fairgrounds and hours of wandering the city, he was ravenous, so when the garçon recommended the escargot with butter and garlic or the foie gras truffes to begin, Theodulf ordered both, along with a carafe of wine and a bottle of Perrier. The wine arrived first. After the sommelier offered Theodulf a taste and then filled a glass, but before he was out of sight, Theodulf quaffed the whole pour.

The long day of exertion had been good for him. Coupled with the charming city, Theodulf finally felt at ease. From his jacket he removed the brochure from the Palais de l'Optique and a pocket-sized French–English dictionary, and while he sipped a second glass of wine began a more careful translation of the information. This bit about the moon affecting the earth's axis and its oceans' tides was news to him. But rather than despairing in the stupendousness of such a notion, he merely filed it away in a lesser-visited part of his intelligence. On the matter of the moon being at once a dead star and influential in helping to divine the earth's origin *and* its fate, well, on that he was less inclined to accept the news.

His whole life he'd been preached to about the Book of Genesis, and God's great wisdom in bringing forth the earth and heavens. Should he really abandon thirty years of doctrine on the basis of a brochure from the fair? A brochure, incidentally, he'd translated himself, from the third of his learned languages? Translated, he might add, with the benefit of two glasses of wine? The thought of all this made him smile, so much that when the garçon delivered the first course, he suggested Theodulf appeared happy. Was the wine so good?

Theodulf felt his smile broaden and relax. "Très délicieux, merci."

"Paris vous trompera à chaque fois," the waiter said wistfully.

"Paris will fool me?" Theodulf said.

But the garçon merely bowed and sauntered back to the kitchen.

Theodulf held one of the snails with tongs and used the small fork to wrest the meat from the shell. He dipped it in the garlic butter and set it on his tongue. It as much as melted there. He ate all six escargots before turning his attention to the foie gras, which, when he centered it before him, sent wafting the earthy smell of the truffe. He had to close his eyes for the pleasure of it, and when he opened them and spread a bite on the baguette and put that in his mouth, he felt a stirring down to his feet. He ate the whole plateful.

Theodulf had finished the wine and was back to his translation with a head swimming in burgundy. He'd closed his eyes to reckon with the notion that we only ever see one side of the moon and was startled when the waiter returned.

"Excusez-moi," he said.

When Theodulf opened his eyes, the waiter continued, "Dormez-vous?"

"Not sleeping," Theodulf said, and smiled again. "Just thinking."

"À propos de quoi?"

"About the moon," Theodulf said.

The waiter nodded at the brochure. "Ah! Oui! You are here for fair!"

Theodulf nodded. "C'est incroyable!"

"Trés incroyable." The waiter nodded in that conspiratorial way again and withdrew a notepad to take Theodulf's order.

"Ah yes," Theodulf said, sitting back to see the menu board hanging behind the bar. "Le poulet à la moutarde avec l'asperges, si'l vous plait."

"Excellente selection!" he said, then leaned closer and whispered,

"Vous nourrissez votre libido, monsieur." The waiter arched his eyebrows.

"Pardon?"

"La moutard, les truffes, l'escargots, l'asperges . . . c'est aliments sont tous aphrodisiaques!" He bowed his head and turned for the kitchen.

"Garçon!"

The waiter stopped. Turned back.

"Auriez-vous un . . ." For the first time in this conversation, Theodulf's French failed him. Scrambling, he merely added, "Papier?"

"Papier?"

"Pour un lettre."

"Ah! Stationnaire, monsieur. Oui, bien sûr. Un moment."

"And more wine, s'il vous plait?" Theodulf held up his empty glass.

The waiter turned and left, returning a moment later with a piece of letterhead.

Theodulf filled his water glass with Perrier and cleared a spot in front of him for the stationery. His first thought had been to write his mother, but now he felt more expansive. So much so that the prospect of writing her sent a wash of embarrassment over him. Perhaps it was the banter with the waiter, or his new wisdom regarding the moon and his thoughts of destiny, or even the simple possibility that his whole course of fare was indeed aphrodisiacal, but whatever the reason, the world was getting larger—not smaller—and he ought to use the notion to be a part of it.

He removed the cap from his pen and pushed aside the pocket dictionary and brochure. Out the bistro window, lovers strolled, arms locked. He smiled to himself, whether at the thought of the lovers or the notion he might write a poem, he couldn't say. Either way, he felt as effervescent as the water. With that lightness astir in him, the moon over the Palais Garnier came out slowly from behind a cloud. It filled the window. He studied it for a long time. Until the waiter brought the glass of wine, which he left without interrupting Theodulf. The lip of the crystal glass caught the moon-shine and he picked it up, as though to gulp its luster. Instead, he sipped the wine and set the glass back in the pool of light. *How de-lightful,* he thought.

When the garçon brought the main course a few minutes later, Theodulf had only written two words: ASTRE MORT.

Seeing those words, the waiter said, "A poet of darkness! Like Baudelaire!" He gestured out at the night with his gloved hand. "Mais, je dois protester. La lune semble la plus vivante."

Theodulf would take those words to heart. By the time he'd fin-ished his chicken and wine only two more words had been scribed. WHAT THEN?

He couldn't exactly comprehend his own question, but later, as he walked along the Avenue de l'Opéra, some answer seemed im-minent. He couldn't say why this was true, but the easiness of his stride through that streaking moonlight left him to feel that the astre mort and his own puzzling were aligned. As if that Parisian av-enue weren't beautiful enough, his contentment—even if fleeting—gave him a resolve he'd not felt since he was a child.

And whether it was the wine and delectable food sloshing in his bowels, or the grand city splashed in moonlight, his good humor on that night was only just beginning. Of course, he couldn't have known this as he passed Le Salle Richelieu and turned onto Rue de Rivoli, or as he paused in front of the Louvre, or even as he walked along the quay opposite Île de la Cité and stood across from Notre-Dame again. He couldn't have known it even as he eventu-ally crossed the Seine onto Île Saint-Louis. But if he'd wondered at the start of that day how he might be made happy, the hours that followed would give him a window onto the possibility.

Forever after, he'd credit the moon and its powers for guiding him to that lesser island in the Seine. As if he were as pliable as the ocean water. Certainly, he was as unconscious of where he went. Across the Pont Marie and onto Rue Saint-Louis en l'Île, under the gas lamps and past the cafés and small hotels. Freely. Easily.

At the end of the avenue, he heard music. Trumpet and a piano. He followed the song to the door of a café, where the maître d'hôtel welcomed him, took his hat, and seated him at a candlelit table in the corner. From there Theodulf could see the zinc bar and the stage. He'd been preceded by dozens of revelers, their romance on the air like the cigarette smoke. He closed his eyes against it and merely listened as the musicians began again. That song that would become his curse but on that night was only divine and virginal to his ears. The pianist started first, the tempo a perfect accompaniment to his mood. Theodulf swayed, his eyes still closed. When the trumpet joined, it was almost as an afterthought. Its forlorn timbre like someone sobbing in another room. How peculiar to think like that! And yet the thought gave Theodulf to discover some chamber in his heart he'd not known before. A true and simple revelation! *My God*, he thought blasphemously. *What a pleasure.* Was it possible that this single day had brought him so far? That he could leave himself—his *former* self—in that previously unknown room? He listened as though the music held the answer.

As the song moved into the second movement, the pianist played solo. Theodulf opened his eyes and watched him. He wore a black coat with tails that hung off the bench and sleeves rolled back to the elbows. The candles on the lid of the piano guttered whenever the café door opened, and in certain troughs of light the dark hair on his arms flashed. He played with light hands, his fingers tamping the keys as though drawn from above by silken strings.

When the trumpeter joined again, it was with a more playful tone. He turned his horn to the ceiling without taking his eyes off his partner and swayed much as Theodulf felt himself still moving. When it came time for his next rest, he turned his full attention to the man playing the piano. Theodulf did the same.

It was hard not to. His elegance commanded the room, but with a playfulness that belied both his appearance and the music he performed. His hair, Theodulf noticed, was slicked back. It also shone in the candlelight, but seemed almost to be lit from within. And while the trumpeter and Theodulf both gave the man their full attention, he in turn gave it to the café audience. As if the song itself weren't enough. Theodulf interpreted it as an act of generosity on the pianist's part and liked him all the better for it.

Only after all this had come to pass did a waiter appear, asking below the music what Theodulf would like to drink.

"La spécialité de la maison, s'il vous plait," Theodulf answered.

A few moments later the waiter returned. An ornate vessel filled with water commanded most of his tray, but there was also a bowl of sugar cubes and a single bottle. After he set the tray on Theodulf's table, he lifted the bottle and held it forward like a sommelier and said, "La fée verte, monsieur." Next he poured a serving of the green liqueur into a reservoir glass and covered it with a silver slotted spoon. He took a sugar cube from the bowl and set it upon the spoon. Finally, he arranged the glass under the fountain and opened the spigot so that water dripped onto the sugar directly. The glass of liqueur turned cloudy as the sugar dissolved. It stayed so after the waiter stirred it and then set it before Theodulf.

The waiter had been there for all of three minutes. Long enough for the song to have grown more ominous. Even the players and the crowd seemed drawn in darker shades. Theodulf, in hopes of quelling the sudden turn, picked up his glass, swirled it around twice, and took a sip. Sweet as licorice, and as heady as the Canadian whiskey he ordered in the saloons on Superior Street back in Duluth.

His second sip brought him deeper into the song, which turned out to be more mysterious than dark. This third movement demanded much more of the pianist than the trumpeter, so the latter gave as much attention to a woman sitting in the first row of tables as he did to his partner on stage. The pianist, in turn, played more seriously now, somehow honoring the shift the song had taken.

By the time they finished their performance, Theodulf had finished la fée verte and was nearly drunk. But rather than turning sour, as usually happened at this stage of his inebriation, he felt rather like he'd drunk the moon.

"C'était notre interprétation de la 'Sonate au Clair de Lune.' Ou 'Quasi una fantasia,' " the pianist announced. He removed his handkerchief and wiped the sweat from his brow, said a few more words, then stepped off the stage.

The pianist went straightaway to a woman who offered him a cigarillo, which she lit. He took a fanciful drag and tilted his head heavenward and blew four smoke rings. When he looked down, he turned to Theodulf and winked.

For his own part, Theodulf had hardly registered the fact that he'd been tracking the pianist's every move. But the wink brought him to the careening realization that he indeed had, and the flush of embarrassment sent him scrambling for the waiter's attention. When finally he got it and the waiter hurried over and asked what he wanted, Theodulf raised his empty glass and said, "Another, please." At that point, the pianist slid onto the chair on the other side of the table and added, "Make it *deux*, Henri."

Henri flashed a sly smile and nodded. Theodulf—startled but also too charmed to risk a look across the table—watched the waiter leave. The din was up and when Theodulf finally found the courage to look at the man sitting across from him, he found him holding his cigarillo to his lips, looking almost ready to bite it.

He said, "Henri is the best waiter in all of Paris."

"You speak English very well."

"I ought to. I grew up in Detroit, Michigan."

Theodulf felt wholly outside himself, yet he still found the wherewithal to ask, "How did you know I wasn't French?"

The pianist took another drag from his cigarillo and put his elbows on the table. "Because a Frenchman would never wear a scarf like that."

Theodulf reached for the silk around his neck as though it were a snake.

"Here." The pianist put his cigarillo to his lips and left it there.

With both hands he reached across the table, untied the scarf, and pulled it from around Theodulf's neck.

He felt naked without it, Theodulf did, with his throat bare and the first few of his chest hairs flowering above the top button of his shirt.

"My own people are from Detroit. Shipbuilders. Sauer is the name."

"Shipbuilders!" the pianist said. "How *grand*." He folded the scarf and slid it across the table.

Theodulf wondered if he were being mocked. He put the scarf in the front pocket of his coat and regarded his guest. Up close, his eyes appeared almost to be outlined in coal; his lashes were long and curled. He had very fine skin and the first shade of whiskers darkening it. His ears were small and half-covered by his inky hair, which caught the streetlight coming through the widow.

Theodulf judged he could have been twenty-five years old, or he could have been forty. "C'est un long chemin de là à ici," he said.

Now the pianist's eyes widened, whether in delight or mockery, Theodulf could hardly guess. When they narrowed again, he smiled. "Tu parles très bien français." He puffed his cigarillo, regarded its glowing tip, and added, "But let's speak English, yes? It reminds me of home."

Henri returned and prepared two more les fées vertes. This time, the water dripping from the spigots on either side of the fountain kept time with Theodulf's own racing pulse. When Henri stirred the drinks and removed the tray from the table, the pianist pulled several francs from his pocket and paid for the round.

"That's kind of you," Theodulf said, embarrassed again.

The pianist lifted his glass and motioned for Theodulf to do the same. "You can buy the next pair." He clinked Theodulf's glass, took a long sip of his drink, and said, "My own people are from Montreal. Mélomanes and riffraff. Gouttière is the name." He took another sip. "But you should call me by my given name."

"Which is?"

"Paul."

"Paul Gouttière," Theodulf said for the first time, then repeated the name seven times in his mind. The better to commit it to memory. Next he took a sip of his drink. The swirling cloudiness in the glass went straight to his head. "I'm Theodulf Sauer."

They brought their glasses up in unison, smiled at the coincidence, and clinked them once more.

"I'll call you Theo," Paul said.

"No one has before."

"Good," Paul said, gulping the rest of his absinthe. "I'll do other things no one has before." And with that he stood. "Don't you go anywhere, Theo. I'll be back after our final number." He plucked the edelweiss boutonnière from Theodulf's lapel, placed it in his own, and joined the trumpeter on stage again, where within moments they played another of Beethoven's sonatas.

But Theodulf hardly registered a note. Instead, he looked down at what remained of his still-swirling, moon-white cocktail and thanked the astre mort for delivering him here—he looked around: Where even was he? What was the name of this café?—as though he were but sloshing seawater.

He knew, of course, the first of the ten commandments. He knew them all. And he knew what his penance would be. First for praising the moon and music. Then for . . .

He dare not hope. Dare not believe. What had it ever gotten him before?

And anyway, of this night, he would never confess. About it, he would never pray.

As Paul and the trumpeter played, Theodulf drank the last of his absinthe. He removed the stationery on which he'd earlier written ASTRE MORT and WHAT THEN?

What had the garçon called him? A poet of darkness? He laughed. Brought his hand to his mouth to stifle it. And laughed again, running the same hand that held his amusement through his hair and considered again the piece of paper.

For all the hours he'd spent in congress with the God his mother and father believed in, for all the holiness those hours should have afforded him, and for all of the emptiness he'd found instead, he gave thanks. Thanks because it gave him the wisdom to see what this singular night offered. Through the haze of smoke and song and his own drunkenness, with the moon shining through the plate glass window instead of the Holy Spirit shining through stained glass, he saw *himself.* He looked at his hands. He joined them for a moment, smiled at what did not come, and took the pen from his pocket instead.

On the stationery, he crossed out WHAT THEN? and added a question mark after ASTRE MORT.

Paul and the trumpeter finished their performance and the crowd applauded. Some of the most jubilant stood and whistled, holding their cocktails in the air.

Theodulf capped and uncapped his pen and with something like vainglory he added: NON JE SUIS UNE ASTRE BRÛLANTE.

Some three weeks later, Theodulf stood at the taffrail on the promenade deck of the SS *La Bretagne* watching thunderheads congregate over Le Havre. Already the shore was but a line on the horizon, and soon—because of the hour and the lowering darkness, because the earth is round—he'd lose sight of it altogether. Just as well. What began as sunshine in May had turned to June doldrums.

Four continental weeks, and all he had was a pocketful of ticking seconds and an eight-word poem held close to his breast. That it remained there at all proved his darkening thoughts. As if the chimerical verse weren't enough. And now the weather bolstered his mood.

He watched the rain running off the shore, chasing the ship's wake. Soon it poured, and he turned for the onboard saloon, holding his ticking watch as though it were the last proof he existed at all. He'd found it on the day after he met Paul. A fateful day for many reasons, not least because it would prove his exile.

Theodulf had left Paul's pied-à-terre on Rue Monge the morning after meeting him in the hotel café, waving goodbye over his shoulder with promises of seeing him again that night. He'd stood on the balcony that Monday, bare-chested and smoking a cigarette, his hair like a blossoming rose, those flowers that seemed suddenly in abundance everywhere he looked. Passing the Panthéon, Theodulf noted some distant pull. Arrogance, surely. But if ever he'd been vain, it was that morning.

He stopped at his hotel just off Le Jardin du Luxembourg so that he might bathe and change his clothes. Being naked again startled him, but only briefly. As he washed himself, he had a fleeting notion of ablution, but that thought, too, was quickly doused. If not in the warm washbowl water, then in the contentedness he felt. That day, he wore a proper cravat. And as he walked back out into the Parisian afternoon, he donned his favorite beaver fur derby, and headed back to the Champ de Mars, where he passed a second day at the fairgrounds.

Later in the afternoon, after surveying the art exhibitions at the Grand Palais and delighting in the Mareorama, Theodulf took the rue l'Avenier—a moving sidewalk that circled the fairgrounds—to the Pont Alexandre III, where he crossed the Seine. Eventually he found himself strolling up the Champs-Élysées. How the city dazzled. As much under the spring sun as moon!

Near the Arc de Triomphe, on the corner of the Place de l'Étoile and Avenue d'Iéna, he paused before the window of a horologist. Inside, on a glass-topped table, hanging from an ornate, miniature model of the Celestial Globe, was the Longines watch that would become his tether to the real world. A bronze placard beneath the watch read: LE LONGINES LA RENOMMÉE—MONTRE OFFICIELLE DE L'EXPOSTION UNIVERSELLE. Theodulf believed, standing on the sidewalk, beholding the watch's elegance, that he'd found the final piece of what he came to Paris looking for.

Inside, from behind the counter, the shopkeeper called, "Bonjour, monsieur." He spoke around the pipe hanging from his lip, and Theodulf could have been forgiven for thinking his entrance into the otherwise vacant boutique had aggrieved the man. Rather than engage him, Theodulf perused the counters, feigning indifference.

After some time, the other man pocketed his pipe, straightened his waistcoat, and approached Theodulf properly.

"Puis-je vous aider?" he said.

"Oui. S'il vous plait—"

"You are American, oui? You are here for the fair?" There was an unmistakable tone of reproach in his interruption, as though already he were weary of assisting foreign travelers.

Reaching for a mocking tone of his own, Theodulf returned, "I am."

The man pushed his spectacles up his nose and eyeballed Theodulf. Apparently satisfied that he wasn't just another rube, he deigned to continue. "You are for watch looking?"

Theodulf turned to the display in the window, lifted his chin, and said, "Je voudrais acheter la montre dans la fenêtre. Le garde-temps official de l'exposition."

The shopkeeper looked over the wire rim of his spectacles. His assessment was slow in coming, but finally, unable to make a judgment, he ventured, "C'est très cher, monsieur."

Theodulf reached into his billfold and removed several hundred francs. He spread them on the counter like tarot cards and said, "Je m'appelle Sauer, Theodulf Sauer. Descendant des Detroit Sauers. Nous construisons des navires. Dans le monde entier." He crossed his arms and again lifted his chin toward the window.

Grudgingly, the shopkeeper went back behind the counter. From beneath it, he removed a leather blotter and laid it out. Next he took a key from his waistcoat pocket and unlocked a cabinet behind him and removed a black box, setting it on the blotter. As he opened it, he said, "Bien, Monsieur Sauer. I will speak English if it pleases you." Without waiting for a response, he continued. "Longines is a watchmaker of impeccable style and precision. This particular watch might be the most beautiful in all the world." He held it by the end of the fob, the watch swaying as though to hypnotize Theodulf.

He explained the many details of its construction and function and told Theodulf that if he indeed did leave with the timepiece, he'd have an heirloom for generations to come.

When Theodulf counted out his thousand francs, he'd yet to touch the watch. When he did, another depth of calmness overcame him. He looped the fob through the buttonhole of his waistcoat, flipped the case open, and noted the hour. Nigh six o'clock. Time to head back to Paul's apartment in the fifth arrondissement. He closed and pocketed the watch, and left with a grin.

But Paul wasn't home. Nor was he at the café later that night. Nor did Theodulf ever see him again. For three weeks he wandered Paris searching, counting the seconds as they ticked off in his pocket. By the last of them, standing with one foot on the train and another on the platform at Gare d'Orsay, searching the crowd for Paul, Theodulf would have traded years of his life for one more smile from that unforgettable man's face.

From his berth on *La Bretagne*, with the incessant rain lashing his porthole, the seconds were as little comfort as they ever were on the boulevards of the city. But at least they proved the world moved. Dead ahead and through the hours. He had a hundred and fifty of them still to endure aboard that ship.

MAGNETIC

JULY 7, 1910

They look so soft and splendorous, the trees on the hill. The way they catch a breeze. The way they hold the night. Especially from out here from on the glassy waters.

But just as the placid water hides its depth, the forest belies a hardness beyond measure. Indeed, the ground beneath the canopy— from the lake's shoreline to the western edge of the Mesabi Range, some two hundred miles west and north—is so ferric as to actually pervert the earth's prevailing magnetic fields. Indeed, it's why, if you pull a compass from your pocket and hold it toward the rising sun, you're as likely to find the needle pointing north or west or south as you are to find it pointing east. Many a ship has learned this lesson by running her keel aground on the very stone that tricked her compass in the first place.

All of which is to say, be wary of the ways you're pulled. Sometime there are forces we can't see. Or understand.

THE DAY DRAGGED like an anchor across rocky bottom. It was only noon and Silje's hands, puckered from salting fish all morning, stung and cramped like her mother's often had. She suppressed an instinct to likewise complain, and instead squatted in the shallows and let her fingers soak in the cold lake. She agreed with her uncle—the lake was many things, including a tonic. She eased her hands under the fist-sized rocks underwater. The weight of them brought still more relief.

His boots on the shore-bound rocks announced him. All this space, and he seemed always underfoot. "Look there," he said, lifting his chin at the passing ship.

The *Lizzie May*, her anchor slung from the hawsepipe on her port side.

"I like the way those whalebacks ride in the water."

"A peculiar thing to like."

He looked at her sideways. "You ought to talk about liking peculiar things."

"I don't like anything."

He smiled and knelt beside her. "I can think of ten things you like right off the top of my head."

The freighter steamed on.

"Singing, carving, swimming, eating licorice, bothering the neighbor lady, sarsaparilla, oatmeal with butter, reading those stories, keeping your old uncle company, skipping stones, that wolf you've befriended—"

"That's eleven things, and I don't like singing anymore. Or the wolf." She lifted her hands out of the water and shook the water from them. "And here's ten other things I don't like: summer, winter, fish guts, salt, waking up too early, the master keeper, that stupid trap I spent all my money on, fried herring, oatmeal without butter, and the way you smell after a day of work."

He sat on his haunches there on the rocky shore and feigned outrage. "How do I smell after a day of work?"

"Like a rotten onion."

He sniffed his armpits. "A *rotten* one?"

She didn't respond.

After a moment he added, "Just look at the way her hull curves to meet the water. She's slick as an otter. Empty like that"—he lifted his chin again—"she's nothing but grace."

"What are ten things you don't like?"

"Wise nieces. That's about all I can think of."

"Not fish guts and salt?"

"Without fish guts and salt, we wouldn't have chisels and sarsaparilla."

"Not the lighthouse keeper?"

"He cuts my hair. I better like him."

She harrumphed.

"The way I see it," Mats said, "we're too busy keeping up to find things we don't like. There are plenty of them, no doubt, but isn't it better to focus on the things we do like?"

The freighter passed them now. In a minute her wake would wash ashore. "When I went to check the trap the other day, the wolf was there," Silje said.

"In the trap?" Her uncle's voice rose in alarm.

"No. Up on the other side of the gully ridge. I talked to him."

"There's a conversation I wish I'd heard!"

"It wasn't a conversation. I'm the only one who talked."

"What did you tell him?"

"That I was sorry I set the trap."

"Why sorry?"

She picked a stone and threw it as far as she could. It landed near the first waves from the wake of the freighter. "I didn't want

to hurt the wolf so much as I wanted to hurt someone the wolf reminded me of."

He waited until the waves lapped onshore. Then he waited another minute. "Who did you want to hurt."

"That man from Gunflint."

He looked at her quizzically.

"Hosea Grimm, I think is his name. He was at the jubilee for
the lighthouse."

"I know Hosea."

"He's a creep."

The last of the waves fell on the rocks. "He's a strange one."

He couldn't know, Silje thought, *else he'd do something.*

"Maybe the wolf is protecting you. Did you ever think of that?"

"I did."

"Well, you got rid of the trap, leastways. That ought to please
him."

"I expect I'll never see him again. Not after what I tried to do."

"I doubt that. Wolves don't have the same kind of memory people do."

She threw another rock into the calm water. The freighter
faded into a sudden mist a half mile offshore. "I'm already forget-
ting Mamma and Pappa. Sometimes I can't remember what they
looked like."

He scooted closer, put his arm around her shoulder.

She rested her head against him.

"Your fingers look like dead smelt."

"It's how Mamma's fingers looked all summer long."

"There's something you remember, eh?"

"I guess."

He cupped her chin in his big, stinking hand. "Here's a true
thing, Silje . . . your mother and father will live in you forever. They
just will. Parts of them might get fuzzy, but they'll always be there.
It's been some twenty years since I saw my mother, and though I
can't hardly picture her anymore, I still feel her love every day."

"I'm not even sure my mother loved me at all."

"I know she did." He stood, arched his back, and clapped his hands. "Your pappa, too." He took a step forward, looked in the direction of the freighter.

Silje also stood up. She dusted her hands.

When they turned back to the cabin, Fenrir sat on the path at the edge of the woods. Silje and Mats both flinched, and the hound answered by cocking his head and pointing its ears.

Mats put a hand on Silje's shoulder.

She shrugged him away and took a step toward the wolf. The dog stood in turn but didn't retreat.

"This is your friend?" her uncle whispered.

Answering, she took another step, squatted, and held out her hand.

"Silje?"

She stood. Her uncle's smile was the same one he wore after his bad jokes. "What?"

"That's no wolf."

She winced. His smile was unrelenting. "What do you mean? Just look at him."

"Up at the Burnt Wood Camp, there's a story about a pack of wolves that came down one bitter winter night. Ate up a horse and made another one crazy. We sometimes see their scat or paw prints in the snow. But for all the thousand hours I spent out in the trees, I never laid eyes on a wolf. If that story about the horses is true, well, I'll eat crow. But the simple fact is, this fella here? He's a hatchet to a wolf's axe.

"Now," Mats continued, "he's a big boy, and easy to mistake for a wolf. If I were guessing, I'd say this mutt came from one of two lines. Either from those mongrels Ollie Odegaard breeds, or from those Alaskan curs the Riverfish family runs. Given the likeness to wolves and the fact he's as small as he is, I'd lean to the latter."

Silje heard him but was intent on Fenrir now. As slowly as the ship had moved in the distance, she now moved toward him. With each step, his ears twitched. But he didn't retreat, and if she were guessing rightly, he seemed curious himself. Halfway, she paused and spoke to her uncle over her shoulder. "Are you sure he's not a wolf?"

"He's no sooner a wolf than I am the governor of Minnesota."

"Does that mean he's just a dog lost in the woods?"

"I'd bet."

"Can we take him in?"

With the back of his hand, her uncle offered his scent. With each step, the dog retreated in kind so that the same twenty feet stayed between them. Three times they danced before Mats turned back to Silje. "He's a handsome mutt, but he'll take some wooing. You should fetch a strip of that bacon left over from breakfast. See if that doesn't sweeten the deal."

When Silje took off running for the cabin, the dog didn't even flinch, only stood watching her uncle as though he were a blackguard. As though, the thought crossed Silje's mind, he were a man like Hosea Grimm. The mere sight of him, even in her imagination, made her as uneasy as it did angry. She thought of the gun. She thought of the dog. She thought of Odd. That man's son, or something like it.

The truth, she realized as she swiped the strips of bacon still on the table, was that already the confusion of her life, of her thoughts, her circumstances, the loss and the labor, threatened to bowl her over. Her fingers still hurt, she was fatigued, dirty, lonesome, unhappy, even, if she were honest, something like hopeless. All this at thirteen years old.

But the dog? Fenrir? He promised to allay all that. As she offered him the first strip of bacon, he let his guard down. His nose shot up in the air and his tail twitched. A great, bushy tail that ended in a black tip. The streaks of gray running off his shoulders and back and down his hind legs quivered at the smell of her offering. Quivered again as he took a step in her direction. With only ten feet between them, the dog extended his neck as though he might reach the bacon without needing another step. She smirked and said, "Come, boy. Come," as she'd heard the boys in Otter Bay call their hounds.

"Give him time," Mats said. "He's working up his courage."

She squatted now, tore a strip of bacon in half, and tossed it at his feet. Almost before it hit the ground, the dog devoured it. His eyes widened and he licked his chops, desperate for more. He closed half again the distance between them and sat, pawing the ground.

Silje tore the half strip in half again and reached forward with it. This time he scooted out of reach. She tossed the quarter strip. This time he caught it midair.

"I've got a whole other piece, my friend," she said.

"Wait for him now," her uncle said. "He's had a taste."

For the first time, Fenrir whimpered. The sweetest sound. His haunches shook.

"You can have more," she said.

The dog stood and circled and sat again.

Silje looked back at her uncle. He only nodded.

"I'm a nice girl. I want to be your friend."

The dog couldn't bear his hunger any longer. He edged close enough that she could have touched his muzzle, but she offered another quarter strip of bacon instead. The dog took it from her fingers, his breath flushing on her greasy hand. After another bite, he lay down and rolled on his back, scratching his croup and withers.

"Your wolf dog needs a new name, Silje."

She fed him another small bite. "Fenrir's a perfect name."

"Fenrir was a god. What you've got here is a goddess."

"Really?"

Mats nodded.

"Then she'll be Freya—the mightiest and most fair."

"Hello, Freya," he said.

When her uncle said the name, the dog scooted closer to Silje and looked between them. Her eyes shining like the lake water, her tongue lolling, still hoping for more bacon.

Which Silje gave her. After Freya swallowed it, she stayed right where she sat.

"Looks like you've made a friend after all," Mats said. "You show her around. I've got work to finish."

THE EMBROIDERY on Father Richter's black vestments was the same burnished bronze as the organ pipes towering above the choir loft. With his mother on his arm, Theodulf followed the acolytes up the aisle at Sacred Heart, the funeral hymn trailing his father's casket. A procession of grieving or grievance? He hardly knew which.

The Requiem Mass his father had long insisted upon was underway, scheduled between nones and vespers, as he'd wished. In the carriage on the way to the church, when he'd asked his mother why his father wanted his Funeral Mass at such a time, she'd said, "He believed his greatest accomplishments were achieved in the afternoon. By his logic, his ascension into heaven would most likely be granted at two o'clock."

"I thought Funeral Masses were usually said in the morning?"

She fingered the curtain aside and watched the streetcar pass. "Your father's largesse landed him in the church's good graces." She let the curtain fall. "Where he stands with God is another matter altogether."

Theodulf had silently scoffed at the notion in the carriage, but here in the church, sliding into the front pew, the candles guttering in the heat, he was reminded of heaven's dominion over hell. What's more, he could imagine his father's superstitions prevailing upon his own better logic. After all, death was the final vicissitude. Better to make any accommodation for it.

To his father's credit, the church crowded with parishioners. Whether to mourn or merely make an appearance, he could not say. But his mother's furtive, over-the-shoulder glances and satisfied sneer suggested their mere attendance sufficed. Theodulf felt only ambivalence. And though he didn't even wish it otherwise, he could not help dwelling on the pageantry. The altar festooned with flowers, the Latin mass, the lustrous mahogany coffin, the incense and stained glass and droning hymns, the crucifix looming above— could it be any more ostentatious? Any less serious?

If nothing else, the mass gave him a chance to reflect, an opportunity he used to contemplate not mortality or the quality of his father's life, but the episode with Miss Haas in the billiard room not twelve hours afore. Already he had a distorted view of the incident. As if his social standing—look at the gathered aristocracy!—and the fact he'd had almost no say in what happened absolved him of moral wrongdoing. If nothing else, God would have been too busy contemplating the resurrection of his father's soul to note Theodulf's own transgression.

He pondered instead the sundering of his own self-perception. Every bit of himself was undone by the tryst. Ten years of calculation and stoicism and abstinence, all of it unbuttoned by a common servant. The realization bent him two ways. On the one hand, he was baffled by his derailment and loathed his lack of restraint. On the other, a certain vibration coursed through him—even here in the church—that intoxicated him anew. That the drunkenness came under these hallowed arches and in the light of the stained glass, in the church of his youth, the place he'd become an acolyte himself, where he'd taken five of the seven sacred sacraments, well, none of these things discouraged his mooning about it. Indeed, he could no sooner ignore his racing blood than he could the hot breath of the congregants.

He looked around at their solemn, empty faces. This sea of Duluth society and nary a true friend in the bunch.

Up in the pulpit, Father Richter stood with his back to the throng, gazing at the rood. What association he might possibly have made between Christ and the man he would now eulogize was even further beyond Theodulf's ken than the dilemma of Miss Haas. But there the priest stood, the thread of his vestments catching the candlelight.

When finally he turned around, he raised his hands heavenward and said, "The Lord Jesus Christ died for us at Calvary. For our salvation, He did. And now He sits in everlasting glory at the right hand of God His father. He is our shepherd. And we are but sheep in His flock." He wiped his brow with a handkerchief.

"We would do well to remember the gospels of Christ's four loyal evangelists. It is they who transcribed Christ's words. It is they who have provided us with the wisdom to live a right and good life. Consider this, from the Gospel according to Matthew, chapter 10, verses sixteen through twenty: *Behold, I send you as sheep in the midst of wolves. Be ye therefore wise as serpents and simple as doves. But beware of men. For they will deliver you up in councils, and they will scourge you in their synagogues. And you shall be brought before governors, and before kings for my sake, for a testimony to them and to the Gentiles: But when they shall deliver you up, take no thought how or what to speak: for it shall be given you in that hour what to speak. For it is not you that speak, but the Spirit of your Father that speaketh in you.*" He wiped his brow again, the church now broiling with three hundred bodies dressed in black.

"*I send you as sheep in the midst of wolves.*" He raised his hands, palms down, and anointed the congregation. "We are, all of us, thus in the world." Now he lowered his hands until only the right pointed at Ernst's coffin there below the altar. "Sheep among wolves, protected by Christ's bounteous forgiveness and eternal wisdom. It is here, as brethren, in this church, which is Christ's vessel, that we are safe from the wolves. It is here we seek—*and find*—eternal life.

"Today we honor the life and death of one of our righteous brothers in Christ. Ernst Sauer. A man I considered a friend and a confidant. A man who believed in the power and glory of God with all his mighty heart. A man whose place at the heavenly table is a foregone conclusion. A man whose soul has surely ascended there with all the haste and resplendence of Halley's Comet. It may well have been carried on that space rock! This man's eternal salvation ought to inspire us all to live more righteously, more closely to God."

Father Richter smiled down on Theodulf's mother. "He was, first, a man of God. And second, a devoted, faithful, greathearted husband." He turned his attention back to the general throng. "He was a man of industry and a man of community. He believed in capitalism and hard work. Dozens of you count yourselves partners and beneficiaries of his labor, and dozens others have benefited from his intellect and stewardship of this city. Indeed, of this whole end of the lake.

"He built railroads and ships; he mined iron ore and felled timber; he fought for what's ours and won what wasn't. Yes, indeed, he was a man of great industry. It might even have been easy to mistake him for a wolf among us, if not for his generosity. In fact, the organ that played his processional is here thanks to it. As is the Christian Brothers Home right next door." For the third time he wiped his brow with the kerchief, as though it were his own labor that had raised the organ and Christian Brothers Home. He gazed down on the casket.

"I take comfort and pleasure in this good man's place at the table of heaven. It brings me peace to know that his earthly toil was such that his reward is with the rest of the righteous flock. That he joins those he loved once, and will be joined again by others he loved, and was loved by."

He stepped down to the casket and put his hand on it. "Our shepherd guides us even in death. We no longer need fear the wolf. No! If we've lived as this good man did, Satan himself, that master of eternal suffering and eternal damnation, has no claim in death. It's only the skeptic who will parley with Satan, who will burn in his unholy and underground house."

Now his aspect appeared smug. As if he'd just saved his own flock by the mere power of his persuasion. Theodulf considered Father Richter a friend, but one several stations below him. That the priest might presume to make any claim of superiority, well, it would normally have offended him immensely. It many times had. But on this day, his distraction compounded by the priest's blathering on about wolves and sheep, Theodulf could only muster a minor pique. Who was the priest, after all, but another of the charlatans his father had surrounded himself with?

As Father Richter turned back to the altar, Theodulf removed his watch. The Requiem Mass must soon end, as vespers would commence in only an hour.

EVEN AT TWILIGHT, the heat of the day persisted. A swarm of mosquitoes smudged the otherwise peerless sky. Willa was as restless as those bugs.

She'd come down to the dock to watch the sunset and relish the coolness off the lake. But clouds had banked in the west, so she watched the moonrise instead. Waxing, gibbous. Her favorite for its promise, special tonight for its brightness. She'd taken extra solace in the moon's constancy since the comet had veered back into deep space. Hanging there now, it inspired another mood: restlessness. Theodulf had been gone some thirty-six hours, and so far she'd only managed to admonish herself for not celebrating his absence more.

But what might she do? The other wives were busy with their men. The girl across the bay was busy with her uncle. Which left Willa free and alone.

So, she began playing the *Moonlight Sonata* across her lap. Just her fingers in the folds of her skirt as she lay back against a dock piling. Herr Volk would certainly have admonished this posture, a realization that straightened her spine. But only for a moment. Herr Volk was fifty miles and five years gone. She closed her eyes against the memory of him, opened them a moment later to two bats flying past the moon. Their wings reminded her of that fateful performance at the Ionic Lodge. The crashing of the gulls and the storm outside. Had a night ever been so at odds with another? As this one was to that?

A dog barked. She watched the night sky darken and brighten at the same time. She brightened herself, even if half of her was as dark as the far side of the moon.

She didn't hear his footfalls on the dock, didn't know how long

367

he'd stood behind her, couldn't have expected him, even as she did. He might not have spoken. Probably knew better than to have been there in the first place. But the dog barked again, and she turned her nose up to the night and the musk of his scent landed on her. Strong and sweet. It made her mouth water before she even saw him.

"I didn't mean to startle you," he said, stepping up beside her.

"Nothing surprises me anymore," she said.

"It's too hot to sleep."

"Sleep," she said, as if she were dreaming in that very moment.

"Mind if I sit down?"

"Please."

The dog barked again.

"Silje has found herself a pet," Mats said.

"That wolf?"

"Not a wolf. And not a fella. Just some wild hound wouldn't leave her alone."

Willa sat up. "Not a wolf? He—she—was the size of small horse!"

"You saw her, then?" He nodded as though that helped explain something. "She'll eat more than my niece and I together, it's true." He sat down, his feet hanging over the edge of the dock.

Willa couldn't look up. Her fingers went back to the folds of her dress, but it wasn't the sonata she sought there so much as some place to hold on to.

"She's intent on rearing her up. My niece, I mean. And that dog."

"How is she? Silje, not the dog."

"Better now, for the dog."

She could see his smile. Could tell the expression didn't often rise. And didn't linger long.

The lighthouse beam passed six times.

"I sometimes work late. In the fish house. That light, it comes in my window. It'll like to make me a madman."

"What are you doing so late at night?"

He took his pipe out of his trouser pocket. He packed it and lit it and the smoke sweetened the night. "Oh, mending nets, sharpening knives. Building fish boxes." He took another puff of the pipe.

"Truth be, sometimes I just sit out there woolgathering. Wondering what the hell I'm going to do about Silje."

His plainspokenness and vulnerability positively entranced her. "Well," she ventured, "this place is good for that."

"It doesn't reach the cabin. The lighthouse beam. In fact, it doesn't reach the back window of the fish house." He pointed across the water, where the front window was lit from within. "But I occupy the front window. The one lit. Silje's got a little cockloft by the back. She sits up there singing songs and reading and whittling wood."

Willa could picture it. Scenes of domestic tranquility. Easiness. She'd not imagined something akin to it since her father passed away. Not once.

The light passed again and again, each rotation pushing them further into the darkness.

"I'd imagine carrying on alone is no small thing," she said.

He shrugged.

"I could help," Willa said, surprising even herself.

"I expect your responsibilities up on the rock keep you busy enough."

She sat up, feeling indignant. "Not really. Mostly I sit around drinking tea, waiting for something exciting to happen. Of course, it never does."

He glanced at her from under his heavy eyelids. "You've darned a net, then? Or salted a hundred pounds of fish?"

She couldn't tell if his tone mocked or played. "Some people might consider that an impertinent, even insulting response. Especially to someone who just offered a hand."

"I don't mean it like that, but only to say it's a specialized thing we do in that fish house."

"I reckon if your child-niece is able, I might be, too."

"She's been darning nets since before she could walk."

"Mr. Braaten, how you persist in doubting me! I'll have you know I've been to the university. Radcliffe, no less."

"I surely did not know that." Another of his halfway smiles there on his easing and most comely face.

"And before you ask, I did not study net darning or fish salting."

He leaned back on his elbows, the slope of him now a gentle grade. "What did you study?"

Her hands flew from her lap and spread wide. "Astronomy."

He leaned farther back, the long and corded muscles in his neck flexing. In the starlight she could see his pulse beating. So slowly. So unlike her own, which she could feel throbbing even in the soles of her feet.

"I imagine there's plenty to learn."

"More than plenty."

"Like what, for example?"

"Everything beyond this earth."

He whistled softly. "Plenty indeed."

"I narrowed most of my interest to the moon."

They turned in unison to behold the half of it visible.

"Tell me something about the moon I should know," he said.

Had he really just asked that? And why? Outside of her father, she'd never been asked a meaningful question by a man. Not even her professors at Radcliffe and Harvard. But she must have been waiting, because without much deliberation she said, "That dark splotch on the bottom quarter of the moon, it's called *Oceanus Procellarum*. Ocean of Storms. We name all of those pockmarks as seas. *Oceanus Procellarum* is the largest."

"Now that'd be a fine place to cast a net." He'd still not looked down, but then he did. "Are they actually filled with water?"

"They're not. But wouldn't it be lovely if they were."

"It's like a shadow."

"Precisely. Each of them is. Scientists tell us each is caused by a volcanic eruption. I hypothesize they're made by collision with some other celestial body. A meteor or asteroid."

"Like our friend the comet."

"But smaller."

He sat up and rubbed his hands together as though some matter were settled. "You've given me an astronomy lesson. The least I can do is repay in kind."

Everything quickened. The light of the stars. The water lapping ashore. The rush of her blood. She braved a glance at him. Even his gaze seemed quicker.

"And teach you to darn a net."

She stood. As if the stars had dropped wires to pull her up.

He let out a great laugh. "You're eager to learn."

She laughed back, at the realization he'd not meant now. A warm breeze came out of the woods to wash the blush from her neck. She privately thanked the night.

"It's awfully late, but I have to get to it in any case. You're welcome to join me. Silje's likely awake herself. She'll come out and help, too."

Willa looked up at the lighthouse.

"I beg your pardon," Mats said. "I guess the summer night has sent me sideways."

"Not at all," Willa said bravely. "I'd love to see Silje. Even in the middle of the night. Maybe especially so."

Freya sent up a wild howl as they approached. She kept her back to the cabin, her eyes watchful even in the dark; her hind legs swinging left and right across the path. As soon as Willa and Mats veered for the fish house, the dog sat. Her barking stopped.

Inside, the lantern's glow quivered under the breeze coming through the open window. It smelled of kerosene and fresh-cut wood but oddly not of fish. Not at all. A net ran the length of the workbench beneath the window, held in place by six evenly placed pegs clearly designed for just that purpose. Silje's cockloft, the fish boxes stacked ten high, the extra oars and glass buoys, the barrels and benches, all of it tidy, like some diorama of a fisherman's life instead of his actual workshop.

"I'd offer you something to drink, but all I have is a ladle and a barrel of water." He picked a pair of leather work gloves off the workbench and slapped them in the palm of his left hand.

"This is exactly how I imagined it."

"Why in God's name would you imagine the inside of a fish house?" He looked at the gloves, put them down in the exact same place from which he'd picked them up.

Willa only smiled and picked up a spool of manila twine.

"That's our fiber." He gathered a handful of net, showed her the gaps. "Tedious work, really, to sit in here like an old lady knitting through the night. But"—he set the net back down, smoothed it like a tuxedo jacket—"since my sister vanished, it's the same as everything: do it myself, or cash in and move to the city."

She tried to picture him jumping on the trolley and heading to a downtown agency to punch a clock there. Tried to imagine him wearing a cravat and jacket. A bowler.

"I know," he said. "I'm no sooner fit for that than I am a starring role in *The Pirates of Penzance*."

"I saw *The Pirates of Penzance* at the Colonial Theatre in Boston!"

"I saw it at the Shivering Timber just outside Gunflint." He blushed. "I saw six of the molls three sheets to the wind singing the songs, leastways."

"Tell me, Mr. Braaten, are you a frequent client of the Shivering Timber?" She'd not meant to sound scolding, but she did.

"I've been a couple times. Not for the molls but for the Canadian whiskey after long winters sawing trees on the Burnt Wood River."

"A whiskey sounds just right about now."

"The best I've got is a pint of rum."

"How about some of your sarsaparilla?"

"There's a little less heat in that, but I do have a batch just brewed up in the cabin."

"Don't disturb Silje," she said, stepping up to the workbench and sliding her fingers into the net. "Show me how to fix this instead."

He showed her how to splice the manila and weave it and tie it off, his hands guiding hers and sometimes getting tangled together.

She hardly breathed for the riot in her belly. It arrived as suddenly as a shooting star and burned as hot. In all her life she'd not known a feeling like it, and yet it was also familiar. Like she'd been expecting it without knowing. Every sense sharpened. She heard—smelled—felt—saw everything. His breathing. His redolence. The heat from the tips of his fingers. The hair between the knuckles on his hands.

Though he was an arm's length away, she could feel the heat from his body. Hotter even than the night. Closer here in the fish house. What's more, she desired it. The heat and his presence both. So many times she'd wondered what the fuss was about. Her classmates at Radcliffe who'd described their dalliances with boys from across the yard. How they mooned about it. The closest she'd ever come to these feelings was watching the comet from behind her bedroom window on the hill above. She could see that same window from where she now stood. Up in the night, beyond her reflection in the glass of the fish house pane.

He was talking. Something about the nets and water and how they required constant repair. Did his voice quaver? Or was it her thoughts that did? The other face in the mirror, was it his? Was his hand lifting from the net? Was it resting on her neck? Softly? Softly. The absence of his voice resounded.

Was he lifting her face to his now? Were his lips—so rough and so warm—pressed against hers? She closed her eyes and hoped. No, she just simply believed.

Goodness, the burning.

"I'm sorry," he said.

She opened her eyes in time to see him stumble backwards. Like a drunk man.

"I'm sorry," he said again, leaning against a vice on the workbench.

"No," she said. She tried to blink the moment into clarity. "Yes," she countered. Then she realized the only reason she didn't reach for his neck and pull him back to her was that her hand was tangled in the net.

THE DOG HAD BEEN WAITING for Silje on the stoop outside the front door. She followed her along the path between the cabin and the dark side of the fish house, sat now at her bare ankle, her tail swooshing against Silje's skin as she craned to see inside. Only her uncle's lantern burned, the wavering light kindling a vision she had to pinch herself against.

"Shh," she hissed at Freya, who sat yet silently. The dog shifted.

Willa's chin pressed into her uncle's bare shoulder. One of her bare arms lay over his right shoulder. Her fingers clenched his flesh. Silje could only see the top quarter of him. Well, that and his right foot, around which his dungarees were tangled. He still wore his boots.

She closed her eyes, saw him the only way she'd ever known him there. Buttoned up and at work. Mending nets or gutting fish or busy at some other chore that seemed to change each day. But never before *this*. She knew that her uncle and Willa—Willa with the pistol, Willa with the piano, Willa with the husband, Frog—stood entangled in the act of . . . what was it called? She couldn't remember, but the feeling in her own middle announced their purpose.

She thought of all the nights she'd lain in her own bunk, her fingers searching out those parts of her body she didn't understand but certainly awoke to. They all fired now. Between her legs. Down deep. A lightheadedness not unlike the one she got that time she stole sips of her uncle's rum. She'd felt it when she was with Odd. She'd felt it again when she set the wolf trap.

This, though? It yawned in her. Made her breathless. Less like jumping into the bitter cold of Lake Superior than like leaping from

374

the waterfall up on the Gininwabiko River. A feeling that at once frightened her and made her wish it would not end.

The whoosh of Freya's tail again awoke her. Her black eyes were visible even in the darkness. Just the wetness of them. She rarely looked away, the dog. It was as if she had all the world to learn and Silje her only teacher. What could Silje tell her about something she knew nothing of?

Rather than explain, Silje raised her finger to her lips. A plea for Freya to keep her barking and howling to herself. Answering, Freya turned back to the cabin path and trotted into the darkness of the woods. By the time Silje reached those shadows herself, she had the first couplet of a song tripping from her lips. *It's deeper than the water dark, this feeling 'twixt my feet and heart . . .*

The happiness of having found that verse distracted her from the rest of the song, but she would track it down. Somewhere in the middle of the night. Sleeping or not. Dreaming in either case.

MARIAGE BLANC

NOVEMBER 26, 1909

Lightness and darkness are not incompatible. It might even be said they require each other. The same is true of most unnatural alliances. The sun and moon. Anger and ease. Sorrow and joy. Heat and cold. April and November. Wolf and raven. Fire and water.

Of this last it might be noted that they share one overwhelming quality. The deeper each gets, the more intense it becomes. Fire in its brightness, water in its darkness.

THE SOLEMNITY of Friday evening mass had always appealed to Theodulf's melancholic nature, but seldom as strongly as it did on this faithful night, the final Friday before the beginning of Advent. Father Richter had said vespers, had sermonized about the coming of Christ and the joy of a believing heart, and though Theodulf was less and less inclined to contemplate the good priest's words, the mere timbre of them had set him right of mind. What's more, the walk from Sacred Heart to meet his mother at the Thibert Hotel was likewise pleasant. It had snowed the day before, but the evening's warmth had melted it, and now after dusk the air smelled sweetly of its evaporation. He would have an hour of solitude before a late dinner with his mother—an hour he intended to spend with a cup of cocoa in the hotel lobby—and taken altogether, he could almost believe he was *content*.

The belief followed him into the lobby, where his cheeks flushed roseate in the whoosh of warm air. A woman played a Chopin nocturne on the piano in the back corner. She possessed an elegant back and it moved wavelike as she performed. Such loveliness. He removed his leather gloves and slapped them across the palm of his hand, a gesture that roused the concierge.

Now Theodulf removed his scarf. "I would very much enjoy a cup of hot cocoa while I await my companion. I'll be just here." He waved at the leather club chair by the front window.

"Indeed, sir." The concierge nodded and was gone in one movement.

Theodulf removed his coat and draped it over the back of a second chair, layering his scarf and gloves atop the lapels. He smoothed his hair and had a look about. The brass spittoons were spread like pawns on a chessboard mid-game. A stained glass bowl in the ceiling cast a kaleidoscopic light that somehow matched the Turkish rugs on the floor. Warmth filled the air between them.

He stretched his back and neck and glanced out the mullioned windows. Even from inside, the evening appeared charmed. The westbound trolley passed, and Theodulf sat and crossed his legs, awaiting his drink. The tapestry hanging between the ceiling molding and the wainscotting was something of a window onto the Sauer family genealogy. At least his mother professed it to be. The man woven into the linen canvas, standing with his cutlass in its scabbard, cock-like, his tricorn angled upon his head and bursting with long tresses, his beard braided, epaulettes fringing his shoulders, was none other than Bleiz Thibert. Legend called him Theodulf's five times maternal great-grandfather, a man said to have built the first proper ship on Lake Superior.

That ship—the *Novantique*—was also woven into the tapestry, beneath a silken line that ran from the lower-left to upper-right corner. A sloop with seven gunports and her mainsail full of breeze, the artist had rendered both the man and the ship in such fine, silken detail that, when paired with the stories his mother told of the Thibert family line, gave Theodulf to believe he wasn't the misfit he'd always suspected himself to be.

A waiter appeared with a steaming cup of cocoa and set it on the table between the club chairs.

"Please charge it to the Ernst Sauer family," Theodulf said.

The waiter nodded and turned and left. Now Theodulf listened to the music. One of the nocturnes. He could never keep them all straight. But this one was played in a style reminiscent of . . . something, he could not quite place it.

It worked like a fine port. Enough that in a respite between songs, he settled back into the chair and imagined the loads of mined copper the *Novantique* was built to freighter across the lake, Bleiz Thibert standing watch with his cutlass hanging at his belt. But what followed his reverie may as well have been that same sword driven into his chest. The song of his life, bounding through the stately hotel lobby like a sloop unmoored! He closed his eyes to Bleiz Thibert and listened only to the music. The sweet, divine, harrowing, and indeed *fantastical* music.

Even after she'd played the last note, Theodulf rested in the chair, his eyes closed, recalling what could only be described as a waking dream, one in which he sailed aboard the *Novantique* across the icy waters of the lake to some heavenly land he'd never before seen, let alone imagined. Goodness, could life really be so plain?

Risking answer and without rising from his seat, he called the concierge again, who hurried to Theodulf's alcove. "Sir?" he said.

"Please extend an invitation to the pianist, that she might join me?"

However could he have known that this singular moment of calm would set him on a course for his final destruction?

MURDOCK ALDERDICE—even his name provoked parody. An hour before, in the room she and her mother kept at the Thibert Hotel, he'd cornered her for the third time. Cornered her and placed his hand on her waist and said, "Your mother's having a social hour with old family friends down in the tearoom." He'd walked his fingers up the ladder of her ribs so they rested in the valley between her arm and breast. "I've had a hundred thoughts about what I would do with you in an hour." His breath smelled sweetly. As if he'd just eaten strawberry preserves.

"You're appalling," she whispered, pushing his hand away. This only emboldened him more.

"Imagine your leisure, if you consented to be my wife."

She ducked under his reach. "I'd sooner live penniless on the docks than spend a minute as your wife."

He sneered. "You'll end up penniless on the docks if I say so."

She didn't doubt this, given their situation and the debt they'd already incurred.

He stood between her and the door, stroking his oiled muttonchops.

"You're disgusting," she said, more forcefully than she thought herself capable. "I'm not half your age."

"I know," he sighed.

"What of my mother?" Certainly Willa was not entertaining the notion of marrying Murdock Alderdice. Nor did she care much about the arrangement between him and her mother. But as often happened, she found herself eager to goad him.

"Your mother has made explicitly clear the conviction she'll never marry again. I believe her first go-round with your father left her . . . wanting."

"She's always shunned decency." Willa raised her hands at the hotel room, damning her present station as proof positive of this very notion.

"I think she shunned boredom and sanctimony."

She took a combative stance. "My father was many things, but sanctimonious? No."

He plopped down on the settee and patted the spot next to him. By his own standards this attempted seduction was clumsy. Even woeful. For a moment she thought he might be sozzled, but the clarity of his eyes and the pleasant smell of him suggested otherwise.

"If you said you'd be my wife, I'd send you back to college before we wed."

"Claptrap."

Now he leaned forward as though he had an ache in his stomach. He moaned and righted himself and said, "Let's set the discussion of marriage aside and talk instead of your dugs. Or better yet, you might show me them."

"Add to *appalling* and *disgusting lewd* and *repellant.* I'll take your leave." She hurried to the door and left in a flourish of skirt.

She replayed his unwelcome and scurrilous advances while warming to Chopin's E-flat nocturne.

She hardly knew which was more stunning: that she had learned so easily and quickly to parley with a man like Murdock Alderdice, or that she had been forced to in the first place. It remained incomprehensible to her that her father was dead. By his own design, no less. That her mother had simply capitulated to this fact, it dawned on her, lent credence to Mr. Alderdice's suggestion that Ann had been unhappily married. Certainly, she'd never encouraged the institution upon her daughter until now, as their circumstances changed, but Willa always understood that reluctance as a nod to her own independence and a future more progressive than her mother's. Now, as she played, that notion vanished as the notes did. It seemed altogether more likely that her mother *had* been bored in her marriage. For all the affection Willa felt for her father, for all his kindness and generosity, for all the ways he indulged her, he did not seem, in retrospect, like a fine husband. A thoughtful man. A decent one. True. But like some great spouse? Did such a thing even exist?

A waiter walked by carrying a tray. From the steaming cup upon it, the scent of chocolate emanated. She brought the melody to a close and thought of getting up. But where would she go? To her room? Likely Mr. Alderdice would still be loitering. Out on the town? Unheard of. Into the restaurant for a bite to eat? She *was* hungry, but she had all of a nickel in her purse. Not enough to eat at the Chester. She pinched the coin to check it was there, and when the waiter passed back to the restaurant, she ordered a cup of cocoa.

Not since her father passed had she rendered Beethoven, but something about the accumulation of the day's troublesomeness inspired her to play. It was as if the music were her own private memory, one she'd only ever experienced alone. As if no such thing as trouble existed. Only beauty and elation and rest.

Could she play it forever, and nothing more?

She might even leave the moon alone.

The cocoa, which she hadn't noticed was delivered until she finished and closed the fallboard, sat on the table beside the wall. There was a note under the saucer that read: *Consider this a gift from Mr. Alderdice.* Simply reading his name was reason enough for her to forget the peace she'd just felt. But she willed her vengeance away and sipped her cocoa.

Not a minute later, the concierge approached, his hands behind his back. His mustache—waxed and curled—twitched in nervousness. "Excuse me, Miss Brandt." He listed forward, nearly tipping over. "Mr. Sauer requests the pleasure of your company."

"Mr. Sauer?"

"Theodulf Sauer, miss." He righted himself. "He's just on the other side of the lobby. In the Thibert Alcove."

"Whyever has he requested my company?"

"I couldn't say with certainty, but I believe he was smitten with your performance." He tilted again, once to port and once starboard, glancing in each direction. "He's sober, miss."

"As opposed to?"

"Soused, miss."

"Is he often soused?"

He lifted a foot now, like an animal caught in a trap. He'd breached the decorum his position demanded, that much she could see. "No, miss," he said flatly. Once more he glanced about. Sighed. "He used to have a reputation. But I believe those days are well behind him."

Willa lifted her cup and saucer from the table. She followed the concierge across the sea of carpets. Even his gait was bobbing and buoylike.

Theodulf stood beneath the tapestry, affecting a posture not unlike the man woven above him. Which is to say he appeared dignified. It was an attitude short in lasting, though. He merely stood there, his hands behind his back, the concierge between the two of them, as if Mr. Sauer expected the mustachioed man to make formal introductions. When the concierge clicked his heels and turned to go, Theodulf finally spoke up.

"Excuse me, sir. I wonder if . . ." He gave her an imploring look. A helpless one.

"I'm Willa Brandt."

"Yes, I wonder if Miss Brandt would like something more than . . ." Now he peered into her cup.

"Cocoa," she said. "No, I'm fine."

Theodulf grimaced. He waved the concierge away.

"Thank you," Willa said to the concierge's back.

Theodulf, mistaking her gratefulness as intended for him, said, "Of course!"

If such a thing were possible, he blundered more on the occasion of this meeting than he had their last. He looked up at the ceiling, putting his face in profile with the one on the tapestry behind him. "There's a certain resemblance," Willa said.

He looked at her quizzically.

"You and the man on the wall."

"Ah, yes!" He turned to look at. "There's no coincidence in that. He was a five times great-grandfather. On the Hogg side. Our lines met at my great-grandmother, Marguerite Thibert." He looked at her, expecting—what—approval? Awe?

"I'm sure she was a wonderful woman."

He turned to behold the tapestry again, as if he might divine just the sort of woman his great-grandmother was.

"That's quite a hat he's got. And his sword!"

"Cutlass," Theodulf said, his back still to her. As soon as he said it, he shook his head. He turned back. "I beg your pardon. I'm insufferable. A quality that comes from my father's side of the family ledger."

She extended her hand, suggesting they sit.

"His hat there," Theodulf continued, "was known as a tricorne. Made famous by French forces in the seventeenth and eighteenth century."

"Yes," she said, rather condescendingly. "I've read Voltaire and the likes."

"Voltaire—there's a proper scapegrace."

Oh, this would be even more fun than she imagined. "That word, did it come from your mother's or father's line?"

"I beg pardon?"

"*Scapegrace.* So severe! So"—she tapped her lips, feigning serious contemplation—"censorious!"

"Well, Voltaire was a heathen. A provocateur. More than anything, a child." He concentrated on the tapestry for another long moment and then turned in her direction without properly meeting her gaze. "Bleiz Thibert built the first ship on Lake Superior. That's it there." Now he pointed at the ship woven into the under half of the linen. "A sloop. The *Novantique*. Over about the Sault, at a yard on Pointe Aux Pins. This was almost two hundred years ago." He shook his head, satisfied but not done. "While you're jesting about my maternal and paternal lines, I might say there are shipwrights on both sides of it. My grandfather was—and my uncles are now—shipbuilders in Detroit. Half the freighters you see out there? Built by Willi and Walther."

"Well, I now know your five times great-grandfather and both of your uncles, but I don't know you."

Abashed, he said, "Forgive me. My name is Theodulf Sauer." He watched his own hand reach across the table between them.

"I know who you are."

Now he blushed. Was it infamy rising in his cheeks? How could a man with so much standing, who did indeed come from such royal Great Lake lines, be so maladroit? She actually found it charming.

"And you've also not told me why you invited me to join you."

"Ah, yes. Simple: I admired your playing and wanted to say so."

"You might have just come over to tell me that," she said. He appeared hurt by her teasing, so she added, "Did you prefer the Chopin or the Beethoven?"

"I have a special fondness for the Beethoven sonata."

She watched an almost chapfallen expression beset him. Gone the blush. Gone the self-consciousness he wore like a tricorne himself. She had no desire to toy with him now. He was like a child who didn't understand the game, and so it would be no fun winning. Instead, she chose a different, more generous tack. "What is it you love so much about that music, Mr. Sauer?"

He interlaced his fingers and considered his hands as though with them he'd built ships himself. Or conducted symphonies. "Is it too much to say that in those notes are everything I thought I might be someday? Some*way*?" He unclasped his hands. "I mean,

Miss Brandt, not just what's happened to me, but a world of possibility I never could have imagined without the music? It's *hope*. It's just simply that. Hope and beauty."

"You've not known much of that, have you, Mr. Sauer?"

He set his hands on his lap and cocked his head.

"Hope, I mean. Or beauty," Willa said.

He sighed. Outside, a horse and carriage drove through the light of the gas lamp. Before he answered, the clomping hooves sounded for a metronomic moment. "Besides from music, I don't think I've ever known a minute of it."

"Oh my."

He reached into his waistcoat and divined his watch. "If I still drank, now would be the time to order an absinthe."

"It's dinnertime," she offered, unsure not only of what she was suggesting, but of every clashing instinct within her.

He seemed not to have heard her and flipped the case of the watch once-twice-thrice. "I sometimes wonder if that music is following me around. Like a shadow." He put the watch back in his pocket. "Or a ghost."

"Surely you don't believe in ghosts, Mr. Sauer?"

"Lord knows it's haunted enough." He readjusted in his chair, crossed one leg over the other, and folded his hands across his knee. "Can you imagine divining that music? From where does something like that come? Perchance from God Himself?"

His voice had softened. Like he was speaking in confidence and didn't want any of the passersby to overhear.

All Willa could think was, what a peculiar man. Did he really have no idea it had been she that'd played it that night four years ago in the Blue Room of the Ionic Lodge? She and not some fictitious cousin from Virginia? Just as baffling as the answer to this was the fact that she felt no compulsion to taunt or tease him now. No urge to make more a fool of this man already orphaned of pride and braggadocio. She sat back, waiting for him to find the answers to his own impossible questions.

Which weren't long in arriving. No sooner had she mirrored his pose in the opposite chair than did he lean forward. "I once saw 'Quasi una fantasia' performed here. In Duluth I mean. At the Blue Room of the Ionic Lodge. A young wunderkind. A prodigy, I daresay."

It seemed impossible he'd be delivering himself so naively, but as surely as he spoke at all, that's what he did. "Where the Masons meet," he whispered, his loose hand covering his mouth.

"This wunderkind, did he play better than me?"

He looked as if he might faint, recalling Willa in her peruke. Willa as Will, the boy from Virginia.

"He played like his hands were on fire. I remember that. It was the night of the *Mataafa* storm."

With each moment that passed, it became more and more obvious to Willa that Theodulf had no recollection of Willa as Will. He'd not made the connection between her father and that night. He had no suspicion. No guile whatsoever. He was merely lost in the fantasy he'd made of his memory. On the one hand, she felt a genuine sympathy for him. A lost soul if ever one existed. But on the other, she recounted his venomous countenance in the lobby of the Masonic Temple. The way he made of Willa as Will simple quarry. *Prey.*

Looking at him now, he appeared toothless. Could a man change so much? Had he been unwell then? Inebriated? Caught in a different languor?

He caught her staring, forced a deferential smile. "Do you know why Beethoven called it the Moonlight Sonata?" he asked.

Rather than punish his ignorance, she said, "I've heard this before. Something about Paris and a gondolier on the river Seine?"

He nodded. Glanced out the window. Then turned back to her. "You played it every bit as beautifully as that prodigy did. And with much more control."

This simple, unadorned compliment felt for all the world like the kindest thing anyone had said to her since she left Radcliffe. She softened more. Might even have blushed. "I believe, Mr. Sauer, that you and I share a sense of wonder about the music. I'd never have identified hope as the thing I see in it, but I might from now on."

"We are kindred, then!" he said without any embarrassment.

"And I am famished," she tried again.

His attention was pulled away, as though by force of the moon itself, to the other side of the hotel lobby. The smile that had rested comfortably turned doubtful now, and he said, "Look, here's Mother." He stood to greet her.

Willa turned to see Mrs. Sauer coming across the lobby. She wore a dress as severe as the expression on her thin face, which was as elongated as the horses trotting by.

Theodulf greeted her formally, kissing both cheeks and holding her hand as he introduced them. "Mother, this is Miss Brandt. Miss Brandt, my mother, the estimable Mrs. Ernst Sauer."

"It's an honor to meet you, Mrs. Sauer."

"I suppose it is." The older woman spoke through her teeth. Her lips puckering on the *pp* but otherwise not moving. Her eyes did roam, though, taking Willa in from head to toe with no small amount of disapproval. "Theodulf," she said, "will Miss Sauer be joining us for dinner?"

"I'd never impose," Willa said.

"Nonsense," Mrs. Sauer said with neither conviction nor enthusiasm. "If Theodulf has somehow found himself in the good graces of a young lady so lovely as you, we'd do our best to extend that confabulation, wouldn't we?"

Willa couldn't help but glance around, as though perhaps Mrs. Sauer were speaking to some other audience.

"We'll dine right here at the hotel. The ham steak and brie is the best dish in this whole wretched town." Mrs. Sauer turned toward the concierge, who was summoned by her mere glance.

"Ma'am?"

"Please let them know we'll be three tonight." She waved her hand but then called him back with her crooked finger. "And tell the maître d' to have a bottle of champagne ready. I'm feeling effervescent."

And so it was that Willa found herself at the best table in all Duluth, seated between Theodulf Sauer, the man who would become her husband, and his mother, who would orchestrate their nuptials as though a maestro of such causes. Before all that came to pass, though, they feasted on ham steaks and brie.

"Are you a Catholic, Miss Brandt?" The first words she uttered chimed like dropped cutlery.

"I'm not."

Mary Sauer looked doubtfully at Theodulf but would not be deterred. "What sort of business is your father in?"

"My father's just passed."

"Oh. You're that Brandt?" She pinched the pearlescent buttons on the sleeve of her gown, one at a time, as if counting back Willa's attributes. *Not a Catholic?* Deduct one. *No father?* Deduct another. "Tell me, how is your mother bearing up?"

The image of Murdock Alderdice dancing her mother around the Thibert Hotel ballroom on the occasion of the governor's visit only a few days earlier waltzed across Willa's mind. "As well as can be expected," she said.

For the first time since they'd taken their seats, Mrs. Sauer considered her seriously. "And you? His daughter? How are you?"

Why did it feel like a trap, that question? Willa resisted an instinct to flee—how different her life might have been had she followed it!—but found herself paralyzed all the same. Paralyzed and as though she'd sipped a truth serum. "In fact, it's been very difficult—"

"Yes, well, best not to dwell on what cannot be undone," Mrs. Sauer offered, her hand having moved from the buttons on her sleeve to the brooch at her throat.

"Here, here!" Theodulf fairly cheered. "If life has taught me anything, it's to move on in the face of adversity."

Mrs. Sauer reached over to hold her son's hand. "Your resolve is matched only by your charms, son."

"You should hear Miss Brandt play the piano, Mother. I've not listened to such sweet music since I was abroad."

Mrs. Sauer let go of Theodulf's hand. "He spent a month in France," she said to Willa. "When was that?"

"Almost ten years ago now, if you can imagine that."

Willa interpreted his tone as wistful. Different than the last time she'd heard him tell of Paris.

"Mother, certainly I've told you of the night I saw Paulette Gouttière perform Beethoven at the Palais Garnier?"

Mrs. Sauer turned to Willa and spoke as though sharing a secret. "Not only has he told me the story a hundred times, but he expects me to know who Paulette Gouttière is."

"I read in *Harper's* that Miss Gouttière has gone on to conduct the Paris Philharmonic. Certainly you *ought* to know who she is," he teased. "But I digress. We were speaking of Miss Brandt."

"Are you a trained musician?" Mrs. Sauer asked.

"I've a pedagogue here in Duluth. Or rather, I did. But I've never performed anywhere."

"And yet she plays every bit as convincingly as Mademoiselle Gouttière," Theodulf said, offering Willa a genuine smile.

"Well then, you'll need to come play for *us*. Mr. Sauer has just had a Steinway installed. I don't believe a single note has been scaled from it."

As simply as that, her fate was set in motion. Their dinner at the Thibert Hotel gave way to the proffered invitation. Three days later, a carriage was dispatched for her first (though not last) performance on the Sauers' Steinway. Three days after that, Willa's mother accompanied her to their manse again, where formal introductions were made. Theodulf was prim and passionless through all their meetings, but not without charms. He presented a corsage on her first visit. A chocolate swan the next. Always he stood with an air of detachment. As though he were already her husband and was being forced to browse lace tablecloths at a department store counter. They socialized with Mrs. Sauer's circle. They dined frequently at the Thibert Hotel. They never once kissed or even held hands, and yet, by Gaudete Sunday, Mrs. Sauer—Mary, as she soon insisted—had not only befriended Willa's mother but somehow convinced her that Willa's conversion to Catholicism was the only obstacle to becoming Theodulf's fiancée.

It was less a courtship than a mugging, Willa would later understand. But by midnight on New Year's Eve, she looked down on the lustrous keys of the Sauer family Steinway and found an engagement ring on her finger. A week later she was baptized. And on March sixth she was married, the mass said in Latin. Willa understood not a word.

THREE HOURS after the first course, and Theodulf could still taste horseradish from the sauce served over the prawns. There'd been seven courses all told—olives stuffed with garlic *pour l'aperitif*, the prawn hors d'oeuvre, trout beurre blanc for the fish course, steak au poivre for the *plats principal*, a simple salad to cleanse the palate, then camembert and profiteroles to finish— served over three hours in the grand ballroom just off the hotel lobby where they'd met. Willa sat beside him, her mother next, and Murdock Alderdice the third in her troupe. A more incongruous family he could hardly have imagined. But what did he care? Willa *was* comely in her wedding gown, and so far she'd not asked for anything they hadn't already agreed upon.

Would that change, now that their guests had gone and they were alone in the parlor suite? He hiccupped, felt the bilious swirl in his guts. At the mirror, he untied his cravat and laid it upon the chest of drawers. Carnations bloomed from a crystal vase. Through their stems he could see Willa's reflection in the mirror. She stood at the window, her back to him, holding the curtain aside. She seemed hardly more than a child. He supposed the queasiness he felt was as much his self-loathing as residual of the feast.

He closed his hand into a loose fist and burped again. Quietly. Thought, *Excuse me.*

For the better part of three months, the terms of their marriage had been negotiated like one of his father's litigations. Willa's mother never pretended to offer a dowry. In fact, she'd as much as asked for a stipend should she consent to approving the betrothal. Not that she had a bargaining position. Willa's temperament, combined with her fatherlessness, made her an unlikely candidate for any marriage at all, much less to the only son of a Duluth scion. But, Theodulf supposed, he wasn't an altogether likely candidate himself. Disgraced professionally and personally, albeit a very long time ago. He knew what rumors milled about him even if he didn't know how to quiet them. Maybe a beautiful young wife would help.

He inventoried their engagement. Her conversion to Catholicism, her baptism. The family teas. The dinners at his parents' house and at the Thibert Hotel. They'd spent not a moment together alone, unless you counted the occasions he listened to her play the piano of an afternoon. Again, at his parents' house or here.

He'd hardly touched her. Four hours ago, when Father Richter suggested Theodulf might kiss his bride, Theodulf had lifted her hand and touched it with his lips.

"I told Mother to insist the prawns be served without horseradish," he said. "And I'd have preferred ham steak to sirloin, but still, the meal was passable."

She answered without turning to him. A sigh. *Thankless*, he thought. "Tell me, what would Mr. Alderdice have sent to your room for supper? Was it often a proper French banquet like the one we enjoyed this evening?" He turned to look at her squarely.

"No. Never."

"Ham steak is my preferred repast. I suppose that's something you ought to know." He put his elbow on the chest of drawers and leaned against it. "With a simple boiled potato and green salad. Of course, there's never much in the way of fresh lettuces at the station. At least not until the garden comes in. We have to make do with canned vegetables. There's plenty, of course. Of ham steak and potatoes and canned peas. Other things. Oatmeal and pilot bread. You'll see."

Was she incapable of smiling? Of gratitude? Of anything but whimpering? Sulking? He turned back to the mirror, inspected the choler rising up his neck.

"I've not spent very much time cooking," she said.

"Yes, well, that's about to change." He removed his cufflinks and crossed the room, as if the new vantage allowed the change in subject. "I've arranged for a private suite here at the Thibert until it's time to join me at the station." He put the cufflinks in his jacket pocket.

"That's a relief. I don't know how it would have gone at your parents' house."

"You'll have your privacy."

She almost smiled. Almost blushed. Turned away again.

After a pregnant pause, Theodulf picked up with their larder. "We'll have to see how the summer goes, but I expect food from the garden by July fourth. Perhaps sooner."

"I'm easily satisfied."

"Good—good. That's the best attitude for life at the station. We'll give thanks for what we have. Which is plenty."

"Yes. And thank you for arranging the room here."

"Suite," he corrected. "This very one. The bell hop will deliver your portmanteaux tomorrow morning." He withdrew his watch, put it away. "I've arranged for passage to Gininwabiko on April the twentieth. Provided the shipping lane is open by then. Given the warm winter, I expect it will be."

"And the other keepers and their wives?"

"We're still making those arrangements. I'll leave in the morning for Two Harbors to meet with the Establishment. Then I'll go directly to the station to finish preparations for her commission." He nodded his head solemnly, as though he were a senator contemplating grave matters of state. "It's unconscionable, the responsibilities they leave on one man." He sat in a ladderback chair and bit at his cuticle. "Especially at a new commission. I'll be there alone most of the month of March."

"I can't imagine," she said.

"No, of course you can't. Not yet. But soon. Your own responsibilities will be many."

"As we've discussed."

He sat up. "I nearly forgot." He passed her on his way to the suitcase he'd delivered earlier in the day. He removed a gift, wrapped in white paper and with a white bow.

Was that a look of gratitude as he handed it to her? It gave him a small satisfaction to believe it true. "For you. For those quiet moments you'll not have many of at the station."

She held the gift lightly, considered it and him in turn. "I didn't get you anything," she said.

"I'm not a man needs gifts."

He made a gesture to open it, which she did, untying the ribbon before tearing at the paper. The expression on her face didn't change. A pall fell over the room.

He knelt in front of her. "You'll be able to read scripture whenever you want now. Your bond with God—your faith in Him—will grow like . . . wildflowers."

Her name embossed in gold on the Douay-Rheims bible caught a flicker of light from the lamp and shot it across the room.

"This book is all you'll need to be happy there. Well, this book and your faith. The former will enforce the latter." He rose. He put his hands behind his back.

A tear fell down her cheek.

"It's a wondrous thing!" he nearly sang. "The profoundest thing! And worthy of your tears."

"On our wedding night?" she whispered.

"What better occasion?" he asked.

She reconsidered the bible. Opened it randomly.

"First Corinthians!" he said, pointing at it. "A husband should submit to Christ, and his wife to her husband!"

She closed the bible and set it gently in the palm of her left hand, which trembled. "I wasn't expecting a bible lesson tonight."

"What were you expecting?" he asked stupidly.

For a long moment, she only shook her head. But soon enough she rallied her voice. "As I understand things, as your mother and mine both explained it to me, as I was *expecting*, we were to adjourn to this room after our celebration dinner—"

"You've been colluding with our mothers?"

Her eyes erupted. She threw the bible on the floor, stood, set herself adrift across the room. Like a boat untied from a cleat. Halfway, she paused, caught in an eddy, her arms came up in anger.

She was about to speak, but he beat her to it. "It's just occurred to me I have a few letters to write before tomorrow," he said, straightening his lapels in just the same way he had as he stepped to the altar at Sacred Heart some hours ago.

"Now?" The disbelief in her voice came in the deepest octave. "*Now?*"

"They're urgent."

"It's your wedding night."

He raised a finger like his father often did, shook it three times, and then turned for the door, which he walked through without saying goodbye.

During the many hours she'd mused about how their wedding night might go, she never once imagined something so uncanny as his sudden departure. She wandered the suite for ten minutes, contemplating the sudden fortune his absence bestowed upon her. At least for now, she'd been freed of her obligation to consummate their union. After those ten minutes, there came a knock on the door. She answered it to find the maître d' himself.

"Good evening, Mrs. Sauer," he said. "Your husband has taken the liberty of having this sent up. Shall I wheel it in?"

She opened the door widely and he brought the linen-covered cart into the suite and left it under a wall sconce.

A pot of tea, a vase of flowers, a note sealed in a Thibert Hotel envelope, her name penned in blue ink. She tore it open.

March the 6th, Year of Our Lord 1910

Dear Mrs. Sauer,

My responsibilities are first to God, then to the Lighthouse Service, then to you. It's unbecoming of a wife to challenge her husband's faith or duty. Naturally you'll require time to learn your role in our marriage, as well as in faithful service to the Lord God. Pray on this.

As I mentioned earlier this evening, I'll be departing in the morning. Our next meeting will be at the Gininwabiko Station on 20 April.

Until then, I'm ever your faithful husband . . .

~Theodulf

She guffawed. How could he possibly have made himself more ridiculous? She cast about the room, imagining someone she might share his missive with. Alas, she was alone, a fact and sentiment that would grow in urgency over the next months, but for now was a simple blessing.

She brought the letter to one of the wall sconces, read it again, then removed the glass and held a corner of the stationery in the flame. It caught swiftly. She dropped it in the teacup and watched it disappear.

WHERE DOES THE LIGHT GO?

AUGUST 23, 1910

Three hundred fifty years ago, at the Paris observatory, a Danish astronomer named Ole Rømer accidentally discovered the speed of light. He'd been studying the orbit of Io, one of the moons of Jupiter, with a hypothesis (one first proffered by Galileo) that by charting the orbits of Jupiter's satellites, mariners might turn to them as a kind of celestial clock, a hypothesis that was eventually abandoned. But Rømer, while conducting his observations over many months, discovered that the eclipse of Io by Jupiter differed depending on earth's relation to the planet. When it was closer to Jupiter, the eclipse occurred earlier than predicted; when the earth was farther away, the eclipse occurred later. Knowing that the orbital period of the satellite wouldn't change, he concluded that the differences were based on the amount of time it took the light to reach earth.

The equation born of Rømer's discover eventually put a value of 186,000 miles per second on the speed of light. Given that earth's moon is some 239,000 miles distant, we can extrapolate the time it takes for her light to get here at between one and two seconds.

Imagine: two lovers adrift on moonlit waters, bathing in light that replenishes itself nearly every instant. Light that traveled through all that darkness to reach them.

S HE MARVELED: how could a light so solemn in the sky become so gamesome on the water? She leaned over the gunwale,
scooped at the shimmer, and laughed at its coldness.

"You'll fall right in," Mats said.

"I'll do no such thing."

He had picked her up on the lighthouse dock not fifteen minutes ago. Their most reckless rendezvous yet. Either Theodulf—
who was on watch—or Silje—who was asleep in the fish house with
Freya—might see them. Especially on a night so brilliant as this.
Two heads in his skiff. Rowing now out past Lindvik Island with
the moon, and moonlight on the water.

Of course, their liaison had been leading to this. To more. After
the first night in the fish house, they'd found every opportunity
to tryst. First on the path between her house and his; then in the
station boat house on a night of warm rain; then again in the fish
house, Freya whining in the corner while they made love; then
behind the Lindvik cabin; and finally on the bank of Odegaard
Creek. Alone at night in the woods, after the mosquitoes put up for
the night, after all the people were sleeping. Forsaking their own
sleep for the requirement of each other's company. And not just
for the pleasures of the flesh, but for the happiness of their conversation, which they picked up each meeting as if days or weeks
hadn't passed. The conversations were greedy and slow and full of
interruptions and laughter. It was as if they were eager to know
each other but only just discovering themselves, too. For Willa, it
was the first bond she'd ever had with anyone. The first glimpse of
love. The first thing that ever distracted her from her father's death.
From the moon and stars.

She watched his face, cocked up and studying the moon. In its light, the muscles in his neck flexed with each pull on the oars. They made not a sound, those rowlocks. He'd arranged nets and the sail between the stern sheets so she had a bed to lie across. The sweet role of the water, its gentle lashing against the lapstrake hull, that and the sound of his breathing—not labored, but impatient, the sound he made after he kissed her goodbye—a symphony for happiness.

"You're a handsome man, Mats Braaten."

He smiled. "I'm just a boy these days."

He was six years older than her, but they were six years spent mostly in the company of woodsmen or by himself in this boat, and so in many ways she was more confident, and certainly she was more worldly. She never condescended, though. His kindness and gentleness and curiosity were the opposite of Theodulf in every way, and for these qualities she was always looking to reward him.

"Where are we going?" she asked, her hand reaching again for the moonlight on the water.

"Farther out," he said.

"Row faster."

He buried the oars in the moonlight, upped his tempo, kept smiling.

"Why did you never find a wife?"

For all their talking, they'd yet to drift into these particular waters. She knew it was a gamble, knew it might spoil their night, but she needed an answer. Just as importantly, he needed to know about her. This first volley? It was an invitation. A suggestion.

"It's hard to court a woman from out here." He gave the sky an apprising glance. "Or from up in the woods. Heck, I've gone three months at a time without even seeing a woman, let alone getting to know one."

"And now that you know me?"

He feathered his oars, put his hands at the small of his back, and arched. "Do I? Know you?"

"What don't you know? I'll tell you anything."

He uncorked his canteen and took a long drink of water. "I guess the big question lines up with the one you just asked me."

"Oh?"

He pointed up at the sky, traced the lighthouse beacon as it passed over them. Passed through them. Corrupted, for that single second, the moonlight.

The light passed again before he said, "You're a married woman."

She sat up on the stern sheets, but that was her only answer. He'd not asked a question, after all.

"What does that mean for me?" Mats said.

"For you, or for us both?"

"I don't think of myself without considering you a part of me. That's probably saying too much, but there you have it."

She'd not expected that.

"I mean no disrespect to Mr. Sauer, but you and he seem about as well suited for each other as the fish and the hook."

"I can hardly fathom how I ended up married to Theodulf."

"That doesn't sound like some great romance."

"Ours is decidedly *not* a romantic story."

"I'd take more than that. If you're of a giving mind."

"I met him in the lobby of the Thibert Hotel almost nine months ago. Well, I met him for the second time in that lobby."

"Second time?"

She told him the whole sordid story. How she'd performed for her father at the Ionic Lodge dressed as a boy on the eve of the *Mataafa* storm; how Theodulf had approached her that night, how she'd escaped him; how, five years later, she met him again; how he'd seemed kinder, less wolfish; how they'd had dinner that night.

"From there," she spread her arms wide, "it seems almost as if his mother and mine had made some sort of arrangement. As if the whole engagement had been premeditated."

"Why your mother?"

Now she told him about her father's death—the whole truth, right down to the cord he'd used; she told him about Murdock Alderdice and his beastly advances; about her mother's bankruptcy (moral and financial); about giving up on the dream of becoming an astronomer; about Ann Brandt's insistence that Willa find a husband; she told him about the tallyho ride with Georg Olaussen; she told him about her loneliness. And her sadness.

Were those tears? Or was it merely the reflection of the moon?

"Do you love Mr. Sauer?"

"I could no less love him than if I'd never met him."

He clenched his eyes shut. "I never laid with a woman before you," he said.

"Nor I with a man."

"Not even your husband?"

She scuttled across the burden boards, sat beside him, took his hand. "Never," she said proudly. "And I never will."

"But he's your husband."

"In name *only*." She felt like she was pleading now, suddenly rudderless.

He lifted her hand and kissed it and said, "Why then did you marry him? A mother's wish is no small thing, I grant you. But a *marriage*?"

"I didn't wish to marry him. I hardly even know him, and what I do know, I find intolerable. As for how I came to accept our marriage, I don't know if I can describe it." Now she closed her eyes as he had only a moment ago. Tight against the memory of her betrothment. "It was as if there were a great blizzard, and when the snow and wind stopped, I was standing in Sacred Heart pronouncing vows I did not comprehend, or ever intend to uphold."

When she opened her eyes, the starlight was another blizzard, and this reckoning another incomprehensible moment in her life.

The boat rocked. Each time it did, she thought to say something more. Each time it fell, she decided against it.

"Surely some reason beyond your mother's will compelled you?" he finally said.

Oh, how she wished there were room to get up and walk around! To spend some of her agitation. True, she'd wanted something like this line of questioning, but now that she was in the middle of it, she felt helpless. She felt like an anchor that's slipped its knot and sinks down—down—down.

"He was not unkind, Mats. Or crass or demanding. He didn't seem to want anything. And as often as not, he seemed as mystified by our engagement as I did." Was she still sinking? She couldn't say, but maybe that's what happened in the depths. She lifted his hand and held it to her cheek. "If Theodulf lacked charm, he also lacked meanness and vileness, something most men I've known have in abundance. But whereas I never quite rationalized our engagement, he seemed to realize at a certain point that a young wife was just what he needed."

"Needed for what?"

"You'd not know it to look at him, but he's ambitious. His family is influential. More than that, really. Much more. And in his occupation, a man without a wife is suspect. I suppose for someone like Theodulf—who's, what, at odds with himself?—having a wife is even more important."

If his expression were any indication, the puzzle of Theodulf and Willa seemed to be coming together. Again they rode the moonlight in silence, the skiff lulling her into a sense of having weathered the first storm in their relationship.

"To think that four months ago I'd never laid eyes on you," he said.

"You sound wistful."

"I only mean, I never thought about a wife. Never knew to want one. Never considered how my life might be made better by one." He gave her an injured smile. "Now it's all I can think about. And the girl I'd choose is already spoken for."

She stood slowly, holding his shoulders against the rocking of the boat. "I don't know what that means, *spoken for*." She put her hand through his hair, thought of a thousand other things she might say, but spoke none of them. Instead, she kissed him. Then she sat back on the nets and sail between the stern sheets, lifting her skirts as she did.

She didn't speak again, but he obeyed her. Already they understood each other effortlessly. He crawled forward, lifted her skirts the rest of the way, and buried his lips in the softness of her belly. She rested her neck in the sculling notch and opened her eyes to the night again. She felt as wide open. The coldness off the water rose to her neck and ears. Without it, she might have caught fire.

Did he know that the callouses on his hands betrayed his gentleness? Is that why he used his mouth instead? Did he know that by tracing the slopes and shadows of her body he was making a map of her happiness? He must.

And how could a man so strapping and strong be lifted like a child? She put her hands under his arms and pulled him up and without looking unbuttoned his trousers. Her face still open to the heavens, she felt it soften—every line, every pinch, every nerve—as he put himself inside her. With the boat moving over the waves, she felt a swelling overrun her. She tried to reach up to him, to grip him, but could only clench the netting. Her back arched to meet him and right away they fell into the same rhythm as the water.

They might have drifted to Michigan before her whole body shuddered. For the briefest moment she thought she might be imploding, but then all at once: an enormous relief. She became as liquefactive as the water beneath them. As bright and as moving and as wide.

He was collapsing in plain sight. His wide shoulders slumped, his waist folded, his eyes fluttered like a moth's wings. But his smile? It defied the rest of him.

"What always happens?" he asked, sitting back on his heels.

"I could drink the lake, to put back what just left me."

Now he got on one knee and buttoned his trousers and took a nightful of air. "Woman," he said.

She sat up, pulled her knickers back on, and patted the spot on the sailcloth beside her. "Mr. Braaten, come sit by me."

As he sat next to her, Mats said, "We've got a predicament."

"I don't see it. Your so-called predicament."

He took her hand again, a gesture that had become his hallmark. "Willa—"

"Just hush." She pushed his hand away, then gathered it again. "And look up at this beautiful night. We're sitting in it. You and I."

He studied her hand for a long time, rubbing the glowing half-moons of her fingernails so long she felt a twinge of apprehension. Was he going to tell her the reasons why they couldn't keep doing this? Or say it had all been a mistake? "Say something."

"I was just thinking about one of the things said in Genesis."

"Genesis in the *bible*?"

He nodded.

"Please don't recite lines from that book."

"I'm not a preacher. No ma'am. It's just a beautiful sentiment, this line I'm recalling. It seems right for the moment." He waited for her approval. When she nodded, he said, "I believe it says, regarding the creation of the world, that God created two lights. A greater one to rule the day, and a lesser light to rule the night."

"Do you believe in God? That He created the moon and earth and sun?"

"My mother taught me to."

"That's no answer."

He took his pipe from one pocket and his pouch of tobacco from the other. As he packed the bowl, he said, "I'm better with an ax in my hand than I am a thought in my head. Which is to say, I've not given much time to contemplating the higher things. And to the question of whether there's a God or not, and whether He created the world we live in, well, I think it takes a vain man to claim he knows." He struck a match and lit his pipe. "I will say this: I'm more wont to believe in something since I met you. Whether that's God or happiness or whatever the hell, I'll take it. The moon's a little more beautiful for it."

She took his pipe from him, gave it a puff herself. The smoke tasted of cherry and wood, and it filled her mouth where all the words might have formed. So much the better.

They sat in his skiff and smoked while a lesser light rained down. After they finished the pipe, Mats went back to his seat on the center thwart. He took the oars and steered them around. Halfway back to Lindvik Island and the dark side of his spit of land, he said, "There's something I've been meaning to ask you."

"I'll tell you anything."

"How long does it take for the light of that moon to reach us?"

She knew the answer. She knew as sure as she knew she loved him.

Love? she marveled. Love. She said, "More than one second, less than two."

"I'd have thought longer."

"Oh?"

He craned his neck around to get a good look at it. "It's as if there's wisdom in it."

"In the moonlight?"

He nodded. He pulled on the oars. "Like all the night's dark taught it something."

"How long has that thought been dancing around in your head?"

"Since the first time I saw you at night. Out on the lighthouse dock."

She was glad for the night now and what it couldn't see. Namely the blush rising from her neck. Instead of answering she thought back to the night in April she'd watched him and Silje from across the cove. As she recalled, it snowed that night, which meant of course that he'd not beheld her in moonlight but rather in the lighthouse's beacon. A trivial distinction, this. His poetry? More beautiful than she'd ever heard. The young memory of it flitted through her mind as the moonlight did across the water.

"I wonder if you know the answer to this, sweet Willa: are there more stars in the sky, or waves of moonlight shimmering on the water?" he asked, gazing up and gazing down.

She didn't know. But for the first time since she was a child, she was happy to let the beauty be in her wonder. "Who could ever say?" she said.

W HERE DOES THE LIGHT GO?

The question dissipated as quickly as the lighthouse beam, and reappeared, too. Since he'd abandoned his study of time— since he'd thrown the Hamilton railroad watch into the waves—he'd found this new obsession. The pondering of things he couldn't possibly know and had no resources to learn.

So instead, he just watched the moon make her meaning. It came across the water at a gallop. It shone on the waves and then the rocky shore; on the treetops and the hills above; on the other side of night. And then?

The question baffled no less in these small hours than it had at midnight, so he finished walking up to the lantern room where he wound the clockworks for the last time that night. He observed the brass gears through the glass box and hated himself.

He wondered, *Had their marriage improved him? As a lighthouse master? As a man? As a child of God?*

Four times, no.

He'd never been more wretched.

Never been less in favor with the Lighthouse Service.

Never felt less virile.

And never been so adrift. In the cosmos or in his proximity to God.

Back in the watch room, he logged winding the clockworks. He took the teacup from his desk and brought it outside, tossing the dregs over the cliff and studying the horizon. Nights like this, the lake ablaze, he thought how closely heaven resembled hell. This thought gave him to wonder why the moon didn't warm the earth like the sun. It exceeded it in size, in proximity, in boldness and brazenness.

And yet, its brilliant light just *vanished*. Like smoke? Like wind? Sound? Fog? Prayer? Like all the ethereal things? It was here, and then gone. Perhaps some reservoir held the burden of all those sublime things.

Up the western shore he saw a fisherman's skiff plying the golden water. Probably Mats Braaten, but who could tell from a mile away? Was he coming or going? Surely going, at this young hour.

He held the empty mug up to the sky. Maybe some of the moonlight would pour into it.

Would he be able to sleep this morning? If he did, would he dream? If he did, where would those dreams go once they were had?

THE THOUSANDTH WATCH

AUGUST 24, 1910

On these autumn days, the darkness becomes insatiable. Brighter minds than my own have calculated this turn and its acceleration. Sine and cosine. Axis. Time. They tell one story (in equations and on tables). I tell another. The simplest I know: as the end nears, it does so with a rapacious quickening. Like the darkness of these autumn days.

EXACTLY A THOUSAND MIDNIGHTS had come and gone under his watch, most of them as unremarkable as this, each of them accounted for in the private log he kept. Earlier, as he ate a companionless dinner of the fisherman's trout and boiled carrots from the garden, it had seemed a consequential occasion. Now, though, standing on the lighthouse parapet as the serenity of another August night spread before him, it felt anything but.

Already two freighters had passed, a mile out, their running lights strung like low-hanging stars. He knew better than to want to sail away on one, and yet . . . well, he couldn't say but that he wished to be *somewhere* else. With just that thought compelling him, he returned to the watch room. The air hung close inside. He could feel the dampness of his shirt and collar, and he'd have given just about anything to quaff a cold beer. But for the second time in as many minutes he resisted his baser instincts.

At the desk he logged his evening's labor. He drank the cold cup of tea he'd absentmindedly made when his watch started and that he'd left sitting since. He swept the floor of the watch room and then the fog signal building and with still five hours to go before sunrise, reckoned the night would never end. And him alone through it all.

And what great fortune would greet him in the morning, if it ever arrived? The walk across the grounds and into his dreary home? A breakfast of oats with his ill-suited and contrary wife? A few hours of sleep on his cot? Each prospect drearier than the next.

Happiness? Contentedness? Meaning? Any of it might as well have been cargo on those distant, midnight ships.

Whenever, as a petulant boy, he'd complained of boredom or skepticism, his mother suggested prayer as the antidote. Sitting there at the desk in the watch room, he wondered how long it had been since he'd prayed in earnest. With the expectation his utterances might be heard, his melancholy cured.

Should he pray now? He made the *signum crucis,* brought his hands together, and closed his eyes. All that greeted him there was an image of the night sky emblazoned with stars. What should he ask for? Forgiveness? Understanding? The subjects darted away as quickly as they arrived. He clamped his eyes more tightly closed, trying harder to see his way to God. But after a minute of this, all he had was more darkness and the surety that whatever intimacy he'd ever shared with God was dead and gone forever.

He unclenched his eyes and hands and sat back in the chair.

Great Christ, am I lonesome, he thought, sighing.

He took a sheet of lighthouse letterhead from the top drawer of the desk. He brought out the inkwell and uncapped his pen, and before he interrupted his instinct, started writing:

August the 24th, Year of Our Lord 1910

Dear Father Richter,

I've lately been remembering an incident from when I was a boy. This would have been one of the first summers you and Father Clovis began your missionary work in Agate Bay, probably in 1883 or 84, between the brothels or saloons along Whiskey Row. Remember how we'd meet in the parlor of Mrs. Marguerite? And then later in the courthouse? Your sermons were half in French to accommodate the Québécois. Father used to say they were like rabbits overrunning the streets, those Montrealers. At any rate, that was the state of things in Agate Bay.

On the day I first mentioned, I was walking home from an afternoon spent fishing. I used to love to fish. It was the summer all those women were murdered, and so people were more on edge than usual. Certainly my mother was. Home before dark, that was the rule. I carried a stringer of fish. Perch, probably.

Maybe a pike. Whatever I might catch from the town dock. Proud, I was. Eager to show my mother the catch. To have her cook them up for dinner. I thought my father would be happy too. He loved a dinner of fresh fish. I mention the fish because I eventually dropped them in the alley. Why, you may be wondering?

The answer is this: out behind one of the saloons, I heard a sound. Like someone was going to be sick. Or perhaps like they were speaking in tongues. In any case, I couldn't ignore it. I wondered was everyone all right. Between the canvas walls of LaRue's saloon on one side, and Dejean's on the other, I saw a priest's black robe. Lifted at the arms. Like he was calling down saints. And this priest—either you or Clovis, surely—was making the sound. I almost interrupted—to show you the fish, or Clovis; to ask for your blessing—but didn't. Just in time, I didn't. For no sooner was I parting my lips to speak when you—or Clovis— groaned. I felt in the souls of my feet! Then you let the arms of your robe down, gazed at the afternoon sky. And do you know what I saw next? Or rather, *who?* None other than Mrs. Marguerite's son, my friend and schoolmate, Alderic, the knees of his trousers soaked through with mud.

What I've been wondering all these years is why was Alderic made to suffer that indignity, if suffering's what he did? I wonder, too, what chance spared me the same muddied trousers.

I've known you most of my life and beg answer if you know. I have a terrible premonition. I keep seeing myself drowning. In dreams and as I look out upon the water. I'd hate for that to happen before I had answer. Thus, I beg you tell.

Sincerely,
Theodulf Sauer
The Gininwabiko lighthouse station

The ink of his signature hadn't dried before he took another piece of letterhead from the desk drawer.

August the 24th, Year of Our Lord 1910

My Dearest Mother,

Even as the nights grow longer, the summer slows. I've hardly slept in a month. When I do, my dreams are less the stuff of clouds than the watery depths beneath the Gininwabiko cliff.

Strangely, my thoughts are no less troubled when awake. Sometimes they occupy those same watery depths, but more often I find myself nearly hypnotized by the night and the beacon strobing across the lake. Mostly the night is black. Whole watches pass without remembrance. As though I were a drunkard again.

I spend so many of those dark hours searching the blackness for Father, who appears practically never. Mother, what does it say about my thoughts of him that they come so rarely? Or that what few memories do penetrate the night are so forgiving? I know he hated me. Know his vision of who he wished I'd be could not have deviated further from the person I am. It seems, though we never had a chance to discuss this, he and I, that not even taking a wife relieved him from the disgrace he believed me to be. And yet, on the rare occasion I see him clearly, I see him with fondness! That I should be so untrue to myself is probably evidence of why he disliked me.

Alas, God hopes—indeed demands—that we forgive those who've trespassed against us. Isn't that what the good prayer says?

Speaking of God and forgiveness, I have another question I hope you'll indulge. Do you remember Father Clovis? From Agate Bay, the first summer we lived there? He used to bring his congregants together in the parlor of the Marguerite family. She had a son named Alderic, if I'm not mistaken, who died of grippe. I ask about him because for all the memories that have failed me recently, some few persist, and one of them is of Alderic being—what? I suppose there's no gentle way of saying it— sodomized by one of our priests.

I wonder if this treachery is just some story I've told myself, or if its roots are in the firm ground of fact. If anyone would know, it's you. Perhaps you'll set the record straight?

I hate to burden you with so many difficult questions, especially as you grieve your husband. As for how things go here at the station, suffice it to say the desperation of my queries is borne by the near certainty I've made grave miscalculations in my life. Aspiring to and becoming a station master is but one of them. Taking a wife another.

But at least I have you, Mother. To console me and to reorient me in peaceful contentedness. I'll await your succoring words.

Your loving son,
Theodulf

His priest and his mother? Could a sadder correspondence be imagined? These questions accompanied him as he folded the letters and placed them in envelopes and addressed each, setting them square on the edge of the blotter and rising to stretch his back.

Outside, standing on the edge of the cliff looking down on the scree below, the lake folding back on itself in gentle waves, he allowed himself to remember his trip to Paris. If tonight was his thousandth watch, that meant twice a thousand that he'd pondered the possibility that he'd blundered his only chance at happiness by misreading Paul Gouttière's vanishing. Perhaps, Theodulf thought for the umpteenth time, the absinthe had clouded more than the glass, and he'd misunderstood their plans for meeting the next night? Had Paul said something about having a concert in Limoges? Why did that ring faintly in his memory? From this far down the line, Theodulf supposed anything was possible. Maybe the whole episode had never actually happened. Maybe he'd dreamt it all after getting potted on *la fée verte*.

Still another ship came into view. This one coming down the lake, the sky so bright he could see the smoke from the stack. Why the boat on the horizon compelled him to write one more letter, he couldn't say, but he turned his back to the freighter and returned to the desk.

August the 24th, Year of Our Lord 1910

My Dear Paul,

It's been all of a decade since our rendezvous in Paris. Impossible that so many years have passed, but I reckon that's what time does. How is it the time has brought no relief in missing you, that's the larger question?

Recent events inspire this letter. My father, a man who dreaded my proclivities almost as much as he adored his own, has recently passed away. Shed no tears for him, or for me—he was a brute and a bastard whose sole purpose oftentimes seemed to be to mold me in his twisted image. In fact, it was his idea that I should have gone to Paris a decade ago. To cure me of my tendencies and sow my wild oats, as he put it. To become the man he thought I ought to be. A man I never was.

What I relish in knowing is that I was never more myself than in the brief time I knew you. What's more, every moment since I boarded the return ship in La Havre has been an insult to my true self. I've lost him day by day, hour by hour, and any thought to reclaim him seems to have died with my father. Perhaps this explains why I'm writing to you now.

I've become, since we met, an important person in the Lighthouse Service of the United States of America, rising to the position of master keeper at the Gininwabiko station on the western shore of Lake Superior. My duties are solemn and I undertake them without hubris. Most importantly, I take three watches each week. These happen overnight and leave me hours to contemplate all manner of things. Lately I've spent those nights sending wishes onto the sea. Silent, beseeching wishes. That any of the hundred ships which pass each week might deliver respite from my desires!

But those ships, they only pass in the distance, their cargo so much ore or coal. That I were made of such strong stuff.

But I am not. I am decidedly not. Instead, I pen missives to twelve-hour friends I knew a quarter lifetime ago. Missives no better than prayers, and as sure to go unanswered. So, another day with less faith.

But who am I to ask God for anything, much less something He abhors? A fool, that is who. A ridiculous jester. And yet! I'll sign this letter and address it to the place I heard you play Beethoven and I will hope.

The fool hopes.

Yours eternally,
Theo

Sealing the last letter was the bitterest, and he did so with a blank mind and teeming heart. Hardly could he wet his tongue to lick the glue. And yet, he found the wherewithal to do so, and to scribble the address of that fateful Parisian café, not even doubtful it would find his intended:

Paul Gouttière
Café le Rêve
rue Saint-Louis en l'Île
Paris, France

He put the last letter with the others on the blotter, capped his pen, and put it in his pocket. In the same motion he removed his watch. Rather than check the time, he merely studied the hourglass on the case. For the first time since he bought the Longines, he noticed the top half of the hourglass was almost empty of sand.

S HE DISTINGUISHED FROG from the other keepers by the slope of his shoulders. Even from her dark window in the fish house she noted them. Of his whole meager constitution.

Why did she dislike him so? Whatever the reason, she couldn't bear the sight of him anymore. She swung around and dropped from her perch on the counter, startling Freya, who whined.

"Now you have something to say?" She reached down and petted behind her ear. "I've been gabbing at you since breakfast, and all I've gotten back is a tail wag."

She stepped blindly through the fish house to the back corner, where she'd stashed her mother's wedding dress in a suitcase. Unfurling it brightened the room, a light that intensified as she hung the dress from a beam in the ceiling, the threadbare cotton filling with moonlight like a sail fills with wind.

She opened the window through which the moon shone and watched the breeze make the dress dance.

"Did you and Papa dance on your wedding night?"

She climbed back into the cockloft and watched the dress. Her mother's malady—her brain sickness, as her father called it—meant she spoke little. When she did, she scolded and scoffed and flitted from one subject to the next like a hummingbird between flowers. Silje saved her inquiries for her father, who was, like most of the men she knew, taciturn and soft spoken and short on answers.

"Uncle's not like Papa was," she said, looking sternly at the dress. "But there are things I can't ask him. Uncle, I mean. Especially now that he's tired all the time. More tired than usual." She bit her cuticle. Wondered if she should tell her mother everything.

Instead, she veered the conversation in a different direction.

"Why were you so sad?" She bit her thumb again. Deeper this time. "Were you mad at me?" She braved a glance at the dress, which twisted in another breeze. "Didn't you like me?" She put her head back on the pillow. "Is there something wrong with me?"

Freya put her paws up on the counter and stretched her neck. Then she went to the dress and sniffed the hem and barked once.

"That's Freya. You'd like her. She doesn't have much to say. She keeps me company. I almost never bother Uncle Mats anymore." Now she rolled onto her side and tucked her hands under her chin.

The dress settled—pearlescent.

"Uncle Mats, he found a girl," she sang, tapping the meter on her chin with the tip of the same thumb she'd been chewing. "They romp all night, and never fight, among the trees, like the squirrels."

She hummed the song again, dozing. But before she fell asleep properly, she said, "Mama, I'm really angry. And sad and lonesome. I wish you were here."

Answering, the left shoulder of the dress dipped on the hanger.

AT LOGGERHEADS

AUGUST 25, 1910

Count the rabble, starstruck and dazed, not even sure what we're hoping to see! Begging of the universe answers to questions we can't articulate. Can't imagine. Some people call it prayer. Others meditation. Still others simply hope or despair. We can't agree on anything

If we only had sight, we mightn't require our wildest imagination. We mightn't bicker like petulant children. We might know that we gazed not only upon stars and moons, but beyond them, interminably beyond them, black holes. Some are but the size of an atom, others the size of a hundred suns. Either is incomprehensively dense. Neither emits a single lux of light.

Now there's a place for answers!

FOOTFALLS?

The moon in the sky through her bedroom window said not yet four, so why? Who?

Willa lifted herself onto an elbow and pushed the blanket down. She was home, yes. There, the familiar iridescence of the curtains in the moonlight. And still the sound of someone moving about the house. She checked again the moon. Remembered the day—Thursday—and that Theodulf stood watch. Or ought to have been. But that slurred ambling? The aimless direction of it? It most certainly held her husband's signature. What's more, it announced his mood. One she knew better than to confront.

So, she folded herself back into the warmth of her bed, letting her hair fall across her cheek. Two more hours of sleep, God willing. As soon as she closed her eyes, though, she heard his tread coming up the stairs. He still wore his boots, a thing he never did. Halfway, he must have realized it, stopped, sighed, and retraced his steps back into the foyer, where he removed his boots one at a time, dropping them on the woven entryway rug first one, then the other. But he did not ascend the staircase again. In fact, the sound of him vanished into some other part of the house. Likely the sitting room and the divan he sometimes fell asleep on after watch.

Willa tried again to sleep, rolling onto her side with her back to the door. The same queasy feeling that so often attended Theodulf's arrival greeted her again, and for a moment she thought she might be sick. But she quelled the feeling by imagining the sound of Mats's feet lumbering through a middle-of-the-night house, then fell asleep dreaming about a life relishing a husband's arrival home.

* * *

At a quarter of six she woke again. Not because new ghosts haunted the house, but because nausea had washed her from sleep with all the eagerness of a freshet. She rolled out of bed and nearly fell from dizziness before stumbling into the bathroom and leaning over the toilet. After retching, she righted herself, rinsed her mouth, and washed her face. She was surprised to discover she felt fine. Slightly feverish, perhaps. But only like she did after cleaning the kitchen or picking lettuce from the garden.

She changed into britches and her chambray shirt, put her hair up, and went downstairs with intentions of making breakfast and the expectation that Theodulf would be asleep on the divan. Instead, she found him standing in front of the cuckoo clock he'd brought home after his father's funeral. The clock didn't work, which she was glad of for the lack of chiming, but its ugliness—like a ghoul escaping the plaster—gave it a presence even worse than the tolling might have been. How often had she seen him standing before it, hands behind his back, face pinched and searching, as if in the grooves and grains of carved wood were answers untold elsewhere? More than once a day; sometimes half a dozen times.

She didn't greet him on her way to the kitchen, only sparked a fire in the stove and started collecting foodstuffs for breakfast. By the time the coffee was ready, he'd made his way to the table, his uniform cravat loose and twisted at a strange angle.

"Did I hear you come in before the end of your watch?"

"I had Axelsson spell me around four," he said without glancing up from his folded hands on the table.

She turned from the pot of oats and waited for him to say more. When he didn't, she said, "Whyever did you need him to spell you?"

"Feeling queer," he said.

"It must be going around," Willa said. "I woke up this morning with the most brackish stomach."

Still he didn't look up, only removed some envelopes from the inside pocket of his coat and set them on the table.

"We'll make a run into Otter Bay after breakfast. You need to shop for groceries, and I have a few matters of business."

"Did you not hear me say I'm feeling unwell myself?" She knew her temper was on the verge of showing, but she also saw some part of him had come unmoored.

"Is that coffee ready?" he asked.

His own tone was moribund, and for the first time since he shared news of his father's death, she felt a pang of sympathy.

She poured coffee and delivered it, then returned to the stove until the oats finished. She served those, too, and rinsed two handfuls of fresh-picked blueberries and placed them on small plates. Then she sat across the table from him. These hours together, her duty, they repulsed her. And yet on this morning at least, her curiosity prevailed upon her bitterness, and she waited for him to emerge from his funk.

Her bowl of oats was empty before he spoke. "I tried to get that cuckoo clock started last night. Despite feeling so peaked, I couldn't sleep. So I took it off the wall and sat at this very table and had a go at it."

She could as much as see it on the wall in the other room. "Where did it come from?"

"The clock?" he asked, looking at her for the first time all morning. "My grandfather made them. In his retirement. He made schnapps and clocks, and he more or less raised me. That clock"—he gestured to the other room—"was his masterwork. The last one he built, as I recall. It stopped running the day he died. Like it required his living soul to tick and tock."

Finally he reached for a spoonful of oats. He took a drink of coffee, wiped his lips with a napkin.

"He used to talk about clocks in the same breath as God or faith. One was the same as the other," he said before scooping another bowl of cereal into his mouth.

"That sounds something like blasphemy."

"Not the way he said it." None of the defensiveness or preoccupation that usually accompanied his answering attended his utterance. "He was as unflappable in his faith in God as he was his faith in time. He kept both very close." He drank the rest of his coffee in four long gulps. "He had faith in me, too."

She stood and offered more coffee. But he declined and wiped his lips with the napkin again.

"Well," she said, clearing the table, "he sounds like an interesting man."

"He was constant." He untied and removed his cravat.

How unlike your grandfather you are, Willa thought. If constancy's the measure. Outside, Axelsson ambled toward his house, his half watch over. His pants were too short. His hair halloing from beneath his hat. Theodulf noticed him, too, and said, "John will make a good master someday."

"Despite his sloppiness?"

He craned his neck, nodded. "I did wake him in the middle of the night." Now Theodulf looked into his empty mug, nodded again. "I've just a few things to gather upstairs. We can leave in ten minutes."

"So early?"

He reached over and set his mug in the sink then tapped his small stack of letters three times. "I want to make sure these make it out on today's boat."

She listened to the whisper of his stockinged feet cross the house. So different from last night's galumphing.

After washing and drying the dishes and laying them back in the cupboard, she wiped the table, moving the letters from one side to the other. Paul Gouttière? A vague memory of the name weaseled into her mind. A kind of déjà vu.

As Theodulf lowered the tender from the boat house, Willa watched across the bay while Mats put his nets in his skiff. He didn't wave. Didn't even glance up. The gentle undulation of his boat on the water—even from the distance between the docks—brought her back to their night on the water, and her mind hurried away.

"Step aboard," Theodulf said, holding the bow into the waves.

As he pushed off and took the oars, he helloed across the water. Mats raised a hand back.

Before they rounded the lighthouse headland, her lover rowed in the opposite direction. Though she couldn't read his face, she was certain he watched. Certain he felt as downcast as she did. Certain that something would have to give, and soon.

Theodulf worked the oars, the back of his balding and hatless head taking the sunrise. Was it possible that for all the thoughts that occupied his simple mind, none of them registered the fact that the same man Willa saw beyond her husband, rowing his own boat in the opposite direction, was cuckolding him? That his wife, sitting behind him, one eye on his glabrous head, the other on her lover, had made love in that shrinking skiff? She didn't know which was madder—that she had, or that her husband was oblivious.

As if to bolster her point, Theodulf said, "He's got an unlucky lot, our friend the fisherman."

"Oh?"

"And that poor orphan girl." His tone fell beyond compassion, into something like affinity. "The two of them living barrel of fish to barrel of fish, no less. I see him sometimes, out there smoking his pipe in the middle of the night." His head nodded as if to agree with himself. "I feel some bond with that man, even as our lives couldn't be more disparate."

Should she laugh or cry? Guffaw or bludgeon him with the spare oar wedged between the burden boards and the bottom curve of the hull? Maybe the right course would simply be to hurl herself overboard. She'd die of hypothermia in August.

Instead of any of this, she merely said, "I think the girl will be just fine."

BETTER TO QUARREL with the moon than an empty dress. This was Silje's conclusion after a mostly sleepless night spent talking with her mother. Or, rather, the memory of her mother through the gown she never saw her wear. Freya would sometimes whine or yawn—the only answers she got—and now in the warm light of morning, she yawned herself. The coffee on the stove in the cabin was still warm. A pan of scrambled eggs beneath a cheesecloth dotted with flies would be fine fodder for the dog, but what Silje wanted was toast and jam.

Her mother had been good at almost nothing, but she could bake a loaf of bread. Chewing her cuticle, Silje could admit that much.

Instead of breakfast, she looked for something to break. Or something to burn. She could not locate the exact reason for her anger—was it anger?—but surely her loneliness was at the root of it. She walked to the window, saw Freya sitting on the edge of the shade before the beach, and then saw Willa and Frog pushing the lighthouse tender off the shore.

Could a world be smaller? Could it be less inspiring?

She walked to the kitchen and filled a mug with the tepid coffee. Bitterest. Bitterest and unkindest. She poured it back into the pot, then looked around the cabin like she was tracing the flight of a bat. Finding nothing, she raised the crockery mug above her head and smashed it on the puncheon floor. The shards scattered like buckshot.

Her uncle was a good and honest man, but she wanted a friend. Who? She thought of the boy, Odd, from down the shore. She'd met him only twice and already counted him among her great confidants. How many conversations had she imagined? How many times already had she rehearsed conversations with the dog she hoped one day to have with the boy? Dozens.

She thought of Willa, who'd been so kind at first. There were probably fewer years between the two of them than there were hours left in the morning. And yet, the lighthouse keeper's wife, her uncle's lover, was more schoolmarm than pal.

She thought of the dog, lying now on the end of the dock, already more at home around here than she'd ever felt, and her born in the same room she now watched the dog from. She turned to see the cabin. Her world. And unable to bear one more minute in the confines, burst for the door and out.

Why she went straight up the hill, for the lighthouse, she could not know. She'd watched Willa and Frog leave in the tender a half hour ago. At the same time her uncle rowed in the other direction, a list of chores clanged around in her mind, but there was no chance she'd do them that day. What she'd do instead didn't even occur to her as she crested the ridge and saw the three brick houses, and the other lighthouse keepers' wives in their garden, baskets of lettuce hanging from their arms.

Silje lay flat on the ground, watching them, Freya's cold, wet nose nudging her ear. She might have delighted in the play, but instead pushed the dog's snout away and told it to stay. When the wives turned up another row of the garden, their backs now to her, she hurried to the front portico of the Sauers' house and slipped inside.

Even above the lake breeze it smelled of butter. For a moment she confused the coats hanging from the stand in the foyer for people, then laughed quietly to herself at the gullibility. She went to the kitchen; from the window over the sink, she could see the wives, now sitting on the lawn with their faces turned to the morning sun, their baskets beside them. What dread, she thought, watching them then looking again about the kitchen. She glanced at the pots hanging above the stove. If I were married to Frog, I'd poison him.

I'd cook him arsenic soup. In the empty chair beside the table, she saw his wan face and sloped shoulders. From nowhere she could hear his nasally voice.

Or maybe I'd just bludgeon him with the cast iron skillet, she thought on the way out of the kitchen.

Upstairs, she went first to Theodulf's room. The fish house was better apportioned. And certainly homier. He slept on a cot. His uniforms hung from wire hangers in the closet and a mahogany valet next to the window. A leather satchel sat on the floor beside the cot, like a doctor's bag. A squat chest of drawers hugged the wall between windows. It smelled funky. Like a swamp.

Willa's room had an altogether different aura. Sunlight filled it. The warmth like a conviction or kindness. The air was easy. The bedclothes lay tousled, half hanging off the mattress, but unmistakably soft and well slept in. Silje walked past them, gathered the blanket in her fist, lifted it to her nose. Sugar. It smelled like sugar. She thought of laying herself down, but knew her dirty clothes would leave a mark. A flash of embarrassment washed over her, and she resolved to launder her dress and the blanket she kept in the cockloft. There was no reason for her to live like a beggar.

She pulled the trunk she sought from the closet and opened it, the layer of vacancy greeting her like all the empty promise of the summer's days. But there beneath it! The rosewood music box, her books, the telescope, packets of unplanted seeds, the portrait of Willa's parents. These things she set aside as if they were nettlesome children. The bottom thing, that's what she wanted. The thing beneath the silk, in the depth of the trunk. The thing Willa had shown her, and about which she'd often thought since.

The heft of it in her hand, the coolness of the black metal, these things settled her. She leaned against the closet doorframe and raised it and aimed at the curtain lifting on a breeze. "Don't you move," she said. "I'll shoot, I swear it."

When the curtain settled, she lowered the gun and just looked at it in her hand, the barrel like a wicked sixth finger. She wrapped the palm of her other hand around it, lifting the gun stock down.

She believed the force of it—the power—might be absorbed by her flesh. She believed she might turn that force into something.

From where these beliefs came she could not comprehend. But as sure as she sat in that room, her loneliness began to fuse with the pistol barrel. She smiled for the first time since she first saw her uncle and Willa rowing into the night.

No sooner had they put ashore the lighthouse tender than the passengers aboard the *Nocturne* disembarked. First among them were Hosea Grimm and his daughter Rebekah, who recognized Willa straightaway and approached her as if they were long-lost sisters. Soon after, Theodulf handed Willa the letters to post and made his way into town with Hosea, the two of them strutting away like popinjays. Both she and Rebekah watched.

"He'll go to Winkler's store pretending business, and end up soaked to his shirt collar and snoozing in the alleyway," Rebekah said, lifting her chin at her departing father.

"Theodulf scorns alcohol."

"The only way to bear Hosea's company is to drink with him."

"I've never partaken of it."

"He buys whiskey from some Fort William roughnecks, then sells it to all the hotels and saloons between Otter Bay and the Canada border."

"A rather strange business for one so learned as him."

Rebekah gave her one of those inscrutable glances, appeared about to scold her, and simply said, "He's a chameleon. It's the truest thing about him."

"Well, their business ought to be interesting."

"There's no business. He makes these calls on the pretense of some, but they're only social musters. That he and the other men of the shore might feel important in each other's company."

"You call him Hosea?"

"When out and about," she said, turning toward the post office. "I'll accompany you if you like?"

"That would be nice."

The prospect of an afternoon with this rather strange woman was not unappealing. On the contrary, Rebekah seemed to embody a preternatural instinct to cut to the chase. It was a quality Willa found herself wanting after so many long summer days with only the gossiping keepers' wives, spooky Silje, and her peculiar, pedantic husband for company.

They stopped at Holzer's dockside office, where Willa posted the letters, then strolled into what passed as town. Winkler Dry Goods occupied one corner of the main intersection, a church the second, and an inn the third, which also had a smattering of café tables in the lobby where they served tea and pastries in the summer. It was there the two women went next.

Before the waiter—who tripled as bellhop and attendant—delivered their tea, Willa divined a mystical quality emanating from her companion. She had the sort of complexion that could have been of a twenty-year-old as easily as someone who was forty; her eyes, beautiful and depthless, might have been a blind person's for all they gave away; and her voice, husky and feline at once, with a faint accent Willa could not place and could as easily have been that of a French courtesan practicing her politest English or a Boston moll hurling nighttime insults.

As the waitress set the tea and scones on the table between them, Rebekah lifted her chin and watched a boy running by with his dog at heel outside the window. Her face flashed with pleasure before she shook the boy's likeness away and picked up her teacup. She took a tight-lipped sip and set the cup back down and said, "The sight of that boy running wild through the street makes me wonder something," she said.

"Oh?"

"Your husband, the lighthouse keeper, he's older than you?"

Willa felt herself shrink, embarrassed by the fact that her husband was the same man who had just walked away with Rebekah's father. She had an instinct to tell Rebekah about Mats, a man more suitable in every way, and certainly more attractive.

"Mind you, I make no judgments whatsoever. Merely observations," Rebekah insisted. She had a look about her, like she held a knife in her skirt, or maybe the cure for the pox. Would she laugh at Willa, or extend a gentle hand?

"I have a very hard time reading you, Miss Grimm."

"I've worked at cultivating my impenetrability."

"Why've you done that?"

"Answer my question first, about your husband."

"It's complicated."

"Complicated? He either is or isn't, no?"

"He is. But our relationship is unorthodox. There's a French term for it—*mariage blanc*."

"An expression I know," Rebekah said, her mouth appearing to pucker. As if she'd just drunk some concoction of vinegar and champagne.

"You look like you've a secret," Willa said. "Like you know something I don't. And that you're taking some sort of pleasure in it. It's disarming."

Rebekah lifted her napkin and wiped her lips, and when she lowered the napkin, the ruck around them had disappeared. "I *do* know something you don't. But it's no great mystery." Now she turned away, as though some commotion were playing out on the dirt street beyond the hotel window. "And besides, you'll know soon enough yourself."

Willa feigned indifference, but in truth she understood Rebekah held an honest and uncanny intuition, and it made Willa mad with envy. How Willa had arrived at this disagreement with herself, she did not know. What she did know, what she was in fact emphatic about, was not wanting to give off the impression of having been cleaved. "Not only is your expression inscrutable, you speak in riddles. It's unladylike."

"Someday," Rebekah said dreamily, "I, too, will share your present condition. I've seen that part of my future."

"My *condition*? Now you're a soothsayer? For your own self and mine? Really, Miss Grimm, that seems unlikely."

"When I was younger—when I was just a girl, really—in Chicago, I saw it a dozen times or more."

"What did you see when you were a girl?"

"Women your age, in your predicament."

Willa sat back, aghast, reconciling the many factors that complicated her life, none of which Rebekah could possibly have known. The same feeling that now occupied her to the marrow had likewise visited her in the company of Father Richter and the convent nuns as together they divined her sinner's heart. At least with those evangelists, she understood their proselytizer's mission. Rebekah held no such office. Not that Willa knew of. She might have simply just left. But where to go? It would be hours before Theodulf finished his calls, and a whole afternoon on the town dock, dodging the ubiquitous gulls, hungry and windswept, well, none of that very much appealed to her.

So instead of leaving, she merely picked up her teacup and pressed it to her own lips, content it would keep her from asking the wrong questions.

"Most of these women I knew—women *and* girls, really—were prisoners, plain and simple. They had nowhere else to go and nothing else to do—"

"I'm sorry, Miss Grimm, but what do you mean, nothing else to do and nowhere else to go? What women are you speaking of?"

"I'm talking about my friends and acquaintances from the brothel."

"I beg your pardon?"

Rebekah sat forward. She crossed her hands over her knee and turned her chin away even as her eyes bore in on Willa. "Surely someone so worldly as you won't shrink from the mere mention?"

"I'm not sure what I or my supposed condition has to do with brothels or the ladies who, well, what do they do there? Work?"

"And *how*," Rebekah said, sitting back now and pretending outrage.

"I do wonder," Willa said, desperate to maintain some semblance of composure, "what you were doing in a brothel?"

Rebekah swept her skirts, as though the scones on the plate before them—which she'd not yet touched—had crumbled in her hand and rained down on the folds of muslin. For a long moment she gazed on the back of her own hands before she returned. "Hosea administered their many needs. I often came along, and so knew many of the girls."

"Administered their needs?"

"Honestly, Miss Sauer, for a woman of the world, indeed one who's been to *college*, you certainly can be daft. Yes, administer their needs. He prescribed arsenic or mercury for syphilis and gonorrhea, salve for their chancroids, things like that. He also performed *operations*." She gave Willa a knowing look.

"He really is a doctor?" Willa said, remembering the letter from Hosea to Theodulf she'd intercepted, and the farcical scientific devilry the former had espoused on the subject of the comet.

Once again Rebekah paused, searching about as though an answer to this simple question might be found in the atmosphere around them. "He does some doctoring," she said, answering three ways at once.

Now more intrigued than ever, Willa said, "And you were witness to his doctoring? You saw him treat these women?"

Her pause in answering this question was the longest yet. So long that for a spell, Willa concluded their conversation, or at least this part of it, had finished.

Willa was forming an apology, though for what she didn't quite know, when Rebekah finally gave her answer. "I did observe them. Some of them. I suspect you've never met a working girl, but let me tell you, they're cagey. You're not. Which is what I guess distinguishes you from them."

"I think more than that fact alone distinguishes us."

"I mean only with respect to your condition."

"My condition, I'd forgotten all about it, so rapt was I with stories of your father's doctoring."

Rebekah sighed. As though Willa were an impertinent child full of nagging questions. But rather than condescend, she said, "I so often do this—spoil perfectly pleasant and ordinary conversations by revealing every twisted thought I'm privy to."

"I must say, pretending this seer's insight—"

"I'm not pretending, Miss Sauer," she interrupted. "And I'm not a seer, as you describe it. I'm just someone who pays attention. Someone who's learned to trust her instincts and intuition." She sat back and again brushed her skirts. "I'm going to have a child."

Willa raised an eye.

"Not now. But someday. I know who the father will be. I know it will be wrong. Well, wrong according to everyone. But that doesn't change anything."

"How, exactly, do you know these things?"

Rebekah brushed the question away as she did the imaginary crumbs. "You're not particularly observant, are you? I've tried at least three ways to tell you what I know."

To herself, Willa admitted the truth in this, that she often misunderstood—or even altogether missed—innuendo or indirectness. She chalked it up to her scientific mind, to the way she understood so much of the world in stark and unambiguous terms. These qualities she'd inherited from her father, even if she hadn't inherited much else. But to Rebekah she declared none of this. Only returned the other woman's abstruse scrutiny with a blank look of her own.

"How well do you know your fisherman neighbor's niece?" Rebekah asked.

"I'll tell you this: for all of her child's attention span, I've had straighter conversations with her than the one you and I are in the middle of now!" She'd meant it to sound playful, but as soon as the words were out of her mouth, she knew they'd sounded cross. Hoping to leaven the moment again, she added, "Which is a way of saying I know her quite well by now. Why do you ask?"

"Hosea is always going on about her."

"About Silje? Why is your father interested in *her*?"

"He's a portraitist. He saw something in her aspect that he hasn't been able to forget."

"Her aspect?" Willa said. "A portraitist?"

"His photographs are exhibited in museums, Miss Sauer."

Willa looked in the direction Hosea and Theodulf had walked, now more than a half hour ago. The street was empty but for the boy and his dog, returning from some errand. "Fascinating," she admitted. "What museums?"

"In Europe. Paris and Stockholm and Helsinki. Places like that."

The boy stopped outside, framed by the hotel window with his dog sitting beside him. He reminded Willa of Rebekah's adopted brother. What was his name? "She's quite fond of your brother."

For the first time since they met on the town dock, Rebekah gave Willa her full attention. "Odd?"

"Odd, yes. I couldn't remember his name."

Something about the expression on Rebekah's face told Willa she'd made a faux pas, though she couldn't imagine how. "Have I said something to upset you?"

"Tell that little shrew she might look elsewhere for her friends."

"Did you just call Silje a *shrew*? Whyever would you do that?"

"She has no business with Odd. None at all." Rebekah stood and dusted her skirts a final time. For all the world she appeared a petulant child. "As for you and your business, Miss Sauer, if what you say about the state of your marriage is true, you'd do well to come up with some excuse for your condition, which, sure as I've spent my forenoon in the pleasure of your company, includes a child incubating in your womb." She pointed her thin, long finger at Willa's stomach, shook it thrice, and turned to the hotel reception without another word

Willa watched her, stunned, until Rebekah ascended the center staircase, presumably to a room on the second floor.

When Rebekah was gone, Willa reached down and cradled her belly. Could it possibly be true? Did she feel, there in the palms of her hands, something more than the softness of her own flesh? Something owing to Mats and their nights together? Something like a *future*?

For the briefest moment she thought of chasing Rebekah. To beg of her the source of her omniscience. To ask for *proof.* But as soon as she thought it, she decided she'd rather linger in the mere possibility instead.

OUT BACK Winkler's Dry Goods, four empty hogsheads sitting around a plank of wood sufficed for a saloon table. Workers from the mill or the docks would meet at sundown, and from the same counter their kids bought butterscotch, and their wives canisters of flour and sugar, they bought bottles of beer and jars of whiskey. For some half hour Theodulf had been sitting there in stoic isolation while Grimm gabbed with Winkler inside.

As weather went, the end of August was about as good as it got in the north country. What summer heat there'd been was baked into the granite around town, and now it paired sweetly with the first suggestion of autumn blowing off the water.

Hosea stepped outside, faced the breeze, lifted his chin, and inhaled. "Fifteen years now I've been breathing that lake air. Sometimes I think it'll keep me alive forever."

Such an unlikely—and unwanted—prospect had never occurred to Theodulf, who pulled up the collar of his coat.

Hosea took a long drink from his bottle of frothy beer and smacked his lips. "You're sure you don't want one? I'll buy."

"I don't have a taste for it," Theodulf said, lying.

Hosea smiled. "I've seen sawyers coming out of the spring woods ogling a Shivering Timber whore with less gallop in their gaze, Mr. Sauer." As if to relieve Theodulf of his lust, Hosea drank the rest of the beer in six great swallows before slamming the empty bottle on the plank. He wiped his lips with the back of his hand. "I've known lots of men too fond of the bottle. What every single one of them required was order. From morning to night: order. It isn't the bottle that gets a man sideways, but his inability to control it." He picked up his empty and looked at the bottom of it.

"By all means, Mr. Grimm, go and find yourself another beer to drink."

"I'll do that."

Hosea was back inside the store before Theodulf could get a good glimpse of him whole. Not one full minute passed before he returned.

"Let's put my theory to the test, Mr. Sauer," Hosea said, setting two more bottles of beer and two shots of whiskey on the plank. "I propose you could drink your share of this, maintain your equilibrium and steadiness, and be no worse for it. In fact, I think it might make you feel finer. All you need to do is decide to make it so."

The head on the beer foamed over the lip of the bottle. The whiskey was as gold as honey. "As I said, I've no taste for it. And no need," Theodulf said.

"Who said anything about need—"

"Nor any want. My sobriety is nigh five years now, Mr. Grimm," he said, neglecting the memory of the eve of his father's funeral. "I'm a steadier, more faithful man for it."

"Faithful to whom?" Hosea asked, picking his shot of whiskey from the board and throwing it back in one fluid motion. "Pray you're not a religious man?" He arched an eye at Theodulf. Burped. "Though I seem to recall now, in one of the letters you sent, an inquiry into some sort of Catholic balderdash."

"You mock my temperance first and now my faith? You're no gentleperson, are you?"

"I speak plain, Mr. Sauer, and I mean no disrespect. If truth be told, I fancy myself a truth seeker. Steadiness and conviction and routine, those are the hallmarks of my philosophy. And my own life proves the veracity of it." He took a long drink from the beer.

"Each morning, I take a constitutional. Out to the lighthouse in Gunflint, where I count the waves against my stopwatch, then back to the town bridge over the Burnt Wood River, where I measure the depth at the eastern piling. I record these things in a log I keep."

Theodulf felt a kinship immediately. It came over him like

warmth. Still, he had questions. "What do these measurements mean to you? Why are they important?"

"They mark me as much as they do the water. You see, no matter how adrift I might ever find myself, I have these constancies to guide me back." He made two fists and centered them on the buttons of his shirt.

Theodulf waited.

"In a manner of speaking, my constitutionals are part of the story of my life. They help me get from one day to the next. And the measurements help to keep me oriented in the physical world. Do you see?"

"I'm afraid not."

He flapped his lips like a child making a farting sound. "Once each month I put on my best shirt and coat. I shine my shoes and oil my hair. My capital look. Dandified, I march up to the Shivering Timber and I lose myself in drink"—he glanced around, leaned in— "and in the molls." Now he sat back, spread his arms expansively. "It's like a prescription. It keeps me young and virile and what harm does it cause? None, that's what. As long as I'm *mostly* virtuous, should I not count myself as constant and innocuous?"

Theodulf couldn't help a mocking smile.

"You see the world too simply, Mr. Sauer."

"Now there's an observation no one's ever made before."

"Come now. This moral certainty? This Catholic faith? This temperance? These qualities, such as they are, don't mask a duplicity? You're really so upstanding?"

"It seems to me there's a fair stretch between moral *depravity*— which is what you've described yourself to have—and whatever chicanery infects the common man." Theodulf lifted the full bottle of beer. He held it up to the light.

"*Infect*. A curious word."

Theodulf knew this sort of man. He'd been raised by one. The sort who could twist their own shortcomings and perversions into moral necessities. They spoke loudly, so as to quash any reasonable retort, and when they found themselves in uncomfortable silence, shouted obscenities and called themselves provocateurs.

"As I recall, you sold me a cure to a disease that doesn't exist," Theodulf said, setting the beer back.

"Bunko, man! The history of the world could be told through its catastrophes." He chugged the rest of his beer. "What I sold you was hope against the next one. Which, by the by, is a whole hell of a lot more than your favorite priest had on offer." Now he patted Theodulf's hand. Like a condescending schoolmaster.

"You'll forgive me for not pondering all this hogwash," Theodulf said. "It's no more a *philosophy*—as you earlier described it—than this patch of mud and bunch of barrels is a Parisian café."

"Funny you should mention Paris and philosophy in the same breath, considering that's where I took my doctorate . . . *on the very subject.*"

"You studied in Paris?"

"At the Sorbonne."

Theodulf sat back and tilted his chin down, trying to see this other man in a new light. "When was this?"

"I left Paris in 1890. After my wife died."

Theodulf tilted his head.

"You regard me queerly, Mr. Sauer!"

"I see a great coincidence is all. I spent a very important time in Paris myself. A decade ago. Time does sail on." Theodulf felt a faraway mien settle on his face.

"A winged chariot."

Theodulf trained his stare on the beer and whiskey. As if they were curios in a museum case. After a moment, he reached down and turned the hooch, as though adjusting a dial on a delicate instrument. He left it there. "Are you truly able to resist temptation on a whim?"

"*Certain* temptations, yes."

"The catastrophes you mentioned . . . what force was it that prevented annihilation for us all? From the comet, I mean. If it wasn't God."

Hosea lifted the beer intended for Theodulf and tipped it toward him, asking for permission to drink.

"Please," Theodulf said.

Hosea took a sip of beer, then stoppered the bottle with the pad of his thumb and tipped it upside down. "Physics," he said, cocking his eyebrow and nodding at the bottle. "That's the simple and accepted answer." He righted the beer and slowly broke the suction of his thumb on the bottle. "But please tell me who would ever be so vain as to look in the sky and pretend wisdom. What scientific hypothesis, given enough time, was never proven wrong? The geocentric universe? Luminiferous aether? Empedocles and his elements? All theories once thought irrefutable. Darwin and Newton, they'll fall next."

"You might put your man from France on the list."

"Monsieur Flammarion. Indeed."

"And yet . . ."

Hosea finished the bottle of beer in several chugs. "And yet we've got to believe in something. We've got to pretend to understand this world, this universe, to keep from going insane."

"A good argument for Christianity."

"As good as any," Hosea said.

A group of three men came from the store, each of them with a bottle of beer, the last of them also carrying a plate of fried sausages. Their beards hung furious, their hair unkempt, and Theodulf might have got up and left if Hosea hadn't stood and extended his hand to the first of them and said, "Mr. LaRue, you're a long way from home."

"Same as you, Grimm." They shook hands.

"You're down here, what, searching for greener pastures?"

LaRue pinched his beer between his knurled knuckles and said, "You find me a green pasture in this fuck-all country, and I'll raise me some goats."

"Excuse me," Theodulf said, stepping into their orbit. "LaRue, did I hear? The same LaRues that ran a tent saloon in Agate Bay some years ago?"

"The ones and onlies. This here's my brother Abel." He nodded at the man with the plate of sausages. "I'm Abraham. That spot on Whiskey Row was right next to Gehenna, sure. I'd done my best to forget about it."

"Me, too," Theodulf said.

"You had your heyday down there, or what?" Abraham LaRue said, sizing Theodulf up.

"Something like that," he replied, his shoulders narrowing more even than usual.

LaRue nodded, then turned back to Hosea. "You've got me tending goats down here. How about you?"

"My daughter and I will be guests of the Winklers tonight."

"You still trying to lure that son of a bitch down the shore?"

"To wider harbors."

"As long as he brings his daughters."

"I'll see to that," Hosea said, a lewd wink as exclamation.

LaRue nodded at the board where the rest of his party sat, already quaffing their beers. "I guess I'll see you on Saturday."

"Have Lucy paint her lips," Hosea said.

Theodulf watched Abraham cross the alleyway, where he joined his party, the three of them setting into the plate of sausages like pigs at a trough.

When he turned back to Hosea, he said, "Tell me, Mr. Grimm, how you've made your fortune?"

"I neither have nor aspire to riches. Lest you count a certain bounty of the intellect among my treasure. No, I'm a democratic man. I want what's best for us all."

"Now you sound like my father's political cronies."

"Not at all. Politicians are as pastors—the crookedest of all. What I am is a citizen."

For the first time since they sat down, the alcohol seemed to have got hold of Hosea's tongue. He leered about the alleyway, looking for a fight or someone to fondle.

A citizen of Lethe, Theodulf thought, inventorying the empty bottles and glasses on the table. *Or of Nysa,* thinking then of the

Shivering Timber. As a way of challenging Mr. Grimm, Theodulf said, "Why did you never marry again? An enterprising man like yourself?"

Hosea feigned expansive consideration. "I thought it best for my daughter that she have my undivided attention. She was of course greatly troubled when her mother died."

Theodulf studied Grimm for a long moment. He was taking on the attitude of a poker player well into the night, one who's given away his tells. "But enough about me! You're the newlywed!" He leaned across the board and whispered, "To a wife so young, no less. How's your marriage bed, my friend? I expect *very* happy?"

Theodulf reached for the knot of his tie, twisted it, and blushed. "I must say, I'm not used to such directness. Especially on private matters."

"Humbug! You're among friends! Nay, *brothers*!"

Upward of seven years of service in the Lighthouse Service had introduced Theodulf to no little vulgarity among his colleagues, but they always directed it into vagueness. That a man should confront another regarding the quality of his *wife*? Why, it struck Theodulf as frankly obscene. "And I say badgering a man about his wife is reprehensible."

Hosea raised one hand and finished the glass with the other. "Then I beg your forgiveness, Mr. Sauer. I was only playing schoolboy."

Hosea excused himself, stepped to the edge of the alleyway, pissed off the pine board plank, and walked back into the Winkler store as he buttoned up his trousers. At the next table, the LaRue brothers and their comrade were elbows up, waving off the flies with their felt hats. From where he sat, he could see the town dock, and Willa and Grimm's daughter sitting on the bench beneath the post office.

He knew the truth—that Willa had married him for his money and for the ease that wealth promised her and her mother—and yet, he couldn't help feeling proprietary about his marriage. Maybe some things simply *were* sacrosanct. He looked down on the dock again. Willa and Grimm's daughter had turned their backs to the sun, which blazed up off the harbor water like lightning.

Her back. He'd spent more time staring at it than any other part of her. Always wondering about the perfidious nature of their union. Always certain that she'd walk away at any moment, just another humiliation to add to his résumé. A weatherman's daughter. Blustery and foulmouthed as a winter gale. And dishonorable men like Hosea Grimm gossiping all up and down the shore.

The wretch reappeared from the rear door of Winkler's store, yet another pair of beer bottles in his hand. This time he stood before Theodulf with one of the bottles extended until he took it from his hand. "That's a good man," Hosea said, sitting heavily on the hogshead he'd recently vacated.

Theodulf felt the slick, cold condensation on the bottle, watched as the droplets wet his fingers, and then he raised the bottle to his lips and took a drink.

"Take your measure, Mr. Sauer," Hosea said coyly. "Steady now."

Theodulf took another swig and nodded slowly. "That's the stuff," he said. "I forgot how good it tastes."

Hosea winked. "Tell me, how often do you see the bachelor fisherman across the cove from you?"

"Hardly ever. It's his season of toil. I can't imagine how he gets it all done. Some days he delivers fifty boxes of fish to the monger. That's twenty-five boxes per hand." Two drinks of beer and already he felt looser of lip. "Mrs. Sauer has made something of a friend of the girl, his niece."

Did Grimm's eyes flutter? Or were they Theodulf's own that did?

"She's often about the grounds. Like Ate from children's stories."

"I should like to shoot her."

"Beg your pardon?"

Hosea let out a great laugh. "With my camera, man! I'm a portraitist. Something about the child beguiled me completely when I met her at the jubilee."

"Beguiled, you say?"

Now Grimm's eyes went faraway, even if they stilled. "Any woman is a third shadow." He drew a figure in the air. A woman's form. "Her hair's a theater curtain. Her eyes the entrance to a mine of fathomless depth and untold mysteries. Her fingers are a magician's sleight of hand. All of it, if you must know, reaching into the deepest of her shadows: the blessed, cursed womb. Do you know, Mr. Sauer, that of all the surgeries I'm called on to perform, the hysterectomy is first in number, followed closely by abortions? I don't think I need to describe for you the thing these surgeries have in common." He wiped his brow, though no sweat glistened there.

"My job as a portraitist aligns exactly with that of doctor. As I remove a woman's hysteria with the swipe of a scalpel and a careful extraction of the ovaries, so I remove the untold and unknowable aspects of a woman's form with my camera. I reduce her. From three or four dimensions to two."

Even the beer in Theodulf's blood did not assist in interpreting Hosea Grimm's riddling.

Between his drinking and rhapsodizing, Hosea had no handle on the realm of the alleyway behind Winkler's store. No, he was like a man enraptured, speaking in tongues. Still he had more to say. "It's the young woman—the girl, even—who's most mysterious. And, so, best to photograph."

"I beg your pardon, Mr. Grimm, but from whence does this predilection to understand women come?"

Grimm let out a guffaw. "If you understand women, you understand three quarters of all there is to know. Where humankind is concerned. *That* is an advantage, no?"

Theodulf watched the figures elude Grimm's grasp, though not for trying. He as much as pinched the air, attempting to capture his own meaning.

"Are you all right, sir?" Theodulf asked.

Abraham LaRue answered for him. "That's midnight Grimm, there." He crossed the alleyway and clapped Hosea on the back.

"Hey, man! It's still daylight! Don't go careening in your thoughts!" He returned to his companions and rejoined their laughter. "That's no philosophy, brother!"

It took a moment for Hosea to focus on the next board and the felt-hatted men three around it. "This whole cursed world is philosoph*ical*." Grimm slurred his words, then pounded the board. "But all that philosophy has taught me one singular thing: we'd do better to try and understand one thing—one single thing—than try to fathom the whole of it. That's another reason for these photographs. They show a lens onto nothing less than human nature."

Now the other LaRue spoke. "Hosea, my friend, what you peddle is pictures of naked girls, not wisdom or learning or whatever the hell you call it from one breath to the next. Don't puff your chest."

Theodulf looked at the empty beer bottle in his hand and felt the first whorls of the whirlpool now drowning Hosea Grimm. "Is this true?" the soberer one asked.

Like a spy with secrets, Hosea reached into the valise at his feet, from which he pulled a small stack of postcards. Handing them to Theodulf, he said, "Tell me the fisherman's niece isn't a right subject for more like this."

Theodulf unsealed the onionskin envelope, inside which were a dozen images, each of them more vile than the next, their subject a young woman mostly undressed but clearly meant to resemble, if not represent, Mary, the mother of Jesus.

Theodulf dropped them as though they might scald his fingertips. He then stood and straightened his shoulders and thought to demand an apology, but he found himself speechless instead. Rather than stuttering, he merely turned and went inside Winkler's store, nary a goodbye spoken.

RIPENESS

SEPTEMBER 1, 1910

Look at that cabbage lying there in the garden row, bigger than a watermelon, its outer leaves curling up like water lapping ashore. All summer it's grown. Ripened. And now at harvest time— coinciding with the leaves on the birch quivering gold—there's but a scant window to pick it. To preserve it. To slaw it. To eat it. Else it turns to rot.

It's a particular green in its ripeness. Beautiful. Soft. Resplendent with life. Not unlike the autumnal shade of water the very lake it mimics dons in the colder months. Is it a harbinger? Am I looking for one?

For someone like myself, whose occupation (indeed, whose whole reason for being) is to find harmony and meaning in the synchronicity, to express it in some artful way, well, it often seems a fool's task. Partly because anyone could look upon the ground and see the cabbage turning. Or at the grove of birches and see their golden leaves whispering. Some would even note the coincidence of their simultaneity. The elegance of nature.

So I ask: what purpose do I serve?

And I answer: only to see this cabbage and this grove of trees, this water turning colder, and describe how they're at once the simplest of things, and the most profound. Simpler and more profound than all the cosmos if you put the right people among them.

ALL NIGHT IT RAINED, warm and sweet and pure. The cabbages they'd all worked together to plant in July were ripe now, and Mrs. Wilson worked a hatchet at the root of one. Once plucked, she rolled it a few inches to the left. Willa came behind her lifting the leafy heads to drain the rainwater they still held before dropping them into the wheelbarrow already full of them.

"That's an awful lot of slaw," Ruth said.

Willa, still uneven after her bout of sickness—which came each day now—delighted at the prospect of the sauerkraut their harvest might yield. She'd never once had a taste for it, and yet.

"We'll set them upside down on the picnic table to drain them," Ruth continued, even as she crawled to the next head, pulled the outer leaves up in a bunch, and hacked again. "Last'll be the corn and squash." She wiped her forehead with the back of her filthy hand, leaving another long smirch on her tanned and weathered skin.

"If only we had a couple of pigs to slaughter, and a tree of apples to pick," Willa said.

"You'd have as much luck with a palm tree up here," Ruth said, satisfied with her quip and leaning back down for the last cabbage. She lifted it herself and carried it across the yard to drain on the picnic table. "Bring that wheelbarrow?"

Willa gripped the handles and lifted and plowed it through the soft ground. A dozen heads of green cabbage, with all the water of the night before, and she might as well have had a load of iron ore for how heavy it was.

Together the two women emptied the wheelbarrow, first tearing the outer leaves of the cabbages off and tossing the waste back into the barrow, then laying the heads out. When the table was covered, the two women sat on either side of their bounty.

"With all that dirt on your face, you look like you grew from the garden yourself," Willa said. How or why she felt the need to constantly tease and joke, she could not say. But she didn't mind feeling lighter of spirit.

Ruth lifted a dirty hand to shield the sun and studied Willa for a moment. "I've not known you to be so sprightly, Willa."

"I ought to be miserable."

Ruth swooshed her hand this way and that. "Our moods, they come and they go."

Willa bit her bottom lip.

"Just now is the first time you've looked your age since I met you," Ruth said. "I sometimes forget you're but a girl." Ida lifted the back corner of her apron to her face and wiped her cheeks. "Why miserable?"

"I believe I'm in a delicate condition, Ruth." It was the first time she'd uttered the suspicion aloud, and voicing it gave her predicament a whole new and greater urgency.

"I see," Ruth said carefully, considering the dirt ground into her cuticles. "You say *believe*. I guess the first question is why? I mean why do you believe it?"

Willa explained her bouts of morning sickness, her sudden and irrational cravings, the fact that she had to use the toilet twelve times a day, and woke on the hour all night, too. "I could sleep from now until Christmas. Or at least that's how it seems." Willa put a hand to her belly. "Do you know Rebekah Grimm? She's Hosea Grimm's daughter. He's the apothecary up in Gunflint."

"I'm familiar with the Grimms," Ruth said, as if she'd just admitted to a crime.

"Last week I ran into her in Otter Bay. We had tea."

"Like old friends."

"Very much like old friends, except I hardly know her. Certainly I don't know her well enough that she should have divined my condition."

"But she did?"

"She did," Willa said.

Now Ruth removed a pocketknife from her apron pocket and began carving the dirt from her fingernails. Willa, meanwhile, rubbed her hands together like she might wring from her very flesh a spark to light a fire.

"First of all, Hosea Grimm is no sooner Rebekah's father than I am," Ruth said. "That's neither here nor there, and I suppose it has nothing to do with whether she has a sixth sense, but it's worth saying all the same." One set of fingernails cleaned, she moved to the other. "As you describe them, your symptoms sound awfully like pregnancy. At least what I can recall of it."

Willa moaned. She'd been hoping for a considerable misunderstanding all around.

"I guess you're not happy about it?" Ruth peeked at her from beneath her raised hand.

Willa shook her head almost imperceptibly.

"I'm going to ask you a question, Willa. It's none of my business, but it might help you see your situation more clearly. Is that all right?"

Willa nodded.

"Does this have anything to do with you and Mr. Braaten running around the nighttime woods like a couple of wolves?"

Now Willa gasped.

"Don't worry. Your secret is safe with me. And I only know about the two of you because I've hardly slept a wink all summer long. You'd think a woman's reward after raising a whole brood of children would be to finally get some rest. But . . ."

"What am I going to do?" Willa whispered, her voice hoarse.

"I guess we'd better examine you, Mrs. Sauer."

"Examine me?"

"So we have more to go on than Rebekah Grimm's spooky intuition and a few mornings of not feeling well."

"But how?"

Ruth stood and folded her pocketknife closed and said, "Come along."

The three station houses were mirror images of each other. Brick foursquares with porticos on the front and sheds behind, the station garden running through the backyards. From the rear door, they entered the kitchen, which was the only room Willa had visited in Ruth's house. Afternoon teas, morning coffees, mostly idle chatter before a day in the garden or cleaning house. But today, Ruth guided her through the kitchen into a world at once familiar and distorted. Like the view of something in a funhouse mirror. Where the cuckoo clock hung in Willa's house, an oil painting—of Ruth's four children, their spouses, and five grandchildren—of modest artistic merit but redoubtable family pride hung in the Wilson sitting room, on the other side of which, where in Willa's house the unplayed piano sat, a shelf of two dozen leather bound volumes— she could see the names Dickens and Trollope and Shakespeare on their spines—and figurines in the form of forest animals lay neatly arranged. Whereas Willa's house usually had a faint air of fetid foodstuffs left in the sink or rubbish bin, the Wilson abode smelled of lemon furniture polish.

"Your home is most warm," Willa said shyly.

"A home is warm or not because of who lives there, not what's in it," Ruth said over her shoulder. "We'll go up here, for privacy."

They ascended the same narrow staircase with the same hand railing and the same wallpaper. Upstairs, they went into the same bedroom Willa herself occupied in the house at the other end of the row. Here was another distortion of the same room: A bed made neatly with an afghan Willa presumed Ruth had crocheted herself and a rocking chair at the window overlooking the lake. On the chest of drawers, a bowl of potpourri and a doily were centered perfectly. The aroma spicy and sweet. Like the tea Ruth was so fond of.

"Sit," Ruth said, pointing at the rocking chair.

Through the window, Willa could see Ruth's husband behind

the push mower cutting the grass between the house and the light-house. He wore suspenders over his bare chest and the wisps of his gray halo of hair flashed from under his cap. Despite being some fifty-odd years old and portly at that, he appeared boyish.

"He's always smiling, your husband," Willa said.

"He's good reason to, considering his wife."

The look on Willa's face must have betrayed her feeling of being in an alternative reality.

"It's possible to be happy, you know. More than that, even."

Her own home was the one that should have been viewed as a reflection in a funhouse mirror, Willa knew that much. She also knew Ruth's suggestion about happiness cried truth.

Outside in the yard, Mr. Axelsson came into view. He leveled the gravel path between the lighthouse and houses with a garden rake.

"I'm going to scrub up," Ruth said, laying a hand on Willa's shoulder and peeking out the window herself. "Mr. Axelsson is a considerable man, isn't he?" She leaned closer, as if the extra couple inches of nearness might bring whole new perspectives. "That rake looks like a toothpick in his hands." She whistled a birdlike tune as she trod to the bathroom.

Willa watched John with his rake outside. His shadow lay halfway across the yard, moving as he moved, slenderer and in some strange way more animate than his body. She reached down to her belly again. Thought of the cabbages on the table out back. There was so much to keep track of in this world.

"I can hardly believe my own youngest child is a mother now herself. She must be about your age? Turned twenty-one in June. Baby was born in July."

"I didn't know that, Ruth."

She dried her hands on a towel. "Edgar Ainsley, they named him. Little Eddie. He's about as cute a thing as you ever saw."

"That makes six grandchildren?"

"Spread from New York to Detroit to St. Paul. I'll be lucky to ever see them all in one place." The tone of her voice was as much resignation as sadness. But she didn't dwell. She never did. Not in Willa's experience. "Of course," she continued, "being a grand-mother is to being a mother what being a match is to the lantern wick. Let's see if you'll soon learn the truth of that."

Now she extended a hand. Willa took it and was lifted from the chair with the same tenderness the cabbages had received in the garden. "Here's what you need to know, friend: I'm going to have to examine you. You're going to have to show me yourself. And be-fore you protest, let me promise you it's better me than just about anyone else on this shore."

Willa lifted her skirt and peeled off her bloomers and clenched her eyes shut tight.

"Good girl. Lie back on the bed."

Willa fell back before she might faint.

"Do you know, that for all four of my children, I never once had a physician examine me? Prudes, every one of them." She folded back Willa's skirt and laid a warm hand on her stockinged foot. "It was always the midwife who confirmed my pregnancies. They al-ways talked me through what they were looking for. What they saw. I suppose for an occasion just like this." She moved her hand from Willa's foot to her hand and said, "Open your eyes and look at me." When, after a moment Willa hadn't, Ruth squeezed her hand. "Good girl. I'm looking for the hue of you. To see what your sex looks like. To see if there's extra blood moving down there, to help the baby grow. I'll touch you, but gently. Just to see the cer-vix inside you. Okay?"

Ruth whistled. Willa felt pressure. Her neck stiffened on the pillow behind her head, and she closed her eyes again.

"Purple as a plum. I'd bet my bottom dollar you're going to have a baby." Ruth stood upright. She went herself and sat in the rock-ing chair, wiping her hand on the towel she'd brought from the bathroom.

Willa pulled her britches up and scooted to the edge of the bed. Her body thrummed with nervousness and embarrassment and the force of new life, the sum of which resulted in a burst of tears.

"That's right," Ruth said. "That's just exactly right. Go ahead and cry now. Cry all you want."

Willa watched her friend turn away, to look out the window again. The clouded sky was framed by the sash.

When Willa had finished wailing, Ruth turned back. As if by magic, she held her small flask, and she offered it to Willa, who accepted it and took a sip.

"You have choices, Willa. There're things certain physicians or midwives can do to induce the failure of your pregnancy. Your friends the Grimms would be a resource in that category of choice. But I know others. In Duluth." She paused, folded the hand towel, and set it on the windowsill. "I won't insult you by presuming to understand all the things that led you out into the woods at night. And I won't pretend to know how hard it is to return each morning to your husband. But I will tell you that your attraction to Mats Braaten is as likely to fade as it is to stay aflame. Don't misunderstand me, he seems a kind man, and he's certainly fair to look at. But he's also a fisherman and a lumberjack, and I'd be surprised if he had ten nickels saved in a coffee can down there. I suspect that a lifetime scrimping and saving and salting fish might not suit you.

"As for your husband, I don't envy you at all. But you married him, and I expect his people could make things hard on you and your mother. The wealthy have meddlesome ways, believe me. And even if the Sauers weren't Duluth gentry, Theodulf is queer enough he might find ways to trammel you just for the sport of it, should you decide to abandon him." Now Ruth gave a nearly imperceptible nod out the window.

She took another sip from her flask and said, "I freely admit it's a little early for these tastes, but sometimes the day just calls for it." After she pocketed her hooch, she pointed out the window and gave the same nod. "You want perspective, here you have it. Come and take a look."

Willa stood and on unsteady feet stepped behind the chair. Down on the lawn, Mats stood with a box of fish in conference with all three keepers.

"Dear lord," Willa said.

"All seriousness aside and from where we stand, there's really only one choice, isn't there?" Ruth said, letting a little laugh trail her thought. "That fisherman is bright enough to stand in for light."

"Mrs. Wilson, that's the father of my child!"

Ruth put her hand on Willa's forearm now and said, "I'd consider having another child myself if it meant a night in his bed."

"Or on his boat," Willa said shyly, but very much wanting to let the lightness of the moment linger.

"I'd even help him choke those herring," Ruth said.

Willa glanced down at her friend's hand on her arm. Such gentle affection. She'd known so little of it in her life. Friendship, that is. And here was this woman old enough to be her mother, even half-way again to being her grandmother, offering it in the moment of greatest confusion. The moment of greatest need. The flattery of it, the kindness, led Willa to free her arm from Ruth's hold and put it around her shoulder instead. The gesture Willa learned from her father, one he reserved for those occasions that called for warmth without wisdom, as he used to say.

Together they stood there, looking down on the men. The four of them became two, as John and Ainsley went back to their chores, leaving her husband and her lover on the lawn. She tried to divine what Mats might be saying. Something about the fish, no doubt. Perhaps he wanted another haircut. The prospect of that sort of in-timacy between the two men—of *any* intimacy, or even proximity—roused plain queasiness in Willa.

As if divining this herself, Ruth squeezed Willa back. She said, "Maybe it would help you understand what you have to do if you imagined that box of fish was a bassinette."

All at once Willa's stomach dropped. Her knees rubbered so Ruth had to catch her from falling. It was as if, until that moment, the whole prospect of her being pregnant had been an intellec-tual exercise. A hypothesis to develop. Now, instead, it became something as fleeting and distant and as unfathomable and beauti-ful as the orbits of the comet had been earlier that year. For some reason, the analogy brought with it a steadying hand that, paired with her friend's, gave Willa the balance she needed for the next couple minutes.

"You've not often spoken of your mother. What little you *have* said leads me to believe there's no great love lost between the two of you. I don't know why that is, and I don't care. I have plenty of my own tribulations to deal with." Ruth swiveled around so she stood between Willa and the window and the men below, her hands raised and resting on Willa's shoulders. "I'm not usually in the business of offering advice, though I'll give you a bit now: talk to your mother. You should hear her counsel." She dropped her hands into the pockets of her apron and gave her slight smile. "You should give her the chance to redeem that part of herself. The mothering part."

MORE AND MORE it happened now that things of ordinary substance took on monumental, metaphorical significance. Maybe the lack of sleep stirred it up in him. Maybe the fantastical thoughts. Maybe the loss of ballast, drip by drip all damn summer long. Hell, he even walked bent now. Tonight, it was the pepper in the slaw that whorled him off into the stars of his mind.

"Ruth told me she'd teach me to make sauerkraut when I return," Willa said.

Theodulf heard her, but merely stabbed at the pepper flakes with the leftmost tine of his fork in answer.

"I'll leave tomorrow. To visit my mother."

The fish at least was fresh, brought up by Mats Braaten that very morning, choked from the nets only hours before he dropped it, asking for a haircut when it was convenient. Theodulf had told him to come back on Saturday. Mr. Braaten was listing himself, or so it seemed.

"Do you suppose men like Mats Braaten are born knowing how to drop those nets? A whole nation sired by Zebedee?" He swirled a bite of fish in the pooled butter on his plate and stabbed it into his mouth. "The funny thing is, when I try to imagine the fishermen of the bible, I see someone an awful lot like Mats Braaten."

"Did you not hear me?" Willa said.

"Yes, yes; go, go." He made a shooing motion with his free hand. "Go see your mother." He stirred the slaw with his fork, raked up a mouthful, and talked while he chewed. "I was talking about Mats. Thinking about him out there on the water by himself. Imagine how strong his hands are. Imagine how tired he must be."

Willa, sitting across the table, her hands in her lap, her food untouched on her plate, the butter and vinegar running together, pressed a napkin to her unsullied lips and said, "Excuse me." She stood and left without another word.

Theodulf, speaking to her absence, said, "No one answers my letters anymore. Not Father Richter. Not Hosea Grimm. Not my friend Paulette. Not even my own mother." He refocused his attention on her seat, and realized she wasn't there, searched over his shoulder for her. Satisfied—and surprised—that she was gone, he took another bite of his fish and said, "I doubt Mats Braaten would fail to write back. Someone that serene, why, he'd probably write extraordinary letters." He thumbed the last piece of fish onto his fork, licked his fingers, then ate the forkful. "Do you suppose he's illiterate? Maybe he only knows how to read the water."

FREYA DOVE FROM THE DOCK, chasing the stick Silje had thrown into the lake. Thirty or forty times the dog had pestered her into another round by dropping the wet piece of birch on her skirt. She'd lost track of most everything in the hour she'd been playing fetch with her dog. The fact of her hunger, of her lassitude, of the coming stars. The first to arrive were always the most beautiful.

Was it the new month today? Willa had told her some few days ago to look for Uranus at dusk. It would be bright and fulsome. That's what she said, as though Silje would be able to tell one star from another. What she saw instead was the first sliver of the waxen harvest moon enshrouded by fog coming off the lake.

When Freya returned the stick again, Silje held it up to the moon. Even wet, the paper bark shone faint as the moon. She hurled the stick again. Again, Freya dove after it. As the dog paddled back, Silje caught a flash of whiteness along the shore. An apparition. A reflection of the heavens among the rocks on the beach, backlit by the darkness of the forest. She reacted not with fear, which might have been a natural instinct, but instead with a wild curiosity. Like the possibility of ghosts suddenly existed.

She whistled for the dog, who shook herself and then hurried with the stick to where Silje knelt behind the bench on the dock. It was as if the faint moonlight had found a cohesive form, moving along the water's edge like a coming wave. Splashing. Hurrying. Stumbling. For a brief moment, as the lightness reached the cabin and hurried right in, Silje wondered if it was a heavenly form paying a visit. But as soon as the light from inside the cabin spilled out, and mingled with the form, she realized it was only Willa coming to call. Earlier tonight than usual. And seemingly more eager. She didn't pause at the threshold to shout hello, didn't wait for a welcoming wave, but walked right in, darkness filling the space she'd just held.

Silje reached down to Freya's muzzle and said, "You keep quiet, understand?"

She crept down the dock and onto shore and up the path to the cabin and peeked in each window as she orbited the house. Willa cradling her own arms. Uncle Mats rubbing his brow. Willa taking the pipe from his hand and having a puff. Uncle covering his eyes with the heels of his empty hands. Willa's skirts—the same that had caught the faint nightlight and held it like a lantern mantle as she scurried to meet him—swirled as she did, like a kite crashing to earth.

At the window beside the back door, Silje dug her fingernails into the space between the sill and the bottom of the frame and inched it open.

"He's been through my things," she heard Willa say. "He's taken my pistol."

"Your pistol?" Mats said, pressing now his ears. As though the news Willa imparted could somehow be avoided if only he closed off the avenues of its reaching him.

Silje put her ear to the space between the window and sill so she might hear better.

"I'm going to visit my mother," Willa said. Her voice cracking and hoarse. As if she were ill.

When Mats did not answer, Silje glanced over the bottom of the window frame. Now he sat with his pipe in his lips and his hands folded together in front of him. Penitent. Willa leaned to him and put her hand in his hair and whispered something. Or anyway her lips moved.

For a long time they remained in that pose. Her uncle and his lover, Frog's wife. Silje eventually reached down and put her hand on Freya's head. She tried to imagine this scene from the vantage of some omniscience. A girl and her dog. A man and his lover. Orphaned and lonely hearted. And all of them caught.

Silje felt the dog stiffen at the same moment the foghorns blew from above. She hadn't noticed the brume roll in off the lake. Hadn't noticed it cape her back and settle into the deepest part of her. The foghorns blew again. They'd be incessant now.

She watched inside as her uncle and Willa held their pose, her hand still in his tousled hair. Silje felt a great discomfort at the sight of them. Almost like she was being relegated, but to what she could not say. When her uncle finally moved, it was to snuff the candle sitting on the table. The darkness made total except for the distant strobe of light from the Fresnel lens on the clifftop. She had the impression of a lever being switched, and now the night in all its darkness came on like some aberrant machine with its strange and secret calibrations to set itself in motion: the sound of waves coming ashore, as if dragged by the fog; the sound, too, of Willa inside, sobs so gentle and in time with the lake it might very well have been synchronized by God or fate or some other deity of the night; her uncle's gentle assurances; the sound of their sighing; all of it interrupted by the intermittent fog signal.

And of course it wasn't long before the wolves started answering, which in turn put Freya on edge. She whimpered and squirmed but wanted to be faithful to Silje, that much the girl could see, so she stroked the dog's ears, which were soft as the silk inside Willa's trunk, while the dog returned the affection, licking Silje's wrist.

Unsettled as she was, Silje could not help but marvel at the turns the night had taken and how quickly she'd adapted to them. As the wolves' howls grew nearer, or louder, she held Freya closer. Together they sat on the pine duff on the ground below the window, the dog arranging herself between Silje's legs. She whimpered again but settled, pressing her flank into one of Silje's knees and resting her chin on the other. Each time the foghorn bellowed, both the dog and the cabin tensed. And each time, Silje interpreted the tension as a reminder of her life.

After a while of this, Silje took Willa's pistol from her pocket and held it up before her face. She could barely discern its shape in the darkness, and certainly could not fathom the reason she held it. Instead of investigating, she merely pointed it at the darkness, put her finger on the trigger, and pretended to pull.

QUEEN OF THE HIGHWAY

SEPTEMBER 2, 1910

For all the stars and moons, the comets and black holes, the darkness and light in eternity, there's one thing more mysterious and expansive than all others. It resides not in the distant reaches of space, it's not a comet orbiting to places unknowable, it's not energy or molten matter. Nor is it a soul traveling among the heavens. Not yet.

No.

In fact, it's a different kind of possibility. More brilliant than any star. More promising than any black hole, and just as dark. It resides in a mother's womb. It is the quintessential beginning. Its prospects are greater than all of the lesser lights. It might even be the fulfillment of them.

This is at least true for my purposes. Why, look at Willa there. It appears she rode the comet to the threshold of that fine hotel, so spent is she in mind and body. Ah, but her spirit! Despite her confusion and befuddlement, she has never been surer of anything. Never.

S HE ARRIVED at the Thibert Hotel just before ten o'clock, belea-
guered and bone-weary and without appointment. When she
inquired of her mother, the clerk, who was new since Willa had last
visited the hotel, said only that Mrs. Brandt had left at dinnertime
and was expected to return and that, should Willa like, she might
have a seat in the lobby to wait. Perhaps they might even arrange
a very late supper for her?

Which is how Willa found herself sitting at the same table she'd
joined Theodulf on that fateful night now almost a year ago, a
warm roast beef sandwich, untouched, stewing in its own jus before her, remembering another unforgettable night, this one from
her childhood.

She and her mother had traveled to Minneapolis by train, leaving her father to his melancholy, which had lately become as glum
and glowering as the gales and first snows of October. Willa remembered it was true he'd been gloomy, but then the change in seasons
usually coincided with a kind of temperamental shift in her father,
whose fortunes depended on seeing things before they happened,
the weather, notably, a task that got increasingly hard to do on the
shore of Lake Superior as autumn deepened. Of course, her mother's motives were not so simple, and the two days they spent in
Minneapolis were as much an education as adventure.

Willa pushed the roast beef sandwich to the center of the table.
Was that trip only six or seven years ago? Willa marveled at the
thought she'd so recently been a child. For a child she was, despite
how her mother behaved.

They'd checked into the West Hotel on a Saturday morning,
spent the afternoon shopping at Dayton's, having lunch, and then

making ready to attend *The Queen of the Highway* at the Bijou Theater later that evening. By and large and as Willa remembered, it had been a pleasant day. She got new shoes and a book by Beatrix Potter without having to plead, and if her mother was distracted, she was also not unkind.

The show starred a bandit dog named Duke and was billed as an action-packed adventure about his heroics. Horses and stagecoaches and wild, marauding wolves filled the rest of the bill, and in fact, the show thrilled. That is, until one of the wild wolves escaped its cage and barreled into the dressing room of the human star of the show—a girl named Miss Charlotte Severson—was hypnotized by the electric lights, and in a frenzy attacked her. The stage lights flickered and the howling that came up from beneath or behind the stage was otherworldly, but the audience understood all the commotion to be part of the act. Not until the compere appeared on stage, calling for a doctor from the audience, did the crowd sense something amiss.

As it turned out, Duke, the hero dog of the show, saved Charlotte Severson from a certain death. Well, Duke and the physician, who happened to be sitting right next to Willa in the orchestra seats, and who climbed over her to attend to the actress. After cauterizing and bandaging her wound, he returned to his seat, the cuffs of his shirt speckled with blood. By then, the theater lights had come up and the compere had already made several announcements—that there was no reason to be afraid, that the show might go on, that if it didn't, patrons would be given a full refund, but that for now they might adjourn to the lobby and enjoy a refreshment from the concession. He looked at Willa, the physician did, then looked at his sleeves and said to her, "A braver young lady I don't think I've ever seen. It's her intention to finish her performance!" He then stuffed the bloody cuffs of his shirt up into his jacket sleeves.

Miss Charlotte Severson did indeed return to finish her performance, though Willa was shocked. That a young woman would be expected to carry on, that she might be able to, had not seemed possible.

All of this was memorable for any number of reasons, not least the simple strangeness. But what Willa remembered most, as she sat there in the lobby of the Thibert Hotel, was that following the performance, when they returned to the West Hotel in Minneapolis after the harrowing night at the theater, her mother put Willa to bed and told her she had to run an errand. She left and was not back until after the sun rose the next morning. All night, the sound of the howling wolves in the theater threatened Willa. If she'd been able to sleep at all, she'd surely have found their fangs in her dreams.

Her mother arrived on the arm of Murdock Alderdice at ten thirty. They came through the lobby doors like young lovers but were both stunned to see her sitting there at the table.

"Willa?" her mother looked around as if there might be some imminent danger. A man with a gun. A wolf escaped from its cage.

Murdock still had his arm around Ann's waist. His hat lay cocked at a very slight angle, and he reeked of rum. "Is there such a thing as a prodigal daughter?" he said, attempting to steady himself and his hat in the same unbalanced motion. He ended up tripping on his own foot.

Her mother handed Murdock the parasol, which he used to prop himself upright before stumbling to one of the divans in the lobby.

Her mother had watched his buffoonery until he fell on the divan, then turned back to Willa and put two loose strands of hair behind her ears. "What are you doing here?" she asked. In contrast to Murdock's, her mother's drunkenness seemed weary, like the sight of her daughter sapped all the fun from her evening.

"I need to talk to you. It's urgent."

Ann raised a finger and turned and stepped over to Murdock. She leaned down and whispered in his ear. He sat up and then stood—again with the aid of the parasol—and left without reply. Her mother watched all this before returning to the table where Willa sat. "Urgent, you said?"

"Perhaps now's not the best time to talk."

"I see a full season of married life hasn't softened you."

"And I see a year of widowhood hasn't sobered *you*. On the contrary."

"Yes, well, can you imagine how unpleasant I'd be if I didn't drink?" She sat down and suggested Willa do the same. "Murdock only knows one direction, and that's down. It's usually fun until it isn't." She removed from her handbag a long cigarette holder and from a silver case a cigarette, which she lit on the table candle. After she exhaled she said, "It *is* a nice surprise to see you. It's been longer even than when you went away to college." She took another long drag from the silver tip and said, "I've not come visit despite some few invitations from your husband. How is Mr. Sauer?"

"He's the same."

"And likely to remain." Now she rolled the tip of her cigarette in the ashtray between them. "Tell me why you're here?"

"Honestly, Mother, I might just wait until morning."

"Morning? Nonsense! I won't be up until noon. Later than that if you leave me wondering all night."

Willa shifted in her seat, as if she were screwing herself up for confidence. "I'm pregnant, Mother."

"Pregnant? That hardly seems urgent. In fact, you might have simply written it in a letter." She started to recline but then sat up again, "I'm surprised Theodulf had it in him."

Answering, Willa merely looked away.

"How do you know?"

"It's been too long between menses. And Ruth—she's one of the other wives at the station—knows what to look for."

Her mother took another very long drag and then crushed out her cigarette. "Well, I can't say I'm old or matronly enough to be a grandmother, but what's to be done?" She pressed a finger under each eye and then looked above Willa. "Murdock tells me this dashing dragoon is the namesake of the hotel, and that there's a rather distinct and unimpugnable line between him and your husband. It really is quite something: to think our family, despite the many disadvantages we've had, will now be directly linked—by blood, I mean—to this noble lineage. I suppose this positively ties the Sauer fortune to you. To us. Bravo, daughter."

Willa puzzled over her mother's logic for a brief moment before saying, "The thing is, Theodulf and I have never yet, well, you know . . ."

"You jezebel!" Ann hissed, but not angrily or with judgment. In fact, she seemed almost inspired by her daughter.

The urge to say a hundred cutting things rose in Willa. But instead of relenting to any of them, she merely said, "Do you remember the time we went to Minneapolis to see *The Queen of the Highway*?"

"I'm tipsy, not blotted. Of course I remember. The star was attacked by wolves."

"*A* wolf, but yes. And we stayed at a hotel in the city."

"A grand hotel, as I recall."

Willa watched her mother visit the occasion in her memory. What other hotel room did she enter in her mind, and who did she visit there? These questions dogged Willa as her mother seemed to relish the thought of them. When her mother finally rejoined Willa there in the lobby, her whole body seemed to have slackened. A certain redness flushed her lips. It was almost as if she'd just painted them.

"I was so scared," Willa said.

"The girl was fine, wasn't she? She finished her performance, even." She twirled her cigarette holder, tapped her lower lip with it, then looked across the table at Willa. "We've gone *very* far afield."

"Not really, we haven't."

"The older you get, child of mine, the more oblique you become. I'd have better luck tracking the wind than the pattern of your thoughts."

What a mistake, to come here hoping for sympathy or counsel or simple love. It was embarrassing to sit at the same table as this woman. Embarrassing that this was her mother. Embarrassing that Willa didn't have better instincts of her own.

"I'm long past seeing myself in the reflection of your eyes, Willa.

I spent too much time trying to understand your judgment." She rigged another cigarette and lit it. "If you have something to say, please, out with it."

"That night, after *Queen of the Highway*, you brought me back to the hotel and then left again. You locked the door behind yourself and left me in that room alone."

"I did no such thing."

"You did. What's worse, you didn't come back until the next morning."

Her mother brushed ash from her sleeve and looked at her daughter with scolding eyes. "Please tell me you've not been carrying that story around for the last five years."

"Seven years."

She waved Willa's aside into the corner of their alcove. "And now, even for all your moral certitude, you wave that old story in front of me why? To lay some blame? To find the villain in me instead of in you?"

"I've made my choices freely. Happily. I thought you might have some advice. I was told you would."

"Advice? Yes, I have plenty. You need to make Theodulf believe the child is his. To protect what you've *earned*, which is to say the security of the Sauer family name. You'd be a fool to do otherwise."

"You have no bottom, do you?"

Her mother blew smoke in a stream toward the tapestry of Bleiz Thibert. Her drunkenness had been replaced with a more general bleariness, one Willa recognized and loathed. She knew more and viler speech was coming and sat back waiting.

Ann finished her cigarette and crushed it in the ashtray. "We all have a bottom," she said. "We're like sinking ships that way. I told you once about marriages. You get out on the seas, all alone, and the weather comes and"—she clapped her hands—"it sinks us. You're in that weather right now. And let me tell you, a strong enough storm always wins."

"So says the woman whose husband was saintly. The woman who was treated to years of undeserved love."

"You presume so much, Willa. Your father was a saint to *you*. He loved *you*. But our marriage? The only thing good about it was you." Her fight had left her, as it often did. But Willa took no satisfaction in this. She had come for advice, and so far, the only thing her mother had offered was the suggestion that Willa trick Theodulf into believing the child was his. The mere thought repulsed her, and yet, somewhere inside, she could see the method. She could see the logic.

"Maybe," her mother said, packing the cigarette holder and case back in her handbag, "you and Theodulf will find some happiness in the child. Your father and I did in you. At least for a few years." She clasped her bag shut and set it on the table, ready to leave. "What time is the *Nocturne* tomorrow?"

"Not until two."

"Then we should have lunch before you catch it." She stood. "If I'm not prone in bed in five minutes, I just might die. I'll arrange a room for you tonight. Let's meet at noon tomorrow. We can see what the light of day shines on your situation?"

"Don't you even want to know who the actual father is?" Willa whispered.

"It doesn't matter. What *does* is that you convince Theodulf it's him."

"And if I don't? If I just go to the man I love?"

"You won't. You mustn't." She wore that expression Willa knew so well from the hundred other admonishments she'd suffered over the years. "You don't actually love this man. You're merely thrilling in the prospect of him. You're mooning over the way he makes love to you. All of that's well and good, but it's also fleeting. Trust me."

Was there truth in that?

Her mother looked up at the coved ceiling, she glanced around, searching, then said, "Remember about the storm, Willa."

"It always wins," Willa scoffed.

"It does," her mother said as though she'd won the argument.

* * *

The following morning, Willa woke early and walked down Superior Street to the incline, which she rode up to their old house. From the platform, she could see into the dining room, and she watched the mother and father and their two toddlers eat breakfast. One of them sat in a high chair and passively spooned oats from the bowl in front of them. A little boy, Willa thought. Then she thought of how many times she and her mother and father had eaten in that very room. The long silences and the yawning spats between them. Why had Willa always sided with her father? Without needing to think long, she remembered it was because he had always told Willa—in the aftermath of that bickering—that she needn't worry, that he loved her mother and their disagreements were a part of the bargain. Her mother had never made such an admission, and so was easier to vilify and blame. Not that Willa needed any extra animus for her mother. She'd been born with plenty of that.

But even by her own standards, Ann Brandt had outdone herself the night before. All that talk of sinking ships! Willa turned now to the railing that overlooked the harbor and the bridge and the long spit of land on the other side of the canal where an amusement park used to exist. Her father would take her there a couple of times each summer for the few years it existed. They'd bring a picnic and ride the Ferris wheel and, from the top of the loop, look back to the city and their house on the hillside. How they'd laughed!

She couldn't imagine the man who bought her taffy and held her hand all the streetcar ride home and returned with a peck on the cheek for his waiting wife was the same who strung himself from his office ceiling. Willa risked another look at the house. She could not comprehend that depth of unhappiness.

Was it happiness with Mats? Could it be? Would living in a cabin in the woods with the orphaned girl and a man who spent his summers on the water and his winters felling trees while she cared for a baby and rubbed nickels together hoping they'd turn into bread be preferable to a life with Theodulf? Maybe her mother was right, and she should try to convince Theodulf the child was his. At least their unhappiness with each other was always in plain sight.

As she walked back to the Thibert Hotel, Willa had all but resolved to implore her mother for help. She'd appeal to what Ruth had described as the *mothering part* of her. It must reside there. It *must*. Willa herself was only some weeks into *her* pregnancy, and she felt her very constitution evolving. It startled her to realize it. She felt protective and tender and proud and like one day soon she'd be able to hold back a gale for whatever child incubated in her now. Surely her own mother had some residue of that instinct. A bushel of sleep—a good, long sobering night—would awaken her to that part of herself.

But when she reached the hotel, not only was her mother's better self absent, all of her was. Instead, Murdock Alderdice greeted her. A sheen of sweat shone on his face and his hands shook as he approached. His breath reeked—the sour smell of wine rotted overnight—and his hair, which he kept curled and coiffed like a society lady, flew in all directions. He wore a coat, but no tie, and, as she looked him down, noticed one of his shoes was untied.

"Where's my mother?"

Speech pained him. "She's unwell," he said, grimacing as he cleared his froggy throat. He spread his hand and gently touched his temples. "She had trouble sleeping last night. She can't get out of bed now."

"Go and get her this moment."

He lowered his hand and sighed. "Willa, your mother is no sooner getting out of bed than the sun is setting now. She's asked me to tell you to be well. And that she'll check in with you by letter. Please believe me when I say I'm certain she can't be roused."

Of the many strange things about this meeting, it suddenly occurred to Willa that Murdock Alderdice not making some lewd suggestion was top of list. "Very well," Willa said, feigning indignance but in truth wanting to weep. "Please have your bellhop arrange a cab for me."

He raised a hand over his shoulder, a gesture so slight she might have missed it if her eyes hadn't been cast down. But no sooner did he make it than the bellhop arrived. "Get Mrs. Sauer a cab,"

Alderdice said to him. Then to Willa he added, "I wish you safe travels home, Willa. I'd better get back to your mother. She needs my care now."

She watched him walk back to the staircase, his shoulders slung low. In fact, he looked not unlike Theodulf heading toward the lighthouse on any given evening.

After some time, Willa finally turned away and stepped through the revolving door to wait under the awning for the cab to take her to the harbor. She'd return to the lighthouse with less than she'd come. She hadn't even told her mother the name of the baby's father. Hadn't even thought it.

OFFING

SEPTEMBER 20, 1910

The water turns verdazurine this time of year. It's colder now, and livening. The crests burst white. My, how they come. Between these pulsing waves and the scintillating green expanse beyond, the effect for an idling gazer like me is hypnotizing.

If you stare across the surface of the lake long enough, through some osmosis I'll surely never understand, you'll see the horizon detach from the lake. Which is to say, it rises.

Why, just this morning, as I stood beside our man, we watched a freighter steaming west at the limit of our sight. Duluth bound, it was, and empty in her holds. How would I know that last? Well, because what coal-laden ship ever rose above the water? What black hull ever held the cold green water in its reflection, an angelic ship among the clouds? For as sure as we stood shoulder to shoulder, that's what it did. It steamed into the clouds, an act of levitation upon a heavenly tide that stirred even my sorry soul. For that moment, I believed in something.

We watched. Long enough for me to lose sight of the ship and remember the horizon all around me. All the time. And onto the rock underfoot I glanced, then onto the green water north did the same once more and saw the water meet the sky again, that ship back upon her waters. When I turned to my friend, he was ambling back to his quarters. I didn't even get to ask him if he'd seen what I had myself. I didn't know.

"I'M ON WATCH tonight, aye?" Ainsley said, his lunch pail hanging from one hand, his ubiquitous pipe from the other. Theodulf didn't approve of the elder man's slovenliness, but by now, he'd abandoned the pretense of governing this station. He still kept his own trousers pressed, but he'd not cajole the other men to do the same. Never mind the shine of their hat bills or the tightness of their cravat knots.

"You are, Mr. Wilson."

Theodulf had pulled the desk chair out from the watch room and put it near the edge of the cliff, and he sat with his feet crossed up on the concrete quarter wall. Ainsley came and stood beside him, puffing on his pipe.

"I've not seen you take a moment's leisure since I arrived, Mr. Sauer. What's the occasion?"

"Season is winding down, is all. I expect two or two and a half months will see us heading home." He turned to face Ainsley. "I don't even know where you live, Mr. Wilson."

"Detroit, sir."

Theodulf shifted yet further in his seat. "I was born in Detroit."

"Ruth's people are from Chicago. She's always badgering me about moving there."

Theodulf smiled affably and turned his gaze back out on the water. Between the time of Ainsley's arrival and now, the moon appeared in the offing, enormous and as orange as the pumpkins ripening on the edge of the garden. "What time is it, Mr. Wilson?"

Ainsley put his pipe between his teeth, set his lunch pail on the quarter wall, and removed his watch. "Half five."

483

"Do you know, Willa can tell the time just by judging the moon or sun. It's uncanny."

"She's a bright young lady. You're a lucky man."

The affable smile remained on Theodulf's face. "You've got a stove to warm. And a lamp to light."

Ainsley doffed his hat. "Aye, sir."

"I'll just sit here a moment longer, Mr. Wilson. I hope I'm not in the way."

"You're hardly in the way."

Theodulf listened to the scuff of Wilson's boots across the way. Twenty paces from here to the watchhouse door. Twenty paces he'd made a hundred dozen times since arriving here. And what had those short forays taught him? He ought to have been agitated by a musing such as this, but tonight he would deflect that agitation. Tonight, he would simply admire the beauty he'd never once found pleasure in.

What an enormous oversight! To have missed this vista all year long. On the horizon, the Apostle Islands rose like mounds of ancient smoke. The water between his shore and that, as placid as he could remember seeing it, seemed to throb altogether—like his own chest rose and fell as he lay on his cot. It was beautiful, the way he felt aligned with it. The way the water, like his heart, seemed to beat to an otherworldly and cosmic time.

He sat there long enough for the light from above to begin its work. A spellbinding winking across the water that only amplified the pulsing of the lake. He knew the Sand Island light was some twenty-five miles across the lake, sending its own light onto the water, light he couldn't see, but was there all the same. For a moment he thought to shout a hullo across the water, but even in his agitation, he knew that was silliness. Instead, he just sat back and counted the rotations of his own light, whispering hello with each pass.

In this repose he heard the piano. At first he mistook it for his own imagination. Some memory inspired by the metronomic passing of the lighthouse beacon or ghost rattling his jewels in the wilderness beyond the station grounds. But no. Though it *did* come from behind him, it was not nearly in those hills.

The light in the front room shone through the window at his house, casting a summoning light on the weedy lawn.

He stood.

The song was unmistakable. *Moonlight Sonata* played against the full and risen moon.

Theodulf waited for the calamity of feeling those notes always delivered. He lifted his ear to it. He clenched his eyes shut, as though some great pain swelled in his belly. Surprised to find so little in him, he focused on the beating of his heart. Of the blood coursing through his body. But nothing attended him. Nothing at all. He might as well have been an empty vessel.

Still, he could not help himself. He walked across the lighthouse grounds. He walked like a man headed to the gallows.

I t was like hearing the voice of God Himself, come now to her wilderness and beckoning her up the hillside. This hour of the day, waited for, this lambent twilight, it made of the music *holiness*. She had no other word for it.

And Freya? Well, the dog had stopped, too, between the sound and Silje. Freya lifted her nose. Then, unable to smell anything, raised her ears like two human hands and praised the sound with canted head. She'd never been so attentive to anything. Not to the foghorns or the whistles of passing ships. Not even to the yowling wolves.

Silje had heard a piano before. In church. Attending the hymns. But always with her mother's mumbling above it. Her father's soft humming below. This music—she didn't even know to call it a song—emanated a mournfulness and beauty that stole her breath and brought a well of tears to her eyes. It was just that simple. She closed her eyes tight. To hear better. To squeeze the tears free.

WOULD SHE EVER UNDERSTAND? Not necessarily what to do about this child taking shape in her, though that question plagued her each moment, but how to live in this world *herself.* How to be loved and happy and something more than a passenger on a sailing planet.

She sat on the piano bench. The first time she'd done so since April. Her fingertips rested on the keys the way they so often lately had rested on Mats's bare chest. But whereas that touch was as warm and comforting as burying her hands in the garden soil, this—the keys of the piano—was like reaching up to touch the moon. She could see it—the moon—out the window, in the offing, a night of promised calm.

A night of calm! She laughed. No such thing had existed since her last night in Boston, one she'd spent at the Harvard observatory with her Radcliffe astronomy professor and a clique of classmates. They'd gazed upon Andromeda, she remembered. But since then? It had been all stormy weather. Even those nights with Mats, the low pressure of them, had not been easy. The threat of thunder always present. The promise of being discovered like lightning.

She'd not seen him in a week. Hadn't even caught a glimpse of him sculling out to haul his nets. So strange was his absence that she began to doubt their affair. What a particular brand of madness those thoughts brought. She'd heard of women losing their minds. Of conjuring whole fantasies. Maybe Mats was just that. An illusion. An idea. Something wished for without consciousness.

None of which explained her condition. In certain, fleeting moments—as now—it absolved her of all other cares. She was but a vessel. Her cargo? The world of possibility within her. Like an empty pirate ship about to plunder, that's how she thought of herself. What booty might come? Well, the mystery of it was handsome indeed!

But even the prospect of all that didn't set her mind at ease. So she sat at the piano. Before these nights and days of tribulation, she'd always felt most vulnerable to the world poised above the keys. So much possibility existed here. The chance for discovery. The chance for darkness. The chance for anything, really. Risky, yes. But most of life was risk. Often as not, if she just simply troubled the keys, the answers would rise on the song.

So, as eager to clear her mind as to risk consequences, that's what she did, there in the dim sitting room, with the windows opened and the moonlight puddling on the floor, she lifted her first song from the neglected piano Theodulf had somehow brought here. For her. And though the music that emanated from it was off-key, she nonetheless wandered in, caught somewhere between herself and the child within.

THE SMELL OF DINNER—he'd forgotten all about it!—was as much on the air as Beethoven. He stood there, watching Willa's shoulders and neck roll with the notes, unworried by the past. No thoughts of Paul, or of the boy that night in Duluth. No, on this occasion it was just the three of them. Willa and the music and himself. He stepped back, saw the dinner on the table—sauerkraut, cooked up with ham and potatoes and served with a warm loaf of bread (courtesy, no doubt, of Ainsley's wife) cooling on the board— and relished the prospect of it. But not until after this. This he would take. As beautiful and as surprising as the moonrise.

He smiled. *Moonlight Sonata*, indeed.

I've botched this, too, he thought, watching her, almost as if she were a painting in a museum. A marriage as full of life, anyway. She was irascible and incorrigible, too modern, bumptious, even, and certainly aloof—she'd not given him so much as a kind glance since she arrived in his life—but what else did he deserve? He wore his disagreeableness like a cloak. Wielded his opinion like a dagger.

He wondered, *what percentage of me is the pleasant, peaceable man watching his wife perform this song*—she'd moved into the allegretto now, her head bobbing along with the frivolity of it—*his slight shoulder resting on the frame of the door, right this moment? What part of me is good? What part of me is agreeable to beauty without condition? A woman at her piano, playing the most beautiful song as if it had been composed for her. He, there in the door, watching her, unannounced and admiring. The night a thousand shades of resplendence. The seas safe and moonlit. Dinner on the table.*

She finished the allegretto and paused—hands poised above her golden hair, above her still shoulders—before the final movement.

489

Just a moment, but it seemed like whole hours passed. He expected the agitato to vex him, to send him spiraling. But it didn't. He merely listened. Contentedly, admiringly. How was it possible to wrest so much from a box of wood and wires! How was it possible that her young body held the knowledge of the song! How was it the sound found him dumb and in awe!

He shook the thought from his head as she made the final dash, her hands rising again for the final pair of notes.

Oh, the silence. After such exquisiteness. He wished he could see her eyes.

EVEN BEFORE THE SOUND OF HIS BOOT shifting on the oaken floor announced him, she knew he was there. The wrong man. She closed her eyes. Just as she had when with hands poised above the keys and saw in the darkness of her mind a choice. The same choice, really. She could either remain as she sat now, or turn to face him.

With as little comprehension or forethought as she'd used making her choice fifteen minutes earlier, when she dropped her fingers to the piano, she opened her eyes and turned to face him, her face as pale and as bright as the pool of light on the floor.

"I've never understood it better," he said, his voice almost a whisper.

"There's not so much to understand. Not really. It's there to be felt."

He nodded. "I've never felt it so profoundly, either. I wonder if the two things can both be true."

She swiveled back and closed the fallboard and then stood, composing her skirts and sliding the bench back under the piano. "I made dinner."

"I could smell it from the lighthouse."

"You're late tonight."

He stepped aside so she could pass, then followed her into the kitchen. "Do you know, I sat on the ledge tonight and watched the moonrise."

"My influence is waxing," she said, embarrassed by her pun.

He smirked. Like they were long and happily wed and their playful banter was standard fare on an autumn Tuesday evening.

"Dinner is likely cold by now, but I made your favorite."

491

He lifted his fork and stirred the sauerkraut. "You made the kraut, yes? You and Mrs. Wilson?"

"From our own cabbage, I did." She pointed at his plate. "The caraway I thought to add myself. She prefers without."

He nearly blushed. "It smells delicious." Now he tucked his napkin into his collar and sliced a bite of ham from the shank. He slathered it in the kraut and put it to his lips. "And tastes delicious."

Appealing to his admiration? She was trying it on.

"I was thinking, out there on the ledge, about the moon. How strange it is. Does it really make the ocean tides?"

"Are you asking me truly?"

He nodded, bashfully.

Those nights slinking around with Mats? They'd taught her to be aware, suspicious, to expect that at any moment someone might be creeping in the shadows, ready to discover them. Despite the fact no one had yet found them—well, except for Ruth—her suspicions became default and constant companions. She looked around the kitchen, half expecting a circus ringmaster to jump from behind the pantry or behind the stove to announce the joke being played on her, so little did she trust this version of her husband. Still and all, she risked answering. "It does."

"How does something so far away do that?"

"Its mass does the work, effecting the gravitational pull on earth. Imagine the seas on a leash, held by the moon."

He nodded. Like a schoolboy who heard the answer to his question, but didn't understand. "Did the comet do the same thing? Does it?"

"No."

"Why not?"

"Because the comet is to the moon what that fleck of caraway is to a head of cabbage."

He rubbed his brow. "Do you know that as the comet came closer and closer this spring, I conferred with Hosea Grimm about the danger it posed? Apparently, he's fast friends with a man named

Camille Flammarion, who's one of the great astronomical minds in all of Europe."

She had to suppress her own spate of laughter. For the first time since they sat down to eat, he gave her one of those scolding looks of his. Albeit a softer, less confident one.

"It's only that Flammarion is a fantasist. I don't know another way to say it. He pretends scientific knowledge, but his gift is in his imagination, not his learning. He writes *novels*. Fantasies."

"Hosea Grimm sold me a potion, one meant to protect me from the poisonous gas of the comet's tail." He took another bite of his ham. "Aren't I a dupe?" he said, chewing around his words.

"That man is full of false cures. His daughter too. They're untrustworthy."

He was listening, but his expression belied a distracted man, one on the verge of a great self-discovery. "I'd rather think about the music," he said, and she realized at once his discovery was perhaps less imminent than she thought.

He cut one of the potatoes in half and ate it. Then he set the knife and fork on the edge of the plate and pushed it forward enough so that he could fold his hands on the table in front of him. He appeared poised to pray, something he had forgotten to do before they started eating, but he only sat there.

After a moment, Willa asked, "What is it?"

He nodded his head slightly and without looking up answered, "I'm just thinking about the Beethoven." He risked a glance up. "How it's worked on me like the moon does the seas, I guess."

"What do you mean?"

"Only that it pulls me in different directions. It occurs to me that single sonata could be the anthem of my life." He pushed the plate of food even farther away. His head sunk. "I know it's grandiose—I'm quite certain grandiosity is my default condition—but it's also true. That music, it stirs something in me nothing else ever has. I feel the dupe again for it."

"You called it hope once."

"I rest my case." He smiled—the saddest expression she'd ever seen from him—and buried his face in his hands.

Willa took a long drink. She watched as the water sloshed back and forth when she set it back down, then dabbed her lip with her napkin. *His kindness is working on me,* she thought. She felt generous. She felt adrift.

When finally he looked up, all expression had washed from his visage. He was once again unreadable. He said, "It's no wonder you despise me."

Did she? Certainly not in this moment, she didn't. But what else explained nearly all her actions since arriving at the station? Her dereliction as a wife? Her confiding in Mats? Her avoidance at all cost of moments such as the one she found herself in now? What accounted for all of it?

"And no wonder you're repelled by me," he added.

To this she had a ready reply, "Oh, Theodulf. It's not me who is repelled. I know who you are."

Judging by his confusion, she might as well have just laid out Kepler's third law of planetary motion. "You know who I am?" he said.

Of all the things he'd asked in the last five minutes, none told her with such certainty that she had but one choice. She reached across the table and put her hand atop his. "I do. And I make no judgment. I lay no blame."

If such a thing were possible, his shoulders drooped even more. His prayerful hands held each other more tightly. "What do you think you know?"

The light in the kitchen was not so different now than it was in the lobby of the Masonic lodge that night five years ago. True, that room was lit by the wall sconces and dim streetlight, and this by the faint light of the gloaming, but when she looked at him kindly, his face shone with the same ashenness in both. "You desired me once."

He scoffed. He sat back in his chair. He crossed his arms over his chest. His confusion was redoubled. "Please don't speak in riddles."

"The night my father ascended to grand master, I played the piano before his ceremony. I was dressed as a young boy."

He pushed himself back from the table and crossed his left leg over his right and looked to the lighthouse. For a long time his vacant and impenetrable gaze lingered there until finally the night was full. By then she'd cleared the table and lit a lamp and washed the dishes. She'd not offered to make coffee. She'd not tried to console him. She only went about her duties.

Fifteen minutes later, she said, "I didn't mean to upset you. I only wanted you to know. It has felt, and I think this is right, like a grave secret between us. We have plenty of those, but I thought we were speaking freely." She stood across the table from him, her arms straight and her hands on the chairback.

He removed the napkin from his collar and laid it on the table and stood himself, looking across at her, his countenance as cryptic as she'd ever seen it. "If, as you claim, you *know* me, then add that to the advantages you have. I surrender. To you. To God. To time. I do. I surrender."

Those words, unresponded to, would be the last he'd ever speak to her.

FOR MORE THAN A HALF HOUR, Silje sat among the ferns beside the barn, trying to understand the scene playing out in the window across the garden. Freya had settled with the darkness and lay beside her, her chin on Silje's knee, ambivalent about everything but her keeper's hand petting her ear. The dog's stillness gainsaid the tempestuous feeling the music had left in Silje. She wanted to believe in something. That's what she kept thinking. She simply must.

She'd lately been counting the passes of the lighthouse beam as a way of distracting herself, and she did that now. One thousand one, she counted. Then twenty more.

"I've hated Frog since I met him," Silje whispered, looking back into their house. "But he looks frightful sick. Like Pappa did when he got the grippe."

Freya lifted her eyes without lifting her chin.

"Usually she bickers with him."

The dog smacked her lips.

"I don't know if I wish you could talk."

The ferns smelled sweet in the cooling night. They gathered the first dew. Silje stood and said, "Look over there" and pointed, and the dog stood and stretched and started in the direction Silje had pointed. Toward home. Before following, Silje removed the pistol from the pocket of her skirt, buried it among the leafy fronds, and ran to catch up to Freya.

THE FAWN

OCTOBER 23, 1910

Rising on marionette legs, a whitetail fawn walks within hours of birth and is surefooted by Sunday. Three hundred–some spots constellate her trunk. Gorgeous. Markers of youth.

I saw one once, bedded in a tuft of soft green grass, alert only to the prospect of her mother and her milk's return. An exemplar of innocence. Nakeder than any star ever was. So, I stood guard. Whole days passed. Then weeks. Months. And soon her spots were gone. Like smoke rising from a fire, they vanished. The fawn's legs grew strong. Her muscles twitched. She chewed on the same grass she'd slept on before. Chased by wolves and cougars alike, she ran through the woods like the wind blowing through it. Effortlessly, invisibly.

I watched all this, and marveled. Already the better part of her youth was behind her. Vanished with her spots.

Every year I watch again. I age. It's the thing I know best, that the spots vanish. They don't ever return.

IF SHE FOCUSED on the sight at the end of the barrel, the fawn standing on the creekside blurred. If she looked beyond it, the animal came into focus. So she tried to watch one thing with each eye—the deer and the sight—but that only made her nauseous, something she already felt at the prospect of pulling the trigger. It had come ambling down the eastern shore of the creek, tentative and alert but oblivious of her position in the lee of a granite ledge not far from where she'd set the wolf trap earlier in summer. It sipped from the creek many times and flinched at each forest sound. No doe appeared beside her. Not in the ten minutes since she'd spotted it.

Silje was positively silent herself. She lay prone on the rock, propped on her elbows, rifle cocked and aimed. Twice she barely lowered the barrel and studied the fawn's hide, and both times she tricked herself into believing she could see its vestigial spots. She knew this was unlikely—if not impossible—but still, there they were. Maybe, she reasoned, they were in some way reawakened by the molting of the fawn's red coat in favor of its gray winter fleece.

The season had shifted the last few weeks. Not only the trees burning yellow and umber up in the hills, but the persistent chill on the air. This morning, the pools on the granite shelving between the cabin and the creek were edged with frozen water. She could see the fawn's breath. She could see her own.

In fact, the changing season was the reason she lay here now. She and Uncle Mats had plotted their winter larder only a couple days ago. Standing over boxes of fish, he'd reckoned a couple hundred pounds of venison—be it caribou or moose or deer—in the cache would get them through. The same amount they tried to store the previous winter, as she remembered. But she didn't ask why so much, and when he went out to his nets this morning, Silje left Freya staked in the yard and headed here.

She glanced once more up and down the stream and still saw no doe. She knew the fawn was as good as dead anyway, sighted it again, watched as the muscles in its foreleg twitched, and settled her aim on a spot right below the deer's shoulder. The fawn fell as quickly as the recoil of the Winchester jabbed her shoulder. A shot just like Uncle Mats had taught her.

Her first thought as she stood above the fallen animal was not that they'd have roast venison tenderloin for dinner, but that they'd not have fish. She was tired of eating fish.

Between the heat of the animal draped over her shoulder and the sun up and warming, she started sweating almost as soon as she took her first step. The meaty and metallic tang of the animal soaked into her hands and generally hung about her. It summoned the ravens, which swooped and cawed like so many thoughts. She had them, those thoughts. About Willa and winter coming and Uncle Mats and school and how everything was supposed to make sense together. She'd never had them before. Not like this.

The whole walk home she labored as much under the weight of them as she did the fawn and cawing birds. When she reached her yard after almost an hour, she dropped the fawn and set the Winchester beside the tree she'd use to string the deer up. Freya strained at her chain and howled at the meat and Silje's return. Before she let the dog free, Silje strung the fawn up by its hind legs. High enough that she thought Freya wouldn't be able to reach it with her bounding.

"You come with me, girl," she said to the dog as she headed to the beach to wash up. Freya followed, sniffing at her. She went to the open side of the isthmus so that she might catch her uncle coming in, excited to share news of the hunt.

But he'd already returned, Uncle Mats had. He'd tied the painter to the dock and was unloading boxes of fish he'd already packed. Not for the first time, Silje admired his unending vigor. In this way, he was his sister's opposite.

"There she is," he called as Silje stepped onto the dock. Freya raced ahead, hoping for a fish to eat. "Looks like you're wearing a shawl. I gather you got one."

"I did. A fawn. But a sturdy one. She's hanging in back."

"What'll you do with a soft hide like that?"

It hadn't occurred to her to think about the fawn's hide, but she saw a pair of mittens as soon as she did. Instead of answering, she shrugged her shoulders and reached into one of the fish boxes on the dock. She took a small herring and tossed it to Freya and said, "Go on, now."

Uncle Mats held his hand up to block the sun and pointed with his other at the fish still in the boat and said, "Then we've got a lot of work ahead of us."

"I'll put the rifle away and come help," Silje said. She was back in two minutes and brought one of the fish boxes to the fish house. Without waiting for him, she started splitting the fish. She filled one full box before her uncle joined her, and together they filled four more, working in companionable silence.

"Better than a hundred pounds in all, I'd think," he said, pausing to slip his galluses over his shoulders and remove his sweater. "We might should have a sandwich before we get after the deer hanging out back."

So, they ate lunch on the back steps—cold fish sandwiches with onions and butter and a jar each of sarsaparilla—three hours until sundown and more than enough time to butcher the deer. It was here, finally, that Silje mustered the courage to ask her uncle the question that spawned all the others. "Why doesn't Willa come around as much as she used to?"

He held the hunting knife in one hand and the deer's left foreleg with the other, so as he turned to her the fawn's upside-down face did, too. "What do you know about Willa coming around?"

She wouldn't let him deflect. "I saw you two in the cabin that night. It's been a month."

"What night?"

"The one she was crying. The one you couldn't lift your face out of your hands."

He returned his attention back to the work and started skinning the fawn. Silje knew he was reconciling how honest he ought to be, so she let him have a moment, watching Freya scavenge the blood and fat and gristle that fell from above.

Five minutes passed, then five minutes more, before Silje gave up. She said, "I'm not a child anymore, Uncle Mats. I see what happens around me."

"I know you're not, and I know you do," he said, still intent on his work.

"Then be honest with me. Treat me better than you did my mother."

"I treated your mother fine, Silje." He hung his head. "Okay, here's the honest truth. It seems like Willa and I managed to fall in love."

"She's married to Frog."

"I know that."

Silje thought of the scene through the Sauer window that night Willa played the piano. "Does she love you?"

"I hope she does. I think she does."

"If she loves you and you love her, why was she crying?"

"She was crying because we shouldn't have let this happen, and we surely should have avoided the consequences."

"Which are?"

"Willa is going to have a baby. The baby will be your cousin."

"Not my brother or sister?"

He appeared baffled. "I guess that's a good question," he admitted. "I don't exactly know. We've not heard from the state yet."

Silje sat there in the yard. Freya came and circled her and then lay at her feet. "What's going to happen? With the baby, I mean? With Willa?"

"I don't quite know."

"You don't *know*?"

"I guess November will tell us."

SILJE MAY AS WELL HAVE BEEN ABANDONED since April for all the attention he'd had so spare. Or anyway, that he'd spared. Now she'd come with all the questions he feared asking himself. Even finding a few he didn't *know* to ask. It was enough that after he skinned the deer and hung it in the fish house to keep cool, he found himself busy with chores that didn't exactly need doing while she sat inside with the dog. He hadn't had the heart to reprimand her for letting Freya in and supposed this simple act would usher in a whole new age of change about the cabin. Hell, it wouldn't be much longer and the mutt would be joining them at the supper table.

The dog. He'd had an uneasy feeling about her from the start, showing up like a goddamned ghost at the same time Bente and Arvid disappeared. He could see the dog through the front window of the cabin now, sitting beside Silje at the fireplace. Her black snout and adoring eyes. That devotion on the verge of religion. It went both ways, too.

The dog ate as much as he and Silje put together. A thought that made his teeth ache. He sat on the thwart of his boat, looped and tied a reef knot around the furled sail and yard, then tied two more, one at either end. For all of the advantages of a sail full of wind, the piddling work of taking care of them grated on him. Give him a good set of oars any day.

He thought for the hundredth time about Bente and Arvid and what must have happened to them. For as much as he noodled on it, the only possible explanation is that they raised their own sail, fastened the boom to the gunwale, and got caught by a gust that knocked them overboard. It was rule number one with the sails on boats like theirs: don't tie them fast. Of course, neither Bente nor Arvid much ascribed to rules of practicality. And certainly once they got screaming and hollering at each other, the prospect of missing a sign on the horizon or even a freshening breeze was altogether likely. He could as much as see them hitting the April water. The shock would have silenced them right off. They'd have been hypothermic in five minutes and dead in ten, if not fewer.

April was nearer ahead of him than behind. Another thought that roused his anxiety. This winter was announcing itself early. He'd had a feeling about it for weeks. Oh, yes he did. Ten years now in Minnesota and it was the same every year. It arrived the same way it did back in Hauknes—in Norway—on the fjord. They were so much alike that way. Here and there. One minute out hauling nets on the open water, the next burning fires to keep from freezing. It hardly seemed right. All this toil just to stay warm and fed. Willa had repaired the part of him that accepted the simple reality of life as he'd known it. The problem was, how could he get everything he wanted now? She'd hardly come around since she told him she was pregnant.

And anyway, his sister and Arvid had shown him what could come of marriage. Was that what he wanted?

As he hopped on the dock and lit his pipe, a whole throng of gulls appeared as if from nowhere. He watched them circling and swooping, the black remiges on their wings calling the darkness. It was then his epiphany arrived. As sudden and loud as the gulls just a moment before.

He checked everything was buttoned down for the night and stepped into the fish house to light the lantern. It smelled musky and peppery with the deer strung from the ceiling beam and the hide draped over a fish barrel. He might have cut a hunk from the ham if he wasn't in such a hurry, but he struck a match against the match safe instead, lit the mantle, and headed to the landward side of the cabin. Arvid's boat was there, upturned, the bottom side of the hull already bleaching if the light told true, and feathered with rust-colored pine needles. He set the lantern on the rain barrel at this corner of the cabin and hefted the boat right side up. The light shone on the boat's deck.

He was right. There on the burden boards and forward thwart, dozens of muddy paw prints. He'd not noticed them before.

He stood upright, rubbing his brow. *Sometimes,* he thought, *if you puzzle things out long enough, the answer will find you. How many times had that been true for him?*

Dousing the lantern, he walked back to the boathouse. He couldn't imagine how he'd manage a child and wife, not alongside Silje and the thousand responsibilities of his workday. But for all he'd pondered—and lord, he had—he simply couldn't see a future without them. It thrilled him to declare it, even to himself alone.

UNDERTOW

NOVEMBER 1, 1910

The primary factors in an undertow effect are two: the rate of decline of an underwater shoreline, and the power of the waves battering that shore. The steeper the decline, the more likely an undertow. Similarly, the more powerful the wave, the more likely an undertow.

The littoral zone along Lake Superior's Minnesota shore is sporadic and dramatic, and rarely along this craggy line of scree and cliff and cold water is it more pronounced in its dramatics than in the league running to the northeast and starting from the headlands at the Gininwabiko station. Not a stone's throw from shore, the water plunges to some thirty fathoms. Another toss from there, and the depth triples.

NOVEMBER FIRST. First snow, an overnight squall that came and went while she slept. The morning sky and the whitened earth hung all as one. From the window, the lake looked black as night.

She dressed hurriedly, and left before Theodulf returned from his watch, her trail of footprints in the snow telltale, tying her cape as she started down the hill toward the dock. Of course, for all he looked down, Theodulf would not notice them even if he saw them—her footprints—never mind recognize their destination. Her destination.

It was not so cold yet, but still the rocks on the beach were glazed with ice where they weren't covered in snow. She stumbled but was resolute. She would catch him before he went out. She must.

At the cabin door, she paused, her hands clenched, her eyes wide open. The snow had shown her possibility. She would take it. Today she would.

She pushed the lever down and opened the door. Mats stood at the stove with a cast iron skillet, the smell of bacon blooming. Silje sat cross-legged on the floor, the dog looped around her, its ears alert but otherwise uninspired by her entry. Silje had been reading a book but dropped it as soon as she saw Willa. Their expressions were nearly identical—Mats's and Silje's were—and Willa merely stood dumb at the threshold, the cold morning air coming in around her.

"Are you here to steal Freya?" Silje said. "Should we stick our hands up and give her over?"

Mats chuckled and moved the skillet off the fire and wiped his hands on a cloth as he came from behind the stove. "She's been reading *The Call of the Wild*."

Willa said, "Do you know, the first time I crossed paths with Freya, she stole my ham?"

"Bad girl," Silje said, scratching the dog behind the ear.

"Silje, maybe you could take the dog outside for a few minutes? I'll call you when breakfast is ready."

The girl stood, eyeing Willa's belly as she put on her coat and mittens and left without a word.

When the door latched shut behind Silje, Willa turned again to Mats. "You're not out at your nets."

He leaned back against the table. "I thought you were a weatherman's daughter."

She looked out the window, then back at him.

He folded his arms across his broad chest. "As sure as I'm standing here, a gale's coming."

Now she walked to the window overlooking the lake and pulled the curtain aside.

"We'll have six inches more snow by lunchtime, I'd bet you a dime," he said.

The water *was* growing, waves blanketing the snow. How had she missed them?

She heard him moving behind her. Heard him set something on the table—coffee cups, she realized—then heard the coffee being poured. Then he stood beside her, steam rising from the offered cup. She accepted it.

"Do you know, Mats, that every morning I wake in the dark and stand at my window? Watching. Waiting."

He leaned against the wall beside the window, facing her. "Why do you do that, Willa?"

"So I might catch a glimpse of you. So your boat rowing out might give me some answer."

"Answer to what?"

She took a drink of coffee. "Never mind."

"I'm a simple man, Willa. I'll require straighter talk."

The lake kept coming. She couldn't stop watching it. "I don't mean to be cryptic. It's just that until now I've hardly articulated to myself what all those mornings meant. But I know now."

He waited. Beatific.

"I suppose I'll learn to live with the uneasy and uncanny feeling of your skiff disappearing each day."

"I've come back every time."

"So far, you have."

She took another drink of the coffee. "It's very good," she said.

"I haven't seen you in so long. How are you? How is . . ."

She finally turned to him. "The baby?" Now she unbuttoned her coat and offered her belly.

"Half a moon," he said sweetly, holding up his free hand. "May I touch it?"

She took his hand in hers and brought it to her belly.

"Sweet lord," he said.

She guided his hand farther and then held it where the baby kicked. His eyes dilated. A huge smile beset his face. "How in the world did this happen?" he asked.

"Mr. Braaten, I believe you know the answer to that."

Now he blushed and leaned back again. "Does your being here mean—"

She raised a finger to shush him. "I have nothing to recommend me, Mats. No dowry. No prospects. The world will detest us."

"There's not much world here." He held his hands wide. The window rattled under the wind off the lake. "And anyway, all I care about is you. We'll find our way. I'm sure of that. You and me and Silje and the babe."

Behind her the door whipped open, and Silje and the dog bounded in as if shoved by the wind, which gusted after them. Silje strained to pull it shut then stood there, her hair blown sideways and her cheeks bitten with cold, an apologetic look on her face.

"It came up quick, aye?" Mats said.

"Quicker than you said, Uncle Mats." Then to Willa she said, "I didn't mean to interrupt you."

"You've done no such thing."

Mats returned to the stove and put the skillet back on the fire. "I think we should all have some breakfast."

The dog went straight to the hearth and fell asleep on the warm bricks before Willa turned her back. Silje, colder and more tentative than the hound, sidled to the table with her coat still on. She sat and rubbed the cold from her cheeks. Mats cooked bacon and sliced bread and then cracked half a dozen eggs and added them to the bacon fat and in five minutes the three of them were sitting together, the only conversation among them the whistling of the flue. No prayer was offered before breakfast. No unpleasant sigh denouncing the food. Just Mats and Silje and a snoring dog, and if ever Willa felt delivered, it was that moment.

Mats covered his eggs in salt and pepper, leaving globs of butter and greasy fingerprints on the shakers, and dipped his crust into the yolks. Whole strips of bacon disappeared into his mouth. It was the first time Willa ever watched him eat. He was ravenous. Wolflike. Nearly as soon as he sat down he was finished, wiping his lips with the cuff of his flannel shirt.

"We've company, Uncle Mats," Silje said, nodding in Willa's direction as if there were a question about who she meant.

"Is she company?" he asked.

Both of them turned to Willa.

This would be her lot. She knew it then, surely. But rather than answering plainly, she teased, "Certainly I ought to get one meal as a guest, so as I won't have to scrub the dishes after eating."

Silje said, "Uncle Mats always scrubs the dishes."

After he washed the plates and cups and set them to dry on the table, after he poured the bacon grease into a jar and wiped the skillet clear, after he unrolled his sleeves and sat down across from Willa in the rocking chair and lit his pipe, Silje said, "I'm going out to the fish house for my carving tools."

Mats looked up at her and said, "Aye, and hurry back." He waved the stem of his pipe about, suggesting the gale and all it held and would soon unleash.

Again the door whipped open, and again Silje was gone. Mats stared at the spot she'd just held, a faraway look about him.

Willa said, "She'll be fine." Whether she meant in the next few minutes or the next ten years, even Willa didn't know.

But Mats nodded again in that way of his and said, "And so will we."

He offered Willa the pipe, which she declined. Instead, she sat back in the rocking chair. The cabin held against the wind, sound in every way, and yet the lantern hanging in the kitchen still casting its hollow glow on the table swayed as though it were hung in a schooner. In the fireplace, the flames guttered and spat.

"My God, this lake has its moods," Willa said.

Mats smiled.

"You're most satisfied by your prediction," she said.

"It's true I take some little pleasure in impressing you. But I'm smiling because I didn't know if you'd ever come back. And now, well, here you are."

She reached over and took his pipe and puffed on it then spoke through the smoke. "I took this long because I couldn't find the best solution. It was like this spring, waiting for the comet to appear and being at the mercy of cosmos."

"The comet *did* appear. I saw it," he said hopefully.

"It seems almost impossible that we should have met, Mats." Simply uttering his name made her smile. "That's all I mean to say. It takes time to recognize a miracle."

"A miracle," he echoed.

A shutter slapped against the house. Both of them looked.

"Silje shouldn't be out there," Willa said.

Mats crossed the room and raised the sash, pulling the shutter closed and latching it before lowering the sash. "My goodness," he said. "It's a circus out there. I'll go find her. Likely she's in the fish house."

"Mats," Willa said as he walked to the door.

He turned back.

"I can't mother Silje, but I can be her friend. I will be. I am."

He smiled and stepped out.

After he closed the door, Willa took a gander about the cabin. The fireplace loomed over the main room, sooty and solid and haloed with a mantel of heavy pine. A pipe box and lantern sat on either end, a vase of dried wildflowers in the middle. The kitchen was tidy. The washbowl mounted under the counter had a drainpipe below and a spigot and pump that connected to one of the rain barrels outside. A table big enough for six occupied most of the space between the rocking chairs and the kitchen counter. There was a sharpening stone and a crock of water at the head of the table, and three knives that Mats must have been in the middle of sharpening. A staircase leading to a loft rose off the kitchen, and behind it two doors leading to two bedrooms. A far cry from the brick foursquare up on the clifftop she'd called home all summer, but preferable in every way.

She took a drink of coffee. Tepid. She got up and put the cup on the mantel and tapped the ash from the pipe into the reeling fireplace flames, then hung it beside a collection of five others from the box. The baby kicked. And strangely she thought of God. She didn't have an inclination to pray or worship, but rather to marvel. And to be humble in her ignorance. She thought of Silje out in the fish house and vowed to dispense this wisdom if ever she was given the chance.

IT HAD HAPPENED BEFORE. A storm like this. One of her earliest memories, in fact: 1905. The storm they named for the ship that grounded outside the Duluth harbor. She couldn't remember the name of it, but she did recall that their dock and fish house had been splintered to pieces that same night.

Sitting now with her uncle and Frog's wife, listening to the gale as though somewhere in its wind her mother was speaking to her, she realized these storms would always be here. It was a relief to know it.

Uncle Mats had insisted Willa not attempt to climb the hill back to the station, had insisted that it was frankly dangerous. She trusted him—or just couldn't leave him—and at noon it was dark as night. The foghorns up at the station bellowed while her uncle dealt hands of whist and they all drank another pot of coffee. Hours passed, threes trumped kings, they ate venison stew at dinnertime, and by six, the light from the station above vanished in the hurricane.

Freya whined, needing to go out to piss, but each time Silje opened the door for her, the dog cowered around, and went back to the hearth for more rest. For more warmth.

Sometime after they all went to bed—Silje offered Willa her bunk and slept on the eiderdown in front of the fire with the dog instead—a pounding came to their door. Her uncle was up and out of bed, strapping his suspenders over his union suit as he lit a lantern and went to answer. It was his skiff, having sailed across the snow-covered beach, with each gust the rowlock knocked hello. The three of them—Willa and Uncle and Silje herself—stood in the doorway, laughing at the folly of it.

When they shut the door and stood in the crepuscular glow of the lantern light, she felt, for the first time and despite the weather, that she finally saw the world for what it would be. At least for now.

Rather than returning to bed, Willa and her uncle pulled the rocking chairs back toward the hearth. He stoked the fire and lit his pipe again and Silje lay beside the dog, rolling herself in the ei- derdown and pretending to sleep.

After a while, her uncle whispered, "Tell me something, Willa?" Silje squinted up at Willa, saw her nod.

He said, "You told me once the moon had a dark side. I've been thinking about that, and it seems to me strange that with all the rest of the universe to light it, it'd still be dark."

"All that other light—those other stars—it's too far away," she said.

He nodded and puffed on his pipe, watching the smoke fog the air between them. After a few more puffs he said, "I guess it's bet- ter that way, aye?"

"Some things ought to remain mysterious," she agreed.

Yes, Silje thought. Like a dog's devotion, like an unsprung trap, like a pistol among the ferns, like the origin of a rhyme, like the perversion of certain men, like the sound a piano makes, and how the blood in your body responds to it, like the promise of a cousin, or like the howling of the wind.

ONLY NOON and already the water wanted out of the lake. It came in heaving waves so thunderous it woke him from his flimsy sleep. At the window in stockinged feet and his boxer shorts, snow blew crosswise with the wind, which already had dominion over this day. He dressed in his uniform, went down to the kitchen with a thought of breakfast, but when he arrived, couldn't muster any conviction and went out to the lighthouse without so much as a cup of tea.

He would captain this station against the storm.

For more than two hours that meant moving from window to window to get a better glimpse of it. The vigor of it astounded him. And he'd been on the shore of this lake for some half a hundred such storms, a realization that brought some resolve but did nothing to ease the uncanny sense that for all the resemblance, this tempest was different. Fate, did it ride these peels of wind?

At three o'clock Ainsley arrived, stomping snow from his boots under the coal stove, which was banked hot with a smoldering fire. He carried a metal lunch box and thermos. Before he set either on the desk, Theodulf wheeled into the cleaning room.

"That's a special blow," Ainsley said.

"I'll stand tonight, Mr. Wilson."

"It's enough weather we might better both watch?"

Though he'd lately been less commanding, he gathered some of his old, exacting authority. "As I say, I'll stand. You're dismissed, Mr. Wilson."

Ainsley shrugged, set his supper on the desk, and said, "Want me to at least get the foghorns going?"

Theodulf only shook his head.

517

"I'll be ready if you need me, Mr. Sauer."

When Theodulf removed his watch and checked the time, he verified that the second hand was ticking, so at odds were the hour it told and the sky outside. Only shortly after four, it could easily have been mistaken for midnight. He lit the light first, and promptly, then started the foghorns. The wind made both the lamp and the bellows impotent. He might just as well have stood on the cliff's edge and shouted at passing ships for all the good the station was doing. The thought discouraged him, but what else could he do?

For two hours more he moved between the lighthouse and cleaning room as though on a yawing ship, stoking the fire, winding the clockworks, whistling *Moonlight Sonata* off-key and out of time. At quarter past six he sat at the desk and opened Ainsley's lunch box. A salami sandwich slathered with mustard, a dented apple, homemade shortbread wrapped in the same wax paper as the sandwich. In the thermos, lukewarm and sweetened coffee. He ate it all in five minutes, then stood at the landward window and nodded his thanks and approval to the Wilson house.

Before he went to check on the lamp flame again, he removed his pocket watch and chain from his jacket pocket, and set it on the blotter. From his holdall, he removed *The Moon*, which he'd recently and shamelessly stolen from Willa's trunk. He would read about lunar craters after he checked the flame. Lately he'd found the subject a perfect distraction.

In the watch room he wound the clockworks again for good measure, then stood under the lamp and inspected its rotation. Normally he could hear the whir of the turning lens. But tonight only the rattling panes of glass heralded. The flame, he could see from here, quivered slightly. So he adjusted the vents in the wall as if he was playing the keys of a clarinet. When he checked the signal flame again, it burned true.

Back at the desk, he poured the last cup from Ainsley's thermos and picked up *The Moon*. Why had he taken a sudden interest in this lie of his wife's? Was it because she had exposed him? He'd not spoken a word to her since. Callow, he knew. But he also could not bridge his own confusion over her knowing. Why had she not ridiculed him? Shamed him? Laughed at him? If ever he deserved punishment, was it not in that moment she divulged the truth? He'd risked a single glance in her direction, and as he saw it from here in the cleaning room, all she gave him was empathy. Perhaps that simple fact is what accounted for his holding this clandestine book on his lap now. He turned to the page he'd left off on and read about the craters.

For almost an hour he read. Occasionally he'd glance up at the ceiling as though trying to imagine what he'd seen in fact a thousand times—the moon looming above him. Most of his life—at least over the past several years—had been spent in some nebulous communion with it. But at best he could barely conjure the sight of it. So he turned to the images in the book. He was no scientist. He knew that. His ignorance had become the thing that more and more defined him this year, beside his learned wife. And yet, he couldn't help but think that the authors of this book were wrong on the source of the craters. They appeared to him to be wounds inflicted from without, not within. He'd have wagered on it.

But alas, his only company that night was the foghorns and storm. He set the book down to listen to them. The foghorns had ceased. Could such a thing be true? He cocked his ear, as though he might catch the throb of them by that simple gesture. But true as the storm still galloped, they no longer bayed. Surely their engines had run out of fuel. He would fill them. He would do his duty.

He set *The Moon* on the blotter, noted the fact of the silenced foghorns in the log, and marked the time. Midnight exactly. Another day done.

At the cleaning room door, he looked through the window to the fog station building. He thought of the men aboard the *Mataafa*, how some of those on the stern deck had attempted to cross to the bow. It was the story of mankind: to get from one place to the next, and yet the simple confluence of snow and wind and the rising lake made it impossible that night five years ago. Some had drowned. Those who did not, died by freezing. One of them washed ashore, into his waiting arms. It didn't seem like much of a choice, and certainly his grandiosity was getting in the way of the simple task at hand, which was to get the foghorns blowing again. His duty beckoned. He would heed it so that another shipful of men wouldn't be faced with the futile choice of crossing the uncrossable or freezing to death. He would play his role in all this.

The ten steps between him and the fog station building were made infinite by the blinding darkness and cutthroat storm. Great lord, it did blow. And the snow had drifted into the doorway so that he could only open it enough to squeeze through. But, duty!

His first step found him slipping on the snow. Falling to his knees. As he stood—his hands plunged into the bottomless snow—a deluge of water slapped him. Impossible that the waves would crest the clifftop, no? he thought. But sure enough, another came, this one knocking him flat on his back. Twenty seconds in the night, and he may as well have been naked before God. Lying there, snow crawling down his neck, he extended his arm above him. He might have been reaching for God, for help from above. But not only did none come to lift him, he couldn't so much as see his hand before him. All of life eclipsed into darkness.

He rose, first to his hands and knees, then to his feet, trying to orient himself by the way the wind blew. From inside it had come across the lake, but now, in the canyon between the lighthouse and the fog station building, it came from every direction. To complicate matters, each step was into an untrodden and knee-deep drift of snow. A wicked gust sent him pirouetting.

Dizzy now, and without quarter in the darkness, he guessed best and kept moving.

DON'T BOTHER WONDERING if what happened next was accident or choice. He did not know himself. *Could* not. And though it was also true that he had sometimes forsaken and forgiven God, the fall was not without its relief. Maybe this was partly true because he did not know he was falling. Not immediately. It seemed, in the first instant, that his own sense of weightlessness had as much to do with the weather as it did anything else. It's also true that between the waves blasting up the rocky cliffside and the snow in such great abundance, he had a momentary impression of falling into a bed more comfortable than the cot he had slept on all year long. So pleasant was the feeling that he opened his eyes wider in the night, hoping for revelation.

Once he splashed into the lake, and the water enveloped him, he knew what he should have from the first: his fate had indeed arrived. Even this might have terrified, for he did have a few moments to understand. Instead, it was simply beautiful. And as unexpected as any of this. There in the undertow, a certain milky light. As if the depths had stores of ancient moonlight ready for the initiates. His eyes widened again at a new prospect, and before he gulped a fatal breath of water, he wondered if that light came from the gates of hell.

As his lungs filled, the rest of the water contrived to keep him underwater and pull him farther out to sea. Were those other souls, leading him into blacker waters?

SPINDRIFT

DECEMBER 12, 1910

I might have introduced myself before now, but the truth is, I'm bashful, and I never know how to offer my hand. I should apologize, I'm sure. I've not intended to be coy or clever. But my greatest charm is my ambiguity, and there's nothing to be done about that. Still, I'll try.

To begin, I'm ubiquitous. When first I spoke and announced my intentions, I suggested some of the things I'd tell you about. I have, I think, been true to my word. What's more? I not only spoke of the moon and the comet and the lighthouse and light, the storms and the softest hours, the clockworks and the watchworks, the shipwrecks and survivals, the hound and the fawn, the drownings and the orphan, the Lord Jesus Christ and His doubters, His sacraments and sins, the most beautiful song, the station master and his wife and the man I've called Mats, the lake and her many moods, the dying . . . I not only told you about these things, I, in fact, am these things.

I am all of them and more. So much it's impossible to comprehend. I contain everything: memory, desire, longing, happiness, sadness, wisdom. Ignorance. Folly. Befuddlement. Love. Perhaps love most of all.

I live among the stars and in the gaseous tails of comets, on the moon and in the light she gives. I live in constellations. I'm even like the constellations. Always expanding, changing, becoming bigger and more beautiful and less knowable. With the right telescope, you might see a fraction of me.

I can see you now, looking up from these words, unimpressed by my riddling, unable to see anything but the vacancy before you. Well, I'm that vacancy as well. I'm a liar. I never lie.

Or, maybe it would be easier and simpler to say: Now? Here? At the end of this version of myself? I also live in this water—this wave—where it meets the wind and is lifted from the crest. I live in its flashing in the bright, full moon.

I am carried in that light. Carried. I am carried.

And am gone.

But I will be back.

I cannot wait to tell you more. Perhaps when next we meet, I'll be a rushing river instead of this spindrift. Or a ship upon the waves. Or the wind that fills her sails.

Even now, I am all of these things.

Yes, I am.

OFTEN AS NOT she felt better walking than sitting, and most nights found her roaming the snow-covered beach, a walking stick in one hand, her belly in the other. This night's constitutional had found her at the end of the lighthouse dock, the waxing moon nearly full and resplendent above the wind.

The wind! How it had played havoc that morning as John and Ainsley lowered the piano with the hoist and derrick onto the lighthouse tender. The wind zithered through the instrument as they lowered it, the most beautiful sound she'd ever heard. Mats had been at the bottom of the cliff waiting with his skiff, and the plan was to use his boat to tow the tender across the bay and deliver it to the cabin. She'd walked along the shore as he made his unsteady progress, the towline slackening and tightening with each small wave the boats crested. John and Ainsley had fastened the piano with ropes tied through the gunwales.

Just past the lighthouse dock, the piano halfway to the fish house dock, one of the lines snapped. The piano teetered, and though John might have carried the thing on his back for all his brawn, the waves played devil, and he couldn't hold it. It tipped and then fell into the cove's water. From shore, Willa gasped but then laughed. Of all the happy places for that battered instrument, she could think of none better.

The other night she and Mats had sat on the fish house dock smoking his pipe together. She'd commented on the moon's loveliness, even thought of ascribing some heavenly and divine power to it, but didn't.

Mats said, "A moon like that's enough to fish by."

A fine and perfect sentiment.

Her best accounting said the baby would be here in April or May. One hard winter pregnant and living in the cabin, then they'd go to Duluth for the baby's birth. Ruth had promised to refer her to an accoucheuse she knew down there. Someone to do the real work of seeing another soul into this world.

A month and a half ago, the morning after the storm, it was Ruth who came knocking on the cabin door. Still the wind howled off the lake, so much that the beach had been washed clear of some twenty inches of snow that had fallen. She apologized for the indiscretion of showing up, but there was either a miracle or a tragedy, depending on how you looked at it.

She said, "The light quit going about two, and when John got there to start it up again, your husband was gone. No sign of him anywhere."

Willa put her coat on and followed Ruth back up the path. At the lighthouse, they inspected the scene like a pair of detectives. His watch was on the desk. And her book. His holdall sat on the floor beneath it. Outside, the snow was drifted into piles as tall as she. The door to the fog station building, she could see, had been shoveled clear by John or Ainsley. She and Ruth looked at each other and labored tentatively toward the cliff's edge. The quarter wall there lay beneath a mound of ice. Water blown up off the lake.

"It's not possible," Ruth whispered.

But of course it was. There was no other explanation.

Willa was never more convinced of that possibility than on this night. She would go back to the cabin in a trice. Go back to her new life. Her fourth in two years.

But for a moment longer she stood on the lighthouse dock, watching the waves come across the harbor, the moon on the water and then again in the spindrift. Whether that shattered light was a song or a soul, she had only a hunch.

ACKNOWLEDGMENTS

Thanks to:

My friend and editor Erik Anderson, whose wisdom is everywhere in this book. And to everyone at the University of Minnesota Press who helped usher it into the world, especially Heather Skinner, Matt Smiley, Laura Westlund, Emma Saks, and Daniel Ochsner.

The countless independent booksellers who have supported me over the years. To list them all would be impossible, but a few who have been there from the beginning (or awfully close to it) include Pamela Klinger-Horn, Kristen Sandstrom, Jessilyn Norcross, Judith Kissner, David Enyeart, Sally Wizik Wills, Ann Woodbeck, Lisa Baudoin, Jessica Peterson White, Bob Dobrow, Alex George, Sarah Bagby, Kate Ratenborg Scott, and Jennifer Wills Geraedts.

Jesseca Salky, my pal and agent.

Friends who make this lonely occupation less so: Matt Batt, Ben Percy, Nate Hill, Leif Enger, and Nick Butler.

Finn, Cormac, Eisa, Beckett, Augie: you all are my inspiration.

I relied on many sources to write *A Lesser Light*, especially Curt Brown's fabulous book *So Terrible a Storm*; *Lost Duluth*, by Tony

Dierckins and Maryanne C. Norton; and *Duluth, Minnesota,* by Maryanne C. Norton.

Before he passed away, my father answered a hundred strange questions that none of those books could. I couldn't have written this without him.

Nor could I have written it without my wife, Emily Hamilton, who is my light in the storm.

PETER GEYE is author of the award-winning novels *Safe from the Sea, The Lighthouse Road, Wintering* (winner of a Minnesota Book Award), *Northernmost,* and *The Ski Jumpers* (Minnesota, 2023). Born and raised in Minneapolis, he continues to live there with his family.